John Steele ___ ___ ___ ___ ___ ___ ___ Ireland.
In 1995, at the ___ ___ ___ ___ ___ ___ e United
States and has since ___ ___ ___ ___ ___ ___ ents, including a thirteen-year spell in Japan. Among past jobs he has
been a drummer in a rock band, an illustrator, a truck driver
and a teacher of English. He now lives in England with his wife
and daughter. He began writing short stories, selling them to
North American magazines and fiction digests. *Ravenhill* is his
first novel and a second Jackie Shaw book, *Seven Skins*, has
already been signed by Silvertail Books for publication. He is
currently writing a third, set in northern Japan.

RAVENHILL

John Steele

SILVERTAIL BOOKS • *London*

This edition published by Silvertail Books in 2017
www.silvertailbooks.com
Copyright © John Steele 2017

1

The right of John Steele to be identified as the author
of this work has been asserted by him in accordance
with the Copyright, Design and Patents Act 1988.
A catalogue record of this book is available from the British Library

978-1-909269-71-2

To Tomoe and Hana
for nine months of inspiration, and all of
the stories yet to come

CHAPTER 1

1993

Stephen Armstrong always thought of himself as a decent kind of guy, so it was a surprise when he found himself privy to a secret that could get a man killed. He mulled this revelation over as Archie Sinclair competed with the drone of the radio for his attention.

'An arms haul was uncovered in a false grave during a security operation at a West Belfast cemetery late this morning. Police said a sawn-off shotgun, two handguns and an automatic rifle were among the weapons found.'

'That was brilliant, like, when yer man turned into metal and all. I tell you, it's all going to be graphics in films in the future, like.'

Stephen looked out of the plate-glass window of East End Video, over the stream of rush-hour traffic to the Ormeau Park opposite. It was a beautiful February afternoon and slivers of light were spilling through the naked trees, bathing the paths in spears of pale golden sunshine. It was almost half five and not yet dark.

'It was definitely better than that other one you recommended. I don't usually go for science fiction but you can't go wrong with big Arnie, like.'

'Police are investigating reports of shots being fired at a taxi office on the lower Newtownards Road in East Belfast this afternoon.'

If he squinted, Stephen could make out the tower block of the Queen's University Ashby Building on the Stranmillis Road, above and beyond the tangle of branches in the park. He wondered if Donal might be somewhere around the tower, drinking coffee in a student hangout. Donal had mentioned last night that he studied some kind of mechanics and Stephen had a notion that the faculty was based in the Ashby. Not that he'd ever set foot in a university.

'A Catholic man shot in the head in the Markets area last night has died in hospital. Detectives believe the killing was the work of the Ulster Volunteer Force ...'

'Wee Minty says yer man who's the bad guy is gay, but I think that's balleeks, like. Sure, he's too hard to be a fuckin' poof.'

Oh Christ, thought Stephen, if only you knew. Here he sat, on his high stool behind the counter of his video rental shop, regarded as a strong man of the road. Tall and broad, he'd been in a few scraps through the years and carried the scars. He'd been at the same school as, and was now on decent terms with, men who had loyalist associations in the area. Men who sanctioned or carried out shootings like the one being reported on the radio.

Men who had no idea that Stephen was assuredly and contentedly gay.

Had they known, his business may no longer have been exempt from the protection money others on the road had to pay, and he may not have been asked to join the paramilitary crowd so many times when having a drink in one of his locals. His refusal was always light-hearted but the recruiters' reactions were unpredictable: from amiable to aggressive. The fact was, he'd drunk in every pub on the lower Ravenhill Road, My Lady's Road, and a couple on the Castlereagh too, just trying to get away from that nonsense. But there was one in every bar, always recruiting, always looking for the next young lad ready to fight for God and Ulster.

'... the man had a Protestant girlfriend from the Lisburn Road. Police believe this may have been the reason for his murder.'

Little did these men know that Stephen had clambered out of the bed of a twenty-six year-old graduate student this morning. A very attractive, very male, very Catholic graduate student from Warrenpoint called Donal, currently studying in Belfast, and who Stephen was falling for at a rate of knots.

'Poor bastard, just because he's a Catholic. And dear help his girlfriend as well,' said Archie.

Archie, too, was ignorant of Stephen's sexuality. Archie was ignorant of a lot of things. He'd left school at sixteen without a qualification to his name. Now, at thirty-one, he was exactly one week older than Stephen and unemployed. At least, he was technically unemployed; Archie was more of a silent partner in the video shop while religiously collecting his unemployment benefits every fortnight. If any inquisitive civil servant should spot him sitting behind the counter next to Stephen, he could claim he was just keeping his friend company in the shop.

And they were friends, Stephen and Archie. Archie's da had been a merchant seaman and ran off when he was still a youngster, and the son had inherited the father's short and scrawny frame. He'd always been a simple soul and small for his age, so he'd been a natural target for the bullies in school. A few of those past fights Stephen had been in were during their teenage years, scrapping to defend Archie. One of his earliest opponents was now a local member of the UDA.

Stephen said, 'Aye, it never ends.'

Archie scratched his broken nose, a fleshy inverted hourglass in his guileless face. 'I watched that film with yer man in it the other night.'

'Yer man?'

'You know, yer man who stopped acting and became a boxer. He was in that sexy film, with yer woman Basinger. You lent me his other one, "*A Prayer ...*" something or other.'

'Ach aye, yer *man*.'

'Load of shite. It's about an IRA man, right? So yer man plays him, but he's all depressed like, because he killed all these kids by accident with a bomb. Then he's moping about through the whole film like he's the fucking victim. Like we're supposed to feel sorry for him.'

Stephen tutted. 'The Yanks probably do.'

By now a customer, Diane Hunter, had walked up to the counter clutching a romantic comedy.

Archie went on, 'And he couldn't do the accent. Sounded mental, so he did, or like he was half-cut. Suppose the Americans think we're drunk all the time anyway.'

Diane joined in. 'Is that that film about the IRA with yer man in it? Yer man's a boxer?'

Stephen and Archie said in stereo, 'Aye.'

'My cousin's a peeler, right? And if an actor or somebody comes here to do research and that, the police have to give them an escort around Belfast in the Land Rover. So my cousin's based at Donegal Pass and he has to take yer man around and they drive up Sandy Row. There's all the usual Union Jack and UVF murals and all. And yer man says, "Why's all these British paintings here?" So my cousin, all patient like, says, "This is a Protestant area, so these people want to stay part of the United Kingdom." And yer man says, "I didn't know there was any Protestants in Ireland!" Fucking eejit.'

Archie said, 'Pity your cousin couldn't teach him to talk right, like.'

Diane turned back to the shelves where two girls of around eight years old were looking at colourful, garish covers in the animation section. Archie followed her gaze and started shaking his leg rhythmically on the leg of his stool. He fiddled with a packet of cigarettes and expressions of panic, wonder and confusion struggled for supremacy on his face.

The girls were giggling, rapidly swapping video boxes around on the shelf.

Diane said, 'Jane, come on you and hurry up. I've to get home and make your tea, and Becky Breslin, you've to go home to your mother before six.'

She didn't have to raise her voice. The shop was the combined space of a couple of small living rooms, the building one of an identical row of red-brick terraced houses standing across the Ravenhill Road like a troop of soldiers in single file. The floor above was silent, locked and empty.

Jane and Becky hung their heads in resignation and began dragging themselves over to the counter. Jane had her mother's hair, an unruly flame of peach-coloured curls, but her rosebud mouth and wide blue eyes were from her father's side. Archie's leg went into overdrive. His own small mouth tightened further.

'How old is Jane now?' asked Stephen, cocking a look at Archie, now apparently engrossed in the video box of an action film.

Diane put her arm around the child's shoulders and gave her a proud hug.

'She's almost eight. It'll be her birthday next month – isn't that right, love?'

Jane nodded. Archie coughed.

Archie and Diane had been an item for a brief period. It hadn't lasted long but they'd stayed on good terms. That would have been about eight years ago. Diane had raised Jane alone, just one of the many single mothers in the area, although older than

5

most. She'd never told a soul who Jane's father was. Stephen and Archie had done the maths and would have laid bets on Archie as her da.

Stephen said to the girl, '*Beauty and the Beast*, that's a good film, darlin'. Isn't it, Archie?'

Archie, now looking as though he were in pain, peered over the counter at the child.

'Aye, it's a great film, Jane.' He shot a loaded glance at Diane, then back at Jane. 'You get it for two days if you rent it. Maybe I can come over and watch it with you, if you fancy it.'

Diane met the suggestion with a meticulously calibrated wall of indifference. 'That would suit me, then I could go out with Sharon for a night. What do you think, Jane?'

The girl looked at the video box again and said, 'Yeah. That'd be good.' It was almost a whisper but she was smiling.

Mark Wilson was also smiling. Over in the war and westerns section, he looked at his friend Danny Gourling. They were standing in front of a row of World War Two classics, hands in pockets, casual as you like. Two rows above the war films, on the top of the cabinet, was a selection of more exotic titles.

Keeping their heads in line with John Wayne and James Coburn, their eyes strained upwards to check out a cover with a pneumatic blonde, arse-out and contorted over a Harley Davidson, licking her lips as though dying of thirst. Mark's parents were away for a couple of days in Scotland visiting relatives and, at sixteen, he was deemed old enough to stay in the house alone. Except he wouldn't be alone. Seven of Mark's mates from school, including Danny, would be keeping him company. Naturally, this had meant bribing his older cousin to make trips to the off-licence to stock up on beer, buying an experimental packet of cigarettes, and now researching some entertainment for the evening.

Mark and Danny weren't alone. A tall man who looked to be

in his twenties with a dark sheen of stubble was standing a couple of yards away. Unlike Mark and Danny, he was openly studying the flesh on show, occasionally glancing at his watch. His hair was tucked under a blue baseball cap and he wore a black leather jacket. He was chewing some gum, smacking his lips. He caught the boys looking at him and swivelled his gaze in their direction, his head not moving an inch. He gave them a quick wink and went back to checking out the porn.

Mark and Danny exchanged a look and sniggered. They didn't recognise the man but it was common for people from the upper reaches of the road, beyond the expanse of the Ormeau Park and the attached golf links, to slum it at East End Video. It was the only video shop on the road and easier than going to other, farther thoroughfares like the Castlereagh or Newtownards Roads.

Their sniggering had attracted the attention of Stephen, who was now monitoring them from the counter at the front of the shop. Seeing this, they concentrated hard on wiping the smirks from their faces. They liked Stephen. He was well respected in the area and he treated them like adults. Like men. He was never condescending and it made them feel as if they were equals when he chatted to them about the new releases, or football, or this actor or that girl. But they'd never tried to rent this kind of video from him before and they didn't want him thinking they were messing around in his shop. They needed him on side.

The man next to them also turned to look at Stephen. He smiled and it was a good smile: open and genuine. Stephen re-turned it.

The door of the shop opened with an electronic chime and the man's smile hardened. To the boys it seemed as if his face actually stiffened, like a freeze frame. He didn't turn back to the videos. Instead, his hand went inside his jacket.

At that moment, two girls in school uniform entered the shop and the boys admitted defeat: their hunt for porn was over. The girls were Sharon Montgomery and Kim Clarke, a year below them in school and, Mark had to admit, both pretty. Especially Kim, who seemed older and more mature than the other girls in school.

The man in the leather jacket relaxed a little but the boys could sense the tension continuing to radiate from him. He still had his hand inside his jacket. Kim gave Jane and Becky a quick pat on the head, the black shawl of her hair falling over her strong features, while Sharon exchanged a greeting with Diane. Then the two girls began walking towards the boys.

The electronic chime sounded again.

The man began pulling his hand out of his pocket. Sharon said, 'Hiya, youse.' The man's hand was almost clear of his pocket. Another man in a bomber jacket and black jeans had entered the shop. He was carrying a sports bag and caught, then held, the gaze of the baseball cap wearer. They nodded at each other, an acknowledgement and signal. The baseball cap wearer's jacket tightened across his body as he turned and exposed his hand. Mark noticed something black and metallic in it. The item looked heavy in the man's grasp and the boy thought how he'd only ever seen it in films, never in real life.

Stephen had seen it too, the man's knuckles white against the black plastic grip. The baseball cap wearer realised Stephen had seen the object and said, 'Fuck!' Then he pulled the gun clear of his jacket. His finger curled around the trigger. Stephen began to rise from his stool. Diane was taking the video from Jane, who was looking at Archie with a bashful smile on her pretty little face. Becky was examining something on her finger and sucking on a couple of strands of her curly red hair. A look of shock was just beginning to flash across Sharon's face as she noticed the gun almost levelled at Stephen. Kim was giving Danny a meaningful look with warmth in her hazel eyes. Danny was, like her, oblivious to all around him as he returned the gaze with an awkward grin.

The man with the bag glared at the gunman and said, 'Shite!'

The gunman said, 'Everybody quiet! Nobody move!'

The bagman said, 'The operation's off. We'll have to abort.'

There was a flash as the sports bag ignited and the man holding it was literally ripped apart. The explosives inside tore through the shop, Stephen, Archie, Diane, Jane and Kate, before engulfing the man in the cap, Mark and Danny. The white heat swallowed Sharon and Kim as the ceiling caved in.

In a couple of seconds they were all dead.

Bomb on Ravenhill Road claims 11 lives

IRA attempt to strike at UDA results in tragic loss of innocents
By Jim Bryson, staff reporter

An incendiary bomb exploded in the East End Video rental shop on the Ravenhill Road yesterday afternoon, killing nine civilians and two members of the Provisional IRA. Four of the victims were of secondary school age. Two were eight years old.

According to sources, republican terrorists had inaccurate intelligence indicating that senior members of the loyalist paramilitary group the Ulster Defence Association were holding a meeting in rooms above the video shop. The rooms on the first floor of the premises were empty. RUC detectives believe the incendiary device exploded prematurely.

Among those killed were Stephen Armstrong, the owner of the business, and his friend Archie Sinclair. Neither are members of a terrorist organisation. Kim Clarke and Sharon Montgomery (15 y.o.), Mark Wilson and Danny Gourling (16, 17), Diane Hunter and her daughter Jane Hunter (8), and her friend Becky Breslin (8) were killed when the device went off. The two bombers have yet to be identified, although the Irish Republican Army has claimed responsibility for the attack.

The bombings have devastated the community on the lower Ravenhill Road and there has been widespread condemnation from all political parties aside from Sinn Fein, who have declined to comment at this time.

Detectives at Willowfield and Castlereagh RUC stations have appealed for anyone with information to come forward and contact them via the Confidential Telephone line. The Chief Constable has called for calm, and warned loyalist groups not to attempt reprisals.

CHAPTER 2

Wednesday

Jackie Shaw grips the arms of the aisle seat on the Airbus A319 as it banks over the thrashing grey reach of the Irish Sea and prays again that he won't die today. He's lost count of how many times he's implored the good Lord to spare him, despite how much he dreads the next five days. But surely one funeral is enough for the week, not that his sister Sarah would shed a tear for him anyway. He glances out of the window to his left, barely tilting his head as if the slightest movement might send the aircraft spiralling into the hungry expanse below.

The woman next to him, an attractive blonde he'd place in her mid-thirties, gives him a pitying smile. It doesn't afford him much comfort but the attention from an attractive woman is welcome.

He is an open-featured man, with solid country cheekbones and hair that is still mostly black with a light dusting of white. His frame is robust and his stomach flat. A farmer's build, his da used to say. He wears a simple T-shirt with jeans and boots.

Now the plane is making its way up the great funnel of Belfast Lough towards the industrial gateway of the Harland & Wolff shipyard and, beyond, the city. It's like a wind tunnel, this gully of mountains on the County Down and Antrim coasts. Another jolt of turbulence rocks the A319 as if the Almighty Himself were trying to shake the passengers from the fuselage like the last drops from a bottle. Jackie's T-shirt is soaking on his back. He closes his eyes.

'I like your ring. It's very pretty,' says the blonde woman. He opens his eyes to find her smile has a hint of intensity. She is English, possibly from the Midlands.

'It's a Claddagh.' He looks down and is surprised to find he's been rubbing the ring, nestled on the third finger of his right hand, with his thumb. The woman's gaze drifts to his left hand, free of jewellery.

'It's Irish.' He thinks he's made it sound like a rebuke and is sorry. Almost in way of apology he adds, 'I'm from Belfast.'

Undaunted, the woman gives him a sideways grin. 'You could *never* tell. So, does it have a special meaning? It looks a little heavy on the symbolism.'

'The hands stand for friendship, the crown for loyalty and the heart represents love.' He thinks he sounds like a museum guide and, in an attempt to close the conversation down, he adds, 'It was a gift,' with some meaning.

Her smile takes on a spiky aspect and her voice lowers. 'As I said, it's very pretty.'

He follows her gaze to the knotted, discoloured blur on his right forearm. The scar, angry and callused, was a favourite topic of speculation with those who worked with him. For those who were old enough to remember his hometown from the seventies to nineties, it was cause for caution too. Jackie tilts his head back and grips the armrest again. The woman turns to look out the window.

He screws his eyes shut. Grits his teeth. Breathes deliberately. The aircraft continues to shudder as it is battered by the air coming up and across the lough. He can hear every pitch and moan in the engines. This fear, this engulfing phobia of flying, came to him in his twenties. When he was younger still, he relished travel. It was something glamorous and placed him at the centre of things: those who knew him would be thinking of him abroad, would be speculating on what he was doing.

To his mother at church, 'Have you heard from your Jackie?'

To his father at the football or in the pub, 'How's your Jackie getting on?'

He'd felt proud that his parents could share in that attention. Even Sarah had a begrudging admiration for him back then. Now he fears dying with unfinished business on his ledger. His mother has been dead these many years, and his father joined her just three days ago. His sister has no time for him.

But more than that, he knows he's done wrong. Real wrong that can't be amended. He doesn't have nightmares, doesn't drink to excess. He doesn't feel guilt in his day-to-day. But when he flies, when his life is in the hands of a pilot he'll never meet – in the hands of fate, or God, whatever floats your boat – he remembers he has blood on his hands. And he doesn't want to die before some form of absolution.

The plane is descending now and he can see his fellow passengers looking excitedly left and right. Across the aisle a small girl with Chinese features yelps in short, high-pitched gulps. He can't tell if she is laughing or crying until her companion, an older woman smiling and speaking what he recognises as Mandarin, leans forward into his line of sight. Even then he isn't sure if the glitter in the older woman's eyes is fun or malice. Cantonese, he can speak to a degree; Mandarin, no. To distract himself, he fiddles with the pre-paid mobile phone he's picked up for the trip. He can't stand the devices, but it's a necessary evil for calling Sarah on the hoof while he's over.

Then East Belfast comes into view.

He's lived in some of the world's great cities: London, New York, Tokyo, Hong Kong. In all of them he's seen a scramble for space, buildings wedged in at awkward angles crowding against one another. But as they finally descend over the Holywood Road and Sydenham, he thinks Belfast has never been like that. Maybe the pounding she took in the Blitz and the more recent years of domestic bombing have aired her out. You can breathe in this city.

And despite all that had happened when he lived there before, despite his apprehension and the coming funeral, he is glad to be home.

He mourns Gordon for a moment.

He wonders if Billy and Rab are still there. He wonders if they are still alive.

He wonders if Eileen is still there. Still in Ravenhill.

#

Jackie exits the baggage claim area through the arrival doors and arrives in the main concourse. A sign reads: *Welcome to George Best Belfast City Airport*. Georgie didn't have his name attached when Jackie was last here and, whatever he thinks of Mr Best, it'll always be the plain old City Airport to him. It's strange, hearing the accent everywhere after so many years. His stride slows as he soaks it all in.

Then he stops dead. Sees *J. Shaw* scribbled in a lazy hand on plain white cardboard. The man holding it is quite tall, over Jackie's five-nine anyway. He is wearing a pair of brown corduroy trousers and a grey shirt with a darker shade of jacket. The jacket is buttoned and Jackie recognises the bulge of a weapon under his left arm, likely a shoulder-holster.

'Mr Shaw, welcome back.' The accent is clipped public school, delivered in a bizarre nasal burr.

It is late Wednesday afternoon. Jackie's father will be buried on Friday morning and Jackie has a return flight on Sunday evening. He set down on his homeland soil less than twenty minutes ago, and a life he left behind twenty years ago has already caught up with him.

He sighs, says, 'It feels like I've never been away.'

The man has large eyes, almost protuberant, in a soft fleshy face with the beginnings of flaccid jowls either side of a prominent chin. A wiry scrub of receding brown hair creeps forward across his scalp as the man's face glides into a smile. The face reminds Jackie of the Toby jugs found in endless antique shops in the West Country of England.

The nasal burr: 'Excellent, excellent. Well, let's be on our way, shall we?'

With that, the man strides off to the car-hire desks. Jackie shrugs his coat on and swings his holdall over his shoulder with just a little more force than is necessary. The man stops in front of a kiosk and begins meticulously folding the cardboard sign, making crisp, sharp creases along the smooth, white surface while Jackie, blank-faced, strides up to the desk and takes care of the paperwork necessary in order to pick up the Toyota Corolla he booked online. They walk together to the car and, once inside, Jackie breaks the silence.

'Judging by the accent you aren't Special Branch, so my guess would be Security Service.'

'Well done you.'

He thinks, So, you're MI5. So, you're a wanker.

Knew which flight he'd arrive on, knew which car-hire company he'd use. The spook probably knows more about the next couple of days' arrangements than he does.

Jackie tries pressing a little more. 'What's your name? At least, what's your name today?'

'Stuart William Hartley, but Stuart will do. And welcome home, Jackie. I hear it's been a long time.'

A bloody long time, he thinks, over twenty years. And yet, as he stole nervous glances out of the window of the Airbus, he was amazed how little had changed. At least from above.

Jackie says, 'What are you, my chaperone?' He looks this man Hartley up and down with a wry smile. 'Bodyguard?'

'Oh heavens, no. Among other things, I'm your welcoming committee. Shall we make a start? It's a good twenty minutes to the hotel and the traffic will be getting heavier.'

Jackie thinks, He wants me aware that he's in control of this situation, that he knows all there is to know. Bastard. He checks his mirror, focuses on reversing out of the parking space, determined not to betray any emotion.

'GCHQ have been busy,' he says. 'I didn't think I'd have merited all this attention. Shouldn't they be listening in on the Russian Embassy and monitoring the emails of Iranian diplomats?' He puts the car in first and nods his head. 'Oh yeah, they monitor everybody's emails these days.'

Hartley is silent, staring out of the window with a look of disdain as they ease into the traffic on the Sydenham by-pass. The roads aren't too congested yet, despite being close to four on a Friday afternoon. As they turn back towards the city on the A55, Hartley begins fiddling with a pen and readjusting his jacket at regular intervals. By the time they reach the Clarawood and Braniel estates, bullying up to the ring road on either side, Hartley is wiping his mouth with a tissue as if he's just eaten something sour.

The scene is a riot of colour and symbol: Union Jacks, Ulster Flags, Saltires. They fly from lampposts or gable walls, at times conjoined to form emblematic Siamese triplets. Red, white and blue bunting is strung above the road, creating a web of colour, and the kerbstones have been painted in the same colours, even a postbox. The day is clear and there is a strong breeze. Every banner clinging to its flagpole is streaming in the chill air.

'What's going on?' asks Jackie. 'It's October.'

'Yes,' says Hartley. 'This kind of display isn't confined to the summer marching season any more. It's been a year-round practice for some time now.'

Practice? thinks Jackie. Dear God. Which Mayfair club did they dig this idiot up in?

Hartley says, 'You haven't kept up with events here while you've been off gallivanting, have you.' His condescension is thickening the air in the car.

'You should know. You've been keeping such a close eye on me.' Christ, in this short space of time Jackie finds he hates this man.

'Things have intensified since the vote to limit the number of days the Union Flag is flown from City Hall. The general consensus among the loyalist population is of an eroding of Protestant, unionist culture. I shouldn't think it's as serious as the bad old days though.'

'You were here during the bad old days?'

'Good God, no. I was off in various embassies occupying myself with our European allies.'

Daddy pulling strings, most likely at the insistence of mummy, to keep Stuart away from those savages across the water, thinks Jackie.

Hartley then says, 'You shouldn't have come back, Jackie, funeral or not. You were out, kept your nose clean and were away long enough for people to forget. You put this life behind you. If you are seen, there's no guarantee that you'll catch that return flight – or any flight ever again.'

'It's my father's funeral. What would you do?'

'My father lives in Cheltenham and spends his days having cream teas and driving in the Cotswolds. He's been dead a long time.'

There is a period of silence as they turn onto the Castlereagh Road, heading out of the city and into the hills.

'Are *they* all still here? In Belfast?' Are any of them landfill out in the lough? he wonders.

He can always hope.

Hartley snorts. 'They all still live on the same bloody road.'

Jackie thinks, Shit.

'Billy Tyrie is in among the middle classes on Ravenhill Park. Probably because of the easy access to his lawyer, who lives a couple of doors down. It's rumoured Billy has the biggest garden in the area because he needs the space to bury the bodies. We believe he has a hand in over 70 per cent of violent crime and 79 per cent of rackets in East Belfast. The only thing we haven't connected him to is the drug trade – surprisingly, considering he's the East Belfast Brigadier of the UDA. Imagine the godfather of East Belfast organised crime attending Neighbourhood Watch meetings ...'

#

The Corolla eases into a parking space in front of the La Mon Hotel and Country Club. It's about six miles and twenty minutes from Jackie's father's house, where he grew up. That's a fair distance in Belfast, where you can take your life in your hands crossing from one street to another, and not because of the traffic. This is far enough away for anonymity, close enough to access the church and cemetery.

He sees a heavy-set man with a short, tidy haircut get out of a dark blue BMW about twenty yards away. The man leans against the side of the car and works hard at looking casual. Jackie would lay odds the car is armoured. By the size of him, the man could be too, and is more likely carrying similar firepower to Hartley. Hartley himself has visibly relaxed.

The La Mon is a pleasant, well-kept hotel on the outskirts of East Belfast. It sits in a pretty rural setting, nestled in the Castlereagh Hills, just as it did in 1978 when the Provisional IRA detonated a bomb that resulted in twelve deaths and more than thirty horrific injuries in the Peacock Room restaurant. The dead were effectively burned alive. The device had been constructed to ignite a cocktail of petrol and sugar, a huge tongue of flame some 40 feet high and 60 feet wide, which would stick to the skin of all those it touched. The twelve who died, swallowed by the napalm-like fireball, were Protestant. Jackie was young but remembers the fury in the community: the vitriol of men his father knew, the empty talk of revenge and violence when they'd had a few jars. One of the dead was an off-duty police officer. The others were civilians.

He rubs his face and rolls his head back, closing his eyes. Without opening them he says, 'Do you know about the bombing here in the seventies?'

'Of course. Quite the atrocity, I believe.'

'Weren't two of the bombing team rumoured to be working for MI5 as informants?'

'Like I said, before my time.'

Jackie sighs and opens his eyes and the hotel is back in his view. Families mingle with businessmen wandering in and out of reception, and a shapely blonde is jogging past their car and heading towards the BMW. The man waiting there doesn't give her a thought as she passes.

'He'll be one of yours then,' says Jackie.

'Well, he certainly isn't one of those thugs you ran with. What I said stands: you shouldn't have come back. Nevertheless, we think Tyrie isn't aware you're here, although I would imagine the thought has entered his mind in the circumstances. He now lives about a mile further up the road from your father's house. Simpson is halfway between. Fingers crossed they won't bump into you.'

Jackie opens his door and clambers out of the car with a little less vigour and grace than he'd like, particularly in front of Hartley. The Security Services man eases himself up and out of the Corolla, unfolding his long limbs with a gentle grunt. Jackie nods to the BMW and the man standing next to it.

'You can tell your man he's a bit obvious. I made him in two seconds. You can imagine how much he'll stick out to the dissidents.'

'That's rather the point,' says Hartley. 'Prevents me from being the target.' His thin mouth slithering into a grin, he sets off towards the BMW and his colleague.

Jesus, Jackie thinks. I got out of this life all those years ago and in twenty minutes I'm already bone tired of it all over again.

He runs his hands over his crew-cut, stretches to straighten out a few kinks, and slings the bag over his shoulder. As he sets off for the front door of the hotel he hears that public-school nasal whine again.

'Oh, and Jackie – Eileen's got kids now. She moved on and so should you. Forget her, go to the funeral, keep your head down and piss off out of here. There's a good boy.'

CHAPTER 3

1993

The sound of the automatic being cocked in the passenger seat was like nails on a chalkboard to Jackie as he cruised the Ford between the Ravenhill and Woodstock Roads. The sodium lighting and drizzle dappling the pavements gave the streets the appearance of shiny orange peel, but the area between the pockets of lampposts remained cloaked in dim shadow.

Belfast was a dark city at night. At another time that would have been an advantage, for himself and Marty sitting next to him, but not at that moment.

At that moment he was craning over the steering wheel as he drove down a deserted Cherryville street looking for Shanty McKee and his fucking Jack Russell terrier. He was gripping the wheel tight, controlling the urge to punch Marty because he wouldn't stop playing with the gun. He was looking for McKee because said gun was supposed to deposit at least one 9mm round in each of his knees.

Jackie glanced in the rearview mirror and spoke as softly and calmly as he could manage to the boy sitting there.

'Harold.'

Not softly enough. Harold still jumped at the mention of his name. Poor bastard, thought Jackie. I'd jump too if I was shopping my best mate to avoid a kneecapping for myself. Harold lived in the Chesham area, an enclave of semi-detached houses a mile away, and had got into a bit of light house-breaking with his mate Shanty. Shanty had been dating a wee girl from the Woodstock Road, who'd broken up with him after he kept pushing her to forego a condom when they drove up to Helen's Bay of an evening for a little back-seat wrestling in his car. It seemed Shanty took rejection hard, because he encouraged Harold to keep watch while he broke into the girl's house one evening and deposited the previous day's dinner, digested and all, on the wee girl's bed. When the girl's uncle, who was a member of the local UDA, heard about the fruits of Shanty's labours, he put the feelers out and poor Harold was grassed up as Shanty's lookout. Shanty went to ground but Harold fessed up to Shanty's one weakness: his Jack Russell, Ally, who had been staying with Shanty's sister since the incident. Shanty still walked the terrier faithfully at the same time every night in order to keep Ally regular. Dogs should reflect their owners, thought Jackie.

'Harold, where is he?' he said. 'We've been driving around for half an hour now.'

Harold's thick lenses were reflecting the sodium streetlight glow, twin orange windows in the dark of the back seat. 'I swear he's always about here,' he said. 'He thinks because it's dark he can get away with walking the dog.'

Marty finally put the gun on the floor of the car, then took his seat belt off and turned to face the kid, hands balled into fists. Jackie had little time for Marty Rafferty. He'd have chewed him out for fiddling with the handgun if the guy's da wasn't one of the top men in the organisation in their patch. In the rear view mirror, he saw Harold shrink into his seat ready for the violence to come. Jackie slammed on the brakes as they hit the end of Cherryville Street. Harold was already so braced for his beating that he barely moved as the car jolted to a halt, but Marty was yanked backwards, causing his head to crack off the windscreen.

'For fuck's sake!' he screeched. Jackie turned to face Marty. 'You arsehole! You want to join that wee shite with a couple of bullets in your fuckin' legs the night?'

Marty Rafferty was actually two years younger than Jackie Shaw who, in his early twenties, was himself a babe in arms in the Ravenhill UDA. Nevertheless, he thought himself a higher rank.

'Marty mate, just braked a wee bit heavy. I was looking out for the kid and the dog. Didn't notice we were near on My Lady's Road.'

'Aye, and you'll not notice when I come up behind you and put a fuckin' round in your head.'

Jackie, nice and calm: 'How're you going to get up so close after I break your fuckin' legs? And you'll be a bit noisy breathing through a tube.'

Harold was wide-eyed in the glow of the streetlight outside. Jackie could see the kid out of the corner of his eye, looking small and lost. He caught a flicker of indecision behind the glasses.

Marty squared his shoulders but hesitated as Jackie followed Harold's gaze directly between the two of them and across My Lady's Road to the entrance of Canada Street opposite. There walked a man in a pair of blue jeans and a parka, with a small Jack Russell terrier on a short lead. There was no one else around.

Marty followed his line of sight and clocked the figure.

Jackie gunned the car, accelerated hard across the road and mounted the kerb in front of man and dog.

He had to admit, Marty did it right. He grabbed the pistol and was out, gun in clear view but held low and no raised voice, just a nod to indicate that dog and owner should get in the car. Shanty reacted well too. He didn't shout or run or threaten. He picked up his dog and frowned, then opened the rear door of the car on the left. He saw Harold but again just frowned and sat next to him in silence. Jackie reversed off the kerb, buzzing on adrenaline, and turned back towards the Ravenhill Road and the Lagan Lodge Bar.

The day shift of drinkers – old men, the unemployed, wasters, alcoholics – had given way to the night shift – the same mix, with men clocked off work and the odd paramilitary thrown in. There were women in the bar too, many matching their male counterparts pint for pint, measure for measure. The atmosphere was one of hard, concentrated drinking with the occasional bray or cackle of laughter scything through the thick fug of fag smoke. In the corner, sitting in a snug with two hulking bruisers, sat a rangy, dishevelled figure with a pint glass in his hand. His hair was lank and tousled, and his wiry frame was draped across the bench like a scarecrow at rest. Small, hard eyes like polished raisins shone from a blunt caricature of a face. Rab Simpson.

Rab was in conference with two men who were twice his size and looked significantly older, sporting thick moustaches and three-day stubble. Their body language telegraphed respect for the skinny man in the dirty Ramones T-shirt.

Rab Simpson was twenty-six and had risen fast through the ranks of the UDA. He was in a constant quest for a suntan in the harsh and dank climate of the Northern Irish winter, but his skin hadn't taken to the tanning beds well. He had a sickly, jaundiced pallor which, along with his prominent overbite, had given him the nickname Homer among some of the rank and file.

Never to his face though.

Simpson's other nickname was 'Sick Bag': they heard a peeler threw up in his evidence bag upon finding some of Rab's handiwork washed up on the shore of the Lagan.

Jackie and Marty, with Harold and Shanty in front, pushed their way through the other patrons. Shanty clutched his dog in his arms. When they reached the snug, the big men stood up.

'Harold,' said Rab, 'thank you for your co-operation in finding young Shanty here. What are you having?'

Harold stared at Rab with his mouth slack. Rab sat, his eyes lidded and narrow, his top lip fat and flared by the great tombstone teeth beneath. Jackie said, 'Our Harold'll have a pint. Harp.'

And probably throw it up again as soon as he has it down him, he thought.

Rab nodded and turned his gaze on Shanty. The teenager maintained his sullen expression but managed to answer that vodka would do.

'Get him two,' said Rab. The big men made for the bar.

Jackie lit up a Benson & Hedges, offering one to the boys, who looked for all the world as though they were in the principal's office. Shanty, smooth-skinned, with clear blue eyes and choirboy looks, took one; Harold, head bowed with a shining trickle of snot tying his pug nose to his thin lips, declined. Jackie lit Shanty to save him having to let go of his beloved dog.

Rab picked up his pint, took a swig, and said, 'You know why you're here, Shanty?'

A nod.

'Why don't you remind me?'

Shanty related the story. The break-up, the revenge, hiding out just a mile away.

'And this wee girl. Who's her uncle?' said Rab.

Silence. Shanty tilted his head to avoid dropping ash on his dog.

'If you don't answer me,' said Rab, quiet, 'I'll take you out the back and put the rounds in you myself. And not in your knees. But before I do, I'll finish that mangy wee rat you're holding.'

Shanty gripped the Jack Russell tighter. For its part, the dog studied a beer spill on the table in front of them.

'Billy Tyrie.' It was almost a whisper.

Rab leaned forward, still the only one of them seated.

'That's right, Shanty. I have to give you credit, son, when you fuck up, you fuck up big-time. Now, here's what's going to happen. You're going to have your drinks so you get a wee bit of a glow on, make things a wee bit easier on you. We're not un-civilised here. You'll have your pint as well,' a sneer at Harold, 'then Jackie and Marty are going to take you, Shanty, out the side of the bar, down to the end of the alley and shoot you in the back of the knees.'

Jackie noticed Rab's face flush when he passed sentence. His fingertips had gone white as his grip on his pint glass tightened, but his voice remained flat and calm.

'Your mate here is going to watch, to see the result of his handiwork in grassing you up. Then he's going to come back into the bar and phone an ambulance.'

Jackie took the cigarette out of Shanty's mouth. It had almost burned to the filter.

'And let this be a warning to you. If youse ever do anything like this again, it won't be the back of the knees next time. We will not stand for anti-social activity in this community.'

The two thugs were returning with the drinks. Jackie and Marty were abstaining as Jackie was lookout and Marty needed a steady hand for the actual kneecapping. He looked like he could use a drink, though.

'Oh, and one last thing,' said Rab, now smiling. His lips were taut and stretched over the aggressive jut of his buck teeth. 'I'll take the dog. You'll hardly be walking him for a month or two so I'll hold onto him. For safekeeping, like.'

#

By the time they slipped out through the reinforced steel door at the side of the bar, it had stopped raining. Shanty's vodkas hadn't made much impact. He had begun to shake and the im-passive front he'd put up in the bar had shattered as soon as his dog became part of the equation. He'd started to rail against Rab, and Jackie had hit him a couple of quick slaps, less to keep him in line than to prevent Rab from taking the kid apart there and then. Rab had pulled a knife and nicked Shanty's ear as a warning and memento. Now Ally was sitting at Rab's feet in the snug being fed snacks by the two goons and Shanty was hugging himself in the damp, cold trench of the alley. There was a stink of stale beer and piss, although the latter could have been coming from Harold.

'It was a fucking accident, you know,' said Shanty. 'I broke into her house, aye. I went to her bedroom, aye. Couldn't get her out of my head, like.' The drink had loosened his tongue. 'I love her, y'see. I took Ally with me. I take Ally everywhere.'

'You took your dog house-breaking?' said Marty.

'Aye. He was just nervous, so he jumped on her bed and did his business. It wasn't his fault. Then I panicked and did a runner. I didn't want to tell Simpson in case he did Ally in. Youse won't tell him, will youse?'

Jackie glanced at his watch. 'Take your time, Marty. Better to do it right than rush the job.'

Marty scowled and gave Shanty a shove towards the low, rough-textured concrete wall of the alley, with broken glass and barbed wire on top. Jackie made for the entrance of the narrow passage that opened onto the Ravenhill Road, about ten yards away. He lit up another cigarette and shooed Harold further towards Marty and Shanty. He checked his watch – 8.04 p.m. – and let out a racking cough.

Marty was fiddling with the automatic while Shanty lowered himself flat on his belly on the cold concrete. The night was settling into dampness; the road was deserted. Jackie could smell the drifting smoke of coal fires coming from the terraced streets a couple of hundred yards away. He strained, but couldn't make out the burned-out shell of East End Video further up towards the park.

What he could make out was a squat grey shape gliding by the shops about 150 yards away. It had two pinpricks of light on the front and was joined by a second, bulky grey shadow approaching the Ravenhill Road from the left. He turned to see Shanty lying flat, Harold tight to the side of the alley, and Marty gripping the Walther with both hands, taking deliberate aim at Shanty's left leg.

'Peelers!'

Marty looked up and cocked his head back sharply: *'What?'*

'Peelers!' said Jackie, somewhere between a hoarse whisper and a shout.

The two armoured police Land Rovers were within fifty yards of the bar now, passing the gospel hall by Shamrock Street. He sprinted up the alley and made for the heavy steel door at the side of the bar. As he grabbed for it he hissed at Marty, who had now lowered the Walther PK and stood staring at him.

'It's the fucking peelers! Dump the gun and get in the fucking bar.'

As he ducked in the door he saw the first Land Rover pull up at the end of the alley and the dark, hulking phantom of a policeman in body armour clamber out, carrying a Heckler & Koch submachine gun.

CHAPTER 4

Thursday

As Jackie drives down from the Castlereagh Hills into the city on a crisp October morning, he can see the patchwork of terraced streets, the maze of the Cregagh Estate and the stalking giants of the gantry cranes in the shipyard, Samson and Goliath.

Jackie is overtaken by a PSNI Police Land Rover and is surprised by how garish the blue and amber check strip looks, rather than the pugnacious battleship grey of the old RUC models. He is conscious that he is unarmed.

By the time he's nearing Bendigo Street and his father's house, he realises the city, or life in it, has moved on. Factories and businesses have gone, to be replaced by startling new steel and glass constructions or left as hollow carcasses by the roadside. Home-grown shops and supermarkets have been consumed by national or international chains. There are pockets of resistance, but the chaotic vibrancy of the local shopping street is almost gone. And the flags are everywhere. It is territorial marking at its most conspicuous. The thought that it could be read as a stark warning to him, that he has no place here any more, isn't lost on him.

Approaching the traffic lights at the bottom of the Ormeau Park, Jackie sees a glass-fronted apartment building wedged between two of the usual terraced houses. Its modernity is stark, like a bright silver cap in a row of yellowed teeth. The cavity that had once been the ruined East End Video building reborn. Just around the corner he spies a small garden of remembrance ringed with freshly painted railings. A small plaque is positioned on the gable wall to memorialise the nine innocent souls who died on that day twenty years ago. The bombers have no such tribute.

A few more yards down the road and he passes another gable wall. In the past it was adorned by a roughly painted mural of two masked gunmen and the crest of the UVF. The other lads had hated that mural: there were no UDA depictions on the road while the local rivals were represented, but Billy had just laughed.

'Who needs to advertise?' he'd said, which was true enough. Billy Tyrie wasn't a brigadier by that stage but he was well on the way and everyone knew he ran the Ravenhill, Woodstock, Cregagh and Castlereagh areas. He said, 'The people know we're here; the peelers know we're here and, most important, the Fenians know we're here.'

And I hope to God you don't know I'm here now, thinks Jackie.

He hadn't intended stopping, just to drive through the old area and take in Bendigo Street from behind the wheel of the Toyota. But it's been so long and the road is busy with morning traffic and assorted pedestrians: it should be safe. So he parks in a side street and strolls back to the memorial, where he stops for a moment to take it in. He catches an older man looking at him. The man, who wears the ravages of time, is walking a scrawny-looking terrier; he greets Jackie as he goes past. Jackie smiles and returns the pleasantry, and feels a little more at home. He had forgotten the simple pleasure of passing the time of day with a complete stranger. He saw the same people every day on the walk to work in England, back when he lived in a city, and never managed to achieve eye contact with them. It is one of Northern Ireland's many contradictions that, while the two communities continue to live in distrust and resentment, people will happily greet and talk to a stranger on the street. He turns and hurries past a convenience store, then dodges traffic to cross over the road and avoid being seen through the front window of the Parkside Bar. Just in case.

He passes a tidy little greengrocer where some locals are already sniffing various fruit and vegetables.

He passes the post office and hears a couple of men chatting in what he takes to be Polish, certainly an Eastern European language.

He passes Mr Ali's mini-supermarket. He doesn't see Mr Ali himself through the window but clocks a large Pakistani-looking guy behind the counter and supposes he's the son. The last time Jackie saw him, he was a scrawny teenager in the local flute band.

A barrage of voices batter his ears. Customers walking out of the mini-supermarket behind him. His hands go to his pockets but he doesn't know what for: maybe it's a reflex from the days when he might be carrying a weapon. It's strange for him, being surrounded by the staccato song of Belfast accents after a time away from the city. He's disorientated.

'... sure, Isabelle ... then he says ... dole ... aye, says you ... catch yourself on ...'

Female chatter with a couple of deeper male voices, indistinct, bringing up the rear.

'... you'll be so lucky ... Sammy Courtney's wife ... I had to laugh ...'

As Jackie approaches the corner of Bendigo Street itself the male voices begin hacking through the older women's babble.

'... Mabel, never again ... 'til next week ... *mine paremale* ...'

He feels the back of his neck tingle, as though one of the women behind had reached out and touched him, and fights the urge to lash out. The female voices fade to his right as the women cross the Ravenhill Road. The Eastern European chatter follows as he turns down Bendigo Street, meaningless blather to him.

'... *ta võib sattuda ... sul on nuga? ... kuradi katkestas teda, kui sa pead ...*'

After ten yards he stops, clenches his fists, closes his eyes for a moment. Jesus, he thinks, no rest for the wicked. When he turns around they stand, unmoving but with clear intent. A morning runner skirts them with a trace of annoyance.

One says in English, 'You come with us. You don't come with us, you come later. We know the car, the registration. If you come later, it is not daytime. It is harder for you.'

Jackie can see there's no malice, it's just a simple statement of fact. Nevertheless, they're big men and carry their bulk with confidence. They look like they have no issue with using violence if necessary. But the pavement between the terraced houses and parked cars is narrow – they'd have to come at him one at a time. And the main road is in view. It's morning, for Christ's sake, he thinks.

'Also, we know your sister, her address. You come later, it is harder for her too.'

Jackie's stomach lurches as though it was back on yesterday's flight, buffeted by turbulence. His legs feel hollow. It took less than twenty-four hours for them to find him. Using these guys rather than home-grown talent is smart. He thinks Billy must be behind this. Fucking Billy. He nods and tries to loosen up a little, raises his palms and they accompany him back to the car. It's only when he pulls back out into traffic that the one in the passenger seat produces the flick-knife and he hears the blade snap open.

#

His passengers direct him to follow the Ravenhill Road to its end then drive across the Albert Bridge Road to the nationalist Short Strand. He's amazed to find the Short Strand is nothing more than a strip of asphalt now, with a couple of new apartments facing onto the river. The sense of menace the place engendered in the past, when it was a nest of PIRA activity, is gone. Following directions, he cuts through the area and finds a vacant lot where Mountpottinger Police Station once stood. He remembers the brick and concrete monstrosity topped by a blast wall which was hammered by terrorist rocket and gun attacks throughout the Troubles.

Now they are on the lower Newtownards Road and the flags are back, augmented by bunting and a long, unbroken mural dedicated to chronicling the very organisation he had run with in a different time – a different lifetime – the Ulster Defence Association.

They turn off into a side street and he's told to stop in front of a small club with steel shutters. It is one of many private drinking clubs scattered around Belfast, Protestant and Catholic, and staunchly working class. Jackie's senses are heightened: he can smell the clean, soapy scent of one of his companions, the heavy, gritty musk of tobacco from the other; feel the crisp, sharp bite of autumnal air and note the cars parked, one of them an incongruous Porsche. He spots graffiti daubed on the door of a house opposite – *Blacks out! White Ulstermen only!* His companions get out of the car with him and one of them approaches the door and batters on the heavy steel. The one with the knife stays close behind.

A heavily-built man who appears to be in his thirties opens the door. Jackie is ushered inside and the other two take their leave. Inside, the big man ups the ante with a leather shoulder-holster and what looks like a Smith & Wesson revolver. Jackie's stomach has calmed but his face feels as though it's on fire. His heart pounds. The man looks solid but is slow and out of shape. Jackie isn't a young man but he has tried to look after himself and it's not a certainty that the revolver is loaded, nor that there is a bullet in every chamber. Then he realises there is a second

33

man in the narrow corridor they occupy, and his pistol isn't in a holster. With his free hand the second man opens a door off the corridor and ushers Jackie through.

He enters a room bare save for a couple of wooden chairs, a stage and some paramilitary banners hung on the walls. Despite the strip lighting, the room retains a gloomy air. With its stark walls and stained concrete floor it could be a slaughterhouse rather than a drinking den. A third man sits on the edge of the stage and watches as Jackie is led to one of the wooden chairs. Jackie's hands are left free and he crosses his arms. The figure, still and silent on the stage, covers its nose and mouth with its hands as if fending off some kind of stench. Then it barks.

The sound is cracked and guttural: a literal, feral bark. The room is so bare of feature that the reverb is sharp and loud. Jackie locks his arms tighter and keeps his eyes levelled on the figure. This man wants him confused and off guard. And he's fucked if that isn't exactly what he's achieved.

What the fuck? thinks Jackie. Struggling to maintain his composure, he hears a snarl. It is a human sound but not coming from a place of reason.

The figure snaps to its feet and takes a jerking step forward. Jackie's hands ball tightly into fists under his crossed arms. There is still a good six or seven yards between them but he is readying himself for a fight. The figure is still taking ragged, jerking steps towards him, the mouth still covered.

The man appears to be unarmed and looks sleek and strong, lean like a bantamweight with a degree of definition showing through the T-shirt. More a Carl Frampton than a Barry McGuigan and in better shape than Jackie. The fact he has a couple of mates with handguns standing at the door could be a deciding factor, too.

The figure gives one final growl, feints forward and drops his hands.

And smiles.

It is Rab Simpson.

But he doesn't exactly look like Rab Simpson. 'Homer' is gone. This is Rab's better-looking, up-market, fully organic brother. There is a healthy colour in the face, the overbite has gone and the man is *groomed*.

'Jackie Shaw, what about ye?'

'I'm all right Rab. You're looking well.'

'What the fuck's wrong with your voice, Jackie? You sound half-fucking-English.'

'I've been living in different places. The accent has rounded out a bit.'

'Watered down, you mean. We not refined enough for you?'

Throughout this exchange Rab Simpson has been smiling, his arms hanging relaxed by his sides and his body language casual. Now he grabs a chair, his movement quick and wired like he's high on something. Jackie is reminded how hair-trigger the change in Rab's mood and movements can be and he is wary of the fact that the man in front of him has lost none of his speed. And that they last parted on less than amicable terms. Most likely Rab Simpson isn't best pleased by the fact that Jackie is still breathing. Rab sits in the chair and crosses his legs loosely, the model of indifference. He asks one of the men to bring drinks and cocks an eyebrow when Jackie defers.

Jackie says, 'Driving.'

Rab says, 'So, the elephant in the room. Where the fuck have you been for twenty years and why are you not dead?' In another of those lightning moves he holds up his hand, palm out. 'I'm not expecting an answer now. It's all pretty much by the by anyway, despite what happened with Tommy and Danny. And now here you are, sitting in front of me large as life.'

He accepts a drink from one of the armed men, some kind of spirit by the look of it.

'Now, I'll not say I was all that cut up when we heard you'd been shot, Jackie. You had a lot of potential and you were handy enough in a fight, like. But you were always a bit quiet, like you were watching all the time. And you're still wearing that Fenian ring, I see. I just didn't trust you. There were times I would've knocked your balleeks in, but Billy liked you, so I had to hold off.'

Jackie fingers the Claddagh ring and concentrates on remaining neutral. That was always the key with men like Rab: neutrality. He'd seen men speak back, just an offhand comment, and be beaten to a pulp or worse for it. He'd seen men kowtow and mewl, and be taken apart for showing weakness. So he breathes, steadily and quietly.

'Then we find out you're alive. A contact in the peelers saw your body – well, *a* body. He took a wee photo for us. The body was your height, your build, wearing your clothes. Even had your tattoo. The face was mashed up because you'd gone through the windscreen when the Army shot up the car. Now, the body was wearing that cheap watch of yours, but that ring, mate, that Fenian fucking ring, wasn't on the hand and you never went anywhere without that ring on you.'

Jackie's concern had been somebody spotting him, word spreading that the ghost of Jackie Shaw was walking around, fit as a fiddle on the Ravenhill Road. But all this time they had known he was alive and, when his father passed away, they must have known he'd come home.

'You couldn't stay away, could you? You were spotted down by the park.'

The old boy at the memorial. He must have recognised Jackie. Maybe it was the bastard Fenian ring. Oul' lad could have made a quick phone call on a mobile when he got round the corner. Then the Eastern European guys were given orders to pick him up.

Rab leans in towards him, elbows on knees.

'I really don't care where you've been all this time. But there's something very wrong with what happened that night and why it wasn't your body the Army shot up. I'm wondering if the Army shot up the car at all, or if it wasn't all rigged. My money is on you being a fucking grass. So why shouldn't I have you shot right now and dumped in the Lagan?'

Is that a rhetorical question, thinks Jackie. The two men at the door haven't budged so he guesses there is no immediate prospect of a bullet in his head, but you never knew with these boys. Rab smiles.

'It's all a question of supply and demand,' he says, leaning back in his chair. 'You see, Jackie, I meet a demand in East Belfast, for high quality illegal substances. It isn't always easy to meet that demand because the youngsters these days just can't get enough of that shite, but I do my best. It's a community service, so it is.' He spreads his arms as wide as his pearly-white grin. 'But I have a potential obstruction to my supply and I need someone to give me a hand removing it. Are you feeling me?'

Jackie cocks his head.

'The bulk of my supply comes from the west of the city. From the Shankill, just like these two boys keeping us company.'

Just like yourself, thinks Jackie.

'They're associates of mine, but they aren't on the same team. They're not taigs, like, but they work for another organisation of a similar nature to ours.'

UVF, thinks Jackie.

'Unfortunately, one of my colleagues in the UDA, a man of some influence, doesn't have the same spirit of enterprise as myself. Things have changed since you disappeared, but this fella doesn't see that we have to move with the times. He's still giving it "No Surrender". So I'm forced to make use of some of our guests from further afield.'

The Slavic-sounding guys, thinks Jackie. He says aloud, 'And your colleague doesn't like the idea of your mates here bringing drugs into East Belfast via their Shankill supply, or you distributing on his patch.'

'Who the fuck said it's *his* patch?' Rab moves forward a fraction, fists clenched. A knotted cord of veins claws up his throat.

'Just trying to understand how I can help you out. I've been away. I'm trying to put things together here,' says Jackie.

Rab gives the armed men a brief glance then continues, an edge to his voice now.

'So here's the craic. I want you to kill Billy Tyrie for me.'

Jackie just manages to catch himself before he can say, *Are you out of your fucking mind?*

'There it is,' says Rab. 'I'll supply a gun, you take him out.'

Jackie is a relative unknown in the area after so long away. He hasn't been in the UDA for twenty years. While Rab knows he's breathing, Billy may not. So Jackie isn't a threat to Rab: he's a resource.

He says, 'You wouldn't be setting me up, Rab, would you?'

'Why would you say something like that to me after all these years?'

'You know, once bitten ...'

Simpson's expression flatlines along with his tone. 'If you do Billy, you can slink off back to wherever it is you were hiding. If you don't, I'll kill you myself in this fucking room.' He flashes those pearly whites again. 'And I'll shoot your fucking sister before my tea tonight.'

CHAPTER 5

1993

The police lifted Marty in the alley and interviewed Harold and Shanty back at Castlereagh RUC station. Later, they'd hear Marty took a kicking in the back of the Land Rover for calling the peelers Black Bastards. He also took up residence in a cell in Crumlin Road prison for possession of an illegal firearm.

That was after Jackie had ducked back into the bar and dumped the jacket he was wearing. The RUC came into the bar and performed a search on the basis they'd had a tip-off there could be an IRA gun attack on the place that night. Those forced to abandon their precious drinks and line up along the walls thought it more likely they were raiding the place for UDA materiel. The Lagan Lodge bar was a notorious hang-out for members. The heavy fug of smoke drowning the bar was thickened with the hatred radiating from the drinkers.

Jackie had lined up against the wall opposite the counter with the rest and was told to face the plaster. He smelled the stench of tobacco and heard the heavy footsteps of the policemen, weighed down by body armour and weaponry, making their way slowly up the line, occasionally asking for ID and throwing the odd question at patrons.

A black-gloved hand touched his shoulder and a clipped voice, drenched in irony, said, 'Evening, sir.'

'Evening.'

'Chilly night out, isn't it, sir?'

'I wouldn't know. I've been in here.'

The glove came off and a large hand grabbed his arm and turned him around.

'You're a bit cold. Are you sure you weren't just outside?'

He looked into the face of a tall, strong-featured man with a thick moustache and intense blue eyes. There were sergeant's stripes on the man's rifle-green coat.

Jackie said, 'I'm not feeling the best, so I'm not. That's why I was here, just having a couple of hot whiskies.'

The police sergeant leaned in closer. 'I don't smell any alcohol on your breath,' he said. 'You wouldn't mind coming outside and answering a couple of questions, would you, sir?' The peeler gave Jackie an exaggerated look of concern. 'Have you a coat you can put on? It really is chilly out tonight.'

'You wouldn't believe it. I'd a jacket on me when I came in here. Then I went to the bog and somebody nicked it while I was away from my seat.' Jackie looked left and right conspiratorially and added, 'They're a bad lot in here.'

He got an appreciative smattering of sniggers along the line of drinkers. The sergeant stepped back and indicated to a couple of constables to escort Jackie out to the Land Rovers parked in front of the bar.

Outside he could see a couple of policemen talking to Harold, one of them holding a notebook and scribbling the odd entry. Another two were talking to Shanty, who sat in the back of one of the Land Rovers while an RUC constable leaned against one of the open doors. He held Marty's pistol in a clear plastic bag. The other Land Rover's back doors were closed. Jackie assumed Marty was inside.

The crackle of police radio traffic was sharp in the night air and the angry buzz of helicopters could be heard drifting across the city. There were at least two up, probably Army surveillance of West Belfast: maybe a shooting or suspect device had been reported. Jackie heard another RUC patrol responding on the radios and it was clear that this unit had called for back-up, probably after discovering Marty's weapon.

On the corners opposite and to their left, policemen with more H&K submachine guns trained their sights on the nearby streets, covering their colleagues from potential ambush. The officer on the opposite corner was sighting his weapon intently down the road leading towards the republican Short Strand.

Jackie's escorts had tightened their grip on his arms as they exited the narrow front door of the bar. Now he could feel the pressure squeezing the muscles of his forearms, although he wasn't handcuffed. He breathed deeply and swallowed as they approached the open rear of another Land Rover. He knew it might hurt to breathe that deep again for a couple of days after the peelers had finished with him. He hadn't been lifted before but he'd heard plenty of stories.

They gave Jackie a shove into the back. He sat heavily on one of the leather bench seats along the side, the two RUC men clambering in to face him in silence. They sat like that for minutes. Jackie didn't know if the peelers had seen him duck in the side door of the bar before they got to Marty; it could have been how cold he was when they got up close to him in the bar that raised suspicion. Maybe they'd smelled the night air on him, or even the smoky coal fire aroma of the chimneys outside. Maybe they just didn't like him giving them lip.

He tried to focus on one of the coppers' boots opposite but found his mind straying. Where was his da? His sister? Would they have any idea what was happening to him? How could they – none of the cowboys he ran with gave a shite if he got his bollocks kicked in; Rab Simpson wouldn't be running to contact his next of kin. The peelers had nothing on him, he knew. He hadn't handled the gun and no one in that bar would grass him at least, but it rankled, the thought of pissing blood for a couple of days for the likes of Rab. Then he thought of what could happen if he didn't take his medicine for the organisation. He crossed his arms, willing himself not to fidget.

He thought of the RUC sergeant in the bar. A big fucker, he reminded Jackie of a boy in his old school called Geordie Plant – a bruiser who'd tortured a few of the kids in his days in the playground. Jackie had spoken back and ended up with a date and time to fight the bastard on the football pitches. He remembered the anticipation, the sickening realization that the hour was rolling around, the long slog to the pitches. The cold tightening in his groin as fear took hold; he felt it now. He'd taken a pretty bad kicking that day too.

The sergeant clambered in with another couple of policemen. The back of the Land Rover was crowded now as they closed the door behind them. The sergeant sat and took his peaked cap off, looking at the badge of a harp and crown on the front, and laid it gently on the seat next to him before he spoke.

'I know that was you ran in the side door. I also know that you're well aware I can't prove a thing.'

And I'm aware of what's coming, thought Jackie, and I wish you'd get on with it.

'Youse think you're something, don't youse?' said the sergeant. 'Think you're fighting the Provos, for God and Ulster, all that shite.'

The first blow slammed his skull off the inner metal skin of the vehicle and the dim interior light flared to searing white in his vision. The second blow, on the left side of his head forced him downwards and into a crouch.

Good for him, bad for the peelers. He curled into a fetal ball and covered his head and crotch and, in the confined space and wearing cumbersome flak jackets, the police struggled to cause real damage. They rained blows on the back of his head, his spine, his side. It hurt, it stung, his kidneys took some punishment, but his face and vitals were protected. And for the rest of the men who delivered the beating, that would probably have been enough. It was a message, nothing more. But the sergeant was determined to make his mark, literally.

Someone took a handful of hair and yanked hard, jerking Jackie's head back long enough for someone else to land an awkward punch on his left cheek. Awkward, but it stunned him, slowed his reactions, and let the RUC men land more accurate, powerful blows on his face. Now he could feel the wetness under his nose as it bled. The gloves were off, literally; knuckles gashed his cheek just under his eye and he hoped it hurt the peeler as much as it stung him. After a couple of good shots his mouth began filling with blood as he bit his tongue and his inner cheek was lacerated.

And then, it was over.

The sergeant said, 'Youse are gangsters. You're animals, just like the IRA. Youse might have some friends in the force, but they're the same as youse: scum. And I'd give them the same if I got my hands on them.'

They held him under-arm and dragged him out of the Land Rover, leaving him lying in the alley where he'd stood guard not thirty minutes ago. He couldn't lift his head, but through the dull throbbing he heard them clamber into their vehicles, and the heavy growl of the engines starting. Then they were gone and all that was left was pain, cold and the pulsing drone of the helicopters watching the city as it tore itself apart.

#

There were sixteen shootings across Belfast that night. The highest body count was in a bar in the Ardoyne area where UVF gunmen walked in and sprayed the place with automatic weapons, killing six and injuring two. A taxi driver and his fare were shot dead in the Woodvale area by IRA gunmen, and an

43

off-duty policeman was gunned down by republicans as he returned home from the cinema with his kids in Dundonald. He was badly wounded but not fatally. An undercover British Army unit passed by a bookies as three armed robbers ran out the front with the late shift's takings. Unluckily for the criminals, the soldiers mistook them for armed terrorists and, after the getaway car was rammed, all three were shot as they scrambled from the vehicle. One survived to stand trial for his crime.

Some time later, Jackie Shaw stumbled home after his beating. He was sore and stank of beer, fags and the piss of the alley. No one from the bar had come out to help him. In the house belonging to his father, he washed his cuts and bruises with freezing water in the kitchen sink, then rinsed his mouth with some Bushmills he found in a cabinet. The whiskey-burn was harsh and he winced as he forced the liquor down. The kitchen and living room were clean and orderly: Sarah had paid a visit. As he staggered to the foot of the stairs he passed his father, snoring in his favourite armchair, lulled to sleep by the soft clink of ice and the swirl of hard spirits.

CHAPTER 6

Thursday

As he drives past a gun-toting mural, Jackie takes comfort in the fact that he is now, at least, armed. A handgun is stashed under his seat, with two magazines stored in the glove compartment.

He is driving through another estate, Tullycarnet, on the edge of East Belfast, bordering the satellite town of Dundonald. The rows of council housing and blocks, set at sharp right angles, are laid out like bigger, boxy versions of the Quonset huts in old prisoner-of-war films. Viewed from the air, much of the city has that regimented order, whether snaking lines of terraced housing or the maze-like patterns of housing estates.

Soon he is in Dundonald. He was born in the Ulster Hospital here. His mother's funeral was held in the Presbyterian church, and now his sister lives in the town.

#

He accepted Rab's proposal because, well, what else could he do? He'd likely be dead by now if he'd refused. And, although family hadn't been considered fair game in the old days, he knew Rab would think nothing of carrying out his threat against his sister and her kids.

As he'd received a Ruger SR9 semi-automatic and pre-paid mobile phone not an hour ago, he heard from Rab how it was thought Jackie had been killed on 'active service'. There had been a few instalments of financial help for Jackie's da, Sam, and the 'funeral' had been taken care of by Billy Tyrie. A couple of fellow volunteers had been killed on the same night and similar assistance had been provided for their families. Billy had even respected Sam's request for no paramilitary trappings at the funeral. Rab told him the UDA hadn't bothered his father when suspicion fell on Jackie's 'disappearance', or when suspicion for the other members' deaths had fallen on Jackie. By then the ceasefire was on, players were making money and political capital, and the disappearance of one missing rogue volunteer wasn't much of a concern. It was assumed any damage that could have been done to the organisation would have already been inflicted and, with prisoners released and tacit pardons for past sins flying like red, white, blue, green and orange confetti, nobody cared much about the Shaw family.

But the rules had changed and, if Rab could use his sister as leverage, then he was happy to threaten Jackie with her killing. Anything to get the job done.

The job being the killing of Billy Tyrie.

Billy had always been one of the most dangerous men in the UDA, because Billy was a believer. Back in the day, many of the UDA brigadiers and hierarchy in the east of the city were seen as soft and complacent by the rank and file. They lived in a Protestant heartland, separated from much of the vicious epicentre by the River Lagan and with only the small enclave of the Short Strand providing a republican threat. By contrast, the UDA in West and North Belfast lived almost cheek by jowl with their republican counterparts. Only the peace walls and a few street junctions separated the two terrorist factions, and the West Belfast boys were very real targets for IRA and INLA violence, occasionally being picked off by republican terrorists.

But Billy was a different animal altogether.

An animal, to be sure, but different to his counterparts in the east. For a start, he was loath to see Catholic civilians hurt in actions under his command. Jackie had seen him order the knee-capping of his own men when a random Catholic had been injured in a local UDA action, even after the Ravenhill bomb in 1993. Not that it was a matter of conscience.

'Irish nationalism's all about self-pity and playing the victim,' Billy used to say. 'Better not to give them any more fuel for the fire.'

He also didn't rate the British.

'The Brits are cunts. They persecuted the Irish nationalists for long enough. They massacred Presbyterians among the United Irishmen in '98. We gave them a bloody nose at the Battle of Saintfield and they slaughtered us for it at Ballynahinch.' He'd lean in close, dropping his voice to a conspiratorial whisper. 'But here's the thing, Jackie. The republicans keep portraying this conflict as Irish against British. We well know, it's Irish against Irish, son. We're as fucking Irish as they are, or George Washington wasn't a fucking Yank, he was a Brit. Can't sell that line to the Americans though, can they? And sure we built their fucking country for them as well.'

Billy would stare at the tip of his cigarette. 'We just came along a bit later. We don't conform to their idea of what an Irishman should be. We're not beholden to the Catholic Church. We're not fucking moaning about British persecution the day long, even though we have our own axe to grind in that department. We have our own identity and that's what I'm fighting to preserve, not some fucking union. I'm not a loyalist, I'm a survivalist.' Finally, he'd take a drag on his cigarette, the dramatic flourish of a quick swig on his beer. 'We're Ireland's loyal rebels. The unpalatable truth.'

Another unpalatable truth was that Billy Tyrie had sanctioned the murder of not a few of his fellow Irishmen, many of his own people for 'antisocial activities', failure to pay protection or simply perceived lack of respect.

He must be in his early fifties by now, thinks Jackie. He had been utterly ruthless in his actions in the UDA and Jackie doesn't suppose age has mellowed him.

#

'Only ten minutes late. Could be worse.'

'Better late in one place than early in the next.'

'No,' says Sarah, 'you don't get to do that. You don't get to quote him. You don't get to put on that show: "Ach my da and his country ways." You haven't earned that.'

'It's not about earning anything, Sarah. He was my da as much as he was yours.'

She looks him square in the eyes. 'But you weren't his child as much as I was, because you just weren't *there*, Jackie.'

This is going well, he thinks. Together five minutes and we're already sniping at each other.

Sarah is right, of course. At seventeen he'd taken off to New York with a ticket saved for with a couple of years of part-time wages. The dishes he'd washed for that fare would probably stretch all the way to America itself. His parents had thought he'd be back in a month: he stayed – overstayed – in the States for a year before his mother got sick and he came home. At nineteen he'd disappeared again, this time to the Army. His mother was gone and with her, the centre of the family. He didn't keep in touch beyond a couple of phone calls each year and his father couldn't keep his hands off the bottle. In the meantime, Sarah started seeing Thomas, now her husband.

Five years later he was back in Ravenhill and running with the paramilitaries. His father, already numbed by drink, took to self-medication with renewed vigour.

'He *was* a culshie from the country though,' says Jackie, his tone light.

'At least he knew who he was,' says Sarah, real venom in her voice. His attempt at levity lies crumpled between them like an unwanted gift.

Stop trying to lighten things, he thinks, it's just baiting her. She is looking at him intently and he realises he is chewing on his lower lip. It's a habit he's had since childhood, something he does when scolding himself for a careless word or deed.

The ghost of a smile steals across her face. She throws a lock of auburn hair behind her ear.

And it is a ghost. He thought the Sarah that could smile at him was long gone.

'At least he didn't sound like he was English. What the hell happened to your accent?'

It isn't much, but it's enough. The dig about his accent, the *smile,* is enough to remind them that they are brother and sister. They begin to talk and trade a couple of stories about Da. Do you remember how he always hid his fags from Mum if she came home early from church? How he always sang in silly voices when he'd had a few? How he used to do a jig with us when he was in a good mood at a party? It made them remember that they had once been close. They had once shared a roof, a bedroom, a school, the same friends. And the same parents. At least until the mortar that had bound them together, their mother, was taken by the spectre of cancer, leaving the family in a pile of broken rubble.

Then Jackie had moved away – run away – after that bloody night twenty years ago. The calls to home, the brief awkward chats between father and son had slowly petered out. Two men bound by blood and blighted by the past with, finally, nothing to say to one another. He had kept up occasional contact with his sister but, he knew, far from enough.

He has to admire Sarah. She is the only one of them who had the strength to create her own family while he and his father ran to violent crusade and drink respectively. The only one to fight for a normal life; a real life. As they talk he sees a softening in her, and he feels a desperate need to protect her, to protect Thomas and her kids, Daniel and Margaret. Her kids, once suspicious little strangers peering around their mother's legs, now surly teenagers, glaring behind mobile phones and tablets.

The mobile phone given to him by Rab chimes.

Sarah hears it, pausing so that he can read the incoming text. He ignores it. She gives him a look but, like him, doesn't want to complicate the moment and so continues.

They discuss tomorrow's funeral arrangements. The service will be held in a funeral home as it is many, many years since his father crossed the threshold of the Presbyterian church. Those in attendance will then proceed to Roselawn Cemetery, followed by a modest wake at Sarah's house. Their father had been a gentle and respected man despite the drink. Sam Shaw's wife was taken by a disease he couldn't understand. His son was taken by wanderlust, the Army, and then an organisation that broke many a family and claimed many a son.

Jackie can see he isn't alone with his guilty conscience, that Sarah has her own regrets. She was there every Saturday in Bendigo Street, some weekday evenings too. She cooked meals and Sunday dinners for her father, changed his sheets and relayed the odd tidbit of news from Jackie whenever he called. But she had left too.

Finally she says, 'Will you stay for your lunch?'

There is a plea in her eyes that he can scarcely bear. Worse still is the hope in her voice. He realises he is dying for a drink.

'I'm sorry, Sarah, I can't today.'

The disappointment makes her look young again and he is back in Bendigo Street, fighting with her as their mother shoos them away from her kitchen. He wants to stay, wants to break bread and be the brother she hasn't had for all these years. Even now, her capacity for forgiveness and love shames him.

'I just have to deal with something but, once it's done, I swear I will stay for that dinner. If you'll have me.'

She doesn't like it. He can see the muscle of her jaw working as she reaches for a civil answer. But they've spoken longer today than in a couple of decades and Sarah won't let that amount to nothing.

'Okay, Jackie,' she says, 'but stay away from *them*. They were scum back then and, if anything, they're worse now that they don't have a cause to hang their violence on.'

'I know,' he says. It's keeping them away from you that's the trouble, he thinks.

Sarah says, 'Do what you have to do and I'll see you tomorrow.'

'See you tomorrow, Sis.'

#

Rab's text is an address on the solidly middle-class street of Ravenhill Park: Tyrie's house.

Jackie is back in the Toyota en route to the La Mon Hotel when his own pre-paid mobile rings.

The road is through typical north Down countryside, rolling green hills undulating away from the narrow strip of concrete. His mother used to refer to the county, with its myriad drumlins, as a 'basket of eggs' and the road peaks and dips like a rollercoaster. There is no other traffic that he can see as he glances at the mobile in his hand and sees the words *unknown caller* on the screen. He taps *answer* and puts the phone to his left ear.

A voice says, 'Jackie Shaw, as I live and breathe.'

It's a rasping voice with more than a hint of amusement. His knuckles whiten on the steering wheel. He crests a rise and sees the road sweep down to a low gully before climbing to another peak. He begins to brake as the car gains momentum on the downward slope.

'Are you there, Jackie Boy?'

The car is climbing again, easing up the slope towards the next crest in the road. He is accelerating, urging the engine to match the steep incline so that, when the car guns over the rise and he sees a makeshift roadblock some thirty yards away, he has to brake hard and turn into the resultant skid, halting side-on to the group.

Fifteen yards away, two cars are blocking the road with six men ranged in front of them. The men wear jeans and Barbour jackets. Two of them are standing in the classic bouncer pose, left hand around right wrist in front of the body. The right hands are wrapped around the butt of automatic handguns. The others are lounging against the cars, feigning an air of indifference – but Jackie can see the tension in their arms, like metal rods, and their faces, set in stone. Two of them part and open the door of the car on the left, a black BMW Gran Turismo. A stocky man clambers out with some difficulty and takes a handgun from one of the men. He strides up to Jackie's car. The man's casual air says he's no stranger to violence: he carries the weapon like it's an extension of his arm.

The man taps the driver's-side window of the Toyota with the gun, and now Jackie can see the owner of the voice that was on his mobile phone moments ago.

He lowers the window and smells the tobacco and whiskey stink of Billy Tyrie.

CHAPTER 7

1993

He couldn't take his eyes off the chair. It sat in the corner like a bad omen, chipped and discoloured. Jackie could guess what had caused the stains. The wood floor around the chair had the same clouds of dark brown, with one large crusted pool surrounding the splintered legs like an ugly birthmark.

The others were engrossed in an account of Marty Rafferty's stay in Crumlin Road Prison. It seemed Marty's stretch after being lifted in possession had become a little more perilous in recent weeks. He'd been targeted by a couple of members of the UVF in the Crum who had an axe to grind with his da from way back. The sins of the father.

Shanty McKee's Jack Russell sat next to Rab Simpson, who fed it the occasional snack and gave it a pat from time to time. Also in attendance was Sam 'Ruger' Rainey, a heavily overweight man with thinning brown hair, compensated for with a bushy moustache. His face had a pugnacious quality, like a bulldog in constant readiness for a scrap, and he packed a solid mass of muscle under rolls of fat. A young man new to the group was sitting next to Rainey. His slim, almost delicate frame and choirboy looks were a contrast to Rainey's haggard appearance, not to mention the young man's shock of dirty fair hair.

At the head of the table, a large, silent figure sat picking splinters out of the table top. He worked methodically, patiently, and once he'd pried a wooden scab off the surface, he placed it in a neat pile. His broad, powerful shoulders made small rhythmic movements as he worked on the splinters, like a Doberman pawing at its kill. The hulking presence had been silent since the meeting began but everyone in attendance knew he was listening intently. The man weighed every remark, calculating the worth of suggestions and the consequences of reports. Those around the table were being assessed, too, judged on their contributions. No one wanted to disappoint.

Billy Tyrie looked up into the light and stole a glance at Jackie. The bare lightbulb above revealed the twisted scar tissue that tore at the right corner of Tyrie's upper lip.

Jackie had mostly recovered from the beating he'd taken in the Land Rover. To his amazement, his nose remained intact. A little purple bruising around his left eye and a healing cut on his lip were all that remained of his wounds. That and the prestige. He'd earned a new level of respect from the men sat around the table for keeping his mouth shut. There was a discernible change in how Rab spoke to him and Billy gave him more time when they were in the same room. And now he'd been invited to this meeting above a small drinking club in the Lagan Village area. It was the first time Jackie had been there, and meetings involving organisation members were being rotated around several venues since the East End Video bomb. No one was taking any chances that the Provos might try another attack.

Ruger Rainey was now detailing a cache of weapons being hidden in Cregagh Glen, paid for with funds from sympathisers in Canada. The republicans had their delusional wannabes pumping money through the IRA terror campaign from the comfort and safety of middle- and upper-class suburbs in New York and Boston. The loyalists had their counterparts north of the border in Ontario.

Ruger was the oldest of the men sitting around the table and, at thirty-seven, he was the quartermaster for much of East Belfast and the Ravenhill cell in particular. Back in the seventies he'd gotten hold of an ancient and not particularly well-main-

54

tained Ruger Blackhawk pistol for one of the trigger men of the time. The shooter's name was Benjamin Wise, and he wasn't one of the more gifted volunteers of the day, mentally or physically. As such, Wise felt he could impress the UDA brass by blooding himself and, being a resolute coward, targeted a Catholic civilian. A baker named Colin McCarthy regularly delivered to a café on the Woodstock Road. In broad daylight and unmasked, Wise strode up behind the fifty-three-year-old McCarthy as he unloaded a tray of buns from his van, and attempted to unload all six chambers of the Ruger into the back of the baker's skull. The pistol was in such bad shape, however, that it misfired, parting Wise from two of his fingers. Sadly for Wise, one of them was his trigger finger and his dreams of religious and ethnic cleansing were shattered. All agreed that Wise was no great loss to the cause. An alcoholic and woman-beater, a couple of years later he drank himself to death in a hovel near the shipyards; but Sam Rainey was never to be allowed to forget the fact that he supplied the instrument of Benjamin Wise's undoing, and had borne the sobriquet 'Ruger' ever since.

Not that he was unreliable now, thought Jackie as he listened to the arms described, currently being buried next to a pretty little waterfall and bubbling stream. Rainey listed a Smith & Wesson.59 semi, a Glock 17, Power Gel explosive materials and a vz.58 assault rifle. There were other items not detailed at the meeting.

Dog walkers would be strolling, ramblers hiking in Cregagh Glen. A local school used part of the glen as a cross-country running course. And all within touching distance of the lethal tools in which men like Rab and Billy traded.

In that other Belfast. The Belfast that many might hear at night, as gunfire was traded, or helicopters circled, or windows quivered to the sudden bass thunder-strike of a bomb detonation.

Billy lit up a cigarette and spoke in a low voice. 'All right lads, some of you know Tommy here, others don't.'

The young man seated next to Ruger Rainey nodded to them. He looked fresh-faced and clean cut. Jackie would have placed him in his late teens or very early twenties.

'Tommy is on loan to us from our comrades over in North Belfast: Mount Vernon. I requested him because an unknown face will be useful on a wee job he's going to do with Rab. And we'd like to promote Jackie here, put him on the team.'

Jackie was mid-toke on his own cigarette and his hand froze momentarily on the roll-up, still clenched between his lips. After the briefest of pauses he took the cigarette from his mouth and emitted a long, swirling stream of smoke.

Thank Christ I wasn't mid-drink, he thought, or I'd have spilled it all over myself.

He said, 'Shite, Billy, cheers.' Thinking, Shite, I didn't expect to work a shooting. Because if Rab was getting his hands dirty, he'd be scrubbing blood off them by the end of the job.

Billy said, 'You done well with the peelers last week, son. It showed you're solid and the boys feel comfortable with you being on board for this one.'

'Well, if you think I'm ready, like.'

But I'm not ready, he thought. It's what I've wanted, it's what I've hoped for.

But I'm not sure I'm ready.

The cigarette had given him something to concentrate on when Billy broke the news but now he could feel the shakes coming on. He stubbed out the half-smoked roll-up and chained another, willing his mind to focus on that simple task.

'The target,' said Billy, 'is James Cochrane.'

#

Back in the late seventies, the Provisional IRA in the Short Strand area of East Belfast brought the activities of loyalist paramilitaries to a standstill for a period of around six months. During that time, the acting brigadiers of the UDA and UVF were shot dead in their houses, the successor to the UDA post was gunned down while on a family holiday on the north coast, and four UVF men were blown apart when the explosive under their vehicle detonated as they were on their way to kill a known IRA member. All of these actions were sanctioned, planned and quite possibly executed by James Cochrane.

Due to the cell structure of the IRA, Cochrane commanded a small but lethal team in the republican enclave of the Short Strand. It was known that he had a senior rank in the PIRA, but what exactly it was no one could be sure. What everyone around the table in that meeting room above a small drinking club did know, however, was that he would be a tough target to hit.

Billy said, 'That bomb in East End Video: what was that, three weeks ago? And how has our side responded?'

The men looked at each other or the scarred surface of the heavy oak table. None of them had responded because they had been waiting on the go-ahead from Billy.

'Jimmy Breslin sanctions some fucking cowboys from Sydenham to walk into a drinking hole in South Down and spray the place. Three Catholic civilians dead and we even manage to kill a fucking prod along with them.'

True enough. Martin Donnelly, Pat McGrath and James Dermot had been murdered in a spray of automatic rifle fire when two UVF gunmen had kicked in the doors of the country pub and raked the place. Their Protestant friend, Samuel Donaldson, had also been killed.

'Indiscriminate,' said Billy, 'and the media all over it, like.' He shook his head in despair and disgust. 'Any fucking excuse for indiscriminate slaughter.'

That was the way most of their cohorts had always seen it. Any old taig would do. A numbers game, thought Jackie; they take out one of our community and we have to take out two of theirs, whether they're connected or not. Doesn't matter who, so long as they go to a Catholic chapel instead of a Protestant church. It sickened him, but until today he'd avoided any involvement in the killings, just putting in hours on the various rackets they ran to fund operations. But the East End Video bomb had taken nine lives on the Ravenhill Road. It would take a while to match that tally, never mind surpass it.

'But we take out Cochrane,' said Billy, 'we avenge the attack and immobilise their operations in East Belfast. There's no Provo activity in this area without his say so. We know he had to have sanctioned that bomb. It cannot go unanswered and we have to send a message, as much to our own community as to the republicans, that there will be consequences if we come under attack.'

And now you could be sanctioning my death warrant, thought Jackie.

The security around Cochrane would presumably be watertight. Not to mention that the target lived four doors down from Mountpottinger RUC station. He was a known IRA entity to the peelers but clean as a whistle. The cops couldn't touch him. Which meant he was smart. And now Jackie was stuck with Rab 'Sick Bag' Simpson and Billy The Kid across the table.

Tyrie said, 'Tommy here has the details of the operation and has worked out the logistics with me. He and Rab will do the trigger work. Jackie, you're the driver.'

Jackie nodded as he eased another spool of calming smoke from his lips. He passed a sigh of nervous resignation off as insouciance.

#

An hour later they emerged from a door at the bottom of narrow stairs into a good-sized room where assorted men were giving serious attention to getting as rat-arsed as possible. The usual blanket of smoke hung heavily in the air. The walls were festooned with a Union Jack, an Ulster Flag and a couple of trade union banners. The club had been founded by linen mill and shipyard workers years ago and many of the men downing pints today were still grafting in Harland & Wolff. There were other local men scattered around, watching football on the TV on the corner wall. Jackie recognised a few. Hard-working, decent enough men gaining some respite from the daily graft with a drink.

He counted a couple of organisation hangers-on drinking in a corner: low-level teenagers asked to lend their weight to the odd riot or back up older members on 'collection runs' around the local businesses. The organisation offered 'insurance' against republican attack for a fortnightly fee.

Because the local butcher is a high-grade IRA target, of course, he thought.

Then he remembered East End Video.

He wasn't up for a drink that night and needed to go home and think through the Cochrane operation, so he headed for the door and the clarity of the chilly night air. But he didn't make it to the exit. The hand on his arm was firm and applied more pressure than necessary to turn him around. Peter Rafferty withdrew his hand and left it hanging by his side. It formed a clenched fist.

'All right Jackie?'

'All right Peter? Are you well?'

'Ach, I'm all right, Jackie. All right for a man whose son is in prison, like.'

'I heard Marty's doing you proud in there though,' said Jackie. 'He's standing up, like.'

Peter edged closer. 'He isn't standing up at the minute, Jackie. He's lying in a bed in the prison hospital, so he is. A broken jaw and two cracked ribs.'

'Sorry to hear that, Peter. He's a good lad, your Marty.'

Peter cocked his large skull, heavy with drink, to one side. 'You've nothing broken though, do you, Jackie? Heard the peelers gave you a kicking that night but you don't look too bad.' Rafferty took a step forward, his broad face and slack features scarlet from whiskey and rising anger. This could only end in one of two ways: someone stepped in to defuse the situation or the two men took chunks out of each other.

'Do you hear me, Jackie? Our Marty's laid out, so he is.'

Jackie was taking in as much as he could in his peripheral vision. They were almost in the centre of the room, too far from the bar to grab a glass or bottle as a weapon. A circle had closed around them at a discreet distance and the anticipation of serious violence was palpable in the air. It was like being back in Orangefield Park for an after-school fight. Sarah was right: men never did grow up.

'Like I say Peter, I'm terrible sorry to hear about that.' It would play better with Billy if he tried to contain this and he hoped he would step in. *Come on now, Peter, that'll do. Leave the boy.*

But he couldn't even see Billy Tyrie at this point, although he knew he was watching. For that matter, Rab Simpson and Ruger Rainey were out of sight, although Tommy was standing casually to his right, expressionless. Peter Rafferty moved another step closer, his forehead almost touching Jackie's now.

'See, the thing is, Shaw, I don't think you *are* sorry. I don't think you liked our Marty in the first place. And I don't like how you're supping in here while my lad's in a hospital bed.'

The fight was unavoidable; Jackie's guts went cold.

He sucked it up and drove a hard punch into Rafferty's left

kidney, then followed it up with a strong fist into the side of the bigger man's head as Rafferty bent in reflex. Instantly, Jackie's knuckles felt a sharp pain. The surrounding crowd swayed a little.

'Fuck!' A bellow from Rafferty as he swung at Jackie, catching him awkwardly on the shoulder. Jackie struggled to maintain balance.

If they went over, Rafferty would dominate through sheer weight and bulk. He could take Jackie apart at his leisure. Jackie aimed another punch at the side of Rafferty's head. He put as much as he could behind it and followed with another hard blow to the temple. His knuckles were on fire and the second blow lost traction on the sweat covering Rafferty's face. A blow from Rafferty caught Jackie on the chest as the bigger man, still stooped, punched upward. It stopped Jackie dead and scared him because the blow was over his heart and it fucking hurt. The big man, now straightening, swung wildly, not connecting with force but keeping Jackie occupied and off balance. Still, he had a flash of satisfaction at the sight of blood over Rafferty's eye where the Claddagh ring had caught him.

But this had to end. Rafferty was now reaching for him, trying to get him close so he could bite, gouge and choke. The watching crowd was making it difficult for Jackie to manoeuvre. The last thing he needed was to trip over some fucker's feet behind him.

Feet, thought Jackie, fucking feet. And mine are in size nine Dr Marten's.

He threw his leg out with force and his right boot connected with Rafferty's left kneecap with a sickening, dull crack. Rafferty roared but his legs buckled and he went down awkwardly on the other knee, the injured left leg straight out at a thirty-degree angle to the bent right.

Fucking knee-capping? thought Jackie. I'll show you fucking knee-capping.

He drove the sole of his right boot, and as much body weight as he could muster, onto the damaged left knee. The image of a branch snapping shot through his mind. He began driving his right fist, Claddagh ring and all, into Rafferty's face, over and over. Some blows bit into the skin, others glanced off the sweat. Blood slicked across the bent and screaming man's face. It felt good.

It felt far too good.

Then someone finally intervened and strong arms encircled him, more than one pair.

He heard a voice – Rab? Ruger? – shout, 'For fuck's sake! That's enough!'

Before he knew what was happening he felt the slap of the crisp, cold night air as he was half dragged, half shoved through the door of the club into the dark sodium glow of the street. He bent over, hands on knees for support, and took deep, wracking breaths. He was shaking and didn't care who saw. He was aware of men next to him and realised they were Billy, Rab, Ruger and Tommy.

Rab erupted in a high-pitched giggle, then smiled a huge toothy grin.

'Fuck's sake, Jackie,' he said, 'you're a fucking animal. Where've you been hiding?'

Billy put a hand on Jackie's back, almost fatherly.

'Welcome to the family,' he said.

CHAPTER 8

Thursday

They had driven to the beach at Cloghy on the County Down coast in a convoy of three cars, Jackie's Toyota sandwiched between an Audi in front and Billy Tyrie's BMW behind. The country roads were quiet.

They had passed the drive in silence, one of the armed men from the makeshift roadblock in the passenger seat, another in the back seat directly behind him. Neither spoke while in the car. Also, neither knew there was a handgun and ammo supplied by Rab Simpson under the passenger seat. It is still there, but now is hardly the time to try fulfilling Jackie's contract on Tyrie.

He stands on the hard, compacted sand in a strong coastal wind with Tyrie next to him and four men keeping watch at a discreet distance. The beach is deserted, much like the caravan park at its southern end, which they begin walking towards. Large clumps of seaweed lie scattered across the sand like shredded body bags.

'So, the Prodigal Son returns,' says Tyrie.

'Prodigal Son? More like the fatted calf – right, Billy?'

Some twenty years ago Jackie had been at a small, disused factory on the outskirts of Belfast with three other members of the UDA on a midnight meet. The following day's *Belfast Telegraph*, *BBC Newsline* and other media had reported that four members of the Ulster Defence Association had been shot dead by security forces in an operation held in the Belfast suburb of Holywood. Three quarters of the story was true: three of the four UDA men had had their lives ended that night. The remaining quarter of the story is now strolling along the beach with Billy Tyrie, who seems as blasé about the fact Jackie is breathing as Rab Simpson was. His 'death' all those years ago has yet to be mentioned.

Jackie suddenly feels tired and his body heavy, as though the sand is sucking him down. The last few days, the last twenty years, is catching up with him: Hartley, Simpson and now Tyrie. Only Sarah gives him hope that something good is left from that time.

'I don't see Rab among the welcoming committee,' he says. The soft whisper of the tide washing onto the beach is the sole reply. 'How's Eileen?'

The thought is out of his mouth before he can stop it: a potentially lethal question. Jackie hears a soft crunch and stops, turning to see that Tyrie halted a moment before and is staring at him intently.

He couldn't know, thinks Jackie, he never knew. She never told him. Because much as she was Billy's gleaming prize to be paraded in triumph, he would have killed her. Tyrie could never have borne the betrayal. Locked in Tyrie's gaze, the four men also watching intently, Jackie feels the night growing colder, even as the sea breeze dies.

Tyrie says, 'Now, why would you ask me about Eileen?'

'Because this is a bit awkward. Because I don't know if someone is going to find my bloated body washed up in a month or two. Because you haven't mentioned Holywood. And because the only civilised, halfway normal topic I can think of to keep the conversation going is your good lady wife.'

Tyrie is still appraising him and speaks slowly as he mulls something over. 'It just seems a bit strange, you mentioning Rab and Eileen almost in the same sentence. I mean, they'd hardly be a pair in word association, would they?'

Jesus, thinks Jackie. Paranoid about what the wife's up to, Billy?

Then he remembers that he was, in fact, sleeping with Eileen Tyrie for a year.

Billy looks out to the heaving grey swell of the Irish Sea and gives a strange little sigh, then starts walking again. Their four companions fall in a good few yards behind.

Jackie says, 'You found me through someone at the car-hire company?'

'Aye. One of the valet boys lives in Sydenham, used to know you from the bars. He saw your name on a spreadsheet. Got your mobile number from your online booking.'

Jackie is impressed that Billy's reach is still so wide-ranging. Then again, the airport and car hire are in East Belfast.

'Why didn't you keep in touch with your da?' asks Tyrie. 'You hurt him, so you did. Not contacting the oul' lad.'

'I thought it was best for him. What he didn't know couldn't hurt him, and, hopefully, you couldn't either.'

Of course, he had been in contact. But always through Sarah.

'Ach now, Jackie, come on. Family's off limits, you know that.'

Does Rab Simpson know that? thinks Jackie.

'Do you honestly think I'd have done anything to your da?' says Tyrie. 'Sure, we genuinely thought you were dead at first.'

'Do you want a refund for the funeral expenses?'

Billy smiles and reaches into his pocket. He says, 'Who's to say I won't get my money's worth yet?'

He produces a packet of cigarettes from his pocket and offers one to Jackie, who declines. Everyone waits as Tyrie battles the wind to get the cigarette lit. Finally, he draws deeply on the filter and exhales with a lazy, blissful expression. 'So here's the thing. I don't know why that wasn't your body at Holywood. We had a couple of contacts in the RUC back then. They told us there were four bodies but we didn't see the corpse so we didn't notice your ring was missing, and I wouldn't have thought to look anyway. It was Rab's pet peeler picked that up.

It was never an issue for me: the Claddagh, all that Fenian-culture-shite. I know better.'

He points at Jackie with the cigarette. The tip is glowing a fierce orange in the wind.

'You disappeared and it doesn't take a genius to see you had help. State sponsored, I'd say. So you were a grass, probably. But now? All water under the bridge. To be honest, why you disappeared and where you went is immaterial. This country has changed and I never suffered because of you. Never did time, never got shot.'

Don't count your chickens, thinks Jackie.

'The shenanigans with Tommy and Danny are another matter. But it was all a long time ago. I'm tired of churning over the past.'

Jackie is weighing his options if this goes sour. He doesn't see any.

'But ... but ... you owe me, son. You caused us all a lot of consternation. And I never made a move on your da when things started looking suspect. Not to mention I was in pieces when I thought you were dead.'

'So ...'

'So,' says Tyrie, 'I need a bit of work done, and I need an outsider to do it. And you are, now, an outsider. You talk like an Englishman for a start.'

Ha, bloody ha, thinks Jackie.

'I want you to be a trigger man.'

Billy flicks his fag butt onto the sand and spits on it.

'I want you to shoot Rab Simpson.'

#

The IRA ceasefire in 1997 brought a glimmer of hope to the people of Northern Ireland and peace became a real possibility.

The Good Friday Agreement became the focus for attempts to establish a political framework which could at least consider all parties involved. For those who lived in Northern Ireland, a healthy scepticism kept the country anchored: *you can't please all of the people all of the time* could have been penned for the conundrum of the Province.

Thanks to the Agreement, many of the agents of thirty years of brutal sadism were given amnesty, released with a clean slate onto the streets of the cities and countryside they had terrorized. But they had no skills beyond butchery and intimidation. Which brings Jackie back to Billy Tyrie and Rab Simpson.

Billy talks about Rab: Simpson is originally from West Belfast, his family burnt out of their home by a Catholic mob during the mutual religious purges which began in the late sixties. Despite relocating to the east of the city, he has kept many of his contacts in the west, and these men had encouraged Rab to look into black-market rackets in cigarettes and fuel. Despite the segregation in prison, many had contacts with IRA and INLA members who were happy to form criminal alliances now that the terrorist wage had dried up. Billy Tyrie turned a blind eye to whatever schemes Rab had cooked up on the side. He drew the line, however, at drugs.

Rab claimed, 'Loyalism doesn't pay the bills no more,' but Billy vetoed any UDA involvement in the drug business in East Belfast. It was like yelling 'Stop!' at a horde of stampeding buffalo. Heroin, cocaine, ecstasy, amphetamines and the rest came streaming in.

Then bodies began turning up. Rab had a contact in the IRA who was also a member of the republican splinter group Republican Action Against Drugs, or RAAD, in Derry. He had told Rab of how they would execute known drug dealers, 'independents', in the city. RAAD could claim they were keeping their streets clean and help alienate the police from their local communities, and they could wipe out the opposition, leaving the way clear to monopolise all dealing conducted on their turf.

In East Belfast, two men were found riddled with bullets in a car near Sydenham. A man was shot in the back of the head at a house party on the Ballybeen Estate. A twenty-three-year-old girl was found dead in her Volkswagen Beetle off the lower Castlereagh Road. She had seventeen bullet wounds in her twisted body. Tyrie was incensed and wanted Simpson dead, but Rab had created a network of paramilitaries across Belfast, all plugged into the drug trade within the city and beyond. Billy had his loyal followers, but he didn't want to risk a feud.

Then Samuel Shaw, father of Jackie, passed away. Billy had known Jackie would come back. And Jackie was deniable, still a ghost for some and unknown to many.

And now he's standing on a wind-scoured beach on the Irish Sea coast under a darkening sky, being contracted to conduct a killing for Billy Tyrie. Just like old times.

#

For the second time that day Jackie knows that, at this moment in time, he doesn't have a choice.

He says, 'I'll take him out.'

'I know you will.'

They reach the cars as darkness settles over the coast like a blackout.

'You'll need something to get the job done,' says Tyrie. 'Don here will deliver a package to your hotel tonight. There'll also be a photograph. Rab has changed a bit down the years.'

Aye, I noticed, thinks Jackie.

'We're going to go for another wee drive now,' says Tyrie, 'just a couple of miles.'

Jackie follows the rear lights of the Audi south along the coast for ten minutes, two men in his car. They turn left through a small pair of gates with Celtic crosses on top. The road winds up and through some scraggly trees already naked of leaves in the dark autumn sky. They pull into a small car park, not another soul to be seen.

They get out of the cars and one of the bodyguards pops the boot of the Audi and illuminates the inside with his mobile phone. It looks like someone has done their grocery shopping. The boot is full of plastic bags of varying shapes and sizes. One of them is the size of a large bowling ball, but egg-shaped. There is a round indentation about two thirds of the way down the bag, a hollow in the plastic. Behind it, Jackie knows, is a mouth caught in a silent scream.

The bodyguards grab the bags, taking a couple each, and as they leave the cars and file down steep, winding steps Jackie remembers the place from a childhood trip. It is Cooey's Wells, ancient and holy, with healing waters and a small, broken altar. In this dark, the trees shivering around them, it is a child's Halloween panorama.

'This place was holy before any of us gave a shite about being Prod or taig,' Tyrie says. 'Norse pirates had a go at raiding here a few times, probably Celts, too. There's always been trouble in this land. It's in our blood, and so much has been shed, it's seeped into the very earth.'

Jackie hears the wash of the tide beyond as they pass through a small iron gate and along a path crowded by long, ragged grass. They stop at what appears to be a gaping hole in the earth, before the moonlight coats the dark ground with a silver gloss and Jackie sees they are standing at the edge of mud flats, the sea churning softly beyond.

'Now, you *will* kill Simpson for me, son,' says Billy. 'I'm not sentimental. This boyo here,' he points to the bags, 'is the godfather of one of my girls.'

Bloody hell, thinks Jackie, Billy has children.

'I remember him holding our Claire in the church at the christening. He was a friend of Eileen's family.'

Tyrie takes the egg-shaped bag from the nearest of his men.

'I found out about a fortnight ago he was fucking Eileen.'

He throws the bag into the black abyss in front of them and turns back towards Cooey's Wells. He beckons Jackie to accompany him. The other men begin burying the bags in the soft, sucking mud.

Jackie wonders again whether Billy could know about him and Eileen. Is she dead, too? Will Tyrie wait until Jackie has taken Rab Simpson out of the picture before exacting revenge for their affair?

As they pass the small holy wells, with signs ordering, *drink* and *wash*, Tyrie stops again.

'The point is, that wanker in pieces back there fucked my wife. In fucking my Eileen, he fucked me, so he did. He made a promise in the church to care for my child if anything happened to me. And then he fucked her mommy when her daddy wasn't around. He crossed me.'

Jackie is meeting Tyrie's gaze as best he can in the deep gloom. One of the bodyguards is trudging back towards them.

'You'll shoot that cunt Simpson,' says Tyrie.

He starts up the steep steps back to the cars. The bodyguard gestures for Jackie to follow suit while the others bury the dismembered body in the stagnant mud behind them. In recognition, Billy stabs a thumb behind his shoulder without bothering to look.

'Don't you cross me, either.'

CHAPTER 9

1993

The Cregagh Road was buzzing with activity as they neared the small shop belonging to James Maguire. Until that point in time, there had been nothing outstanding about James, other than his status as the youngest retailer on the road. Golden Discs did well, saving the youth of the area a trip into the city centre if they wanted to pick up the latest dance, indie or rock CDs.

Those milling about the road at two in the afternoon were generally older than Golden Discs' customer demographic. Plenty of pensioners visiting the local bakeries, butchers and greengrocers, or housewives picking up provisions at Stewarts, the local supermarket. Many knew Jackie's face as his mother had often shopped here. Some of the people strolling by had visited their house from time to time in the past.

Today, he couldn't meet their gaze. Those who dared to look at him at any rate.

He couldn't stop his face reddening at the thought of these decent people, people who had loved and respected his mother and pitied and despaired the alcoholic wreck his father had become, seeing him walking next to Rab Simpson on a clear spring afternoon.

Rab was well known in the area. His latest claim to fame had been an incident at the King James public-house last week. Rab had been enjoying an afternoon Harp at the bar when a sales rep for a drinks supplier called in. The rep began a pitch on the joys of Jameson whiskey. The King James offered Bushmills, and only Bushmills, as an Irish. The barman said as much. The sales rep wasn't having it. He'd had the same experience in many bars east of the River Bann, he said, but had yet to meet an unsatisfied convert.

Rab had already put a few Harp lagers away. He was also blissfully unaware that Harp was brewed in staunchly Catholic and republican Dundalk, just over the border in the Republic of Ireland. The town was a popular spot for fugitive republican terrorists and IRA hit teams enthusiastically pursuing a policy of religious cleansing by assassinating Protestant farmers and their sons in the borderlands of Counties Down and Armagh.

But all that mattered to Rab was that this sales rep, probably a *Fenian* sales rep, was coming into a good loyalist bar in a good Protestant area and bad-mouthing a good Protestant whiskey – Bushmills; not to mention selling papal piss like Jamesons. So he sacrificed the rest of his pint and smashed the glass over the rep's head. Then he excused himself and nipped out the back of the bar to a storeroom, to fetch a hammer and nails. Returning to find the rep kneeling on the floor, a sickly pink blend of blood and lager soaking his lacerated scalp, he hauled the man to his feet and led him to the front of the bar before nailing the rep's right hand to the door.

So it was no wonder that Mrs McCauley, a member of the Ravenhill Presbyterian Church choir, the Women's Institute and good friend to his mother in her last days, gave Jackie and Rab a withering stare before she entered Gibson's Newsagents.

The Prodigy was playing as Jackie and Rab entered Maguire's shop. James Maguire, standing behind the counter, looked up with a pre-packaged smile for the punters when the chime above the door jangled.

He had refused to pay his fee to the UDA for two weeks. The fee was a subscription in order to keep the road a safe and prosperous environment for local residents and for those from further afield to do their shopping. Protection money by any other name.

Looking at the delicate man behind the counter, mousy hair scraped back in a severe ponytail, Jackie was surprised and impressed by Maguire's resolve. He looked like you could spit through him, yet Maguire had told four goons to fuck off in the space of a fortnight. But not Rab, who didn't handle such low-grade work as doing the collection rounds. He was only called in when there was a problem to be dealt with. And with Jackie's newfound status in the gang, he was being tutored in the finer points of paramilitary violence and intimidation from one of the best in the business.

Maguire didn't know Jackie from Adam, but he obviously recognised Rab Simpson. Colour draining from his hollow cheeks, he said, 'Look, I don't want trouble. I'm just trying to make a living, you know?'

Rab turned the sign on the door over, from *Open* to *Closed*.

He walked up the centre aisle of the shop, flanked by racks of CD cases as drum and bass hammered off the walls. As he got closer, Maguire said, 'I've no problem with youse. I'm local, live just off the road, like. But I can't afford to be giving my money to youse when I'm competing with Virgin in the centre of town.'

Jackie hung back at the door and kept an eye on the street outside through the large shop window, while watching Rab and Maguire.

When he reached the counter, Rab said, 'Come round here a wee minute, will ye? I can't be talking to you over this counter.' As Maguire sidled around to the shop floor Jackie was taken aback by just how rail-thin the man was, tottering on gangly legs like a newborn foal.

Rab turned to Jackie and said, 'Who's this we're listening to?'

'The Prodigy.'

'Load a' shite.'

73

Maguire, with a dumb look on his face, said, 'Do you want something else on?'

Jackie said, 'We'd need to make a move soon and head on. Maybe it's better just to get this done.'

At this Maguire's skin seemed to tighten across his skull-like face, as though someone were turning a tourniquet at the back of his head. He said, 'I swear to youse, I'd give youse the money if I could, but I'll be out of business if I just give my profits away like that.'

Rab said, 'You'd be surprised what you can do, if you put your mind to it.' He plucked a CD case from the rack behind him and popped it open, revealing the shiny silver disc inside. 'Taking a bit of a chance keeping the CDs in the cases, aren't you?' he said. 'Some wee fucker'll have it and be away out the door before you can stop him.' He squinted at the disc and read out, 'K-L-F. Are they a splinter group of the UVF then?' Pleased with his own joke, he gave a chuckle. Jackie glanced outside again. Rab took the disc out of the case and held its edge between his thumb and forefinger, giving it a gentle squeeze. The disc warped in his grip, then returned to its original flat shape.

'They say you can do anything to these things. Scratch them, burn them, whatever, and they'll still play.' He tensed his wrist and the disc warped further. Maguire was gaping at the shiny plastic. After a couple of seconds the disc splintered in two with a sharp crack. 'But, you see, mucker, anything'll break if you put enough pressure on it.'

Jackie turned to check out the street through the large shop front window. Mrs McCauley had exited the newsagents and was standing in front of the shop, sorting out her shopping bags.

He turned back at the sound of a high-pitched yelp and a grunt of effort. Rab had Maguire in a headlock and was gripping a jagged shard of the broken CD in his free hand, inching the barbed point of the shard towards Maguire's right eye. Maguire was frantically trying to hold Rab's arm away from his face. Neither man spoke but Jackie could hear a whine from Maguire piercing the thud of the drums and bass line. His head began pounding with the rhythm. Stupidly, he tried to listen if this was the same track as when they'd entered the shop before realising it was his own pulse. Rab's hand began bleeding as the CD bit into his palm. 'You wee fucker,' he said, half laughing. 'You'll fucking pay, d'you hear me?'

Just tell him you'll pay, Jackie willed, *just tell him*. The splintered point of the shard was an inch away from Maguire's eye and Jackie could see the gaunt shop owner was weakening. He looked out at the street again. Mrs McCauley was still fiddling with her shopping bags in front of Golden Discs. Turning back to the struggle inside he saw Maguire had a frenzied look, his mouth silently agape, his eyes wide and frantic. When they settled on Jackie the man's fear felt like a physical force, gripping and shaking him, and he turned away.

'Ach, Mrs McCauley, how are you?' shouted Jackie. 'I haven't seen you about the road for a while.'

He stood in line with her through the window, blocking Rab's view. The old lady looked up, startled. The music had stopped in the shop, the track ended along with the sounds of struggle. Mrs McCauley gave him a look of suspicion and peered around him.

'Aye, I know Mrs McCauley, I must call over and see you for a wee cup of tea. I've just been a bit busy, like.'

The woman's scornful look became sharper as she slowly approached the window.

'This is my mate, Rab Simpson. Do you know him?'

There was a murmured *fuck's sake* behind, then quick footsteps. Rab appeared next to him a moment later, scowling at the old lady, who took that as her moment to move on. More people peered in at them. Rab took in the spectators scattered about the pavement and turned back to Maguire, who stood gripping the counter for support, tears in his eyes.

'You're a lucky bastard,' said Rab, 'but I'll not let this go. You'll not be making a living at anything by the time I've finished with you.'

With that he made the shape of a gun with his hand, aimed it at Maguire, then walked out of the shop, blood dripping from his fingertips.

#

As they strode away, Rab whirled on his heel and began walking back. 'Fucking wanker, I'll fucking have him!'

'Rab, wait,' said Jackie. He grabbed Rab's arm. Simpson turned on him with a snarl.

'You can't touch him. Everyone on the road's seen you in that shop. Plus, you've just shouted all over the Cregagh that you'll fucking do him.'

Rab seethed, breathing hard.

'Leave it for now and act later when we've had a chance to think it through.'

Rab's lips were drawn back in a grimace, gums and teeth exposed like a shark in attack mode. But he was thinking. He looked down at the hand on his arm and stared at it hard. Jackie left it there for a couple of seconds. Just enough to prove he wasn't *that* intimidated.

Rab said, 'I'm away for a drink. Coming?'

'No, mate, I have to do some stuff for my da. Sure I'll see you the night, in the Tartan Star Club.'

Rab nodded and headed off with a backward wave.

Jackie considered going back to check if Maguire was okay – as okay as you could be after a violent psychopath has tried to blind you in one eye – and reason with the guy. But it wouldn't look good to the boys if he was seen and his stock was high at the moment. Walking back to his Ford, parked a couple of streets away, his face reddened. He breathed deeply and thought of his mother. Being seen in such company, in such circumstance, by his mother's friend. Such shame.

He knew there were plenty who whispered to his father: 'Terrible about your Jackie with that crowd. It's not your fault, Sammy, sure there's nothing you could have done.'

You could have stayed off the bottle and had a go at being a father once my mother left us, thought Jackie. You could have been a bit less unbearable so our Sarah wouldn't be living with her boyfriend's family now.

As he turned the corner onto a side street he spotted a young lad checking out his car. The teenager was in a T-shirt, despite the biting chill in the air. He saw Jackie and made off at a run, disappearing into the rabbit warren of streets between the Cregagh and Castlereagh Roads. Jackie couldn't work up the enthusiasm to give chase, burned out after the violence in Maguire's shop, but he had recognised the young lad. It was Shanty McKee.

#

Groups of uniformed kids wandered the city centre like regimented gangs. The City Hall was ringed with commuters waiting for buses, always late, to North, South, East and West Belfast that branched across the spider's web of thoroughfares from the central hub of City Hall, to the outskirts that stretched like a giant pincer, snaking up the Antrim and Down shores of Belfast Lough and clinging to the banks of the Lagan River in the south; and the trunk of the city in the Lagan Valley, stretching up to the Castlereagh Hills to the east, and hugging the Black and Divis Mountains to the west. Above it all, a couple of Army helicopters kept vigil.

Jackie had driven in, fast and smooth, and parked in a multi-storey. Last week, traffic had been disrupted on a daily basis with those in the east facing RUC and British Army roadblocks on all the major bridge crossings into the centre. Today, aside from a couple of RUC sporting rifles outside a chocolatier, Belfast could have been any regional city in the UK or Republic.

He walked past Virgin Megastore on the corner of Castle Court, bloated with schoolkids and university types, and thought James Maguire had his work cut out. Strolling through the shopping mall, he made for a brace of public phones out the back of the complex, next to Smithfield Market.

He dialled. On the fifth ring a smooth, rich voice answered.

'It's me,' he said. 'Can you talk?'

'I'm alone for the next half an hour or so.'

'I'll be in the Tartan Star tonight. Will you be there?'

'Just to show my face. He likes me to show my face, for appearances' sake.'

'Who can blame him? It's some face.'

'It's not my face you're interested in.'

'No, it's your generosity of spirit and engaging conversation. When's he away?'

'He'll be in Glasgow in two days. Business and a football match, so it's overnight.'

'Can we meet?'

He was careful not to sound needy or desperate. She wasn't a woman to counsel a man she thought weak or grasping.

'I've already told him I'm going shopping in Dublin while he's away. I said I might stay overnight.'

'I might see you tonight and I'll ring you tomorrow about where to meet.'

'Make it the afternoon, he's playing golf with a couple of his friends.'

She hung up. He felt his face flush and his blood quicken.

Then he remembered the real reason why he was there at the bank of phones, and his face went pale.

He hit the redial button and punched in a number committed to memory.

#

They were all there in the Tartan Star Club: Sam 'Ruger' Rainey, Rab 'Homer' Simpson and the quiet man, Tommy. Jimmy Love, East Belfast Brigadier, was in deep conversation with a wiry, long-haired man high-ranking in the UVF.

Jackie was usually happy to have a couple of pints and leave it at that. He liked a drink, but he'd known plenty who liked it a bit too much, his own father included. The others drank for Ulster. Sam Rainey, in particular, was a Rolls-Royce. The other reason Jackie was pacing himself walked in the door at about half eight. Eileen Tyrie strode into the bar in front of her husband Billy, turning every head. The other women gave her side-glances and forced greetings. The men worked hard at not staring. Jackie caught Rab clocking her over the rim of his pint glass as he took a swig. Rainey was having a laugh with a guy from the shipyard workers' union at the bar, but he cocked a sly glance at her legs as she eased her way through the drinkers. Tommy was enthralled, although what was going through his mind was probably best not known.

And Jackie just thought she was the most beautiful woman he'd ever seen.

He couldn't understand how she could have married Billy Tyrie, but that never dampened his desire for her. Eileen wasn't your typical Colleen by a long shot. She was around five feet five inches and slim, lithe. At least 4 feet of her height seemed to be taken up by her legs, which were sheathed in black stockings and perched on simple black heels. She was radiant in a short black skirt and mustard sweater under a long winter coat, now open. Her hair was the colour of her shoes, a brush-stroke of inky black, her skin a beautiful olive hue.

Like pale gold, thought Jackie. He was convinced that the Spanish Armada, shipwrecked on the coast of Ireland, left more than their treasure behind. The fine nose, full lips and dusky eyes of Eileen Tyrie were living proof. She was in her early twenties, a decade younger than her bullish, sweating husband.

'Can I get you a drink, pet?' said Rainey. As oldest and ugliest, the others felt it prudent to leave the offer of a drink to him.

'Vodka, thanks, Sam.'

Jackie felt stupid and awkward, and hated himself for it. In bed with her, he was powerful and confident, free yet in total control of himself, of the moment. Now he felt like one of the schoolkids he'd seen slouching around that afternoon.

She laughed with and indulged the men around her while Tyrie, gorged on her presence, sought out mates and connections from the organisation. Jackie watched, fascinated yet sickened when he thought of her with Tyrie. Not just his age and sweating bulk, but the ugliness of his brutality. Nausea at the thought of her with Tyrie was his edge, what kept him from tripping up and committing a fatal error that might expose their affair.

He knew Eileen was strong, self-sufficient and beautiful. She was sexually aggressive and intoxicating. But he didn't idealise her. If she could be with Tyrie, she wasn't a woman you could spend your life with. God, but he wanted her though.

'Do you want her?'

'What?'

'Do you want her?'

His stomach contracted. Rab swayed before him, all crooked smile and hungry eyes.

'Leanne?' said Rab. 'Fuck's sake, are you with us?'

Eileen, in mid-flirt with an older man connected to brigade staff, flashed him a look like a slap across the face. It brought him back to the moment.

'Sorry, Rab, I was up late last night and the drink's making me a bit slow.'

'That wee girl over there, Leanne. Youse went to school together, didn't youse?'

Across the room stood a pretty girl in a denim skirt in a group of young women drinking halves. He remembered her from his days in high school.

'She's interested in you,' said Rab. 'You should go over and talk to her.'

Jackie shrugged. 'Maybe later.'

As he turned from Rab, he caught sight of Eileen's back as she headed for the door, this time unaccompanied. Billy was chasing a pint of lager with a shot of whiskey and howling at one of Ruger's jokes. For a moment Jackie thought of offering to walk her back to her house, but thought better of it. She needed no escort: no one was going to mess with Eileen Tyrie on the streets around Ravenhill, day or night.

He felt a blaze of desire as he watched her slip out of the club.

#

Later, he felt a blaze of guilt as the image flashed through his mind again, Leanne's face contorted below him as she struggled not to cry out, her body bucking under him. His knees were stinging on the carpet of her living-room floor, her parents asleep upstairs. He hesitated, afraid he might be hurting her, but she grasped for him and clutched his head, pulling his face to her. She kissed him hard, her tongue fierce in his mouth. Her lips widened in a silent scream and he came.

Later again, he slid the key in the door of his father's home.

The house he lived in but a home no longer, on Bendigo Street. He was spent, a wave of fatigue washing him into the hallway like a lazy tide. The drinking, the violence. The desire, always frustrated. Using Leanne, the girl silly with excitement, stirred by the promise of more.

Just a surrogate for his own grubby desire. The fetish of another man's wife.

He needed to talk, to vent. He wanted someone to listen to him, to the real Jackie Shaw. To tell him that everything would be okay. He was tired of living in his head and he craved a confessional. As he shambled to the door of the small living room he found himself hoping, for once, that his father would be awake.

I can make him a wee cup of tea, thought Jackie, just talk with him. It's been so long since we just talked.

But he knew from the smell of booze and the low hum of the unwatched TV screen, that his da would be passed out on the other side of the door.

CHAPTER 10

Friday

It's a good day for a funeral, dry but with a slate-grey sky, the city brooding beneath. He dons the black suit, the shirt crisp and scratchy with starch. Jackie feels he shouldn't be comfortable. He should suffer on the day his father is laid to rest.

Also, he isn't comfortable because there is a Smith & Wesson .357 Magnum now nestled at the bottom of his suitcase, delivered by Tyrie's man as promised. A revolver: old-school. Very Billy. And another pre-paid phone. He'll be needing extra pockets. Billy's phone has an address on Ardenlee Avenue in its contact book. Rab Simpson is living among the herbal tea and coffee-morning set now. There is an instruction to await further instructions.

As he sips the coffee he's made with the room's facilities, Jackie drinks in the solitude with the hot liquid. He's always enjoyed hotel rooms for this very reason: they segregate and seclude. He tries to remember the face of the old guy at the memorial on the Ravenhill Road, walking his dog. It seems likely the old man is on the UDA payroll. It also seems likely that, whoever he is, he doesn't know Tyrie and Simpson are in the midst of a clandestine war and plotting bloody murder on each other. An old hand like that is hardly a player in the drug trade.

The other question is what happens when Jackie executes one of the hits. They are both happy to give him firearms but he's a loose end and he can't imagine them not wanting to see him disappear on a more permanent basis. He considers going to Hartley, reaching out through the authorities and telling all. But he knows enough about the Spooks to trust them only marginally more than the paramilitaries. MI5 will use him, exploit him, and put his sister's family in danger in the process; or they'll ship him out on the next available flight and put his sister's family in danger in the process. Either way, it ups the stakes even further at this point. He knows his people, Belfast people, and that these men will cut Sarah's throat at the first hint of security force involvement.

And, much as he hates to admit it, he wonders about Eileen. Is Billy really ignorant of their affair? Twenty years is a long time; plenty of opportunities for the truth to out. Where is she in all of this? Not with Billy if the poor bastard in Tyrie's boot is anything to go by. How many others have ended up in a bog or shallow grave because of her? And they have kids?

He shakes his head and despairs of himself. Not the time to be mulling over old liaisons.

Now is the time to mull over old regrets.

#

The church is small. Sarah calls it compact. There is a smattering of mourners from down the road but the numbers can easily be accommodated on a couple of pews. Sarah is there with Thomas and her kids, Daniel and Margaret. The funeral church staff are along the walls, professionally solemn and swelling the numbers. The minister is from the Presbyterian church, but his father hadn't set foot over its threshold for some twenty-five years or more. Sarah's kids are putting in a good shift, looking suitably grave, but Sammy Shaw was a virtual stranger to them too. He had a title, Grandfather, like the Duke and Duchess of Gloucester or the Executive Vice Chairman of the board, a meaningless office held in their family for a man as distant as an absentee landlord.

The minister, an earnest man, sincere and decent, does his best to circumnavigate a life that began with much promise, lived through the Second World War and the Belfast Blitz, then kindled with the love of his mother, the angel in the room. Two children followed, says the minister, offering a smile to Jackie and Sarah. He can feel its warmth glowing from the small, polished pulpit at the front. Sarah came first, then Jackie, both the pride and joy of their loving parents. His mother often said how his father would call him my 'son, moon and stars', and neighbours had laughed at how Sammy had danced in the street when he heard he had a boy. Jackie had been the quieter of the children, while Sarah was a boisterous child and a light sleeper. Samuel Shaw, a welder in the shipyard and a true rough and ready Belfast man, had crept downstairs with his young daughter and indulged her in fantasy tea parties, or shopping trips, in the middle of the night when she couldn't sleep.

And then, in their teenage years, the horror of the Troubles was trumped by the personal terror of the cancer that claimed their mother. Like the leaves of St Patrick's shamrock, they'd fallen apart without their anchoring stem. Sarah had clung to a caring man who could offer her a comfortable life and the family she craved. Jackie had begun to run wild, travelling abroad followed by a short-lived spell in the Army. And Samuel had escaped to the bottom of whichever bottle, pint or shot glass he could lay hands on at the time.

The minister says, 'Friends, God remembers. He has a memory far beyond you or I, a memory far longer than the lifespan of the oldest among us. And He remembers the victims, the meek.'

He leans forward on the pulpit and says, in true Presbyterian style, 'And He remembers the guilty, friends. He remembers the guilty and He will bring them to account. He will punish the sinners, and none shall escape His wrath.'

They are leaving the small church, Jackie with the casket on his shoulder, Sarah's husband Thomas on the other side. The Ormeau Park is across the road. The trees along the railings sway gently in the gathering breeze. He can see people huddled on the pavement to watch and recognises some. It is impossible to read their expressions, these 'ordinary' people from down the Raven, but he knows that they must be burning with questions. He is here, in the flesh, Lazarus returned from the dead.

His father had an old friend, Harry Clarke, whose daughter was one of the schoolkids murdered in the East End bombing. But a heart attack took him some years ago and his surviving son moved to Canada. Few of his parents' generation remain on the road. But there is Mrs McCauley.

And Jackie is back on the Cregagh Road for a moment, shouting through the window to spare a young shop-owner from Rab Simpson and his psychotic whims.

The coffin in the hearse, Jackie gently takes the old woman's arm. Her look is stoic, but she manages a perfunctory, 'Jackie.' She nods. 'Sorry about your daddy.'

'Thank you, Mrs McCauley. I can promise you I'm not the man you think I am. Or was.'

'Jackie, it's not for me to judge you. As the minister said, we'll all be brought to account when our time comes.'

'You've no reason to help me, Mrs McCauley, and you've every reason to think I'm a waster. But I am trying to be a better man and put the past behind me and there's people here won't let me alone.'

Then he describes the older man at the memorial to the nine innocent souls taken at East End Video all those years ago. He describes the man's weathered face, his clothes and the mangy wee terrier with him. Mrs McCauley listens, stern-faced, then says, 'From what you tell me, and that wee skitter of a dog he had with him, it sounds like McKee.'

His face has always been dangerously easy to read, and his surprise is scrawled all over it.

Mrs McCauley says, 'You know him, then. I suppose you would, considering your past. Aye, he's changed a bit but it sounds like you saw Shanty McKee.'

#

Roselawn Cemetery is the home of thousands of departed souls, a city of the dead. In among the graves of the good citizens of Belfast can be found the odd headstone engraved with the crest of the Royal Ulster Constabulary or a British Army unit. Look hard enough and graves bearing UDA, UVF and other terrorist groupings markings can be found. Their opposite numbers in the republican IRA and INLA are housed over in Milltown Cemetery in the west of the city.

Samuel Shaw is laid to rest on the outer reaches of the graveyard in a fresh row of plots. His wife, Jackie and Sarah's mother, is at rest in Dundonald, in a grave too shallow for a second burial. Even in death, Sammy is alone.

Jackie can see a woman standing a few graves away but focused intently on the small group of mourners. She is a striking figure, in a black winter coat. Her hair is like a dark waterfall streaming down the sides of an olive-skinned face. Even with this distance between them, he can see that she has lost none of her beauty.

Once the minister has given the last blessing, Jackie thanks him and excuses himself for a moment. Eileen Tyrie waits for him a short walk away, attempting to dim her radiance with a subdued expression. It's a losing battle.

Once he reaches her, he is lost. He simply says, 'Eileen.'

'Jackie. I'm very sorry about your father.'

'You know, I always used to scoff when people would say things like "At least now he's at peace" at funerals. But I really pray that's true of my da.'

She smiles. 'And you? Are you at peace these days?'

'Well,' he says, 'I'm not fighting any good fights.'

'I knew you weren't dead. I just knew.'

'Look, Eileen ...'

'It's okay,' she says, urgent, 'whatever it was, you must have had good reason. Anyway, what were we going to do? We couldn't have gone on behind Billy's back like that forever.'

No, he thinks. He remembers the body, sectioned in bags at Cooey's Wells. They stand in silence and Jackie looks back towards his father's grave, signalling to Sarah that he'll be over in a minute.

'Will you come back to Sarah's for a wee while? For the wake?'

'No, I'd better not.'

She looks at her black-gloved hands for a moment, fiddles with the strap of her handbag. He is about to make his excuses when she speaks, a resolve in her voice.

'Take my mobile number and give me a ring,' she says. 'If you want to.'

He punches her number into his own mobile and she tells him to call in four hours: she should be alone then. Billy doesn't know she is here, at Roselawn. A wave of nostalgia washes over him, followed by a bubbling foam of anticipation. They part, but as he is walking back to his sister and her family, he sees a familiar face, a Slavic face, watching from next to a mausoleum, some distance off.

CHAPTER 11

1993

He got back to the house on Bendigo Street around ten to find it empty. Sarah was probably out with her boyfriend but she had been busy. The living room was clean and tidy and there were fresh vegetables in the fridge. His father was probably in one of the bars, pissing away the little pay he still picked up at the shipyard. Jackie collected his unemployment benefit regular as clockwork, but shipyard work had been drying up for years. Opportunities for his da to grab a couple of hours' paid labour were increasingly unpredictable.

Much like the daily movements of IRA commander James Cochrane. Jackie knew that the men and women of Northern Ireland's police force, the RUC, routinely avoided routine in order to make assassination attempts more problematic. Cochrane had followed suit. The bulk of surveillance had been done by Tommy thus far, since he was an unknown face in the area and more at liberty to move around. Jackie had observed the target to a lesser degree and Rab had sat back, waiting until the actual hit. He was a known quantity among republicans in East Belfast and a liability when it came to surveillance.

A short time ago, Jackie had been sitting in a Vauxhall on Mountpottinger Road watching Cochrane visit his estranged wife and daughter. They lived next door to Cochrane, three doors down from the local RUC station with its blast walls and towering reinforced gates flanked by sangar security posts – huge concrete blocks with a single observation slit in each.

Now Jackie sagged in an armchair and lit up a cigarette,

drawing deeply and letting his head rest on the back of the threadbare cushion. He was relieved his father wasn't home. The two of them circled èach other like boxers in a ring, their daily chatter harmless sparring while both ducked the knockout blow: Jackie's connections and the threat they presented. Awkwardly, he took a handgun from his waistband and laid the ugly weight on the floor next to him. Sitting exposed like that in the car, in a republican area where, at any moment, someone could walk up to the side window and put a bullet in his face, had sapped his energy. He'd been living on his nerves for days now. His thoughts turned to the call he had to make and he dragged his weary frame to the phone and dialled the same number he'd dialled out the back of Castle Court. The number he'd dialled after talking to Eileen yesterday. The number he'd committed to memory, like the combination of a safe containing the secrets of his life. The key to his precarious existence.

#

Jackie parked his Ford Escort in the small car park at the foot of the path up to Scrabo Tower and switched off his lights. The tower stood like a stone lightning rod on Scrabo Hill overlooking Strangford Lough. He sat in the late-night darkness, ten miles from Belfast, and waited. He could not see another soul. A restless mob of clouds blocked the moon and threatened a downpour. The gravel car park was a web of deep shadows surrounded by gorse. It was almost midnight. He was tired, his eyes raw from lack of sleep. He knew that tired wasn't good. Tired meant careless. But he was sure he hadn't been followed.

As sure as he could be after a couple of Black Bush on five hours sleep.

After five minutes, another car eased into the car park and came to a stop at the opposite end of the gravel enclosure. A small torch inside the car flashed: *Oscar-Romeo-Romeo.* Jackie tucked the 32 ACP Walther PP into his jeans, took a deep breath and opened his car door. He sprinted across to the waiting Astra, its back door already open.

Once inside, he lay across the back seat while the driver leaned over and closed the door.

'Jackie, how are you?'

'I've been worse, yourself?'

'Can't complain. BRC passed your call on yesterday, said you'd phone today when you had the chance.'

'Sorry about the hour, Gordon. I hope Rebecca wasn't too pissed off at me.'

'It's hardly the first time. Better you than some asset who's a player.'

'That's ninety per cent of your job.'

'Aye, I suppose. But she sees me take the Astra and she breathes easier. She knows I wouldn't be driving soft-skinned if I wasn't confident about a meet.'

Not that Jackie wouldn't have been happier in an armoured vehicle. Still, he knew it was hard on Gordon's wife, Rebecca, being married to a police officer. Wives and kids struggled with the thought of their husbands and fathers being 24-hour targets for republican terrorists. Thanks to Gordon Orr handling 'assets' – or agents – in the UVF and UDA, he was a target for loyalists too.

'Sorry about the beating you took at the Lagan Lodge. The sergeant is a transfer from D Division, took a bit of abuse in Tiger's Bay and Mount Vernon. Rubbed up against some bad apples colluding with the UVF, so he has a thing about loyalists. He's out to prove a point.'

'He's an arsehole is what he is.'

'That's no sort of language to be using about a colleague.' So said the Burning Bush: Gordon Orr, evangelical conscience of Special Branch East.

Colleague, thought Jackie, a good word. A word with gravitas and a sense of respectability, the very qualities expected in a police officer. Not like undercover, with its clandestine, cloak-and-dagger connotations. 'At least they got the time and place right,' he said. 'And we prevented the kneecapping and got Rafferty. That's a result.'

'Sounds like you got Rafferty senior.'

Gordon, his partner in E Division Special Branch, East Belfast, was a tall, broad man in his late forties with a shock of rapidly greying hair and a trim moustache clinging to a generous mouth. A devoted husband, father and churchgoer, Gordon was the moral guardian of Special Branch East. Jackie often wondered at how he had navigated his way through the murk of the Branch for over a decade and kept his integrity intact. He had run various assets, including one IRA member in the Short Strand, and did his best to keep Jackie sane during meets.

Sane in an insane position: Jackie was wedged between the huge, well-oiled policing machine of the Royal Ulster Constabulary and the largest terrorist organisation in Ireland, the UDA. He was the only undercover RUC officer that Gordon worked with. In fact, Jackie was the only undercover RUC officer that he knew of inserted in a terrorist organisation in E Division. Probably in Belfast. He wasn't even Special Branch. He was on secondment after a superior who liaised with SB had mentioned him to one of their officers.

Born and raised on the Ravenhill Road, Jackie had known some of the players since his days kicking a football up and down Bendigo Street and coughing on stolen Benson & Hedges in the alley behind his parents' house. He'd gone to the Army, then the Constabulary out in the country regions, and effectively disappeared from the community. His father was a private man and hadn't discussed his son, no matter how much he loved the drink. His sister, Sarah, had largely been absent. Jackie was perfect material for an undercover operative in the local paramilitary cell. He'd come home, drawn the dole, drunk in the bars, and made the right noises until an approach was made. Now, beyond the highest ranks in Branch, Gordon was the only living soul who knew the truth of Jackie's association with Rab Simpson and the rest. No other officers could know he was police: the risk of a leak was too great. And if the UDA were to discover he was RUC there'd be baseball bats, cigarette burns and, after a long, painful ordeal, a bullet in the head.

The austere big man facing Jackie was his sole friend, his confidant, counsellor and minister.

Gordon said, 'Do I smell whiskey? Tell me you didn't drive here under the influence? Do you know what would happen if you were stopped at a VCP and the uniforms picked you up?'

'Relax, Gordon, I know what I'm fucking doing.'

'And I meant it about the language. You're not in one of those holes drinking with Tyrie and Simpson now.'

'You want to try going to some of them holes yourself. Get out of Divisional HQ and spend a bit of time with the players in their natural environment.'

They sat in silence for a minute, Jackie clenching and unclenching his fists and jaw. He thought of insults he could hurl at Orr, interspersed with hurling a little self-loathing at himself. Gordon was right, he didn't behave like a policeman. He didn't *feel* like a policeman, Special Branch or otherwise.

He knew Gordon was waiting until he calmed himself, like a father with a tantrum-throwing child. It was textbook handling for a volatile asset, someone who was a violent and unstable player, a terrorist, informing on his comrades. Is that what I am now, he thought, one of them? Even through the dense gloom he could see concern on Gordon's face. Was Jackie more at home now in a dive like the Lagan Lodge, knocking them back with Tyrie, Simpson and the rest?

'Look, I can't begin to know what it's like being with them; *being* them. But it's undercover, son. It isn't real, you're playing a character. Your warrant card and dress uniform is still at E Division HQ. You're still a policeman. One of us.'

Jackie exhaled with a whistle, scratching his head a little too aggressively, like a junkie without a fix. He was dying for a cigarette but Gordon forbade smoking in his car.

'I'm all right.' He relaxed a little. 'I'm all right.'

He took a small notepad from his hip pocket, sparked up his cigarette lighter and squinted at the book as he related the protection run at Maguire's, Simpson's violence and threat to the shop-owner, and suggested intrusive rather than static surveillance of Maguire in case of further intimidation.

'I think it's to our advantage to keep Simpson in play for now, so a decent uniform presence around the Cregagh Road, the shop and Maguire's house. Enough to scare Simpson off doing something rash.'

Next, he gave an account of the altercation with Peter Rafferty, how he had been forced to confront the man in order to maintain his cover. He had used non-lethal force and established further credentials with Tyrie, Simpson and Rainey. Gordon wasn't happy. Rafferty was in bad shape and wasn't the type to forgive or forget. However, it had boosted Jackie's credibility and standing within the Ravenhill group.

They covered Shanty McKee and how Jackie had seen him checking out his car. Why would he be doing that? Did he recognise Jackie's Ford from another, previous meet with Gordon?

'I'll have DRU look into him and ask CID if he's come up anywhere in their files recently,' said Gordon, 'but I doubt it. You were driving your car when you picked him up for the kneecapping. He probably just recognised it from that night.'

Jackie knew the Divisional Research Unit probably wouldn't find anything. CID had likely never heard of the kid.

'There's an arms bed in Cregagh Glen,' he said. 'Big gear: an assault rifle, explosives and handguns.'

'How do you want to proceed on that one?'

'I'd go camera surveillance for now; there's no harm to the public that I can see. It's buried well off the hiking path and the bed is pretty deep. The explosives are Powergel, useless without a precursor to mix them with. The guns aren't loaded, but the ammunition is stored in the same dump.'

He wondered if any of the weapons had been marked for use on James Cochrane.

And there it was. The elephant in the room; or in Jackie's head, at any rate. There was a plan to kill a senior commander in the Provisional IRA, a guy who would love to put a bullet between both Jackie's and Gordon's eyes. Jackie remembered a colleague, John Wilson, blown apart in a rocket attack on the sangar at Mountpottinger station. It could have been Cochrane holding the launcher. Jim Magee, shot in bed with his wife wailing next to him and his kids screaming in their bunk beds in the next room. Might have been Cochrane pulled the trigger.

But Jackie should tell Gordon about the hit and prevent his death? Save the bastard?

He cleared his throat and said, 'Any information for me?'

'Not much at this end,' said Gordon. 'We think something must be brewing because Tyrie hasn't responded to the Raven-hill bomb yet, but we have nothing in terms of intel.' He rubbed his eyes. 'Rainey is seeing some girl somewhere near the Shore Road. We got that tidbit from SB North. D Division passed the intel on.'

'Vera won't be too happy if she finds out. And a wee girl? He's well into his forties, the dirty oul' clart.'

This was much of what they did on meets: gossip like a couple of bored housewives. So much of surveillance was observing routines and looking for anomalies in everyday existence, the tiny exception in the unexceptional, wading through so much daily grind. Jackie pushed Cochrane further to the back of his mind.

He said, 'There's a new face working with Tyrie's crew now. Name's Tommy, apparently from North Belfast. Mount Vernon. Don't have a surname at present. Young, about five foot seven, 120 pounds, fair hair, pale eyes, clean-shaven and boyish in appearance, although I'd guess he's in his early twenties.'

'I'll look into it.' Gordon checked his watch. 'Take care of yourself.'

'All right then. Cheers.'

Jackie opened the door again and sprinted back to his car. By the time he was settled in the seat and turning the key in the ignition, Gordon Orr's Astra was gone and Jackie was, once again, alone.

#

The sex was ragged and frantic.

They hadn't fucked for weeks and, like binge drinkers, they gorged on each other. And after she had drained him, they lay back on sheets soaked in their sweat and retreated into their own lives for a moment.

Jackie had risen late and run through the Ormeau Park to get the booze out of his system and allay the feverish anticipation of her time, her body, *her*. She had boarded the train for a shopping trip in Dublin, as she had told Billy she would, then disembarked in Portadown, where he had picked her up and driven to Newcastle.

Now they lay in a queen-size in the Slieve Donard Hotel, named after the greatest of the Mourne Mountains, which stood watch over the town. Jackie rolled onto his left side and took in the smooth, glowing body lying next to him.

'You could go, you know,' he said.

'I thought we just came, Jackie.'

'I'm serious,' he said. 'You could just go. Across the water, away from all this shite. At least until it's all over.'

She laughed. Too hard and loud. It sounded cruel.

'What, the Troubles? I'd be in a wooden box when I came back. This is never going to end.'

'It could end for you. You have money. Go to England. Scotland.'

Eileen propped herself on her right elbow.

'Are you trying to save me, Jackie?' She reached out and touched his face.

As always when he was with her, he felt younger than his years, awkward and foolish.

'I just think you're better than Billy, better than the life you have now.'

'Jackie, I left school with hardly a qualification to my name. I don't know how to do anything other than what I do now, and that's make all the right noises when Billy climbs on me after a night in the bar, or look good for the man when he wants me on his arm. I can read him, I know him, and he can protect me because he's the head of the pack. Call me cynical but this is the best I can do.'

He began shaking his head but she said, 'No,' with a force that stopped him dead. 'I know I have looks, Jackie. If I'd been born somewhere else, I might have been able to do more with them. Jesus, if I'd been born a bit further up the road. But where I am, I make the best use of what God gave me.'

She was on her knees now, legs neatly folded under her.

'Billy has guile and ruthlessness. Rab is a psychopath. Frankly, Jackie, I deserve them.' She leaned forward and touched his lips. 'But I don't know what has brought you close to them. You're smart, no matter how much you pretend otherwise. You're hard when you need to be but you've no stomach for their violence.'

He felt suddenly exhausted. Used up.

'You bring me here when you want me. And at the minute, when you're finished you still want me. But that won't be forever. Someday, I'll not be enough for you to stay around. So you might fool yourself otherwise, but I'm no more than a good-looking fuck to you either, Jackie.'

Eileen kissed him before he could speak.

'Don't spoil this by lying. To me or yourself.'

Then she unfolded her legs, locked them around him, and salved the raw wounds of his existence.

CHAPTER 12

Friday

He doubts they are armed and counts his blessings. The Slavic man disappeared from Roselawn, but he and his companion were parked a few doors down and across the street from Sarah's house as he left the wake. It was a good old Presbyterian wake, which is to say it was like the cliche of an Irish wake – loud, boisterous, plenty of craic – with tea and sandwiches instead of booze.

He's thankful. He needs his wits about him now. He said his goodbyes with promises of a call later. Now, the two men are a couple of car lengths behind him on the Knock dual carriage-way. He nears Belvoir Forest Park in the south-east of the city. As a young teenager, he would follow the river tow-path; five minutes along the path and you wouldn't believe half a million people lived around you. Long grass, trees, a sheep meadow; then thick, silent forest, a favoured spot with joggers, dog walkers, lovers. It has had darker patrons too: bodies, some of them children, have been found buried beneath the trees or bobbing in the river.

He pulls the car into the parking area at the edge of the forest, locks it with the Ruger inside and takes off at a jog through the evergreens. He hears the tailing car crunch to a halt behind as he keeps a steady pace into the forest. Jackie thinks the men will follow because that is what Simpson would have told them: *Keep the fucker in sight, don't lose him.* He listens for feet on the dirt path or snapping twigs on the forest floor and hears only cloaking silence, so he slows his pace and crouches in a clump of tall grass. They are probably debating what to do, forestalling the inevitable. Perhaps Simpson is bawling them out on a mobile phone, screaming at them to follow.

Jackie is glad he resisted the impulse to bring the gun. It is an obvious advantage, but a liability against two men should he be overpowered. What he did bring is the jack from the car, which he pulled from the boot through the gap at the bottom of the rear seat back-rest. He's confident they will not try to kill him: Tyrie is still breathing, the job not yet done.

Sound disturbs the perfect solace of the forest, a deliberate whisper of boot on dusty forest floor and hoarse, ragged breathing. He sees them walking through the trees like characters sneaking around in an old cartoon. They don't appear armed, although they could be carrying concealed weapons.

When they are within spitting distance he stands and walks at a brisk pace from the grass and drives the car-jack into the base of the nearest man's skull. The man crumples and begins screaming. His companion barks in a foreign language and freezes, stunned. Jackie approaches him at speed, seeing him flinch with each step, and batters the left side of his head with the blunt metal. This second man falls to his knees and begins sobbing.

He returns to the first man and delivers a sharp kick to the kidney. He has worked enough on their heads and knows it is much more difficult to render a man unconscious than most people think. Besides, he wants to deliver a message and needs at least one of them sensible. A final kick to the testicles is enough. Satisfied, he returns to the sobbing man. Blood covers the man's face on one side. He looks terrified. Compliant.

Jackie brings the car-jack down on his right shoulder. Another scream follows.

'Where are you from?' he asks.

He is met with a shambles of foreign invective. Pink spit

bubbles and flies from the man's lips, mixed with tears and snot. Jackie slaps him hard across the face, avoiding the congealing blood on the battered skull.

'Poland? Slovakia?'

'Estonia.'

'You work for Simpson?'

'Sometimes.'

'You're following me for Simpson.'

It isn't a question, but he kicks the man's leg to get confirmation.

'Yes!' It's a child's cry, frantic.

'Not any more. He asks you to follow me again, you say yes. Then you go for a drink. Go to the beach. Fuck your girlfriend.'

The man nods, eager. Jackie looks back at his companion, lying in a heap, shoulders rising and falling in exaggerated gasps.

'Names.'

'I am Petri, he is Ion.'

'Give me your mobile phone, Petri.'

The man pauses, unsure. His fear of Jackie is wrestling with his fear of Rab Simpson.

'Give me the phone or I'll break your arms.'

He hands over his mobile.

Jackie says, 'Do you know Shanty McKee?'

'The junkie? Yes, I know him.'

'Where does he live?'

'Toronto Street. Number 42.'

Jackie nods, then glances at the fallen Ion. 'If I see you or him again, I'll kill you.'

'I understand.'

He nods and walks back towards the car park, swinging the car-jack as he goes. It was a chance he'd had to take, confronting the men. The blow from the makeshift weapon looked bad but wouldn't do lasting damage, and violence was a language everyone could understand.

Christ, I buried my father this morning, thinks Jackie.

#

The creature stares out from a pitted, ravaged face. A broken face on what is left of a broken man. His features have contracted as his teeth have rotted and fallen from his head, and his eyes look lidded and stupid. His ears seem huge as his skin has stretched, crawling over his skull and revealing the ugly skew of a broken jawline. The skin is old parchment, blistered and burned through in places, as though someone has taken a lit fag-end to it. The arms, covered in tattoos and track-marks, are sinewy threads hanging limp from a sleeveless vest.

Shanty McKee is a heroin addict.

Jackie says, 'You haven't changed a bit.'

A phlegmy cough. It could be a laugh. Shanty says, 'You haven't either. I recognised you soon as I saw you at the memorial.'

'You must be, what, late thirties now, Shanty.' He looks twice his age. 'You'll be dead in a year or two if you don't knock this on the head.'

'Sure, I'm dead already.'

Jackie is shocked by the change in the man, a withered wraith sitting in a living room bare save for a TV and battered sofa. The room is dominated by the blackened maw of a derelict fireplace strewn with fag butts and needles. Piles of dog shit are scattered around the carpet.

The back door was unlocked. Jackie had parked a few streets away, then sprinted through the rabbit warren of back alleys forming the spine of the terraced streets on the lower Ravenhill Road. Counting the wooden gates into the tiny back yards of the houses, he'd climbed over and been ready to force the back-door but it gave with a gentle push.

Shanty looks like he'd give with a gentle push himself. Fold in on himself, his ribcage snapping like the bones of a bird carcass, dried in the sun. The dog had greeted Jackie. No yapping or growling, just a brief sniff. He'd found Shanty in the living room, lying with his back against the wall in a shaded corner holding a shoe-polish tin. There was a dirty brown mixture in the tin: heroin and water. Gollum and his precious.

'Give us the needle, will ye? Once I shoot this skag, I'll tell you anything you want.'

The drug slang sounds strange coming from the old-man face. Jackie has the needle in his right hand. He's squatting on the carpet, down on his haunches. He doesn't want anything but the soles of his boots touching the surface.

'So you knew me soon as you saw me. Who'd you call to report? Petri? Ion?'

'Them Russian boys live next to the One Stop?'

'Estonian.'

'Same thing. No, never had a word to say to them. They're shit scared of Simpson, just work for him so they aren't burned out of the road. 'Mon Jackie, give us the skag.'

Shanty scratches his left arm. His tattoos are blistered with track-marks and scabs. The Red Hand of Ulster on his upper arm is stretched and bloated, an infection festering beneath it.

'Who did you report to when you saw me, Shanty?'

'Ade, Adrian Morgan.'

'Don't know him from Adam.'

'He's from somewhere about the Holy Lands, near Queen's. He supplies Rab sometimes.'

'With drugs.'

'Aye. Wingers, some heroin.'

'Wingers?'

'Y'know, ecstasy. Wingers. When you're winged off your tits, like.'

Jackie examines the syringe he's taken from McKee, just long enough for Shanty to get a good look at it, before he lets it dangle close to the floor.

'Where would I find this Morgan? What's he look like?'

'He likes the Realm, the club near Botanic station. He'll be there tonight. Beard, shaggy brown hair. Has a tattoo on his neck, some kind of Buddha thing. He's young, mid to late twenties. Can I shoot up now?'

'You were always a sleeked wee shite, Shanty. But working for Rab Simpson, after all the man did to you ...'

'Ach Jackie, you have to put things behind you and move on, isn't that what all the politicians are telling us now? It's all in the past.'

'No Shanty, it's all in here, isn't it?'

Jackie taps the syringe, tosses it over and stands up. His joints crack. He watches, fascinated, as Shanty injects himself with the filthy water from the shoe-polish lid. The man pierces his ankle as his arms are used up. Shanty looks like he's being eaten alive by a monstrous parasite.

Which, Jackie thinks, he is.

#

Eileen answers on the second ring. He can't deny it still gives him a rush to hear her voice. Every man has his drug, he thinks.

They arrange to meet in the gardens of Belfast Castle as the first dark descends over the city.

Irish people laugh at Americans for so few of them possessing a passport, yet there are some natives of Belfast who have never seen swathes of their hometown. There are those in West Belfast who have never ventured five miles to the east, and vice-versa.

This is why here, in the gardens of the Scottish baronial-style great house, the couple feel safe from detection.

Eileen looks more beautiful than he ever imagined, untouched by the years. Motherhood has given her face an angular edge – serene, he thinks – and the lines that bracket her mouth fascinate him. He is shocked to find how much he wants to kiss them.

'You have kids,' he says.

'Two girls, Wendy and Claire,' says Eileen, 'sixteen and eighteen. And you?'

'No. Probably just as well. I've moved around a lot since leaving.'

She glances at his hand. 'The heart is still pointing out on your Claddagh.'

He keeps his counsel. In truth, he's surprised by how intense it is being near her again. After a time, he says, 'I'm sorry.'

'For what?'

He is that wee boy in her presence again, stumbling over his words while she is poised, in control. 'For going. No word. No goodbye.'

'It was a long time ago. It wasn't like people didn't just disappear then. When we realised you weren't dead, well, I was disappointed.' She looks at the far eastern shore of Belfast Lough. 'The betrayal was worse. Your betrayal of me. You weren't the man I thought you were. You were no angel, but I thought you were better than them. And then, when it looked like you killed the others …'

'Eileen, whatever I was in those days, the only time I felt like the man I wanted to be, was when I was alone with you.'

What would she think if she knew he'd been RUC? Would it be better? Would he be less of a fraud? Maybe she knows already. Billy and Rab have danced around it, but if they had contacts in the force, something could have leaked. Whatever the truth, she doesn't ask why he ran.

He says, 'I saw Billy. Claire's godfather was with him.'

'Mark,' she says, 'his name is Mark.'

'*Was* Mark. If anything happens to yourself or Billy, God forbid, somebody else'll have to step in to take care of your Claire, because Mark certainly won't be doing it.'

He waits for a slap, physical or figurative, but none comes.

'He can't bear for another man to have me, but he can't be bothered to touch me himself. I suppose two decades and a couple of kids, people do grow apart.' She straightens the hem of her skirt. 'He doesn't know about us. Never even suspected. But he does think you were a tout.' She studies his face. 'You don't have to worry. It's all water under the bridge. He came out of Good Friday with a clean slate, like the rest of them. He doesn't want to get his hands dirty again.'

'And my da? If Billy suspected, why was he left alone?'

'He was never a threat. Billy felt sorry for him, thought he'd been betrayed by you too, left alone in that wee house to rot.'

'And he kept Simpson off my da too?'

She gives a soft snort. 'Rab couldn't have cared less about your dad. If it didn't involve hurting Catholics or making money, it was a waste of his time.'

Twilight is advancing at speed now and the lights are blinking on across the city below. Jackie thinks of Shanty's arms and says, 'I saw Rab, too. He's changed a bit.'

Eileen's eyes flicker in the dying light of the day. 'He was shot in the face. Some kind of feud with some cowboys over in West Belfast. He had reconstructive surgery. Had the money to iron out a few kinks while he was at it.'

She says she has tried to keep Billy's past and present dealings as secret from her girls as possible, but now they're older and beginning to suspect. She wants to get away now, spits out a brittle laugh as she remembers Jackie's pleas for her to leave all those years ago. But it's too late. She's scared of what Billy might do, she'd have nothing, she's too old to start over now.

Excuses, thinks Jackie. You'd be amazed how you can change the entire fabric of your life in a heartbeat when you don't have a choice. He remembers the flight to England, relocation in a Home Counties town that felt like living in a retirement home. He petitioned for relocation abroad, took a posting with the Royal Hong Kong Police Force in the last days before the handover. A new world, huge and welcoming, that opened up and gripped him like Shanty and his drugs. He travelled; he consumed foreign lands, cultures, people, living his life in far-flung corners.

But now, in the deep, black pool of the lawns in front of the castle, with the lights scattered below as beautiful a sight as any he has seen in all his travels, he says, 'Aye, well, I'd better get back into town.'

Her profile is like a cameo. You're still a beautiful woman, he thinks. But you're tainted, like the rest of us. And you're the death of any man who thinks he can have you.

He turns and walks back to his car, conscious that despite this time together, he hasn't felt the touch of her skin once.

CHAPTER 13

1993

Jackie fingered a revolver, heavy and reassuring, tucked under his left armpit. He didn't usually wear a shoulder-holster, didn't usually carry a gun on his daily business, but sitting in a car in the incendiary Short Strand, he felt better with a little loaded heft.

It was a chilly day, not like spring at all, in the first week of April. The Ravenhill bombing was over a month ago and some of the local boys felt it was high time for a response, but Billy was all about the long game and hitting IRA commander Cochrane when the time was right. So Jackie was sitting in a rented car, tarted up to resemble a taxi, waiting for Danny Moore to walk around the corner. Danny worked in the bus depot in the Short Strand. Jackie or Tommy could squeeze thirty to forty minutes of surveillance on Cochrane's house at most. Their cover: a bored taxi driver waiting for his pre-booked fare to finish a shift at the depot. Danny, a Ravenhill man with quiet sympathies towards the UDA, worked there and could keep an eye on developments in the republican area for long stretches.

Jackie had never been in the RUC's E4A so he was no surveillance expert, but he knew they were doing this as well as could be expected. Tommy and Jackie rotated static surveillance on Cochrane, never staying in one location for more than around forty-five minutes. At night they could use the roof of a building opposite which Danny had scouted.

But it was still anathema to Jackie. When the IRA shot a police officer, or any other poor bastard, it was almost always from behind.

The surveillance had yet to yield much. Like any good terror-ist commander, James Cochrane was well aware of how many of his counterparts among loyalist factions, members of the se-curity forces and, possibly, rivals in the republican INLA would sleep better at night knowing he was six foot under. He strin-gently avoided all routine and at night a reinforced door protected him, along with a couple of discreetly placed guards in their own parked cars.

Danny turned the corner and strode over to the car in his Citybus uniform, opening the passenger door and collapsing onto the seat.

'How's our boy?'

Jackie smiled. Danny wasn't in the UDA, but was clearly en-joying the residual thrill.

'I don't think he's at home. The wife was talking to a neigh-bour a few minutes ago and she looked happy enough. She looks pissed off when he's there.'

'She wouldn't look pissed off if I was her man. I'd fucking give her one, so I would.'

'Well, you can step in and give her a shoulder to cry on when Hubby isn't around any more.'

Jackie gunned the engine and took off, doubling back a few streets later and driving to the Lagan Lodge on the lower Ravenhill Road. Danny headed off for a bite to eat and unwind after his shift and Jackie walked into the bar, a smattering of hardened drinkers chasing their pints with shots at the counter. In a small room above the main bar, he found Rab playing pool and Billy looking over the *Belfast Telegraph* while drawing on a pint in the corner.

Rab sank a stripe in the middle left pocket, and said, 'Well?'

'Nothing. I don't think he was there, the missus was in too good a mood.'

'Fenian bastard. We'll never fucking get him at this rate. He must be over in the west or north half the time.'

'He's wily enough. You don't survive as a commander in the 'RA in this part of the town without having some smarts.'

'No,' said Billy, 'our colleagues are just too fucking lazy to put the effort in. Easier to go out and shoot some poor fucker on his milk-round.'

'Aye, some Fenian fucker,' said Rab.

'But not the *right* Fenian fucker,' said Billy.

Jackie said, 'We'll get a break. We just need him vulnerable for a few minutes.' He was freaked by the genuine enthusiasm in his voice.

Rab lit a cigarette and took a drag. He leaned over the table, cue in hand, and eased another striped ball into the top left pocket. 'That fucker Maguire is another one,' he said. 'We can't get near him for RUC patrols. The wee shite probably called the Black Bastards after I near skinned him.'

Jackie said, 'Sure, leave him. Wait'll we've sorted Cochrane.'

'Fucking wee shite,' said Rab, loud and shrill. 'Fucking wanker.'

Changing the subject Jackie said, 'Here, where's Shanty's dog? I haven't seen it in a while.'

Rab tipped some ash on the floor and coughed up a chunk of phlegm.

'Sure, I shot it,' he said.

'You what?'

'The fucking thing was yapping away at me so I took it to the park in the middle of the fucking night for a walk. Must have been about one, had to climb over the railings with it and everything, but when you're drunk, you know ...'

No, I don't know, thought Jackie. I've never executed a Jack Russell when I've had a couple.

'I had a gun with me because you hear all these stories about the park at night, you know: fucking sickos running about. And it was still yapping and I was tired. So I put my coat over the dog's head and shot it.'

Jackie tried to keep his expression neutral while his mind raced for something, anything to say.

Billy Tyrie to the rescue.

'Enough,' said Billy. 'Ruger will be here in a wee while and we can discuss Cochrane. Jackie, away and get yourself a drink from downstairs.'

And so it was that twenty minutes later they were standing around the pool table

'I know youse are champing at the bit to get at Cochrane,' Billy said, 'and I know youse are frustrated. It's over a month since the East End bomb and it grates even more that the 'RA bastards who did it were looking to hit us, UDA command. But we have to do this right.'

Rab fingered a cigarette burn in the green baize.

'Do you hear me, Rab?'

Rab nodded, not taking his eyes off the burn. 'Right,' he repeated.

'It doesn't look like we can hit him at his house,' said Billy. 'Rab set up a couple of video cameras when Danny took him up on a rooftop a couple of nights ago. Cochrane's place is under constant guard, probably because they expect retaliation. We don't want the car surveillance drawing any unwanted attention, so we're knocking it on the head.'

Jackie breathed a sigh of relief. He hated watching from the 'taxi', literally a sitting target. He wondered at Rab's hidden talents for electronic surveillance, though.

Billy continued, 'Now, youse haven't seen Tommy for a couple of days because he's been doing a bit of work for us over in the west. Turns out Cochrane's domestics are worse than you think. His wife's not happy because the fucker's shagging some wee doll on the Springfield Road.'

Jackie wasn't surprised. Many of the players in the city had at least one mistress hidden away somewhere. It was a point of weakness Special Branch had tried to exploit in the past. Billy was the exception rather than the rule.

'This wee bint,' said Billy, 'took a tumble last week coming out of a shebeen when she was full. Now she's in the Royal with a spinal injury and Cochrane's been going to see her. This is it, lads. Time to make the fucker pay for nine of ours we lost in that bomb.'

Rab looked up from the scarred surface of the pool table and smiled. Rainey's face had lit up and Jackie gave his best shit-eating grin in response. This was exactly what they'd been looking for. Cochrane was restricted by hospital visiting hours and locked into a schedule of sorts. The Royal Victoria Hospital was a sprawling complex with a wealth of hiding places and it was possible to enter with a good chance of remaining undetected. The busy Grosvenor Road on its northern perimeter mainlined directly to the city centre, although they'd have to be wary of the joint police and Army base located halfway along it. Alternatively, they could escape up the Springfield Road onto Ballygomartin and loyalist Woodvale, or continue on into the mountains on that side of the city.

Tommy had done his homework and noted the hours and days when Cochrane visited the girl, Shona Doherty. Cochrane visited without fail between 4 and 6 p.m. It would be rush hour, but easier to blend into traffic after the target was taken out, with plenty of crowds if they were forced to escape on foot. They could use a contact of Tommy's within the hospital to gain access, study floorplans and hide weapons there in advance. Cochrane would have bodyguards but, crucially, would be alone in the room with the girl during the visit.

Jackie was surprised to find that the preparation was solid and the hit feasible. Risky, but what operation wasn't? He would call Orr. Gordon would probably move the girl, maybe to another hospital under some administrative pretence. He might put a man in another room nearby with a uniformed guard on the doors. That would discourage the hit and piss Cochrane off, having to pass a couple of peelers while he visited his woman-on-the-side.

Half an hour later they were downstairs for a drink. The revolver and shoulder-holster had been placed in a safe upstairs by Rainey, the quartermaster. Jackie ordered a second pint.

Just this one and I'll head off, he thought. Maybe two, just to get my head right.

Business over, Billy and Ruger began an earnest discussion as to whether Ally McCoist could do the business against Marseille. With Hateley out, the consensus seemed to be that the UEFA Champions League probably wouldn't be coming to Ibrox this season. Talk turned to English football. Rainey was a Liverpool fan, Billy a Manchester United man. Billy was gently riding Ruger about United's win at Anfield last month when the barman cut in.

Eddie McMaster was a new face behind the counter . Young and cocky, the Lodge's landlord had hired him because he was cheap labour paid off the books, and in a desperate but doomed attempt to bring in a younger crowd. Eddie was also a fervent Liverpool fan. Cloth over his shoulder, he leaned on the oak bar and said, 'Good result last month, Billy.'

Billy and Ruger nodded earnestly.

'Hughes and McClair, eh? Yer man Hughes is quality, so he is.'

More nodding and a sly grin from Billy, enjoying the gloat over his mate.

Eddie McMaster said, 'Too bad it was an ex-Celtic man scored your winner.'

There was barely a flicker of annoyance from Billy. But a flicker nonetheless, like a hand passing through a naked flame.

Eddie said, 'Then again, is there any such thing as an *ex*-Celtic man?'

Sam Rainey stepped in, his voice an octave higher. 'Ach, Eddie, sure we'd Dalglish for years and he was a legend for us.'

'But wasn't he a Rangers supporter as a kid? I can't see McClair ever having a season ticket for Ibrox, like.'

All this time Eddie McMaster had had a small, conspiratorial smile on his simple face. He had even winked at Rainey. Before he could say another word Billy smiled and said, 'You'll never walk alone – right, boys?' then strode off to the toilets.

Sam Rainey lit on McMaster: '*You fucking eejit, is your head cut? Winding up Billy Tyrie?*'

Jackie turned away, looking for an opportunity to make for the door and find a phone box. The sooner he could get the details of the Cochrane hit to Gordon the better. Picking through the finer details of the operation had brought home the fact that a man was going to lose his life and, whatever he thought of Cochrane, he didn't want that on his ledger when he stood before Saint Peter. As he took in the swelling crowd of drinkers, he spotted, in the corner near the front door of the bar, two oul' lads hunched over their pints. One of the men was in a bad way. His shoulders were shaking and even from across the increasingly busy room Jackie could see the man was wracked with large, gulping sobs. His companion, a ruddy faced boozer, his nose an explosion of shattered blood vessels, sat with a hand on the other's arm. He leaned in close.

Jackie hadn't seen his father for a few days. When he had come home his da had been busy with a dedicated bout of drinking or passed out in bed. He walked over.

'Da, are youse all right?'

He nodded at the other man, curled over his pint as if protecting it, head down and focused on the cracked Formica table-top.

'Aye, we're grand, son. Harry's just feeling a bit under the weather, like.'

Jackie bent to take Harry in. It was Harry Clarke, father of one of the wee girls killed in the bombing last month. Jackie remembered there had been two schoolgirls, friends, in East End Video at the time.

He put a hand on the man's shoulder and said, 'Mr Clarke, if there's anything I can do ...'

Harry Clarke looked up, his eyes fierce and red raw. Jackie took a step back, shocked by the venom in the man's stare.

'I don't need nothing from you, or your boss.'

Samuel Shaw said, 'Ach, c'mon now, Harry, that's our Jackie. You don't need to be talking to him that way. Our Jackie isn't a bad lad.' His father nodded at him: *best if you go.*

Harry Clarke straightened his frame in the chair, as if ready to deliver a sermon. As soon as his chest had risen and his back become rigid, he collapsed in on himself, deflating and returning to a wretched hunch over his half-empty glass. At first Jackie thought grief had got the better of the man. Then a voice behind him gave him a start.

'Mr Shaw. Could I borrow your son, here?'

Jackie's father nodded at Billy, who returned the gesture before guiding Jackie gently through the bar.

'Upstairs. Now.'

The order was non-negotiable, but Jackie felt desperate to get to a phone box and unload the details of the Cochrane hit on Gordon before the drink and the stress washed them away.

Eddie McMaster stood next to Rainey in the upstairs room. There was a metal cashbox on the pool table, popped open.

Billy said, 'Milburn pays you cash, doesn't he, the tight oul' shite?'

Eddie nodded. 'That's right, Mr Tyrie.'

'Don't be taking this the wrong way, Eddie,' said Billy, 'but I can't be having you spout shite like that at the bar to me. It's a lack of respect. People could hear.'

Jackie felt a hollowness in his gut. He didn't want to see another young man beaten. He was tired and scared and just wanted to be outside in the cool evening air. To make that fucking phone call.

Billy said, 'So you won't be working here again. I have to be seen to do something. I've told Milburn. No hard feelings, eh?'

Eddie let out a long, slow breath. He said, 'Mr Tyrie, I am so–'

Sam Rainey put a hand on his arm.

Billy pointed to the cashbox. 'Like I said, no hard feelings. Take what you're owed and be on your way.'

Eddie rubbed his hands on his hips and thanked Billy. Ruger walked over to the cashbox with him, trusted companion. Eddie smiled, Sam smiled. Eddie started taking ten-pound notes from the box. Sam Rainey took hold of him. Eddie jerked but Ruger was a big man. Billy was next to them in a second. The metal lid of the cashbox slammed down on Eddie's right hand with a wet snap. He screamed. There was blood on the lip of the lid already and Ruger held McMaster's neck as Billy slammed the lid down again. And again. The cashbox must have come smashing down on McMaster's mangled hand at least ten times. Jackie lost count.

When it was over, Billy had barely broken sweat. He said to Jackie, 'Take this piece of shite out and get him to Casualty. Make sure he keeps his mouth shut,' then turned and began a conversation with Rainey. Jackie helped McMaster down the stairs and out to the alleyway where Shanty had had his escape from a kneecapping. He gave Eddie, a mass of tears and snot, a couple of ten-pound notes and told him to get a taxi to the City Hospital Casualty Department.

Then, mercifully, he was alone, a fine drizzle falling. He walked the short stretch home to Bendigo Street to grab a coffee before calling Gordon and was relieved to find the house empty. He turned the TV on while he searched for a jar of coffee in the kitchen.

Fifteen minutes later he was in the hall putting on his jacket, ready to go out and find a phone box. He picked up the remote control to turn off the TV when a solemn-faced reporter on the ten o'clock news began the daily tally of deaths in Northern Ireland. A young man had been shot on the junction of the Albertbridge and Mountpottinger Roads. The police were treating the killing as sectarian. A couple of bomb scares. And an RUC constable had been gunned down by two PIRA gunmen in the car park of a hospital in Antrim. He was ambushed and shot in the back of the head as he left the maternity unit after visiting his wife and newborn daughter. His wife heard the shots from her hospital bed. She was now a widow, the child fatherless.

Jackie took off his jacket, threw his keys on the coffee table and cracked open a can of lager. He was going nowhere.

CHAPTER 14

Friday

A mist has descended on Belfast and it clings to the city like cordite to a gunman's hand. It chokes the roads with slow-moving traffic and cloaks pedestrians in anonymity. Even Botanic Avenue, with its fast-food outlets, bars, nightclubs and hotels, is clogged with the fugue, like the inside of some giant drinking club from the old days, when you could double up on the poison you fed your system with tobacco as well as alcohol. It is 8.30 p.m.

Jackie thinks of Gordon Orr. A teetotaller and non-smoker, he was too gentle a soul for the world of E3A and E3B, the RUC Special Branch divisions targeting republican and loyalist groups. Jackie had received a phone call from his sister Sarah a few years ago to say Gordon had suffered a stroke. Not massive or fatal, but enough to force retirement and a plan to emigrate to the warmer climes of Australia with his wife. He never got on the plane, his health declining rapidly. He passed away four years ago.

As he parks in a side street and wanders around the corner towards Club Realm, Jackie thinks how aghast Gordon would be at Botanic Avenue tonight. Kids high or dulled by drink are strewn across the pavement and the homeless huddle at the entrance to the train station. For the first time since his arrival, Jackie sees a police presence. A PSNI patrol car is parked in front of a pizza joint and a foot patrol is making its way along the avenue at leisure, Glock handguns snug in hip-holsters.

There is an indistinct hum drifting from the closed door of the club, further muffled by the heavy mist. The facade of the building is an old church; Gordon would be distraught. He pushes open the door to be greeted by two bouncers with regulation shaved heads and ill-fitting suits, sporting small earbuds for radio communication.

The bar is filling with a mix of students, young professionals and wasters. At the far end of the room is a stage, set up for a band, with more toilets next to it. Jackie looks along the counter on the left of the room for a man with a Buddha tattoo on his neck, Adrian Morgan. There are clumps of people laughing, drinking and chatting, but no shaggy-haired, bearded, tattooed drug-dealer types. Jackie eyes the bar again. He hasn't touched a drop since he touched down at the City airport and now is not the time to start, but he makes for the counter and orders a fruit juice. As he sips, a door on the right of the stage opens, a *Toilets* sign above it, and a man walks through. He looks to be in his late twenties and is wearing a scruffy T-shirt and black jeans. Jackie catches a glimpse of biker boots. The man has greasy-looking, unkempt hair and a desperate attempt at a beard, which he scratches vigorously as he walks towards the counter.

Adrian Morgan, thinks Jackie, pleasure to meet you. The man adopts a swagger as he nears the bar, oblivious of Jackie.

Morgan says, 'All right, doll, how's you?'

The bar staff gives a stale smile. 'Hi Ade, I'm tired. My flat-mate has an exam, so always I have to be quiet at home. She gets angry when I make noise.'

'Maja, darlin', you can always come and make some noise in my place.'

Jackie calls it: the guy's a first-class wanker. A wannabe.

Morgan orders a pint and persists with the girl, other staff saying hello as they pass. As he moves to a table, Jackie keeps an eye on the bar. He doesn't want Morgan to notice him, and that's a problem with an orange juice in his hand. After about fifteen minutes Morgan makes for the toilet again.

Broken the seal, thinks Jackie.

The ritual is repeated again when Morgan returns: drink, craic, piss, taking around twenty minutes this time.

Jackie makes his way towards the steps at the far end of the balcony, next to the exit for the toilets. He zips up his leather jacket, keeping watch over the bar from a distance, and takes a white wire and earbud out of his jacket pocket. It's for his iPod, when he runs back in the West Country, and purposely only for one ear: he likes to be aware of his surroundings as he runs. He shoves the bud in his ear and walks into the toilet. A punter is washing his hands in the Gents. Jackie, looking like a bouncer, tells the man to finish up and leave, the toilets will be closed for a while. He takes in the room: chess-board tiles on the floor, long urinal, cubicles, two sturdy washbasins with brass taps, and a long light-cord hanging next to the door with a ceramic ornamental handle on the end. Then he follows the man out and stands in front of the toilet door. He hopes that, as these toilets are at the opposite end of the club, the real bouncers won't notice what he's doing. A young man with a Queen's University rugby shirt approaches the door. Jackie turns him away, gives him a line about a damaged toilet. Morgan is laughing at the bar with another girl.

Come on, you bastard, thinks Jackie. You couldn't hold your water half an hour ago and now your bladder's a world-beater.

Another young man approaches and he waves him away with the damaged toilet line. He wonders how long he can maintain this charade.

A third young man appears in front of him and he feeds him the line about the damaged toilet, telling him to use the Gents at the entrance to the club. When he turns back to the bar Morgan is heading straight for him, checking his mobile phone as he walks.

Jackie yanks the bud out of his ear and stands aside as Morgan pushes through the toilet door, then waits for a moment, monitoring the punters nearby, and slips into the Gents. Morgan is mid-stream at the urinal as Jackie takes the earbud and wire and quickly ties the inner door handle to the light cord, locking the door from the inside. It won't hold for long, but, he hopes, long enough.

Morgan shakes himself dry at the urinal and says, 'What're you–' when Jackie punches him in the throat. Morgan stumbles back, almost bouncing off the wall behind as Jackie slaps him hard across the face and says, 'Shut the fuck up or I'll kill you. Understand?'

The man goes pale, gagging and retching, trying to hold his throat and cover his shrivelled penis, and managing neither.

Jackie runs a cold tap and says, 'Take a drink.'

Morgan gulps water, spluttering. Jackie moves in close.

'I don't want to kill you, but I will if you don't follow my instructions, Adrian. Do you understand?'

'Who are–'

Another slap. 'No questions. Do you understand?'

Morgan still hasn't had a chance to put his dick away. His eyes are huge and filling with tears. He nods.

'Good lad. Do you have any spliffs on you?'

'Is that what this–'

Slap.

'Spliffs.'

The door is pushed from outside. Morgan stares at the Claddagh ring, now tightening against Jackie's finger as his hand curls into a fist. Morgan nods.

'Light one. Now.'

Morgan fumbles for a rolled spliff and cheap lighter. The Buddha on his neck is pulsing. Swearing drifts from the other side of the door. The cheap lighter sparks, then dies.

A kick at the door. More swearing. The lighter catches the paper and a deep red glow blossoms at the end of the spliff.

Jackie says, 'Hold it high above your head, like you're stretching for the ceiling.'

Morgan stares at him, dumb. Jackie draws his fist back sharply and Morgan snaps out of it and holds the burning spliff high. There is another kick at the door. Muffled snippets of sentences: ... *wanker* ... *need a piss* ... *open the fucking door!* The wire gives a little. It is slipping on the smooth surface of the metal door handle.

Another, brutal kick at the door. The wire gives some more.

Then the smoke detector goes off, followed by the fire alarm. Jackie grabs Morgan's arm and says, 'Put your dick away.'

There is a general uproar coming from the other side of the door: ... *smell grass* ... *fucking dope* ... *fucking students* ... He hears deeper, louder shouts. The bouncers: ... *make for the doors please* ... *make for the exits please* ...

As he rips the wire from the door handle, Jackie says, 'You're with me. Anyone talks to you, you smile, you keep walking. Signal you're in trouble at any point and I'll do you permanent injury before anyone can stop me. Understand?'

Morgan says, 'Yes,' earnest and eager to please, frightened by Jackie's savage calm. They step out of the Gents to find the crowd already bottlenecked at the far exit. Stragglers are gulping down the remnants of drinks at a couple of tables but the area around the toilets, stage and bar is clear. Now for the bouncers.

If anyone describes a third bouncer in a leather jacket and jeans closing off the toilets, there is potential for further trouble. As they near the exit, Jackie whispers, 'What else are you carrying?'

'A wee bit of coke, some E.'

Shuffling towards the cold night air, Jackie hopes he is right about the reputation of the area. As they clear the double doors, a firm grip on Morgan's elbow, he sees several PSNI officers standing outside speaking to the bouncers. RUC uniforms and

Vice always kept an eye on Botanic, with its proximity to the university area and Golden Mile entertainment district. He had been banking on uniforms being nearby and arriving quickly on the scene. The bouncers would be kept occupied and a drugs possession charge might deter Morgan from trying to alert the cops.

Outside they reach the car and Jackie unlocks the passenger door, pushing Morgan down onto the seat.

'Stay calm and relax. I just want to talk. But if you try anything, I will break your arms. Understand?'

Satisfied by the sobbing reply, he puts the car in gear and drives into the mantle of gloom oppressing the city.

#

They sit in the rented Toyota on the Rocky Road, sloping down to the city of Belfast at a twenty-degree incline from the Castlereagh Hills to the east, like a giant concrete water-slide. Somewhere beyond the lights, on the other side of the city, is where he walked with Eileen hours earlier. Jackie is looking ahead but Adrian Morgan is clear in his peripheral vision, sharp in the car's inner light.

'Whereabouts do you live, Adrian?'

'Markets area.'

'Oh aye? Which part of the Holy Lands is that then?'

There is a small moan from the passenger seat.

'Make no mistake, Adrian, if you lie to me again I'll hurt you. But I don't want to, and if you answer my questions you'll be fine. Understand?'

'Yes.'

'Where do you live?'

'Damascus Street.'

'Where do you deal?'

'Mostly about Queens: students, squatters, that crowd. You're not Drugs Squad, right? You're not wired up or anything?'

A backhanded slap. Not enough to really hurt. Just a reminder.

'Focus, Adrian, focus. Where do you get your stuff?'

'I know people. People over in West Belfast. People in Derry.'

'And do you supply anyone?'

'Look, I can't–'

Slap.

A moan.

'Adrian, I know you're scared. You don't know who I am and you never will, I can promise you. All this mist, open fields on either side of us, hedgerow – I could end you right now. Nobody would find your body for weeks. Maybe longer.'

'Please–'

'But I won't hurt you if you answer my questions. You have my word.'

Morgan's head goes down. 'There's this guy in East Belfast. He's somebody big there. I'm like a middle-man.'

'Name?'

'I don't have a name.'

Jackie considers the semi-automatic now taped deep under the steering column. No: he wants Morgan calm and coherent. No good beating the face and head for the same reason, and the stomach or balls will just slow this down.

'Are you a smoker, Adrian? Aye? Get us a fag from the glove compartment, will you? Take one for yourself.'

It's a simple manoeuvre to snap the compartment shut on Morgan's hand. He feels the smallest give in the tendons between wrist and knuckles as the sharp edge bites hard. He lets the howl continue for a moment.

'No permanent damage. Yet. Now, give me the name.'

Of course, Jackie knows the name. He despises the mention

of the man, but he needs to trust what Morgan tells him as far as possible.

'Rab Simpson ...'

'When're you next due to supply Simpson?'

'Next weekend, Friday afternoon.'

Far too late. Simpson and Tyrie expect each other dead by Sunday night. There is silence for a moment, blessed silence. He considers just getting on the first available flight tomorrow. Rab and Billy are all sound and fury. Hartley will be glad to be rid of him. They'll never go after his sister and her family.

As if resurfacing in shallow water, he hears a muffled, 'Adlea-surnoraad.'

'What?'

'At least you're not RAAD.'

Jackie notices the man eyeing his ring.

Morgan says, as though talking to a slow child, 'I thought you might be Republican Action Against Drugs. I mean, you're not a Prod,' and nods towards the Claddagh.

'I'm a tourist,' says Jackie. 'Why would I be RAAD?'

'They were sniffing about a while ago. Shot a mate of mine from the Markets last year. I know they don't like competition coming into the Short Strand. That fucker would take out Simpson too, given half a chance, although they're supposedly partners. Here,' he says, 'Shanty McKee called me about some fella Simpson wanted followed. I stuck them Transylvanians or whatever they are on it. You're not him, are you?'

'Like I said, I'm a tourist. And which fucker would take out Simpson?'

'Don't know his name. I've never seen him, but everybody on the lower Ormeau and Markets has heard of him. Some big name in the republicans, gets the nickname Madra. Madra Mor.'

Jackie stares at him.

'Irish for dog, or big dog. This fella's bigger than Simpson in the Prods. That's why Simpson deals with him: it gives him more clout.'

'And Simpson, do you meet directly with him?'

'Mostly, yeah,' says Morgan, warming to the subject. 'Sometimes he sends men but he's there most of the time. Sleeked bastard doesn't trust anybody, always wants to see he isn't ripped off.'

'Where do you meet?'

'Out in the country, wee small hours. Nutts Corner, Ards Peninsula, Lough Neagh shore.'

Jackie gives Morgan a smile. Morgan smiles back, his mouth at any rate. His eyes telegraph confusion and fear.

'Now Adrian, you've been very cooperative but there's one more thing. I need your mobile phone.'

Morgan hands the mobile in his back pocket over.

'Just the one?'

Morgan nods and says, 'I swear,' with true conviction.

'Good man.'

Then Jackie reaches under the steering column for the semi-automatic.

CHAPTER 15

1993

It was a beautiful, sunny spring afternoon. St Paddy's Day had passed with barely a glance in the loyalist communities of Northern Ireland. Easter Sunday has been and gone too, and with it the beginning of the marching season. This, in turn, marked open season for Jackie and Eileen, as Billy was a committed marcher with a blood-and-thunder flute band. So it was that he was at Portadown for a minor Orange parade.

And so it was that Jackie and Eileen were lying in the long grass of the County Down coast near Kearney, facing the shining glass surface of the Irish Sea, the horizon blanched with haze for the first time that year. Somewhere beyond was the Isle of Man and, farther still, England.

Over there, people were still shocked at the horror of the James Bulger murder and the IRA bomb in Warrington. The youth of the country were listening to Lenny Kravitz, Depeche Mode and Suede while they drank their carry-outs on a Friday night, then munching on ecstasy and dancing in underground clubs until dawn. Arsenal and Sheffield Wednesday were preparing to do battle at Wembley for the League Cup.

And Jackie Shaw and Eileen Tyrie broke off from a deep, intense kiss and looked each other square in the eye. Jackie held her gaze and Eileen, guarded, searched his face, then smiled despite herself. He wondered what this was, passing between them. Not love; certainly desire. For him, at least, it was ever more difficult to keep things in perspective. He thought of Leanne, the two of them sweating silently on her parents' living-room floor. He hadn't seen her since but had heard she was asking after him. Life was frustrated temptation: Leanne couldn't have him, and he couldn't have Eileen, except for stolen afternoons.

'Have you ever wanted to live over there?' She pointed to the shimmering line in the distance, separating the two hues of blue: sky and sea.

'Nope, never considered it. Apart from when I went through training in the Army.'

'Where was that?'

'Wales. Nice place, but not like here. Not home. What about you?'

'Same. I've been to Liverpool a couple of times: we've relatives there. Been to London as well. Hated it. It's so ... lonely.'

'I know what you mean,' said Jackie. 'I went to Bristol for a weekend when I was at Catterick for infantry training. Didn't speak to another soul from the time I got there until I left, and I was surrounded by people.'

Eileen laughed. 'It's funny, isn't it? We're all about being British and no interest in going there.'

'Aye, but England's not Britain, is it? I love Scotland.'

'But do you want to live there?'

'Probably not,' he conceded. 'It's just not the same.'

Eileen looked out at the water. 'It's strange, isn't it? I've more in common with someone in Donegal than Devon, but we're all fighting to keep that border in place.'

'It's fear,' he said. 'We're scared of losing something. Identity, rights, religion, whatever. And we've been fighting too long to give up now.'

'That's a man talking. People fight *for* something, and youse fight for the right to keep fighting? That's pure Irish, that is.'

'Talk like that to Billy of an evening, do you?' he said, then immediately regretted it.

Eileen's face hardened. 'There's not a lot of talking of an evening in our house. Half the time he's drinking somewhere with you and his cronies, half the time he's drinking at home and staring at the telly or reading the *Telegraph*. When he's in the mood, he'll climb on top of me until he's done heaving away.'

He reached for something to say, to change the subject. He feared her scorn and couldn't stand when she shoved the reality of her marriage in his face. And much as he loathed his weakness, he was afraid of losing days, hours, like this.

He settled on, 'I'm sorry, I didn't think ...'

'No, you didn't. You look at me and you don't see a woman. You see a quick fix. You might be broken, Jackie, but I'm not the answer.'

Maybe she was right: she was a fix. She took him out of his life for a time and gave him a high. Of all the men on the road, it was him she was willing to risk these trysts with. But when it was over, they'd had a shower and washed the scent of each other away again, he went back to his life of cowboys and Indians and put her back on the shelf like a library book.

'I really didn't mean anything, Eileen. It was a stupid and careless dig, I'm sorry.' It sounded disingenuous even as the words tripped over themselves leaving his mouth.

'Take me home,' she said.

He had had trouble getting a good night's sleep since going undercover and, aware of how much of a crutch alcohol could be, had treated drink with reverence. He only had to look at his father to see what it could do to a man.

But he'd had Eileen.

Lying next to her for a precious hour or two, he was at peace. It wasn't much, but it was enough to survive on the broken slumber with a gun to hand. Now that wouldn't happen.

He dropped her off at Dundonald bus station, leaving her to

make her own way into the city, and considered his options for the day.

He could call Gordon, arrange a meet. He'd watched the news and seen the funeral of the police officer shot at the maternity hospital. Poor bastard's wife had followed the coffin, clutching their baby while her brothers had supported her. The same scene would follow Cochrane's death, but with masked gunmen, volleys of shots over the coffin and the pinched, bitter face of the widow beaming spite to the assembled media. The thought of a world without James Cochrane was a tempting proposition.

Jackie screwed his eyes shut for a second as he sat at traffic lights then shook his head. Cochrane's death would be the catalyst for another murder: possibly a police officer or civilian. When he opened his eyes again, he was surprised to find how far he had driven. It scared him a little to think he'd been driving the last few miles on autopilot. The Holywood Arches were to his right with the statue of local boy C. S. Lewis opening his wardrobe, and a line of buildings on his left, masking Connswater Shopping Centre. On the green light, he swung left towards the complex.

He parked in a corner of the car park, then sprinted over to a bank of phone boxes to the right of the rear entrance and punched in the contact number for Gordon Orr. He was met by a metallic click and an automated invitation to leave a message, and a beep.

'This is *Katana*. I want a meet at 13.00 tomorrow: designated location Sierra-Charlie-Bravo.'

As Jackie replaced the receiver, a younger man walked past him, close enough for him to smell the man's body spray. The man had his hand locked in a pretty young girl's hand. Jackie recognised Shelly Kerrigan, daughter of Marty Kerrigan, husband of Jennifer. Jennifer's maiden name was Tyrie. Shelly was Billy Tyrie's niece. The young man was Shanty McKee.

Jackie's legs turned to water.

When he was sure they hadn't seen him, his cheeks burned and he swore sharply under his breath. He stood in the phone box, stupid expression on face and heart racing, for a few moments until a leather-faced older woman yanked the door of the phone box open and said, 'Are you using this, love?'

'No, it's all yours.'

'Thanks, love. Our Sylvia's in the hospital so she is, and my husband's at the football, so I have to get our Davy to pick her up from the Royal. She's getting out the day, so she is.'

The Irish habit of pouring out your life story. It grounded him and he caught sight of the couple walking in the direction of the Albertbridge Road. The weather had kept up and the sun lit the girl's golden hair as it bobbed in the breeze. Jackie kept a good number of yards behind on foot but Shanty and the girl weren't professionals and far too interested in each other to pay much attention to what was happening around them. They stopped at the outer edges of the car park and stood behind a painter and decorator's van. It wasn't difficult to imagine what was happening on the other side of the vehicle. Jackie hung back, playing with a packet of cigarettes and, a couple of minutes later, watched the girl walk off with a spring in her step.

Two minutes later, Shanty sauntered out from behind the van, finishing a smoke. There was playing with fire and there was full-on arson, and Shanty was in danger of getting a lot more than his fingers burned. If Jackie was going to protect a murderer like James Cochrane, he had to step in and keep a wee eejit like Shanty McKee out of harm. So he began closing the distance between them across the car park.

Then a blue Ford Cortina came to a screeching stop on the sun-baked concrete and two masked figures leaped from the left-side doors. Shanty's face seemed to crumple even before one of the men took a savage grip on his balls; the other wrenched his right arm behind his back. Jackie was between two cars, frozen, his breathing harsh. He barely registered the attack unfolding in front of him, it happened with such speed and ferocity.

Survival instinct kicked in: fight or flight or keep your fucking head down. He went for the last option.

Shanty's head was up, his face scrunched in a silent scream as the attackers threw him into the back of the car like a scrap of discarded paper. There was a shriek of rubber as the Cortina took off at speed, leaving black scars on the concrete. Then it was over. No one had screamed. No one had moved to help because no one was there.

Except Jackie.

He surveyed what he could see of the rest of the car park. There were faces straining in the direction of the fleeing Cortina, but at least sixty yards off and they hadn't witnessed the snatch.

'Who the fuck was that?' he whispered.

Masked, but not republicans: what interest would they have in a scrappy teenage kid? Security Forces weren't likely either. The style, aggression and speed had been in line with MSU or SAS work but again, there was no reason for Shanty to be a target for those boys. They'd have the sense not to do a lift near a busy shopping centre on a Saturday afternoon, too.

Which left Billy and his mob. Shanty had escaped his kneecapping, then given them the finger by going back to the cause of his punishment, Shelly Kerrigan. The ball-grabber could have been Rab. Same height and build.

A tattered rag of cloud blighted the afternoon sun. Jackie prayed that, against the odds, Shanty would turn up unharmed. He didn't want to report another body to Gordon tomorrow.

'You, Lodge, one hour.'

That was the extent of it. The other end of the line went dead and Jackie slowly lowered the receiver back onto its cradle.

He'd gone back to his father's house after Shanty was snatched. At first, he'd taken the stairs two at a time up to his bedroom, ready to grab his warrant card from its hiding place and tour the local UDA haunts in search of information. Fuck the undercover work, fuck the surveillance, fuck the Branch. If Shanty was shot because Jackie hadn't acted, well, that was something he didn't want to live with.

Then he'd thought of his family and the possible repercussions for them. Would Billy move against his da, maybe Sarah, if he found out Jackie was a peeler? The initial punishment for Shanty had been a kneecapping, nothing fatal. It was unlikely that Billy would escalate the sentence to a killing and Rab, psychotic as he was, wouldn't make that kind of move without Billy's permission. No, it was more likely Shanty had been picked up to put the frighteners on him. Maybe given a bit of a hiding as a reminder: past transgressions hadn't been forgotten.

I'm a coward, Jackie had thought, or I'd march over to Billy's house right now and beat what was happening to the kid out of him.

Instead, he'd gone to a phone box near the park and called in to Gordon again, bringing the time of tomorrow's meet forward.

He'd needed a strong cup of tea and a quiet few moments to settle himself, get his head together. After, as he sat in the bedroom upstairs, the window open to ease the rising heat, the insect whine of a helicopter began drifting across the city again. West Belfast, maybe North.

Give my head peace, thought Jackie, just for one night.

But how could you get any peace in this city? The choppers shuddering overhead; two-tone sirens; the dull thump of a bomb detonating, shaking the window-panes. Hellish 'political wing' spin doctors using misdirection and diversion to justify atrocity. Even funerals were all sound and fury: masked gunmen firing volleys of shots over flag-draped coffins and mourners brawling with the police, sometimes each other.

And in the middle, the James Maguires and Mrs McCauleys. Gareth Hunter, who lived next to his father, worked shifts in the Co-op dairy, and lost his sister and niece in the East End bombing. John Wilson from two doors down who lost his wee brother. Tom Breslin who taught in Park Parade school and lost his little girl.

Then the phone rang and there were four words, barked down the line.

'You, Lodge, one hour.'

Jackie hated the phone. He was a police officer, and reminded himself of the fact when he could. He read people, read faces. On the phone, that edge was gone.

His mother always said, *be sure your sins will find you out.* He ran through his: sleeping with Eileen, beating Rafferty senior, seeing Shanty snatched and doing nothing. And, for Billy and the rest, being a traitor. A traitor to 'Ireland's Loyal Rebels'.

He didn't carry a weapon at meetings, but he considered tucking his personal issue Special Branch Walther in his waistband. But if he were searched going into the Lagan Lodge it would be an indictment. Instead, he drove out of the city for a couple of miles, checking as best he could for a tail, then stopped at a petrol station and left another message on Gordon's machine detailing the summons to the Lodge. At a little after six, he walked up the stairs to the room above the lounge bar. Billy was sitting next to the pool table sipping a mug of something.

'Do you want a cup of tea? Something stronger?'

'No thanks, Billy, I'm all right, so I am.'

'Sure? You might need it.'

Jackie dragged a wooden chair across to sit opposite Tyrie, looked him in the eye and said, 'I'm grand, Billy.'

Billy's attention turned to the battered surface of the pool table. His hands, huge and pitted with scabs, picked at the green baize. He said, 'You're a single man. Keep it that way.'

Jackie's guts felt hollow, as though someone had carved them out of his body.

'Billy ...'

'The ring. Your Claddagh.'

The ring. Jackie's mother had told him what it signified. When your heart wasn't claimed, the tip of the heart pointed outward. When you were in love and your heart taken, the tip should point inward. Not that someone didn't have some claim on his heart, but he wasn't going to advertise the fact.

'Oh, aye.'

'Like I say, keep it that way. It's better in our business.'

Billy stroked his chin, his head miles away.

'Fuck!'

He threw a punch at the corner pocket. It cracked and the net drifted lazily to the floor.

'Fuck! Fuck!'

Jackie prayed that if this was a domestic, Eileen had kept him out of it.

'I sound like Simpson,' said Billy. '*Business*. It's not a business, it's a cause.'

Drunk and angry was a toxic combination. His thick arms, further swollen with tension, hovered in search of a target. Then his head drooped slightly, as though wilting in the heat, and he slumped.

'At least Rab's handy with the video and camera stuff, I suppose. He's done some sort of course at the polytechnic. Timers, automatic shutters, sensors, all that shite. Not that it's been much help. I remember the day a balaclava and a baseball bat was all you needed to bring the government to its knees.'

He was silent, probably lost in hazy memories of the barricades of the Ulster Workers' Strike in '74, manned by hooded paramilitaries wielding clubs and iron bars. Then his face seized in a scowl.

'Sometimes I think it's my fault.'

'How's that?' said Jackie.

'Those nine. Sometimes I think their deaths are on me. The East End bomb.'

'Ach, sure Billy, how's that on you?'

'The fucking Provos wouldn't have bombed the place if they didn't think I used the upstairs. Nine people, Jackie. Those wee girls.' Tyrie's reptilian eyes drifted closed for a moment. 'The op's off,' he said. 'Cochrane's girl's been transferred. The Fenian bitch is on a ward with a city councillor now. There's a police presence twenty-four hours a day. The Black Bastards are all over it. We can't hit him at the hospital.'

It sounded for all the world like a Branch response to intelligence from an asset. Relatively low key, no obvious specific response to the threat at hand; a manoeuvre to neutralise the hit. But Jackie hadn't informed Gordon of the plan yet. He didn't even have a confirmed day. He stared at the broken pool-table pocket, now a sharp metal splinter.

'Sorry, kid,' said Billy. 'You'll have to wait a bit longer to see the fucker dead. But we'll get him. We ... will ... get ... him.' His head sagged further into his chest with each word, his hand moved to his face and rubbed across his scalp. Billy pointed at Jackie.

'I'll see you right. You'll be on the team. When that murdering Fenian bastard is on the ground with a bullet in his head, you'll be there, pissing on his corpse, Jackie.'

CHAPTER 16

Friday

Adrian Morgan could have been lying dead in a ditch some-where in the County Down hinterlands, a bullet in his brain. Instead, he is safe and sound back in the Holy Lands with a couple of quid in his pocket. His mobile phone is also safe and sound – in the glove compartment of Jackie's rented Toyota.

Jackie showed him the gun and painted pictures of various bodies he's seen: headshot wounds with eyeball haemorrhage, lower jaws blasted clean off the skull. He told Morgan what death could look like, and to keep his mouth shut about tonight.

Just to be sure, Jackie has left him with a promise that, should Morgan get any word to Rab Simpson of their meeting, Jackie will contact the police with the mobile in question. The message will have Morgan's address, bank account details and drug contacts in-cluded. Whatever befalls him, he will have time to hit 'send' before his life is ground out. It is just past midnight on Saturday and over twenty-four hours until the next 'business' day rolls around, so there's no hope of Morgan changing the mobile account before Monday. By then, Jackie hopes to be boarding a plane.

But for now he is parked in a street off the Ravenhill Road. The road is deserted save for the odd taxi shuttling lost souls around the city. The local pubs have shut; the city centre bars and clubs are still open. It's Friday-night-limbo for those too drunk to carry on, yet too far gone to find their own way home.

He walks quickly to Bendigo Street. The mist still cloaks the city and he enjoys the cover it provides. He is also wary of others it may cloak in turn.

The key turns smoothly in the lock and he quietly slips into his father's house. Easing the door closed behind him, he stops and listens. There is a silence, which crowds him in the dark, smothering him. There had always been a clock ticking, timber settling, the general sighing and moaning of the house. No longer.

His eyes begin to adjust to the dark and he makes his way into the small, narrow living room at the front of the house on the ground floor. The curtains are closed and there is no illumination from the street outside. The armchair, his father's favourite, is still there, looking miserable. He takes in the sofa along the wall, the TV in the corner, the empty fireplace. He sees an ornament on the mantelpiece, a brass figure he picked up on some Boys' Brigade outing in Scotland. Its silhouette stands proud, kilt billowing in the stagnant air.

They lived as strangers, his father and he. The drink had crippled their relationship: Jackie couldn't trust his da with details of his work and had fed him the bare minimum. He was RUC; he had insinuated himself into Billy Tyrie's gang; if Tyrie or his hoods ever found out, Jackie would die. This had terrified his da. Sam Shaw had never said so but the look of panic on his face when Jackie came home in a mood or the phone rang late at night spoke volumes. This mutual fear and distrust had sapped the life from their bond as father and son. They talked about meaningless trivia, circled each other like wary guests at an awkward gathering and lived much of their respective lives in bars and clubs.

He crouches and picks through a pile of books under the TV. He recognises landmarks and landscapes, and feels a thickness in his throat. They are all guidebooks and travel books about the West Country in England, where Jackie has been living for the last few years. Tucked beside the chimney flue, he can see a large coffee table volume and, straining through the gloom, he makes out the vague shapes of a junk and tall, angular buildings. Hong Kong, where Jackie served in the RHK Police Force.

He sits heavily on the sofa and stares at the armchair. He would sit in it but he feels unworthy. He imagines the delicate frame of his da, shrivelled by age and ravaged by drink, flicking through these books. Perhaps he just stared at a picture imagining Jackie among these stock photos of oriental skyscrapers and rolling Cotswolds hills. He breathes evenly but his eyes begin to burn and he lets it come, crying quietly in this dark, roped-off museum exhibit of a room.

He doesn't have a da any more.

After a time he rubs his eyes, raw with hot, salty grit, and walks past the mirror above the fireplace to the kitchen. He is an inky wraith in the glass, and thankful that the dark disguises his wretched face streaked with tears. He fancies a cup of tea, but there isn't a tea bag to be found in the place. He wonders if there is anything stronger lying around. The cupboards which held a constant supply of vodka, gin or whiskey now contain only cups with faded patterns, relics from the warm summer days of his life when his mother was still alive: the Age of Mabel.

And now the dawn of what? The Age of Jackie? The Autumnal Age? The Dead at the Hands of East Belfast Gangsters Age?

Back out to the hall and the telephone stand where he used to call his mates, then girlfriends, then fellow paramilitaries. The phone is new but the table is exactly the same as twenty years ago. The Land Where Time Stood Still. He is shocked by a creak and puts his hand on the back of his waistband, feels the angular jut of the Ruger SR9.

It takes him a moment to realise the sound was his footstep on the stair. Nevertheless, he takes the rest of the steep flight slowly, with his hand on the plastic grip and his finger across the trigger. The landing has a vacuum cleaner propped in the corner. Sarah's been busy. His father's room is at the front of the house on the first floor. He pauses before entering. As a child, his parents' room was off limits without permission and he can't shake the sense of intruding. Still, he pushes the door open and sees a neatly made bed, a wardrobe looming in the corner which terrified him as a child, and a bedside table with a couple of books and a horse-racing magazine. The curtains are drawn and the room is bathed in dim streetlight glow. There is a scent, possibly summer fruits, tussling with the sharp ammonia stench of urine.

Jackie takes a moment to wipe his eyes, then walks across the narrow landing. Past Sarah's old room, to his bedroom.

It is all here: a football club poster circa 1985; an AC DC poster, 1988 vintage; a photo of a Bond girl. His books are lined neatly on the shelf, although many of the spines are bleached by years of sunlight. There is an old Atari video game console in the corner with a few cartridges piled next to it, a football award from school and, of all things, a Bible study cup from the Boys' Brigade.

Jackie Shaw circa year zero to year zero. Birth to impostor: the make-believe Jackie who lived with his father like a character in an elaborate drama. Producers: Royal Ulster Constabulary. The posters, the books, the wallpaper: it is Jackie before the Army, before the police, before Mabel Shaw was taken by cancer. It's Jackie when he was his father's son, the wee boy his da used to bounce on his knee.

He is dying for a drink. He pumps his hands in fists, balling and flexing his fingers and blowing air through his lips in a low whistle. After a time he hides the Ruger in the house, calms himself and walks down the stairs and out the front door, locking it behind him and sealing the time capsule once again.

#

He is surprised that it is already past 1 a.m. He hasn't checked his mobile in hours. It has been in silent mode and Sarah has left a text asking when he'd like to come over again. He is irritated with his disappointment at no further contact from Eileen.

Rab Simpson has sent a text message: *Sorry for your loss. Now your da's at rest, be sure your sister doesn't join him.*

Nothing on Tyrie's mobile. He wonders what Hartley is doing now, wonders if maybe it might be best to reach out. He has no idea what to do.

Jackie walks back to his car through the mist. He approaches the small garden of remembrance for the East End Video victims and notices another plaque on the wall next to the monument: *Best-kept street in Belfast 2007.* He stands at the immaculate railings and takes in the painted mural of the innocent victims. They look at him with warm, smiling eyes. Filtered through the haze they look like soft focus matinee idols in a film. Many of the more dubious murals around town juxtapose the sinister shadow of a gunman, machine gun in hand, with a comical face, a child-like scrawl of features in the holes of a rough balaclava.

But the East End victims are beautiful, smiling as if from a family album: Stephen Armstrong, Archie Sinclair, Diane Hunter. The two wee children: Jane Hunter and Becky Breslin. The schoolboys: Mark Wilson and Danny Gourling. And the two schoolgirls: Sharon Montgomery and Kim Clarke. Jackie had known Stephen pretty well, could pass the time with him. He was a strong character who'd commanded respect in the area with his decency and obstinate rebuffs to join the UDA or UVF. Diane had been a good girl. Big-boned and honest to the point of bluntness, she'd doted on her daughter Jane and was popular with a lot of the kids in the area. The pupils from the primary school had left wee mementoes at the bombsite in the days after it happened. The teenagers he hadn't known but he'd seen Kim from time to time about the road and had looked away from her gaze on occasion. There were times he'd thought that gaze was a wee girl trying to grow up too fast. Her father had been a good friend to his da but he'd locked himself away after losing his daughter.

The memories fog his mind and he barely registers the movement behind until the three men are within a couple of yards. Black leather jackets, black jeans, black Dr Martens. Their faces are uncovered but it is difficult to discern features in the dim canopy of mist. Still, he judges them to be in their mid-thirties. They stand three abreast, a yard or so apart.

The man in the centre says, 'Mr Shaw, if you'd like to come with us.'

The voice is quiet and the accent broad. The tone is polite and reasonable. They are under orders to treat him well.

Jackie says, 'And if Mr Shaw doesn't want to come?'

The man says, 'Kempey,' and his companion takes his hand from his pocket to show a solid black object. A handgun.

Jackie says, 'Now this presents us with a problem. See, I don't want to be going anywhere with youse. And youse have orders to pick me up, but you're not supposed to rough me up.'

The two men on either side look to the centre man. The leader says, 'I guarantee you're not going to be hurt. Someone wants to talk to you and we've just been told to come and pick you up. That's it.'

'Simpson or Tyrie?'

'Neither. Now you can drive your car and I will accompany you with one of these men. No one's going to hurt you while you're at the wheel. The other man will follow behind.'

Jackie thinks the men are praying he'll go easy; there will be consequences if he's molested in any way. He nods and makes for his Corolla parked another two streets away, beckoning the gunman and his companion to follow with a wave of his hand.

CHAPTER 17

1993

Life goes on.

It was a favourite refrain around the road, around the city, the country.

The length and breadth of Northern Ireland, families watched the news: today, three painters shot dead by the IRA because they were contracted to paint a police station; a suspect device detonated by an Army bomb disposal robot near a telephone exchange in the city centre; a weapons find next to a children's play area in a park; and a man and woman gunned down in a shopping centre in Newtownabbey, believed to be a case of mistaken identity. The woman was pregnant.

After the shocked comments, the condemnations and cries of shame, people ate their breakfast, or lunch, or dinner and said, 'Life goes on.' What else was there but to plough on and hope the next day had a lower body count?

The question now was, did Shanty McKee's life go on? Jackie sat in a car in the early hours of the morning watching Shanty's sister's house. The condensation on the windows gave him a glaze of anonymity but interfered with his view of the small semi-detached across the street.

He saw shadows pass in front of the windows of Charlene McKee's house, neatly sliced by venetian blinds. Jackie would meet Gordon Orr in another couple of hours and didn't want to hear that Shanty had been found in an alley with a bullet in his brain. So he had sat watching, in his car, through the night. Now, in the freezing early light, he kept his vigil. This was where Shanty had hidden when the kneecapping was ordered.

Jackie was about to run around the corner and find a quiet spot for a piss when a stooped, hooded figure stumbled into view, lurching down the gentle slope of the street. Grasping for the odd gatepost or garden fence for support, it took ten minutes for the figure to cover twenty yards to the patch of lawn at the front of Charlene McKee's house. There it paused, almost bent double over the small iron gate. A flutter of movement at the front window, and Charlene appeared at the front door. Her hand went to her mouth. She ran to the figure, opening the gate and almost collapsing under the weight of the human ragdoll as it fell onto her.

Jackie's hand went to the door handle of the car; then he cursed under his breath. He shouldn't make himself known just yet. He had to wait a little longer, ensure that no one had followed Shanty, for it must surely be Shanty. He wasn't keen on being seen by anyone, the sister included.

As Shanty and his sister retreated into the house, the paperboy sauntered by, casually tossing newspapers into gardens between slugs of Coke. Other kids in various school colours left doors with a wave and hooked up with neighbourhood friends to trek grimly towards the day's study. Some jumped into cars with harassed-looking parents. Men and women in suits rushed to Fords, Renaults and Toyotas. And, finally, Shanty's sister edged out her front door. She locked it, touched the blistered wood for a moment with her fingertips, and walked to a small Fiat Panda parked on the street a couple of doors down from her house. Jackie watched as the car turned the corner up the gentle hill at the top of the street, and checked his watch.

It was eight fifty-five and he was due to meet Gordon in an hour. The meet was at Smuggler's Cave, Whitehead, on the other side of Belfast Lough. He had to leave.

The figure had to be Shanty and, satisfied that McKee was alive and safe for the time being, Jackie coaxed his car to life and pulled out into the morning tumble of the city.

#

The concrete was slick with water where they stood on the Blackhead path. The choppy grey sea surged madly towards the rocks a short distance in front of them, while Smuggler's Cave yawned behind.

'So, the lad's turned up safe and sound?' said Gordon.

'Well, he's turned up. In what condition, I don't know. Judging by the state of him, he'll not be going anywhere for a while so I'm hoping I can catch him when he leaves the sister's.'

'Lucky wee boy,' said Gordon, his shoulders hunched against the cold wind blowing in off the Irish Sea. 'Looks like he got away with a slap and a warning.'

'As I said, I don't know what state he's in yet.'

Gordon was swaying on the spot, as if standing on the rolling deck of a ship. It was a habit he claimed to have picked up from his father, a merchant seaman on the north Atlantic convoys during the Second World War. But he was agitated, too. 'He's luckier than yer man Maguire anyway.'

Jackie turned sharply.

'What?'

'Maguire. Och, he's all right, physically, but his shop's gone.'

'Gone? What the fuck do you mean, gone?'

Gordon's eyes flared with blood and thunder at the profanity but he let it go and said, 'The shop was burned down last night. Looks like a firebomb. Caused some damage to the properties on either side.'

'And the uniform patrols? Where the fuck were they?'

'Keep your voice down.'

145

Jackie spat, 'The man's lost his livelihood.'

'Ach, catch yourself on. He could've lost his life if you hadn't been with Simpson and reported to me. You know yourself we haven't got the manpower to dedicate uniform patrols for protection work on an indefinite basis and his home address was still being monitored. He'll claim on insurance and set up somewhere else.'

A young boy appeared at the corner of the path on the Larne side with a dog in tow. They waited, Jackie fighting against the wind to light a cigarette. After several drags on his fag, Jackie said, 'Sorry, Gordon, you're right.'

Gordon nodded. Jackie went on, 'There's something I need to tell you.' He related the details of the Cochrane hit, and of Tyrie's fury at Cochrane's mistress being moved to a ward with an RUC protection detail.

'What's the craic? Is there another asset among the Ravenhill players?'

Gordon shook his head. 'Not that I'm aware of – and I don't think CID would have any grass in there. If we had someone in the group I'd think we'd have been told, but I'll look into it.'

'Cheers. You don't think Cochrane's a protected bird, do you?'

'If he's an asset, he's not one of ours.'

They began walking back to the car park as the wind picked up whitecaps offshore, rolling them into the angry swell and hurling them back onto the rocks next to the path. Jackie could taste the salt in the air. It was a fresh spring morning, the kind of day to blow cobwebs away.

As they reached their cars, Gordon said, 'Play it careful, Jackie. If we don't have an asset in East Belfast Brigade and CID aren't running a source, it could be Army Intelligence or Five. If it's MI5, they'll do anything to keep their asset in play. Watch your back.'

Jackie lit another cigarette as Gordon's car pulled out of the empty car park. He smoked it to the filter to put some time between their departures, then climbed in behind the wheel and headed for Belfast.

#

He got back to Chesham just before one. When he pulled into the kerb a couple of doors down from Charlene McKee's house, on the opposite side of the street, he swore softly. Her Fiat was parked out front. She must have come home during lunch break and might have let Shanty leave, if he was up to it.

Jackie settled a little into his seat when he saw two shadows move behind the venetian blinds and cursed that he hadn't picked up a sandwich on the drive back. He considered lighting up again but his mouth tasted like ash and he was sickened by the tobacco. Drinking too much, now smoking too much, he thought.

He felt for Charlene and the fear and concern she must have felt for Shanty. Brothers had an infinite capacity to visit stress and worry on their sisters and he wondered if Sarah had any sleepless nights fretting over the tightrope he walked in his job.

Thirty minutes later, Charlene McKee left the house and drove off. Another thirty minutes passed and Jackie became restless. If he dropped off the radar for too long, Simpson and Tyrie might get suspicious. He'd have killed for a coffee.

Around forty minutes after his sister had driven off, Shanty walked out the front door and slammed it behind him. Shanty had a short start on Jackie as he fumbled with his door handle and, as quietly as possible, climbed out and locked the Escort. He crouched next to the car and prayed Shanty didn't recognise the Ford.

Jackie followed him at a jog, controlling his pace and keeping it steady. He turned the corner in time to see Shanty follow the

147

bend of Earl Haig Park towards the shopping thoroughfare of the Cregagh Road.

It was difficult to maintain a discreet distance without alerting Shanty, and the smokes weren't helping. Jackie's breath was already ragged and there was a dull burn in his chest. Shanty was almost at the top end of Titania Street now, the first in a small grid of terraced housing running parallel to the Cregagh Road. They were less than five minutes' walk from where James Maguire's shop had stood. Jackie was swallowing hard and another ragged breath caught him. He tried to clamp his jaws shut and swallow to fight off a cough but he lost control. A harsh, angry bark escaped him.

Shanty turned at the sound. His face was frozen for a moment in an expressionless mask, then moved up through the gears of confusion, recognition and comprehension. He bolted, taking off at pace. Jackie had to leg it around the corner and give chase fast. Shanty could duck down one of the narrow streets splintering off like ribs from a spine and be lost from view. The pavement was deserted but Jackie could see and hear the bustle and noise of the busy Cregagh Road at the end of the terraced streets as he passed them.

Running at full pelt, Shanty looked at ease.

Jackie was finding a rhythm for his breathing now, his back already soaked in sweat. As they neared a T-junction ahead, his legs began to ache from pounding on the split and chipped concrete.

Shanty still looked comfortable up ahead and capable of another gear.

There was a primary school on the corner and Shanty veered left and out of view, almost bowling a couple of kids into the path of a post office van. An old lady walking past with a shopping trolley stopped to check on the kids and yell a reprimand. Jackie lost sight of Shanty behind a hedge and high wooden fence in the moments before he turned the corner, and ran onto the road to avoid the woman and kids. A small car clipped him and screeched to a halt.

He ran on.

Shanty was once again in his sights up ahead, perhaps seven yards in front. The wee bastard was headed for the Cregagh Road, was almost there. A steady stream of traffic was buzzing past up ahead. More kids were being picked up by mothers and grandparents as they finished school. Shanty ran onto the Cregagh Road, literally on the road, to dodge the crowd milling in front of the school.

Jackie followed.

Car horns blared as the two men recklessly headed towards the highest concentration of shops. Someone connected to Billy could easily see them as soon as they neared the local cafés, greengrocers and butchers, Jackie thought. But then Shanty suddenly veered right across the oncoming traffic, heading for a narrow street.

Jackie hissed, 'Shit! Shit! Shit!' as he pelted over the broken white line in the middle of the road. A saloon car hit the horn and swerved, and he had the mad thought that he'd die a road traffic statistic. Then he was almost losing his footing as he half tripped onto the kerb on the other side. Thank God there was not an RUC Land Rover in view. The last thing he'd need was interference from a uniformed patrol.

He cursed again. They were leaving the busy road for narrow Ladas Way – which was about 300 yards long and leaned crookedly to the right. At the end of it was the thoroughfare of Ladas Drive. And on Ladas Drive, opposite the end of Ladas Way, was Castlereagh police station. One of the biggest and most heavily fortified RUC stations in Belfast and first port of call for any suspected terrorist to be interrogated. Shanty was headed for the cop shop to seek safety. This could blow Jackie's cover and compromise him with fellow officers who didn't know he was undercover Branch. If he were recognised in the station, Shanty would know he was SB. And much as he hated to admit it, there was always the outside chance that one of the rank and file could leak his cover to the UDA.

He sprinted hard. The smokes, the aching legs, the burning lungs were gone. All that remained was the figure ahead, the hood of the jacket bouncing crazily. There were about five yards between them. Jackie's hands punched the air as he gained. He could almost see the station.

Five yards became three. Jackie forced his legs and lungs to cooperate.

Two yards. The green hood bounced in front of him. The railings of a small playground were coming up on their left. He could hear Shanty's breathing, now more desperate than his own. The high, blast-proof wall of the station compound was in view at the end of the street. In another couple of moments the upper floors of the station buildings would be in sight. He reached for the hood.

For a moment it went slack in his hand as he grasped it and he thought it had come away from the jacket. He saw Shanty in his mind's eye sprinting the rest of Ladas Way and heard shouts from the officers on duty in the security sangar lookout posts. Then he realised his momentum had almost overtaken Shanty; the hood was still attached to the jacket and the jacket was still on Shanty. He yanked it hard, swinging the teenager left and into the playground railings, then shoved a hand over Shanty's mouth and went close to his face.

'Quiet, now,' he wheezed. 'I'm not going to hurt you.'

Shanty's eyes stared back. Had he heard? Was he too frightened to take in what Jackie had said? There was no one around but a small block of flats sat opposite, and anyone looking out of an upper window would see them.

'I'm going to take my hand away from your mouth, okay? Don't run. I don't want to hurt you.' He took his hand away.

Shanty said, 'What do you fucking want, then?'

'I saw you being snatched yesterday from Connswater. I've been looking for you – I was worried.'

'Why do you care about me? You were going to kneecap me a while ago.'

'I was under orders. I didn't want to do it.'

Shanty gave him a quizzical look. Jackie said, 'It could bring trouble for the organisation.'

'Some organisation,' said Shanty, his face screwed in a sneer. His contempt was almost a physical force.

Jackie took a hold of the zip at the front of Shanty's jacket and zipped it up to the teenager's neck. He then grabbed a fistful of material at the back of the jacket and said, 'Walk into the playground.'

A minute later they were sitting side by side on a pair of children's swings, rocking gently to the soft groan of the chains hanging from the frame. Shanty began to talk and Jackie lit a cigarette, offering one to the teenager who took it with a nod.

'It was Rab Simpson, so it was. You saw, they picked me up in Connswater: him, Sam Rainey, some fella called Tommy and another fella – Danny something. They drove me to a bar in Lagan Village and took me up the stairs to a room with a broken oul' chair in the corner.'

Jackie remembered the night in the drinking club when he'd taken on Peter Rafferty and won the respect of Simpson and the rest.

'They didn't touch me at first, like. Just started getting rounds from the bar downstairs. When they'd had a few, they began to slap me about a wee bit. Then Rainey disappears down to the bar and comes back up with a couple of bottles of whiskey. I thought they were going to get full, then really go to town on me.'

He drew deeply on the cigarette and flicked its glowing remains on to the grass a couple of feet away. He exhaled the rest of the smoke in a smooth, continuous stream and shivered, despite the warmth of the spring afternoon.

'Instead, they kept forcing me to drink it,' he grimaced. 'I hate the stuff. I'm not one for spirits. They were having a right oul' laugh. Then I was sick and Simpson gave me a kick because I got some on his trainers.'

Shanty smiled.

'Anyway. I drank most of the two bottles, so I did. I managed to spit a bit out and a bit came out natural with me coughing and retching, but most of it went down. Afterwards, I couldn't stand up. They took me down the back stairs to a car. It was dark, so I must've been in there for hours.'

A small pulse flickered near his ear. His eyes were red and moist, but he wasn't crying and Jackie knew he was fighting hard to make sure it stayed that way.

'I never said a word. I mean, they never asked me nothing but I didn't shout, or cry, or beg them bastards. I never wet myself either. I was fucking scared, but I didn't want to give them any-thing, any excuse to laugh at me or give me a worse kicking.'

Good lad, thought Jackie.

'I've no idea where we went in the car. I was too hammered, but we were driving for a while so I don't think it was East Belfast. Maybe the Shankill. They carried me out of the car and took me into this building and a room. Really bright, like. I could smell disinfectant and they put me in a chair, like a dentist's chair, and held me. I couldn't have moved anyway, I was so drunk. I closed my eyes and thought I was going to die.'

He rubbed his eyes with nicotine-stained fingers.

'I heard them laughing and felt a pain. Like I was stung or something. That was it. Can I've another fag?'

Jackie offered the pack. Cigarette in mouth, Shanty took off the jacket. He was wearing a Guns 'n' Roses T-shirt underneath, black with just the name of the band written across the chest in red.

But his arms were a patchwork of Ulster flags, red hands, stars and crowns. There were Union Jacks, a St Andrew's Cross and crossed Armalite rifles. His arms had been tattooed from shoulder to wrist. *For God and Ulster* unfurled across the left, scrawny bicep. Jackie rubbed the single UDA tattoo on his forearm distractedly, the most permanent aspect of his under-cover work. He hoped.

Finally, Shanty lost his battle with the tears.

'Bastards,' he said, '"So you won't forget". That's what Simpson said. They branded me so I won't forget my crimes.'

CHAPTER 18

Saturday

Stuart Hartley is sitting in an ergonomic office chair nestled behind a large oak desk in what had been a warehouse overlooking the Lagan River downtown. Now it is an office building with large panoramic windows and views of the river, with the lights of the city centre glittering off its lazy murk and the brooding hulk of Cave Hill beyond. The mist has begun to lift, leaving a delicate film of moisture clinging to Belfast. Hartley is fiddling with a paperclip as Jackie is led into the room by his three minders.

As they enter the large space, all stripped-back red-brick walls and natural wood flooring, the broad-accented Belfast man, leader of Jackie's escort, gestures for him to take a seat opposite Hartley. Jackie declines. Hartley nods and motions for the three men to step back.

'Mr Shaw, how delightful to see you again.'

Hartley looks older under the stark strip-lighting. Jackie is dog tired. It's been a long day.

'What the fuck do you want?'

'My, we have rediscovered the vernacular, haven't we?'

Jackie sighs heavily, then sits down as heavily again in the chair.

'Your boy there isn't the same as the clown at the hotel – Mr Oilskin,' he says.

'No. Darenth is on secondment with me from Thames House. He graduated, as did I, from Cambridge and Sandhurst. Ray here is local talent.'

Jackie turns and says, 'Well, Ray, you're a lot more convincing than Darenth from Thames fucking House.'

Ray's face betrays nothing.

'Any weapons?' asks Hartley.

Ray shakes his head. They'd frisked him before getting into the car and Jackie had breathed easier knowing the SR9 was in the attic of his father's house, taped behind the water tank twenty minutes earlier.

'You've been a busy boy, Jackie. Two Estonian gentlemen, rather the worse for wear, were seen stumbling out of Belvoir Forest Park shortly after you'd been there for a stroll. Seems you visited a local "character" named Shanty McKee this afternoon, too. A couple of meetings with Eileen Tyrie and a visit to a local club this evening. All on the day of your father's funeral. Let's not forget an hour in a drinking club with Rab Simpson and a trip to Clocky with Mr Tyrie on Thursday.'

Jackie says, 'Next time I'm abducted by local paramilitaries, feel free to step in at any point. That's what I pay my taxes for. And it's *Cloghy*, not *Clocky*.'

'And what grounds would the security services have had for interfering? You appeared to go with both parties of your own free will. There was no violence involved. Times have changed: we don't have stop and search privileges any more.'

'Your lot never did, far as I know. Isn't it more about reading the nation's post and emails between watercress sandwiches and cream teas?'

Hartley heaves a sigh, the disappointed patriarch. He fiddles with a pen, grasping for control of the situation but plainly intimidated by the presence of men who have been to the places he has glimpsed in memos and heard stories of in the club at lunch. Jackie throws his car keys on the desk with a sudden clatter and watches Hartley flinch.

He says, 'I've been under surveillance. You may have seen me meet Simpson and Tyrie; more likely you got the intel from sources. The forest park was a black spot because there aren't any cameras. I've hardly used my mobile, so not much to track there. There was heavy mist and a general melee outside Club Realm, so my guess is you lost me and sent this team to my da's house thinking I'd end up back there at some point. Maybe Darenth from Thames House was at the La Mon with another team. You've searched the room but found nothing out of the ordinary, you think Morgan could be dead by my hands and so you decided to move on me. I am more tired than I can remember for a long time and I really need a couple of hours' kip so, once more with feeling, what the fuck do you want?'

Hartley leans back in his chair and Jackie catches sight of the great glass dome of Victoria Square, brightly lit like a giant firefly's arse, behind him.

'What do we always want, Jackie? Information. What did you discuss with Simpson?'

'Old times. The weather. The price of milk.' Jackie crosses his legs and says, 'I've a question of my own. These boys – Simpson, Tyrie, the players – are all still walking around without a care in the world. They may be smart enough to keep themselves distanced from their rackets now, they might not be a big enough threat for your lot to bother with any more, but you have enough from the old days to put them away, surely? Why aren't they locked up?'

'Haven't you heard, Jackie? The *war*,' Hartley's face contorts in a wry grin, 'is over.'

Jackie remembers Shanty McKee beaten and branded for life. James Maguire losing the business he had built and loved. Others dead, maimed and destroyed by Tyrie, Simpson and the rest.

'Bygones are bygones, eh?'

'Yes. Who knows, one of them could be deputy First Minister in a couple of years. So, no hard feelings towards you?'

'They claim they knew I was alive but don't know why I disappeared. They suspect I was a grass. Nobody seems that eager to extract their pound of flesh yet.'

There is a pause and Jackie is struck by how silent the city is in these wee small hours: no choppers, no sirens.

'The dissident republicans have been stirring again,' says Hartley, 'mostly North Belfast. A couple of explosives finds, isolated shots fired at PSNI patrols, but nothing major. We want to know if there are stirrings on the loyalist side. The UVF, through the usual channels, has assured the government their ceasefire will hold.'

Hartley tosses this out with the insouciance born of privilege: doesn't everyone know *the usual channels*?

'Your Billy Tyrie is still a bit of a firebrand, however, and the UDA have been more active recently in their pursuit of criminal enterprise so the weaponry, manpower and expertise is readily available for a loyalist response.'

Jackie looks at the ceiling in thought and then says, 'No. Simpson is too busy working on his fake tan and selling heroin to give a shit. It was always more an excuse to kill a couple of Catholics and throw his weight around than the whole *Quis Separabit* waffle. Tyrie seems occupied with his wife sleeping around and keeping an eye on Simpson. So long as nothing major kicks off in East Belfast, he'll stay under the radar.'

'Good to know,' says Hartley, adding, 'and Eileen? You met her. Anything important?'

'Nothing. She just offered condolences at the funeral. We had a short meet at Belfast Castle where she talked about her kids, a wee bit about Billy, our past. She told me about Simpson, why he looks a bit ... different these days.'

'Yes. Ironic, isn't it?' Hartley shifts his weight in the chair and says, 'We'll keep an eye on you for your own safety and because a rogue element like you has the potential to upset the applecart.

What I said at La Mon stands: lay low and go home in a couple of days.'

Jackie considers mentioning Sarah, asking if the machinery of the state will keep an eye on his sister and her family, but any extra activity around them could tip off Tyrie or Simpson that something's amiss.

'Oh, and by the by,' says Hartley, 'Shanty McKee is dead.'

Something warm begins to kindle in Jackie's centre and spread throughout his body. He is charged and, for a moment, believes he can light the whole city with his anger. He tenses in the chair and, despite the knowledge that Ray and the other two men are behind him, launches himself across the desk at Hartley.

He connects with a strong right to the bridge of Hartley's nose, the Claddagh biting into skin, then makes a grab for the back of his head. Ray gets to him before he can slam Hartley's face into the desk with full force. He still manages to glance the man's temple off the edge of the polished oak. With satisfaction he sees a gash on Hartley's smooth, pink skin, the nose off-kilter, as Ray yanks his head back in a vicious lock. Another man rabbit-punches him in the side and he feels as though his kidney has just popped. He crumples in the chair.

Ray relaxes his grip a fraction. Enough for Jackie to butt him with the back of his skull. He hears a grunted 'Fucker!' from behind before a blow is delivered to the side of his head, leaving his mind wading through mud. He makes a final lunge, the fire still glowing in his belly, but his limbs have turned to lead. A strong hand grips his shoulder and pins him to the chair.

There is what seems like a long moment of silence; the only sound is some harsh breathing and a soft murmur from Hartley, nursing his nose. His face is difficult to read. Then he speaks.

'I'd heard of your reputation for violence. I'd hoped not to encounter it first-hand.'

'With some men it's drink, others violence,' says Ray. Jackie turns his head to look at him and feels a deep, dull ache in his skull. Ray continues, 'Get started and there's no stopping them until they've had their fill. That's our Mr Shaw, I think.'

Hartley dabs at his bloodied temple with a linen handkerchief. He is trembling from fear and adrenaline and finding it difficult to meet anyone's eye. The others are breathing evenly again. Jackie is studying a bruised knuckle. He can sense the body-guards standing directly behind him. Professionals to a man, this is just another day's work.

'You are angry about McKee,' says Hartley. 'I know you tried to help the man when he was younger. But his death is not my or the British government's responsibility.'

'He'd be alive if the likes of Simpson and Tyrie were off the streets.'

'Don't be so bloody naïve, Shaw. The Troubles had to end and that meant compromise, on both sides. The terrorists may be free but so are the people they once terrorised.'

'You want to tell that to the people on the Newtownards Road. The Shankill and the Falls. Derry. But don't worry, Stuart. In a year or two you'll be back to the house in Surrey, the seven-thirty to London and lunch at the club with Darenth. Then you can continue to plot what's best for the people of Northern Ireland with a thirty quid glass of single malt in your hand. You patronising cunt.'

Hartley's face is grey. His hand is shaking as he dabs at his ruined nose. There are flecks of blood on his tie.

'Harry and Tom will drive you back to your hotel. Get some sleep, keep your head down and, on Sunday, go home.'

Jackie bit the lining of his cheek during the fight. He flashes a scarlet smile, his teeth smeared red as the goons behind lift him from the chair.

'I *am* home,' he says.

CHAPTER 19

1993

Jackie's mother had been a great believer in the benevolence of the Almighty and regularly went to converse with him at Ravenhill Presbyterian Church. His father was less conscientious in his dealings with Our Father, although he regularly invoked the Lord's name, if often in vain.

Jackie was somewhere a little further down the scale. Having been dragged to church until his teenage years, he had a firm grounding in the burning bush, but hadn't exactly been giving the faith the attention his mother would have liked. But he had to admit, someone might have been looking out for him the night of his discovery that Shanty McKee had been branded with paramilitary tattoos by Rab Simpson.

He trawled the bars of the Ravenhill and Woodstock roads, full of piss and vinegar, hungry for a fight. He burned with the desire to take Simpson's tombstone front teeth and ram them down his putrid throat, then crush his larynx with his boot while the bastard choked on them. He was ready for a brawl with any of them: Simpson, Tyrie, Rainey, or Tommy if the pond scum was all he could find. Fuck them, fuck the job, fuck Gordon Orr and his sanctimonious peeler shite. Jackie needed to crack a few heads, do this old style and stop another life being damaged or ended by these gangsters.

But in every bar, they were nowhere to be found. The Lagan Lodge, the Crown Jewels, the King James, the Lagan Village club. Jackie asked at the counters, his rage crackling in the air. He got drunk. He tried to pick fights but was known to be connected and no one was biting. And finally he slunk home and collapsed on his bed, staring at the spinning ceiling until his fury burned itself out and he drifted into a restless sleep.

It was, of course, just as well. He awoke with a head full of Lagan mud and a stomach lurching like the ferry to Stranraer. He heard his father whistling in the kitchen. He smoked a couple of cigarettes out of the open window of his bedroom – a habit picked up in his teenage years – then gagged as the tobacco had a violent disagreement with the alcohol and Chinese takeaway still swilling around his guts.

Shanty had wept for a time on the swing, then begun bawling when he heard the fate of his dog. Jackie had sat mortified, waiting for the tears to run their course. After a time, he'd told Shanty to get out of the city for a spell. The lad had family on the north coast and Jackie had given him some cash to help him get there.

Making his way gingerly down the narrow stairs in his father's house, he could hear the TV babbling from the small living room and the whistle of a boiling kettle in the kitchen. He shuffled into the living room and peered through the open kitchen door.

'All right, son? Fancy a wee cup of tea?'

'I wouldn't say no, thanks, da.'

Five minutes later they were supping. His father was in his favourite armchair. Jackie was on the sofa. He could see the street through the front window behind his father. It was a fresh spring day and Mrs McCutcheon across the way was out scrubbing her front step. Edna Withington joined her, en route to pick up her pension . Both exchanged a greeting with Winslow McCartney, something of a local celebrity as the only black guy on the road.

Life goes on, thought Jackie.

His father was in a good mood. He had managed to pick up a little work from the shipyard and would be going in next week to do some welding on an oil tanker in the massive dry dock. Better still, he'd won a few quid on the Down Races and treated his mates to a couple of rounds last night.

'Where were youse?' Jackie asked. 'I was in a few places and didn't see you.'

'We saw you,' said his father, 'up at the counter in the Crown Jewels. By the look on your face I thought better of talking to you.'

'Aye, I wasn't in the best of form last night.'

His father turned to the TV. Silence passed between them for a time. His da slurped his tea.

Jackie was about to broach the eternal leveller of football when his da said, 'Why'd you look so angry last night, son?' He held up a placatory hand. 'I know you don't like talking with me about what you're up to. God knows I don't want to know half of it but you'd murder in your eyes.'

'Ach, I was a bit wound up. I'd had too much to drink and wasn't handling my booze too well.'

His da gave him a smile that didn't reach his eyes.

'Don't be worrying, Da. You don't know what I'm doing because I want you away from it.'

'Son, I live on this road. I can't get away from it. Look at Harry Clarke. Decent man lost his wee girl in that bomb. And now I have to keep him from doing something stupid.'

'Something stupid to Billy Tyrie?'

'That's enough,' said his father. Jackie felt a pang of shame at the realisation that his da didn't trust him enough to continue.

'You know, Da, if there's something I need to know about Billy Tyrie, you can tell me.'

His father shook his head and said, 'There's nothing.'

'I'm your son. You can tell me.'

'There's nothing!' The anger had a frightened edge.

Jackie couldn't remember the last time his father spoke to

him like that. He sank further into the sofa, a reflex left over from his younger years. If he'd had a tail it would've been between his legs.

He stood to put his mug in the kitchen and have a smoke in the back yard, but his father said, 'Don't go.' It stopped Jackie dead in his tracks.

Samuel Shaw said, 'Do you fancy a drive?'

#

They had done this when he was a kid. On a Friday evening his father would take him down Templemore Avenue in their beat-up old Morris to the sweetie shop for chocolate-covered fudge, caramels and Italian ice cream. Sometimes they'd take a drive up to the fire station on the Upper Newtownards Road and, if the engines were in, the firemen would let him sit in the cab.

Now they drove in Jackie's Ford towards the city centre with his da holding sway like a tour guide.

The Markets: 'Ma Copley was a hard woman, used to organise the bare-knuckle boxing just over there. There used to be grass, Chapel Fields, and men from all over Belfast would come to fight. I saw Cuthbert Carr and Barney Ross box to a standstill there. The peelers never did much about it and a couple of them got in on the fights.'

Sandy Row: 'Billy Moore used to sell fruit and vegetables off a horse and cart. In the evening he'd ride the horse to the pub and tie it up outside, like a cowboy. Sometimes he'd leave it overnight if he'd had too much to drink and the landlord would feed it.'

The Shankill: 'There was a man, "Stormy" Weather. He was a fighter, used to fight "Silver" McKee down at the markets. Great trade union man, Stormy. Always fair, so he was.'

It was a different Belfast. A past Belfast full of larger than life characters and all of them from the working-class areas. His father knew more tales of the Protestant areas but Jackie knew there were similar stories and legends in the Falls and beyond.

Driving back home they passed by the end of the Short Strand. The road was quiet save for an RUC Land Rover patrol.

His father said, 'I used to work on Mountpottinger Road, just off there. I worked for a man called McManus, owned a print shop, hauling paper stock and ink rollers.'

Jackie hadn't known that his father had worked in the sole republican enclave in East Belfast.

'You were just a wee baby then, but things were really bad. You could lie in bed and listen to the gun battles all over the city. My mate on the Lisburn Road had rounds ricocheting off the tiles of his roof. But I never had no trouble at McManus's place. Everybody knew I was a Protestant and nobody cared.'

The car was entering the Lower Newtownards Road now. A republican tricolour mural was facing off across the thoroughfare with King Billy, resplendent on the wall of a warehouse opposite.

'So one evening, I was locking up the print shop and a British Army patrol came along. They stopped me and asked for ID, so I showed them my driving licence. One of them, an Englishman, says, "What's a proddie from the Ravenhill Road doing working in the Short Strand?" and gives me a shove with his rifle.'

The squaddie had probably used stronger language, but Sam Shaw had always been shy about swearing around his children.

'I said that I worked for Mr McManus and I was locking up. They put me up against a wall, spread-eagled, and searched me. Of course I'd nothing dodgy on me. Then one of them whacked me in the back of the legs with his baton and the lot of them gave me a pasting. I tell you, son, never let it be said your average British soldier isn't impartial; they hate us just as much as they hate the Catholics.'

He laughed then, this man, without a trace of bitterness. It was a genuine, if hopeless, laugh and Jackie thought that he had never met a gentler soul than his father. The oul' lad might be fond of the drink, but he was too tender for this world, especially Belfast, and he'd been paying for it for years.

'They made a right mess of me,' said his da, 'and then they drove off. Left me lying there, all bloody, like, in the street. And do you know what happened?' His father laughed again. 'A fella came up to me and says, "Are you all right, Sam?" He was a young fella at the time. He helped me into a bar on the corner and I knew rightly it was an IRA bar. But they cleaned me up and made me a cup of tea. Offered me something stronger but I had to get home to your mommy and she'd have smelled the drink off me. The fella says, "Any more bother, Sam, you let me know. I'll make sure you're all right," and then I thanked him and I walked home. Walked home, through the Short Strand.'

His father shook his head in wonder and tutted.

'Your mommy wasn't too happy at me being late, but they did a good job of cleaning me up in that bar, so I didn't look too bad. She was shocked at my bruises and what-have-you, but a lot worse could have happened to you back then, and you were thankful for small mercies. I never told her what happened and she never asked. Sarah never knew. You're the only one I've ever talked to about it.'

His father sounded surprised at his own revelation. Jackie was silent. He was afraid to speak in case he might cry. Then his father said, 'I never saw that fella again. Your mother made me leave the job, for me own safety, like. But the fella who was so kind to me was a big man in the Provos, so he was. Name was Cochrane. He was shot by the Army back in the eighties.'

His father shook his head slowly.

'I think he had a son, though. Probably still lives about the Short Strand.'

It was late afternoon when they got back to Bendigo Street and schoolkids were making their way home. Scruffy boys were kicking footballs against gable walls while awkward-looking wee girls tried to talk to them and huffed when they were ignored. Wee girls not far off the age of Kim Clarke and Sally Hunter.

It was a good story his father had told. Sam was from a generation who'd known life before the Troubles and still had faith in the kindness of strangers. Jackie marvelled at Belfast. An act of kindness from a terrorist to his father; that same terrorist's son might be culpable in the bombing murder of innocent men, women and children; and the man who received that kindness has a son, a policeman, who considered neglecting his duties to see that second-generation terrorist dead.

Small world.

He shook his head as he opened the front door of the house.

'Are you all right, son?'

'Yes, Da,' said Jackie. 'I was a wee bit confused about something, but I'm clear as a bell now.'

And then Sam 'Ruger' Rainey approached and said, 'You've been summoned.'

#

In actual fact, they'd all been summoned, the core of the Active Service Unit. They were in Billy's house, a rarity for all of them. Billy shared the sofa with a disconsolate Rainey, all hangdog jowls as he sucked on a cigarette. Rab was quietly fuming in the corner, his wiry frame all awkward angles on an armchair. A crackle of violence charged the air. Jackie couldn't help feeling he was being sized up by Simpson and wondered if word had somehow got out about his catching up with Shanty and his subsequent bender. Tommy sat on the floor, his back propped against the wall, eyeing the Sega Megadrive and Desert Strike game cartridge under the TV.

Billy ground out his smoke in a glass ashtray, and said, 'Un-fucking-believable.'

Rainey scratched his head. Rab glared at his Converse train-ers. Tommy sat calmly. Jackie didn't have a notion what was going on, which seriously scared him. He held his peace.

Billy went on, 'This fucker's charmed. I mean, he's been blessed by the fucking Pope or something.' He hurried to add, 'If I actually believed in that shite.'

Rab said, 'He must have known. He had to have known. This kind of thing doesn't happen twice.'

'I don't know, Rab,' said Rainey. 'Once is chance, twice is co-incidence.'

'You're full of shite,' said Rab, glaring.

Jackie said, 'Look, I don't mean to be slow but what are we talking about?'

'You don't mean to be a cunt, but you are,' spat Rab.

The others stared at Rab and it looked like Simpson was burning through all the self-control he could muster not to launch himself at Jackie, all knees, fists and feet.

'Enough!' said Billy. 'This is exactly what I don't want hap-pening. Back-biting, people turning on each other.' He pointed a finger at Rab as if training an attack dog. Simpson sucked at his tombstone teeth in aggravation, his skin the colour of old paper.

'We'd another day and time to hit Cochrane,' said Billy, turning to address Jackie. 'Everything worked out, all the logis-tics. Rab's video surveillance had shown a short window of opportunity when Cochrane's bodyguards change over outside his house. Danny Moore was going to help set it up from the bus depot on the Short Strand. It was going to be quick and simple:

shoot him on the street, use the confusion to get away. Sounds risky but it would've worked. Now the fucker's street has a police and Army checkpoint set up in it, outside the RUC station. Another at the opposite end. The whole street's sealed off.'

Jackie felt his pulse quicken and he willed the hairs on the back of his neck to lie back down. He forced his tongue, swollen and clumsy, to move.

'And when were youse going to tell me about the job? I was going to be in on the hit, wasn't I? Or am I out to pasture now?'

'You'll watch your fucking tone, Shaw,' whispered Rab. 'You're just a fucking driver. A lackey. Lackeys don't have a say.'

'I'll not tell you again,' said Billy. He kept his eyes on Jackie and winked. 'It's no small thing, being the driver on a job. Man runs most of the risks of the trigger men without taking the glory.' Then he turned to Rab and said, 'You'll be relying on this man to get you in and out when the time comes, so let's have a bit of respect.'

'So, what's the next move?'

It was Tommy. His eyes were hooded, as if he were bored by the bickering.

'We bide our time. I will see that bastard shot dead, and all good things come to he who waits.' Billy turned to Rainey, sitting next to him on the sofa, a nodding dog. 'Now, Ruger, I'm dying for a cuppa. Away and wet the tea, will ye?'

CHAPTER 20

Saturday

He awakes to the sound of his mobile phone's shrill alarm at 08.30.

A couple of hours' sleep. Better than nothing but he craves a strong coffee. Jackie drags his carcass out of bed and showers in scalding water, then towels himself off vigorously, his skin tingling. Calling room service, he orders a pot of hot coffee and dresses for the day ahead. As he pulls a sweater over his head, he takes a look at himself in the mirror.

He's in good shape for his age. Jackie could give plenty younger than him a decent run in a half marathon. Last night has left him with no more than a small cut on his lower lip, but he'd winced as he towelled his hair off this morning. The legacy of Ray clouting him in Hartley's office.

The coffee arrives, delivered by a pretty girl who vaguely reminds him of someone from the past, and he asks her if he might borrow a screwdriver from maintenance as he has a problem with the wheels on the bottom of his suitcase. The girl smiles and says she'll take care of it, not noticing that he doesn't actually have a suitcase, only a holdall.

Taking stock of his situation as he drinks his coffee, Jackie concludes that things are pretty grim. He's due to fly to England in two days and, before then, is expected to kill two powerful players in the UDA, Billy Tyrie and Rab Simpson. He is no closer to achieving either hit and probably has MI5 watching him day and night.

What to do, he thinks, but take the initiative?

The pretty girl returns with the screwdriver. Five minutes after she leaves he throws a jacket on, locks the room and goes for a walk in the grounds of the hotel, all wide expanses of lawn edged by clumps of trees and bushes. The trees are almost bare as winter approaches. He wanders along the perimeter, keeping an eye out for anyone following or hotel security cameras. No one is there and the cameras are pointing towards the hotel, or the fence that rings the property. A little before the fence, beyond the skeletal trees, is a small, sunken stream with a shallow but steep bank edging it, below the range of the cameras' view.

Jackie wanders towards the stream then turns, having another quick check for anyone watching him. A cook walks around the corner of the building with cigarette and lighter in hand. There is no one else outside. Dropping to a crouch, he eases himself quickly over the edge of the bank. Digging in his heels to arrest his fall, he makes his way down to the water and the small branch he left upright in the darkness in the wee small hours, wedged in the silt of the stream bed as a marker. Rolling up his sleeve, he digs under the silt and finds the dark package he has hidden. The revolver is carefully wrapped in a plastic film then sealed in a plastic bag. Glancing up at the lip of the bank to check he is alone, Jackie removes the gun. It and the rounds inside are dry.

He buries the plastic and tucks the gun into his jacket pocket, then picks his way carefully along the stream to a point a few yards away from the gate of the hotel, where the lip of the bank is crowded with shrubbery. The hotel cameras are trained on the gate several yards away and the area is quiet. After scrambling up the bank, he walks on to the driveway leading back up to the front door of the hotel and makes for his car. He has his hands in his pockets, negating the heavy sag that would be clearly visible thanks to the .357 Magnum.

Nearing his car, he sees a man standing by a flower bed having a smoke. When the man sees him coming from the direction of the gates, he stares for a beat. The Toyota was driven back by Ray last night, and Jackie had to wait in his room before slinking his way through the grounds and burying the revolver. As Jackie opens the Toyota's door and climbs in, the young Five man now on baby-sitting duty throws the cigarette on the ground and says something under his breath. Jackie puts the car in gear and heads for the city.

#

Ardenlee Avenue is a broad, tree-lined artery connecting the Ravenhill Road around its mid-point with the Cregagh Road to the east. Once a modest middle-class area with a mix of professionals, civil servants and self-starters, the real estate at its Ravenhill end has increased significantly in worth. Large, three-storey Victorian structures or bulky, squat detached houses are the order of the day. Jackie parks his car in a cul-de-sac a couple of minutes' walk away. Evading surveillance is generally easier on foot. As is breaking and entering.

He walks to a broad expanse of school playing fields, the property of a preparatory school for Belfast's sole public school. It is 09.30 now, but the street is still quiet as he slips through a gap in the railings and strolls around the periphery of the fields, keeping an eye out for anyone following. A school minibus is parked near a small concrete structure he takes to be changing rooms. A rival school ready for a rugby match.

When he exits the fields through the open gates, Ardenlee Avenue is ahead, running across the top of a short street. Jackie makes for it at a good pace. Turning on to Ardenlee, he finds himself in the middle of its affluent stretch. He sees Audis and Mercedes parked in driveways. And there, parked two houses down opposite where Jackie stands, is a silver Porsche. In a sense, it is just as out of place among all of the modest but expensive automobiles as it was on a small terraced side street off the lower Newtownards Road.

Rab Simpson's house is the last of a slew of large detached homes next to a row of tall Victorian townhouses. A narrow alleyway separates the property from the first of the townhouses and, Jackie knows, continues behind them. Jackie makes a pass on the other side of the street, taking in the exterior of Simpson's property. There is a camera above and to the right of the front door, another perched on the eight-foot wall running along the alley-side of the house. A six-or-seven-foot brick wall surrounds the garden at the front. No doubt there are another couple of cameras at the rear.

Jackie walks for another thirty yards, stops and checks his mobile. Satisfied that any tail or surveillance unit has lost him, he crosses over the avenue and doubles back. As he nears Simpson's place he hunches his shoulders and slouches, taking in the front of the property out of the corner of his eye. He can see a security alarm box above the large bay window at the front of the house.

Jackie walks on past the row of Victorian townhouses next to Simpson's home. At the end of the row is the other end of the alleyway which curves behind the houses. He enters the alley, looking for all the world as if he belongs. Behind the houses, high brick walls crowd in on either side of the narrow concrete walkway. The highest floors of the townhouses can be glimpsed above the wall on one side, the tops of trees in expansive gardens on the other.

As he walks towards Simpson's place at the end of the alley, Jackie sees a discarded, empty plastic crate. He picks it up and carries it with him. Near the end of the alley is a large green wheelie bin, half-full. He lifts it to prevent the wheels causing a small racket on the rough concrete and carries it a couple of yards to the high wall of Simpson's property. Two cameras are positioned on top of the wall, taking in the path leading from Ardenlee Avenue, and Simpson's back garden.

Jackie works fast, nervous that anyone passing the end of the alley will see him. He props the wheelie bin next to the wall of Simpson's property, below the cameras. Ducking out of sight of the avenue again, he shoves the revolver deep into the back waistband of his jeans. The last thing he needs is for it to fall out in the next thirty seconds. Next, he carries the crate to the foot of the wheelie bin. Then Jackie backs up, takes a run at the crate and springs from it on to the lid of the bin, bouncing on the plastic and levering himself on to the top of the brick wall. His stomach flat on the lip of the wall, he quickly yanks the wire leads out of each camera then drops into the garden.

He estimates there are five or six yards of lawn to the window at the rear, north-eastern corner of the house. The room behind it is darkened and unoccupied. Jackie takes the mobile Simpson gave him out of his jacket pocket and, concealed by shrubbery, texts: *Trouble. Need meet now, Low N'Ads Rd club. Will be there in 10 mins.* Mobile on silent mode, he places it on the earth at his feet and takes the Magnum revolver from his waistband. No further cameras cover the patch of garden between him and the window. The wall is high enough, the garden big enough and the neighbours far enough, that Jackie should be unseen if he makes it to the window, and there is no sign of guard dogs. Things didn't exactly work out with Shanty's terrier, after all. The thought of McKee drives a dull, cold wedge through his stomach. After ensuring the rounds are in the chamber, he tests the trigger pressure of the gun.

The mobile vibrates and he involuntarily jumps. He is thankful that the .357 trigger-pull is hard and he hasn't taken out the rose bush a couple of feet away.

Simpson has replied: *Be there in 20. Don't fuck me about.* Jackie's mobile is pre-paid and he was concerned that Simpson wouldn't be checking his own; the number from which Jackie had received his text after the funeral was probably one of several Simpson had at any one time. He takes cold comfort in realising he is a priority.

An upstairs window opens suddenly. Jackie retreats a couple of inches, flattening himself against the wall. Simpson has probably been in bed, and the sounds of a TV blathering loudly drift from the first floor. A short time later there is a clatter as the front door is opened and pulled roughly shut. There is a hollow growl as the Porsche grumbles to life and a minute later silence returns as the car takes off.

A couple of seconds later Jackie is crouched at the windowsill at the back of the house, peering into the rear room. All is quiet. Simpson's desire for privacy and seclusion has afforded the time and space to work. Jackie places the revolver in the back of his waistband again and takes a folded sheet of tinfoil from his pocket. After some fiddling, he manages to slip it through the window frame. The house is old and the wood of the windows warped and callused by northern weather. The magnetic alarm sensors disable. Jackie takes the hotel screwdriver from his jeans pocket and begins to lever at the window frame.

As the wood at the bottom of the frame splinters and cracks, an image of a broken Shanty McKee lying dead in his own filth creeps into his mind and, for a moment, he is no longer in the cool light of a bleak autumn morning. Instead, he is in a dark, cold place and he knows he must clear his thoughts and focus his mind. As he slides the window up, he keeps the tinfoil in place and squeezes through into the darkened room. It is shaded from the sun, a dining room. He leaves the window open for a quick departure.

He should have around thirty minutes until Rab comes back,

spitting fire at the waste of time. Jackie pulls the Magnum and makes for the first floor and the room he saw the window open from fifteen minutes ago. The smell of strong cologne seeps from the room, a bedroom. It looks like Rab was awake in bed when he received Jackie's text. A couple of cigarette butts are clogging up a cut-glass ashtray on the unkempt duvet cover and the remote TV controller is lying on the pillow, like a priceless item presented in an auction room. Jackie begins to look through the drawers of the bedside cabinets, but it occurs to him that he doesn't actually know what he's looking for.

He is sure that Rab is responsible for Shanty's murder and hopes he can find something here to use against Simpson: evidence, a skeleton in the closet, some kind of leverage. But, again, he has no idea what he'll do with such an item. He could take it to Hartley, but doubts the Five man would be interested. The PSNI would take him in for housebreaking and he couldn't protect Sarah and her family in the meantime.

He continues to search. The bedroom, like the dining room, is immaculate save for the dishevelled bed. Simpson lives in a virtual showhouse. The drawers reveal socks and underwear with a penchant for silk boxer shorts. Moving to the wardrobes, he finds a couturier's wet dream. A gallery of shirts to rival Gatsby.

The next room has another double bed, an en suite and a large built-in wardrobe. On a shelf running the length of the wardrobe, Jackie finds an impressive collection of comic books. Most of them are American with a couple of old-school British war comics here and there. He picks one out to have a flick through it and spies a small leather case behind. It is the kind of case a small girl might keep trinkets or a diary in, with a small latch and keyhole. The case is locked. He grabs it and takes the screwdriver to the lid. It pops open to reveal its contents.

It reveals a lot.

Lots of skin, some pale, some tanned like Simpson himself. There are prints but the majority are Polaroids, taken in the bedroom where he now stands. There are wicked smirks to camera and coquettish grins. Some of the subjects are wearing masks, hiding identities and nothing more. He sees a tear-streaked woman's face, her ass in the air striped red with violence. There is a girl in a choker necklace with a blank expression, her legs spread wide and sheathed in black stockings. A naked man gives a wolfish leer to camera, his knotted body slick and shining with oil. Simpson isn't in any of the photos. Jackie supposes he is behind the camera, directing, orchestrating and consuming this flesh in front of the lens. The date of each shot is scribbled by hand on the back of each photo.

Jackie had never seen Rab Simpson with a partner. He'd never heard of a partner. The man's social life back in the day had been male companionship within the UDA and the pursuit of violence. Now Jackie thinks 'Homer', with that sickly pallor and alarming overbite, must have been desperately lonely. And in the years since, he'd certainly made up for lost time. Thanks to the reconstructive surgery – thanks to a bullet in the face – he'd become the proverbial swan. Judging by these photos, he'd gone on a rampage of debauchery. Men and women. At least there weren't any signs of bestiality, although Rab never had been much good with animals.

Jackie continues to flick through the images. Some are coiled bodies in aspects of intimacy, hands holding faces, inches apart as they couple. Others are cold, men wrapped in concentration pounding away at disinterested young women who look anywhere but at their partner in coitus. Some of the women could be from anywhere, others have a distinctly Slavic tinge to their features and Jackie remembers Petri and Ion in Belvoir Forest. Rab may have had more than Eastern European muscle in his employ.

The angles are different in later shots: more remote and fixed, rather than the closer, more intimate photos of before. There is a voyeuristic quality that suggests a hidden camera. The next photo seems to confirm this. A prominent unionist politician, eyes screwed sternly shut as he toils in the missionary position. The girl is staring at her reflection in a mirror propped on the wall to her left. The next image reveals a leading figure in Northern Ireland's business community, a property magnate. He is bent over a young man from the rear, as though about to administer the Heimlich manoeuvre. The young man is craning his head back, a smile on his sweat-slicked face. There is a campaigner from the city's Chinese community. Another business leader. Even a republican politician with a young girl wearing the hat of a PSNI policewoman, the rest of the uniform strewn across the bed. The irony, thinks Jackie.

He can look at no more and shoves the photos in an empty plastic bag in the bottom of the wardrobe. Beneath the photos in the case are a couple of football stickers, random players from random clubs in England. There are ticket stubs for Paris Disneyland, of all places, and a couple more Polaroids at the bottom. If he could access Simpson's hard drive, God knows what he might unearth.

Ignorance is probably bliss, he thinks.

Jackie is about to replace the case on the shelf when he spots one more Polaroid, wedged up against the inner lining. He has to prise it out with a fingernail and takes a look.

A woman lies on a bed. She is naked and her body is contorted in embarrassment. This is not the playful bashfulness of some other shots, but sharp, cringing unease. Her left hand is in front of her face, a gold band visible on the ring finger. Despite the attempt at anonymity, an angry frown creases her high forehead and some of her long black hair is tangled in the fingers. He can see from the delicate creases around her mouth, apparent below a knuckle, showing that her mouth is turned sharply down. That skin is dulled by the Polaroid, almost a matte finish on the cheap print. But he can still see the rich olive hue. And despite the twisted aspect of the body, it is lithe and beautiful and familiar.

Eileen Tyrie.

Jackie sits in silence in a lotus position on the carpet, the photo in his right hand, the gun at his feet. His face is burning and his insides churn.

He sits like this for several moments.

Then he remembers where he is and checks his watch. Simpson left the house about twenty minutes ago. Jackie should leave.

He tucks the Polaroid of Eileen into his wallet and closes the clasp on the case, then replaces it on the shelf. He closes the wardrobe, shoves the revolver back in his waistband and the screwdriver in his jacket pocket, and grabs the plastic bag full of photos. He makes his way back to the stairs, holding the bag of photographs. Taking the stairs two at a time he reaches the ground floor of the house and walks down the hallway towards the front door. He wants to rifle quickly through a pile of post on a cabinet next to the door before slipping out the back window and making his way back to the Toyota. When he is a couple of feet from the front door a shadow appears in the frosted glass of its upper half.

Jackie just has time to wrench the Magnum revolver from his waistband before the door opens and Rab Simpson, murder in his eyes, is standing before him.

CHAPTER 21

1993

'We need to put these boys away.'

'We need to contain the violence.'

'Gordon, they *are* the violence.'

They sat in Lady Dixon Park, on the southern outskirts of the city, side-by-side on a park bench. Despite being a warm spring morning, the park was virtually deserted at this time on a weekday. It was a fair whack out of the city, sprawling beside the suburb of Finaghy. Jackie took in the wide lawns, which would be flush with roses when the rose festival swung around in July.

Gordon said, 'I know how you feel and no one wants these animals locked up more than me, but we can't just move without the say-so from E Division. You know that.'

Jackie loved this time of year, when the greenery was returning to the trees. Leaves were bobbing in the breeze, but the branches weren't yet smothered in them. If you were so inclined, you could count them on each towering tree.

'And the fact is there may be another asset in the East Belfast Brigade. Maybe more than one and we can't afford to compromise them if that's the case. If they're a protected bird, we need the go-ahead before they're red-lined.'

Jackie lit up a cigarette to a look of disapproval and said, 'Ach shite. Talk to Shanty McKee. Look the wee lad in the eye like I did. There's a life forever marked. James Maguire: another life ruined. It has to end, Gordon. None of this "acceptable level of violence" bollocks.'

To give him his due, Gordon Orr was swallowing his disdain at the language and the smoking and was taking what Jackie said on board. A good man, earnest, he folded his arms, sat back on the bench and crossed his legs.

'Okay, Jackie. One thing at a time. You've told me they cancelled another hit on Cochrane. They'll try again, so let's sort that out. Keep your ear to the ground and I'll see what I can do about making a move on Tyrie and Simpson as soon as possible. Fair enough?'

It wasn't fair enough, not really. Jackie was worried that he'd been excluded from planning the last attempt on Cochrane's life, and there was Rab's increasing hostility. He knew there was little Gordon Orr could do if MI5 were running an asset on the same turf. But he also knew the man was sincere and would do what he could. And Cochrane, despite what he was and what he'd done, was a husband and father: it would be another life saved if they could stop the hit. Probably a slew of lives if you considered the tit-for-tat that would follow. So he nodded and patted the older man on the elbow.

'Okay, Gordon. Now I'll treat you to an ice-cream.'

#

That night, the whole crew were in the Tartan Star Club off the Holywood Road. It was a birthday party held for James 'Doctor' Love, the top man in East Belfast, and the great and the good of loyalist paramilitary cognoscenti were there.

South and West Belfast Brigadiers were in attendance, although the north's commander was conspicuous by his absence. Several representatives from the UVF had made appearances, along with a couple of faces from Scotland. Billy was at the bar next to Jackie, deep in conversation with a grinning Love about a forthcoming republican rally in the city centre and how they might disrupt it. Love was hammered with the drink and in a less than political state of mind. Hunched over a shot glass, Tyrie leaned into the much smaller man with an arm around his shoulders, like a Silverback with a small child. Sam 'Ruger' Rainey eased through the crowd to the counter, surprisingly agile for such a big man.

'All right, Sam?' said Jackie.

'Ach, Jackie, what about ye? I haven't seen you for a couple of days, like.'

'Ach, I'm all right. Some bash, isn't it?'

'Sure, this crowd'll take any excuse for a piss-up. Are you heading to the shebeen after? Wee Jonty's organised one down Templemore Avenue.'

Jackie had no idea who or what wee Jonty was, and wasn't really in the mood for a locked-door after-hours all-night boozing session with a crowd of vicious terrorists. But he said, 'Aye, sounds like good craic. Here, how's that wee girl up in – where is she – the Shore Road?'

Rainey was oiled up with alcohol, sweat glistening on his broad forehead as it creased with raised brows. Generally cagey about his sweet young thing up in the north of the city, now he smiled like the cat with the proverbial cream.

'Ach, she's great, like,' said Ruger, sloppy with his shirt hanging out of his piss-stained jeans. 'It's the real thing, so it is. The two of us just, like, talk, you know. We're up half the night gabbing but I don't see the time going.'

A frown crossed the great expanse of his skull.

'I still love ridin' her, like. She's a fantastic arse on her and a great wee pair of lungs.'

Jackie said, 'Sounds like true love, Sam,' and patted the big man on the arm before turning to head for the door. He was a twenty-a-day man, but the heavy cloak of smoke in the air was beginning to sting his eyes and he needed a breath of fresh air.

There was something else in the atmosphere, too. Despite a healthy smattering of women in the club, it was all testosterone, ego and booze with this crowd. Violence usually followed. He'd been at this kind of bash before, in the forces, and RUC too. It always included a barney between a couple of bulls the worse for wear, butting heads. Jackie was pacing himself carefully, a pint an hour at most. He'd been cradling his current lager for forty minutes already. At some stage, something would kick off and he'd have to be on his toes. When he spotted Rab Simpson standing alone by a wall, he counted another good reason to stay sober. Jackie wandered over to say hello and test the water.

Rab was fixated on something or someone across the room and was running his tongue along the rim of his upper teeth, jutting like the snowplough on an Old West train. Following his line of sight, Jackie saw Rab scrutinising the quiet man, Tommy.

Leaning on the wall he said, 'Fancy a fag?'

Rab turned his head slowly. His eyes were bloodshot and seemed to drag the rest of his features down as though his face was melting. His entire lower jaw was lost in shadow. Rab was a living skull. He said, 'Aye, go on then.' His voice was thick and his words slurred.

At a loss for a better ice-breaker, Jackie said, 'Some "do".'

'S'all right.' Rab's gaze returned to Tommy. His head was bobbing gently.

'You going to Jonty's shebeen after?'

'Prob'ly.'

'Yer man Tommy's a funny one, isn't he?'

The slack features turned back to Jackie again. 'Oh aye?'

Jesus, thought Jackie, he looks like he's had a fucking stroke. 'You know, the way he's so quiet. Never really says much. And he's from North Belfast. Where's fucking Gilroy tonight? We've Porter and Wilson, the only brigadier hasn't shown is Tommy's.'

'He's quiet, is he?' said Rab. 'And that's a bad thing, is it? At least he doesn't ask a load of fucking questions.'

A finger pointed like a stiletto blade.

'Y'know, you're a sleeked one, Shaw. You're always watching. Just watching. Then you ask your fucking questions. Jesus, you're like a fucking peeler.'

Jackie felt a shot of adrenaline, like a belt of whiskey, and gripped his pint glass a little harder.

'And you're soft. You won't do what's necessary. Look at you with that cunt Maguire. I'd have put his eye out and he'd never have missed a payment again and he'd never fucking forget me. I know you were raging about McKee too, what I done to him. But he'll not forget me either. And you, Shaw. You'll not forget me. You'll see.'

The glass smashed with a heavy, liquid explosion in Rab's face. His forehead was lacerated, his eyes blinded by the stale lager as Jackie yanked and gouged, tearing at Rab's shredded skin. *And you'll not forget me, you bastard!*

And then Jackie was back in the room and the brief fantasy was over. There were those who might back him, stand up for him at a UDA tribunal, but glassing Rab Simpson in a crowded club during the Brigadier's birthday party probably wasn't the way to go.

'C'mon Rab, what's the bother, eh? Relax and we'll have a drink.'

Rab moved a step closer. 'You think you're too fucking good for us. You think you're better. But the taigs aren't decent. They're fucking killers, and if we don't match them, they'll win and we'll be gone, driven into the fucking sea.' The purple lips had receded behind snarling, jutting teeth. The Great White shark look Jackie had seen in Maguire's shop. Except now it was directed at him.

Rab looked dully at Jackie's hand gripping the glass. For an awful second, Jackie thought Simpson was reading his mind. Then Rab said, 'You and your fucking Fenian ring.'

Then a hand settled on Rab's shoulder. A slender, delicate hand. A quiet, measured voice said, 'All right Rab, Jackie?'

There stood Tommy, cigarette in mouth and glass of Bushmills in hand, an easy grin plastered across his face.

'There's some wee girl here asking after you, Jackie. Leanne. Nice-looking girl. You might want to go and have a chat with her.'

Jackie, silent, nodded and walked off. He glanced back to see Tommy escort Rab away, his arm straddling bony shoulderblades. He saw a young girl with a trim figure make for the bar counter, and Rainey's face light up in a warm grin. Miss Mount Vernon, Ruger's mistress. He saw James Love sit in state with his hard-bitten wife beside him, his son and two daughters at the adjoining table. Billy was chatting with a local UVF commander and waving his arms about expressively, the two men laughing. Jackie walked out of the emergency exit at the side of the room to drink in the warm spring evening. The door swung shut behind him.

He craved a smoke and absently waved his hand in front of his face as he lit up in the side alley, then rubbed his nose.

Bloody spiders' webs, he thought.

He ran his hand over his face more vigorously, determined to shift the gossamer strands, then turned to the right and said, 'Fuck!'

Standing next to him, strands of errant hair tickling Jackie's face, stood Eileen.

'You're jumpy,' she said.

'What are you doing? You don't stand right next to people and not let them know. Are you stalking me?'

'I was here first.' Her tone was light and easy.

He scowled for a second, then looked at the ground and

smiled. He offered Eileen a drag on his cigarette but she declined.

'I didn't think you were coming,' said Jackie. 'Aren't you meant to be in Coleraine visiting a relative?'

'She had to work a double shift. She's a nurse.'

Eileen looked, as always, stunning. In keeping with the balmy temperature she had a light dress on and every ripple of the breeze highlighted the soft curve of her small breasts, the smooth sweep of her thighs, the flat bank of her stomach. He wanted her, ached for her and had an image of them frantically clawing at one another, her dress hiked up under his arms as he supported her ass and drove into her.

Instead, he said, 'Billy's inside, up at the bar.'

'Of course he is,' she said with weary resignation. 'And you're out here on your lonesome. How come?'

'I just needed a breath. Rab's getting a bit feisty with the drink, so I thought I'd get offside for a minute or two.'

She shuddered – actually shuddered – at the mention of the name. The corners of her mouth creased in delicate lines, like petite brackets, as her mouth formed a scowl.

'He's an animal,' she spat. 'Billy's a bastard, but at least there's method to his madness. Rab just likes to watch things suffer.'

Jackie was unsure what to say. He was a member of the group and couldn't mouth off against one of his 'mates'. Not even to her. So he changed the subject.

'What are you doing creeping about the side door anyway?'

'Ach, there's women at these things always make a big deal when I show. You know, the whole bow and scrape at the big man's bird, and I can't be bothered with it. I just wanted to slip in, quiet.'

'Well,' said Jackie, gesturing to the door, 'slip away.'

And with that she went up on her toes, took his face in her hands and enveloped him in a kiss, sliding her tongue into his mouth and pushing her body against his. For a moment he was lost to all doubt or caution, and he returned the kiss with intensity.

Then she shut it down with a firm hand against his chest and a step back.

'I'll see you in there. And I'll see you in three days. He's away on business. London.'

'Okay.'

She nodded and yanked the door open, slipping into the light and noise seeping out from beyond.

He lit another cigarette and smoked it with relish. It was Saturday. Tuesday and he'd be with her, he'd have her.

He paced the alley, hummed a New Order song and –

'Jackie.'

'Shite!'

'Sorry.'

Leanne stood against the wall of the alley. She wore a tight white T-shirt and a pair of ripped jeans. And an expression he couldn't quite decipher.

'You all right, Leanne?'

'I'm okay.'

He could see the contours of her body. The T-shirt, clinging to her small waist, her hips straining against the jeans. She wore a hair band, scraping her shaggy bob back from her forehead, but her eyes were glinting pinpricks in the low light.

'What brings you out here?' he asked. 'The party's inside.'

'Not from where I'm standing.'

How long had she been waiting there, in the shadows? If she'd seen anything, he wanted to beg her to keep her counsel, or threaten her if needs be. Desperate times called for desperate measures, he thought, and dropped the cigarette, grinding it underfoot.

Then he did something worse than grabbing her throat.

Worse than threatening her, slapping her and bullying her into keeping what she might have seen secret. And he did it with the best of his effort because it might buy her silence, at least for now. He pulled her to him and laid his lips against hers.

#

They fucked on her parents' living-room floor again. As he left to take a taxi back to his father's house, he heard the drone of helicopters hanging over Belfast.

Five people were shot dead that night. A soldier on foot patrol in the Ardoyne area; two friends walking home from a city centre club; a policeman closing the gate of New Barnsley RUC station after a civilian car had driven in; and a young man walking on the Woodstock Road, not three streets away from the local RUC station.

CHAPTER 22

Saturday

'You're fucking kidding.'

Rab is all wide-eyed rage.

Jackie is holding the Magnum in his right hand, his left locked around that wrist and his feet planted firmly and evenly. The plastic bag of photos is on the ground at his feet, where he dropped it. He says, 'Close the door.'

There is a heavy sound as the reinforced front door shuts tight.

'Windows double-glazed?'

Rab nods. 'Blastproof.' The colour has drained from the deep tan, a residue of sickly yellow pallor showing underneath. Rab looks momentarily shrunken in a quilted jacket as he glances briefly at the bag. His arms hang at his sides, limp, and his hands are curled in half-moons aside his black designer jeans.

'Right hand on right shoulder and vice versa. Walk backwards, back to the dining room.'

'Jesus,' says Rab, 'you sound like a fucking cop.'

Jackie says nothing.

'Christ,' says Rab. The penny drops. 'You *are* a fucking cop.'

'Dining room, now.'

Jackie grabs the bag of photographs and keeps his distance, gun trained on Simpson's chest as they walk through the hall to the back of the house.

Rab mutters, 'A cop. A fucking cop.'

In the dining room Jackie says, 'Close the window.'

Rab does as ordered, glancing at the foil on the frame.

'Shoulders.'

Rab once again holds that pose, as if playing a child's game.

'Take your jacket off and throw it in the corner of the room.'

Rab does as he's told, then resumes the shoulder position. His torso looks lean in his tight-fitting T-shirt.

'I'd you all wrong, Jackie. I thought you were a grass, and there's you a peeler all along.'

'Is that why you set me up that night?'

'Ach, behave yourself. I just thought you were a cunt. But until I saw you handle that gun and give them orders, I never clocked you as a peeler. And I know a Black Bastard when I see one.'

'Right hand, pull out the lining of your right jeans pocket.'

Rab does so, keeping his left hand on his left shoulder. A couple of coins fall out. He repeats the action on the left pocket, revealing a cigarette lighter, keys and a mobile phone. He lets them fall on the carpet.

'Push the table over to the wall, the chairs, too.'

As he follows the orders, clearing a space in the centre of the room, Rab says, 'One thing I don't get. You were a cop; how'd you get away with murder? I know the Fenians complained about the whole shoot-to-kill thing and that, but I thought somebody would have pulled you up for gunning a man down. Aren't youse accountable? Not that you didn't do a good job, like. One shot in the forehead.'

'I didn't kill anybody,' says Jackie. 'Maybe you're confusing me with one of the psychotic bastards you call mates. You must have known a few.'

Rab shakes his head, serious. 'You shot Tommy that night in ninety-three. Shot him in the face.'

'Not me.'

'Fuck off. I got the ballistics report from that night. The round that killed Tommy wasn't security forces issue, it was from his own gun. You took it from him and fucking killed him.'

189

'It wasn't me.' Jackie despairs at the thought of Simpson having access to that kind of intel from a police source.

'Then who? It wasn't that other prick, that's for sure.'

'You wouldn't believe me if I told you. And I don't have to explain myself to you.'

'What were you? Branch? CID? Maybe HMSU?' Rab spits on his valet-cleaned carpet. 'Sure youse were all trigger-happy in the day. You shot him, you cunt. And that makes your sister guilty by association.'

Jackie takes a deep breath, swallowing the urge to lunge at Rab. If he loses control, Simpson gains it.

He says, 'On your knees,' and circles behind Rab. The Magnum is weighing heavily in his hand, the tension he is keeping on the trigger not helping. Simpson looks comfortable despite the stress position.

'Did you kill Shanty McKee?'

Rab snorts, then looks over his shoulder at Jackie and smiles. A catalogue model smile rather than the ugly mask of twenty years ago.

'What kind of a question is that? Don't you want to establish a rapport first? Maybe a threat? I haven't asked for a solicitor yet.'

'I'm not in the job any more. I haven't been a police officer in this country for twenty years and I've already broken the law a couple of times today.' Breaking and entering, possession of a firearm, abduction. 'Now, the question remains: did you kill Shanty McKee?'

'Of course I fucking killed him.' He tut tuts, as though disappointed with a foolish child. 'You'd know by the state of him I done it. I'd usually just give the word these days, but me and Shanty go back so I did it myself this time. As a courtesy.'

'How?'

'Poker.'

Jackie gives him a solid kick between the shoulderblades. Rab takes it with a grunt and his arms fly forward to arrest his fall. Then he settles his weight back on his legs, knees on the carpet, and returns his hands to his shoulders.

'He was off his face on something. The dog was sniffing round him when I arrived, I think he'd pissed himself. There was an old poker lying next to the fireplace. I caved his head in with the first blow, then went to work on him for a while. I took as many of his teeth with me as I could, just to piss the crime scene boys off a bit. That was that. I took off and left the dog eating away at what was left of his face.'

'Why'd you kill him?'

'Stupid twat called me, told me he'd spoken to you and gave you information about me. About Morgan. Thought coming clean would buy him another fix. Sure, I was putting him out of his fucking misery.'

The truth of this statement doesn't detract from the cold, white fury Jackie is channelling to the tense knotted rope of his right arm. He struggles to control pressure on the heavy trigger of the revolver.

Rab says, 'I've been looking for that Fenian bastard, Morgan. No sign of him though.'

'Seems you're cosy enough with the Fenian bastards these days. Call them that when you're cutting your heroin together?'

'Just a manner of speech,' sniffs Rab.

'And Billy isn't too fond of your new playmates?'

'Billy Tyrie's a fucking dinosaur. He still thinks it's the nineties. There's no money in terrorism any more, and the taigs are smart enough to see that. See these splinter groups: Real IRA, Continuity IRA, Part-time-professional IRA? They're just the bottom of the barrel, the ones not smart enough to make money out of the peace.' Simpson loudly sucked some stray spit back in his mouth. 'Billy still gets by on the usual UDA rackets, but that's nothing to what we're making.'

Jackie shifts his grip on the .357. Holding it one-handed, his arm is beginning to burn and he can see it beginning to shake. 'Nice wee box of memories you've got upstairs,' he says. He struggles to get a random Polaroid out of the bag with the other hand, and tosses it in front of Rab. The shot is of a woman in a dog collar, her face wrenched in agony or pleasure; it's difficult to tell which.

'Quite a collection: some hand-held, some hidden camera jobs. Pretty good work from a surveillance point of view.'

'Nikki,' says Rab. 'Russian bird worked behind the bar in the Tartan Star Club.' He leers up at Jackie. 'Them immigrants'll do shite our girls'd throw up at the mention of.'

'Like Eileen Tyrie?'

The leer freezes for an instant. Then the features relax, unfurling into a bright, open smile. He looks like a kid who's just been given a glowing report on parents' evening at school: Eileen is an A+.

'Ah, seen that one, have you? Doesn't get better than shagging the boss's woman, does it?'

'Been there, done that.'

'No chance,' says Rab, with a flicker of doubt.

Jackie keeps his distance but drops to his haunches, on a level with Simpson's head. He rests his right elbow on top of his thigh, easing some of the weight of the revolver.

He says, 'Did you find the wee mole on her right buttock just where her arse ends and her leg starts? I used to call it her Coco Pop.'

The grin melts and Rab's forehead knots into a frown, his teeth bared. But his eyes are his biggest tell. There is pure bloody murder in them.

Simpson probably couldn't believe his luck. Survives being shot in the face, his currency rockets in the organisation and his legend on the street grows. Into the bargain, the reconstructive surgery gives him looks. Takes what pleasure he can from women, maybe men too, and records it all for posterity. Eileen must have been the greatest prize of all: the boss man's missus. Now he finds out that the traitor in their midst had already been with her.

'It's a wonder you haven't shagged Billy, too,' says Jackie.

'I'm a bit old for him,' says Rab, flecks of saliva in the corners of his mouth. 'I don't have a school uniform for a start.'

He wants to press Simpson on the comment but time is short and he focuses on Rab.

'You were running girls?'

'Whatever pays the bills. These birds come over here, all lawyers and accountants and what have ye. But they can't get anything better than stacking shelves or cleaning bogs. I'm doing them a service. They make ten times working for me what they would for Tesco.'

'On their back.'

'It's a living,'

'I thought it was all "local houses for local people" with the UDA these days. Burn out a couple of Polish or Blacks when there's no football on TV.'

'They have their uses,' says Rab. 'At least the fucking Eastern Europeans are white.'

'And they get to meet famous people,' says Jackie, thinking of the politicians in the photos.

'Ah, you found *those* shots. Funny, the Catholics are generally less kinky than the Prods. Must be all that fucking guilt.' He laughs. 'The photos are just a wee insurance policy.'

'I hope you've life insurance too.'

Jackie tosses the bag in the corner and takes a cushion from a chair. He shoves it on Simpson's head with his left hand. With his right, he pushes the muzzle of the .357 hard into the fabric. He psychs himself up: thinks of Shanty McKee. The young man ruined by sectarian ink; the older man broken and ruined by drugs pushed by Simpson. And the broken and bloody corpse, unrecognisable. Dog food.

'I'm going to end you now,' he says.

There is silence but for their breathing, ragged and rapid. The trigger is a hard pull. He extends his left arm, as if to avoid blood splatter. Rab feels the movement.

'Wait. There's more. More photos upstairs.'

'I don't think I could stomach more.'

'There's one,' says Rab.

Jackie shoves the muzzle of the revolver hard into the cushion and Rab's head jerks forward.

'There's one with me in it. The only one. My reflection in a mirror behind somebody, riding them.'

'Who?'

'Cochrane's missus.'

Jackie eases the pressure on the cushion. 'James Cochrane?'

'Aye,' says Rab. 'I work with him. With Cochrane.'

Madra Mor, thinks Jackie, Adrian Morgan's 'big dog' in the republicans. So Cochrane and Simpson are sharing the drug trade in East Belfast, UDA and RAAD working together. Brave new world. He kicks the cushion under the dining table and takes his previous stance with the revolver levelled at Rab's head.

'I'm listening.'

'He was away in Cork. Some of our gear comes up from there. I'd been working with him and that shower from RAAD for over a year. He'd shot a young lad who was a friend of Morgan's.'

Morgan's mate from the Markets, thinks Jackie.

'I went over to his house to ask him to lay off my dealer, didn't know he was out of town. His wife was in next door and saw me through the window, offered me a cup of tea. She can't abide him, but you know what the taigs are like about divorce.' Rab's face creases in disgust. 'She'd do anything to spite him and she's pretty fit, so I fucked her here, upstairs.'

He looks at Jackie and winks. 'She was a good ride.'

'And your partner doesn't know?'

'Of course not. The photo's under the bed in my bedroom. It's in a briefcase, not even locked. Take it and fuck off.'

Jackie is unsure what angle Rab is playing here. Maybe just buying time. Maybe moving to take more control of the business. Maybe just desperate. But the photo would be of value and he isn't going to kill Simpson, he knows that. Not like this, in cold blood; he isn't sure he could do it in anger.

Then the door opens and a man stands in the entrance. Solid build in a Barbour jacket with faded black jeans. Cropped black hair, heavy stubble.

He looks at Rab on his knees, then Jackie.

Jackie looks at him.

The man begins reaching into the pocket of the jacket.

The next second is filled with Jackie levelling the .357 Magnum revolver at the intruder, exerting pressure on the trigger and firing a round at a range of around seven feet.

The recoil punches Jackie hard, a shockwave shuddering up his right arm. The bullet rams home in the man's abdomen, opening a small geyser of blood. The sound is deafening, the muzzle flash a lightning strike. The man goes down, crumpling like a collapsing tent.

Jackie never sees him hit the floor.

Rab swings both hands hard and hits Jackie's gun-hand like a hammer, sending the .357 flying into the wall and landing just inside the threshold of the room. Just behind the screaming, writhing stranger on the floor.

Rab is silent as he goes to work and rugby tackles Jackie, toppling him in the centre of the room, then aiming a couple of vicious blows at his temple, driving a knee into Jackie's throat and raining blows onto his face. Jackie feels the dull thud of cartilage against cheekbone as the rigid knots of Rab's knuckles connect. Rab's face is all concentration and Jackie is already finding it difficult to breathe, the weight of the knee crushing his larynx. He is bucking and writhing under Rab but can't shake him. Something sharp is stabbing in Jackie's side. His fists slap against Rab's thighs to no effect. Panic seizes him.

He can hear the shot man moaning and crying, 'Fuck! Fuck! Fuck!' He hears the pain and fear, the accent broad and local.

Rab is grunting, picking his shots. He glances a blow off Jackie's left eyebrow, leaving a throbbing ache in its wake. He then draws back his hand, taking aim, and lands a hard, sharp punch on the bridge of Jackie's nose. The cartilage gives way with a thick liquid sound.

It provides some clarity. Jackie pulls his arms close to his sides, working them up as far as he can under the inside of Rab's thighs. He breathes in deeply and leverages his fists upwards, connecting – with all the force he can muster – with the soft groin. There isn't much in the blow but it's enough. He grabs Rab's bollocks in his right hand and with a force born of fear and madness wrenches with everything he's got. Rab's face seems to collapse in on itself and he yells.

'Ya bastard!'

Jackie twists and throws Rab off, rolling away from him in the process.

They form a ragged triangle, the three of them. The mystery stranger is the tip, now whimpering quietly near the doorway, the gun just beyond him on the cusp of the hall. Jackie is leaning against the wall opposite the window, breathing hard. His face is a mass of throbbing pain sewn deep in his skull. Rab is coming to his feet in the centre of the room, his back to the window, smiling a hideous, rictus leer. There are a couple of yards between them.

Jackie moves away from the wall and Rab comes at him, ducking low as Jackie throws a right. The Claddagh gouges Rab's ear along with Jackie's finger. Rab grabs Jackie's jacket and hauls it up over Jackie's head, pulling it down to trap his arms. The toe of Rab's boot connects with his hip and more pain blossoms. Something is now stabbing at his right shoulderblade from inside the jacket and he vaguely remembers the hotel screwdriver. Pulling Rab down, he begins throwing punches upward, connecting anywhere he can. His fists find stomach, ribs and, as he hauls further at the neck of the fabric, Rab's face. The ring bites into the skin above Rab's left eye. They are hot now, and Jackie's knuckles are slicked with sweat from Rab's face. He hopes there might be some blood on there too.

They dance, locked in close embrace for a moment. Jackie has the better position, punching hard at Rab's stomach and face, although the weight of the jacket is tiring him. Rab's tactic has backfired and he can only hammer at Jackie's shoulders and back. Without a weapon, he can do limited damage.

So he finds one. Rab grabs his keys from the floor. He pulls Jackie's T-shirt up and, holding the keys by the fob, slices the skin of Jackie's side, like a kid scraping a car door. Pain sears into Jackie's side and he slackens his grip on Rab's T-shirt, giving the other man a chance to shove him. He loses balance and lands hard and awkwardly on his back, his jacket bunched up around his shoulders.

Rab looks at Jackie, then the gun lying just beyond the fallen stranger. His face is shining with sweat and blood. A cut has opened up above his eye and his lip has a wicked split. Jackie tastes blood and realises it's leaking from his nose, which is surely broken. His side is on fire. His left eye already feels as though it is swelling up and his strength is waning.

Rab smiles, his perfect teeth red, awash with blood, and lunges in the opposite direction of the shot man and revolver.

At first Jackie thinks it's a feint and drops to the floor, scrambling for the gun. It's still out of reach when Rab brings a wooden dining chair crashing down on his back. Jackie arches in pain as Rab brings the chair down again, this time across his right hip.

Jackie yells. He's frightened. He can't reach the gun. He's winded and tired and the jacket seems to weigh a ton, dragging him down. He twists on the carpet, enough to have another blow of the chair glance off his kneecap with a ringing sensation. It gives him a sight of Rab's feet and he traps Simpson's ankles with his own, his legs like pincers. Rab loses balance and falls with a grunt.

But he falls on Jackie. Jackie lands a good, hard right on Rab's jaw with a satisfying crack and follows with a left, connecting with the man's neck but doing little damage. Simpson batters a couple of vicious blows into Jackie's face, but he hardly feels them now. He can read Simpson's eyes: he knows the end is in sight. Rab's fingers lock around his throat.

He claws at Rab's arms with his left hand, but it's useless. He is gasping and the crushing pressure on his throat is too much. He tenses his body, trying to find a surge, but he is slipping away. He tries to shout to Sarah, his da, his ma in his desperation. He knows his sister and her family are doomed by his failure, but he can't make a sound beyond a wheezing gurgle. His right hand dances in spasms on the floor as though playing a keyboard. The edges of his vision are blurring and he wonders if he'll meet his father when he dies. Rab laughs in triumph, his mouth a yawning chasm. Simpson is growing hard as he straddles Jackie's stomach.

Then Jackie finds the screwdriver on the floor to his right. The object that has been digging into him throughout the fight and has just fallen from his jacket pocket. He grips it and rams it, with the strength of the damned, like a stiletto blade into the gaping hollow of Rab Simpson's mouth. He feels the soft tissue give under the sharpened bite of the metal tip. The palate is ripped in two and Rab's grip goes instantly slack. He stares, his eyes, wide with triumph a moment before, now wide with disbelief. The screwdriver is hanging from his open mouth like a lever to be cranked. Jackie's breath comes in harsh, ragged sobs. He is aghast at the sight of the obscene handle, blood now running down its length. Rab is gurgling, but his jaw remains locked open as blood fills his mouth. He can't swallow; he can't close his throat because of the metal shaft and some gore is bubbling and spitting from his mouth.

Jackie pushes Rab to the ground and, to end it, he grips the handle of the screwdriver – but his hand slips on the blood and saliva. He finds purchase again and pushes deep and hard. The screwdriver shudders and scrapes into Rab's cranium slowly. More blood bubbles and blurts from his mouth in small geysers.

Rab won't last long, but he is still not dead. Neither is the stranger lying on the floor beyond them, although he is still. Jackie detects shallow breathing.

It is a question of whether anyone heard the initial gunshot now. The house is set back a small distance from the street. The blast-proof windows and reinforced door may have helped quell the sound but a Magnum is loud. Jackie's clothes are flecked with blood and he gags, a sharp pain tearing at his side. He swallows hard, then steadies himself against the table as though he's downed a string of doubles at the bar. He tears the lining from the pockets of his jacket and wipes down the .357, then places it in Rab's hand. With the lining wrapped around his right hand he searches the pockets of the mystery man and finds another handgun, a Beretta semi-automatic. He places it in the stranger's hand. Returning to Rab, still quietly bubbling on the floor, he wrenches the screwdriver back out of his mouth. It is grim and tiring work, the blood and gore sucking at the metal shaft as he strains. Once the screwdriver is free, Jackie takes off his blood-stained jacket and wraps the screwdriver in it. He grabs the plastic bag of photos and goes to the hall. He takes one of Rab's jackets from the small cloakroom under the stairs and throws it on. He searches the kitchen and finds a sports bag, then places his bloodied jacket with the screwdriver wrapped inside, and the plastic bag of photos, in it.

Running upstairs, he locates the case under Rab's bed and sifts through the contents as quickly as he can with the pocket-lining 'gloves'. The shot of Cochrane's wife, Rab straining behind her in the reflection of the mirror, is near the top of the pile. He is about to close the lid when he spies more photographs beneath. These are of other couples in various positions, all rutting on a double bed in a simple, threadbare room. There is an older, faded, worn quality to these and the room is not in Rab's house. Jackie grabs them and throws them in the sports bag, then closes the case and slides it back under the bed. Returning to the dining room, he shoves the tin foil in his pocket and ensures the window is firmly closed. Rab and the stranger are still not dead, each lying in a pool of blood. There's about to be more.

Jackie hauls the stranger over to Rab's side and fishes the man's wallet and mobile from his coat pocket. Danny McCardle from the Short Strand. Jackie would put money on Danny being an associate of James Cochrane. He scrolls through the contacts list of McCardle's mobile with interest and pockets it, then thinks better of it and returns it and the wallet to the man's coat. He retrieves Rab's mobile from the corner of the room and pockets it, then wraps one of the pocket linings around the tip of Danny McCardle's trigger finger. He pulls and the semi fires twice into Rab's mouth, obliterating traces of the screwdriver's damage and some of the upper face. The noise is deafening in the confines of the sealed house. The shots leave powder residue on both men's hands and a ringing in Jackie's ears. Rab's catalogue looks are consigned to history.

The bodies are left, finally dead, sprawled on the carpeted floor. With luck this will pass as a drug meet gone wrong. Chances are the PSNI will be less than convinced but the narrative will suit their agenda. Two players gone, one of them a celebrity in paramilitary circles.

Then Jackie zips up Rab's jacket to cover his blood-stained shirt, slings the sports bag over his shoulder and steps out into the chilly autumn light, slamming the front door shut behind him.

CHAPTER 23

1993

They were in bed, the three of them: Jackie, Eileen and Billy Tyrie. No matter when they got together, Billy's presence was always looming somewhere in the background.

It had begun with the ring. The Claddagh. Everyone was fascinated by it in some way. Rab detested it as a symbol of papal idolatry. A lot of the younger lads had no idea what it was but liked the look of it, the style. The crown on top appealed to your average true blue loyalist, too. Eileen was romanced by it, by the sentiment. And now she was holding forth on how Billy loved it, and loved Jackie wearing it. Apparently, it made a statement.

'Rab and Ruger keep saying it's a Catholic thing, but Billy says that's not true at all. He says the man who made the first one, some Joyce guy from Galway, was even a friend of King Billy.'

'There's a story,' said Jackie, 'that Joyce came up with the Claddagh and then got himself enslaved by Algerians. William III demanded his release. At the time he would have been a subject of the crown.'

Eileen was delicately fingering the silver, turning it gently on Jackie's finger.

'Billy's right,' he said. 'The Claddagh has nothing to do with religion. I'm hardly the pious type, am I?' With that, he cupped her left breast in his hand and stroked the dark swirl of nipple. Eileen pulled the ring from his finger and began rolling it between thumb and forefinger. He continued, 'But it is Irish. I think that's why Billy's so keen on me wearing it. He's big on the Prods having their place in Ireland.'

Eileen flipped the ring, the tip of the heart facing inward towards Jackie's wrist, and began sliding it back onto his finger again. He took his free hand from her breast and placed it on her arm, gently putting a stop to her.

'No.'

She looked up into his face and saw his expression, then drew back and said, 'Sorry.' She turned away, ostensibly to search for cigarettes.

The ring was a gift from his mother, a religious woman in the best sense of the word, all God is love and ripe with forgiveness. But she was also fiercely superstitious, growing up in the country town of Saintfield where such sentiments were respected, and would have baulked at him wearing the tip of the heart inward when not married.

Jackie and Eileen were in a small hotel on the Antrim shore of Belfast Lough and they smoked while listening to the gulls calling to each other outside. Eileen ran her fingers over the skin at the sides of her mouth.

'Am I getting old, Jackie?'

'What?'

'Am I getting old? Are these lines longer? Deeper?'

'Not at all,' he said. He saw a woman who knew she had made poor choices, and was only now waking up and realising that the world turns on and won't always be falling over itself to keep her happy. But she was still beautiful and probably always would be.

'What's brought this on?'

'Nothing.'

He could see she already regretted showing the chink in her armour, and was turning inward.

'Is Billy having an affair?'

As soon as he said it, he mentally slapped himself. Subtle as the proverbial brick, he leaped into a mental trench and prepared for the onslaught.

But instead, she said, 'I don't know.'

'You suspect him?'

'No,' she said. 'I mean, I don't know if you'd call it an affair. Or just the odd fuck. Always with the same person.'

He almost recoiled at that. What was he, if not *the odd fuck with the same person.*

'How do you know he's been with anyone?'

'A wife knows.'

'Not always. Archie Nelson was at it with his case worker for a couple of years before Gertie found out.'

'*This* wife knows.'

'Well, *this* fella has to get back to Belfast,' he said. 'We'd best be going.'

He got out of the bed and began searching the room for his boxer shorts. It was cowardice, changing the subject, but he was hardly qualified to counsel her. He looked at her as he pulled the boxers on and could see she was somewhere else entirely.

#

Death was waiting for Jackie when he got back to the Ravenhill Road. He'd dropped Eileen off at York Road station in the north of the city, then driven on to the outstretched finger of the Albert Bridge. When he pulled up to the kerb in Bendigo Street, a young guy of around sixteen approached and told Jackie that Sam Rainey was waiting to speak to him in the Park View Bar.

Jackie walked a couple of streets towards the Ormeau Park, a beautiful mess of greenery, and entered the pub. It was mid-afternoon and, aside from a couple of oul' lads watching the racing on TV, deserted. He ordered a Coke and was just settling at a table by the wall when Sam Rainey entered.

He scanned the place and gave Jackie a quick nod, then went to the counter and ordered himself a pint of heavy. Settling his bulk at the table he said, 'What, you sick or something?' with a look of distaste at the untouched Coke.

'Bit early for me, Sam,' said Jackie. 'I can't handle it as well as you, mate. You're a machine.'

Ruger smiled and sank half of his pint in three gulps. His face flickered in satisfaction, then assumed an aspect of concern.

'Where have you been? The boys have been worried about you.'

'I went up the coast road for a drive,' said Jackie. 'I took that wee girl Leanne home the other night and I needed to clear my head this morning.'

'I know where you're at, mate. My wee honey's the same. Mad about her, like, but does my head in. Boys like us, we're hardly the pipe and slippers type.'

More the pipe bomb type, thought Jackie.

'Now,' said Rainey, 'I have to talk to you about Saturday night. I don't know when you left the party but at least now I know you were with this wee girl, Leanne.' Ruger was turning the pint glass in circles on the table top, agitated. 'A young lad about your age was walking home on the Woodstock Road about half twelve on Saturday.' Ruger took another swig from his glass. 'Apparently, a Cortina pulled up next to him on the road and two gunmen jumped out, shot him about six times, then took off in the car. Probably to the Short Strand.'

'And the punchline is?'

But Jackie knew what was coming and it was no joke.

'It was the Provos. A source in the peelers tells us you were the target.'

Jackie downed his Coke. The fizzing gas burned the back of his throat.

'Any idea why I'm being targeted?'

'Haven't got a handle on that yet.'

'And your source in the peelers is sound?'

'As a pound,' said Rainey. Then he drained the dregs of his pint and walked to the counter for a refill.

Jimmy Brevin had been in his early twenties and the only child of two doting parents. He'd left school at sixteen and taken an apprenticeship in welding at the shipyard but, as the contracts dried up, so did the work. The Jericho fish and chip shop on the Woodstock Road was owned by a couple with a strong Christian faith who were friends of the Brevin family. They'd given Jimmy what hours they could to help him out and he'd been walking home from the late shift when he was murdered. The Provisional IRA released a statement declaring their sympathy with the grieving parents, and sorrow at the case of mistaken identity.

Had they hit their intended target, Jackie's father would have been left with a letter of condolence from the RUC and his bottles of booze to toast his dead son.

At least, Jackie thought, an innocent would still have been walking the streets.

#

Sam finished his third pint in thirty minutes and stood to leave. He and Billy felt it was best if Jackie had a personal firearm. Jackie had thought of his police issue Walther, tucked away in his bedroom in Bendigo Street. He was to take possession of a Glock buried up in Cregagh Glen in the arms bed they'd discussed weeks ago the night Jackie had crippled Peter Rafferty. He should meet Rainey there after nightfall to pick it up.

Ruger shuffled his considerable girth towards the doors as Tommy entered the Park View. They gave each other a nod of the head, and then Ruger excused himself and eased his heavy frame out into the late afternoon sunshine.

Jackie walked to the counter to leave his glass with the

barman.

Tommy said, 'What are you having?' It was the longest sentence Tommy had ever directed at him.

'I'm all right, thanks.'

'Ach, c'mon, let me buy you a drink. By way of apology for Rab's performance on Saturday.'

'Hardly your fault.'

'Ach, I know. But that tight bastard'll never stand you a round, so I'll do it instead.'

Jackie took the path of least resistance and relented, having a pint of lager. They raised glasses, then took a sip each.

'How's Mount Vernon?' said Jackie.

'Revealing,' said Tommy.

'What?'

'Nothing.'

A silence followed which Jackie thought he was expected to fill. Then he realised Tommy didn't expect anything of anyone. Except, perhaps, the worst.

'You must see big Ruger up there sometimes,' said Jackie.

'How's that?'

'His girlfriend being from up there, same as yourself.'

'Oh. Aye. Anyway, Saturday night. Rab was out of order. What was it set him off?'

Me talking about you, thought Jackie.

'The drink, probably,' he said.

'Aye, he's a terrible man for the drink. Did you find that wee girl, Leanne?'

'I went out the side for a bit of air and bumped into her.'

'And then headed home, aye?'

'Aye. Actually, I headed over to her place.'

'When was that? I didn't see you after we talked.'

'About ten, twenty past twelve, maybe.'

'Does she live near you?'

'Other direction,' said Jackie. 'Cregagh Estate. I'd to get a taxi home from hers later.'

Tommy nodded his head. He lit a cigarette, offering one to Jackie, who found himself surprised that a smoke hadn't entered his head since arriving at the bar. He took one and accepted the light offered. They stood at the counter, smoking, taking mouthfuls of alcohol to season the tobacco, poisoning themselves in silence.

Another minute passed.

Then Tommy said, 'Heading out tonight?'

'I think so, aye,' said Jackie. 'I don't want to be at home after what Ruger told me.'

'About the Provos, aye?'

'Aye. Don't want to be around my da in case he's affected either. I'll probably head over to that new place on Templemore Avenue, the Windsor. Safety in numbers.'

He wondered if Tommy knew about him taking the Glock for personal protection.

'Good place, aye,' said Tommy. 'Sure, maybe I'll see you in there.'

With that he finished his smoke, drained his glass and took off.

The Windsor. Now he'd told Tommy he'd be there, Jackie whispered to himself, 'I wouldn't be caught dead in the place.'

He immediately regretted his choice of words.

CHAPTER 24

Saturday

It is a gorgeous day now. As he makes his way back to the car, the sun has found its full morning glory and shines on the telephone wires strung across the street, giving them the look of giant spiderwebs.

He isn't as sharp as before the fight but still doesn't see a tail. He works hard not to limp and keeps his head low. His face is a patchwork of welts and he doesn't want any passers-by to remember him so close to the house. Beyond the elegant Victorian facade, Rab's home was a fortress. He might be lucky. The roar of the handguns might have been smothered by the reinforced doors and windows. He hears no sirens.

Back at his car, Jackie checks his face in the mirror. His nose is skewed to the right, hammering away at his nervous system in protest. His left eye is swollen, although not as badly as he feared, and a quick check reveals that his teeth are still intact. But he doesn't look pretty. Caked blood is smeared around his face. He needs a place to wash and recharge his batteries.

His pre-paid mobile rings. It's Sarah. For a moment, he considers her house. But he can't let her see him like this and it may still be watched.

'Hi. Do you want to come over? I'm making pasta for lunch.'

'I'm really sorry,' he says. And he is. Then is taken by a notion. 'I promised Rebecca Orr I'd call in for a chat about Gordon, old times. She's making lunch for me. What about we do something tomorrow, like Sunday dinner?' It's hardly likely but he needs to believe in the fantasy right now.

'Okay,' says Sarah. 'Ring me later to sort out a time and stuff.'

He promises he will and hangs up. Then he guns the engine and turns for the Holywood Road and the shore of Belfast Lough.

#

He called Rebecca Orr just outside Holywood to check she'd be in. She still lived in the same house that she had with Gordon on the outskirts of Bangor, an ever-growing coastal town on the knuckle of the North Down coast. As he drives up to the house, he almost passes out with a sudden wave of emotion – emotion he doesn't understand. He doesn't have the energy to try. He is confused and out of joint, and bone-tired.

Rebecca Orr opens the door and does a sterling job of hiding her revulsion at the bruised and broken face in front of her. A copper's wife, thinks Jackie. This isn't the first time she'll have put a policeman back together. Then he remembers he's no longer a copper.

'Jackie,' she says, 'come inside.'

She treats his injuries with care and an economy of language, quietly sponging his cuts. An ice pack on his eye and nose, a strong cup of tea to keep him busy and help calm him. She's twenty years older than when he last saw her and looks a little harder, but she's still a handsome woman with a quiet strength and dignity. He spots a Bible on the coffee table. It looks well thumbed.

It is a long time since Jackie has given himself over to the care of a woman. It is a long time since he has seen a Bible, come to that, recently read or otherwise. Not since his mother sat at the kitchen table and read a passage each morning while the kettle was boiling.

The first tears come hot and salty, and take him by surprise.

Moments later, he can't keep his eyes open and his shoulders are heaving. He tries to keep the sound in, to internalise, but it's all too much and he collapses in great, wracking sobs. Rebecca takes him in her arms and she holds him on her sofa in the clean, neat and ordered living room. She is a fragile-looking woman but, when she pulls his head to her chest, he feels warm and safe.

Later, when he is calmed some, he feels ashamed. Ashamed to bring his own sordid world to this woman's home. Ashamed that he has spent his life hiding, whether behind a job or on the other side of the world, from those that love him. And ashamed that he has taken two lives today.

Rebecca Orr brings another cup of tea for him on a tray with a plate of biscuits. He hasn't spoken a word to her beyond, 'Sorry.'

'I don't want to know, Jackie,' she says, 'why you're in this state. And I'm sorry about your father. I read it in the *Telegraph* death notices.'

He looks wretchedly at the carpeted floor and nods. There is one of those silences that can't be measured in minutes.

'He had a lot of time for you,' she says. For a moment Jackie thinks she is talking about his da. Then she says, 'Gordon.' He thinks she probably likes the sound of her husband's name. She is fingering her wedding ring and smiling faintly.

'Gordon kept me right,' he says. 'He reminded me who I was back then. Why I was doing what I was doing.'

'Jackie,' says Rebecca, 'I'm glad you came to me. I loved my husband very dearly, but I hated what he did. Did you know we used to live in the city? Willowfield? I loved that house. There were lots of kids around, always playing outside in the summer. Then the Anglo-Irish Agreement was signed. You'd have been a teenager then. The loyalists turned on the police. The Thompsons lived six doors down from us. He was uniform in

Strandtown station. They burned the family out one night, left them homeless, and then Gordon knew it was only a matter of time before we were targeted. We found this place and got out of Belfast.'

She picks up the plate and offers him a biscuit. When he declines she frowns and, to please her, he takes a Rich Tea. Nodding, she says, 'When he was taken, I was glad it wasn't by that world that he had to live in for his job. He never brought it home, but God knows what he saw when he was a policeman in this country.'

Rebecca Orr takes his hand in hers.

'You've been tainted by that world too, Jackie. You still are. I think most of the men and women who did your job were, to some degree. But you are a good man, just like Gordon. He said so himself and he would have known.' She sighs. 'You're a lost soul, mind you. A Sunday morning in church wouldn't do you a bit of harm. But you're a good man. And a good man needs all the help he can get in this world.'

#

Forty minutes later he is in the woods at Helen's Bay on the shores of the lough, bent double and retching violently into the undergrowth. A wild hare watches with mild interest a few feet away.

It isn't that Jackie has never seen death. He's seen it ugly and peaceful. He's dealt with the terrible anguish that follows and, he has to be honest, celebrated it a couple of times. HMSU took out an active PIRA cell in Armagh back in the day, a group of players responsible for the deaths of two police officers, a soldier and three civilians. There'd been a couple of drams mixed in with the tea in the canteen that evening.

But the thing is, death isn't an end, despite what most people think. His mother would have said it was a new life in Heaven, but for Jackie it's a chain reaction. Someone carries that death around for the rest of their days, be it through guilt or loss or anger. They might pass it on to others around them. Others still might carry the flame of revenge as a result of a death, burning their insides until they're hollow. And now he is responsible for two lives being taken. He clings to the thought that they deserved it. But they both died slow and Simpson died bad. And what chain reaction has he set off?

He can hear kids laughing and a dog barking eagerly somewhere.

He feels totally, coldly alone. He is living another existence, in another world to the families and dog walkers enjoying their afternoon stroll beyond the treeline. He fears that his only company from this day forward will be Rab Simpson and Danny McCardle, visiting him of an evening to reminisce.

Jackie wants to call his sister and tell her he loves her and is proud to be her brother. But he is damned if he'll contaminate her with what he has done, with his world, and holds off on contacting her just yet.

So he fishes his sim card out of his pocket, slots it in his mobile and texts Eileen Tyrie.

#

After things had gone pear-shaped in Belfast, Jackie travelled. He spent a year in New York, then went to Hong Kong and got a position with the Police Force, staying a couple of years until 1997. Following the handover, he travelled in Asia.

But the pull of home was strong. He caught snippets of the peace process on TV: the leering grin of the British Prime Minister, 'the hand of history on his shoulder'; the earnest gaze of the Irish Taoiseach, looking faintly uneasy as though he wasn't quite sure what he was getting the Republic into. So he moved back to the British Isles and settled in England, close enough to home and family to feel connected, far enough to ensure the past remained where it belonged.

He picked up a position working as a groundsman and nominal security guard with a racehorse trainer and stables in the West Country. The job was mainly centred in the Cotswolds but he had the occasional trip to London. It never ceased to amaze him how huge cities like London or New York consumed their residents, almost enslaved them. Whether you lived in Tsim Sha Tsui or Tower Hamlets, Wan Chai or Chelsea, that district and by extension the metropolis around you, became your world, ignorant of life beyond your postcode. The Battersea biosphere.

The same was true of the Tyries and Cochranes of this world. It was true of those who lived with violence and criminality the world over. And he can see that the same is true of Eileen. He stands opposite her in the living room of her home in the affluent enclave of Ravenhill Park, Rebecca Orr's car parked around the corner. She has given him its use while his rented Toyota sits in her driveway in Bangor.

As she simmers in controlled fury, he can see that Eileen is calculating. Calculating how to drink her coffee without leaving a smear of red lipstick on the rim of the cup. How much flesh to give him as she crosses her legs on the sofa. How long it will take to get him out of her house.

'I hardly need to say it,' she fumes with polite bile, 'but you shouldn't have come here.' She smiles with no feeling beyond malice. 'And you look like shite.'

Her daughters are out with friends. He is standing and wants to stay that way, just in case Billy should decide to visit. But from everything he's heard of their marriage lately, that doesn't seem likely.

'Your text said you'd meet me later, at your hotel,' she said. 'He'll kill you if he finds you here. He might well kill me, too.'

'I don't think you need to worry,' says Jackie. 'If you're still breathing after what he did to Mark the Godfather, I think you're bulletproof. You are the mother of his children.'

'Don't bring my kids into this.' Her tone is even, but the anger scratching to get out behind her eyes is anything but.

'Mind you, they're hardly kids any more,' says Jackie. There are photos framed around the room of one or other of the girls, a couple of the three Tyrie women together. None with Billy. 'I'm guessing that's your oldest, Claire. Quite a heartbreaker. Is she away to university now?'

Eileen clasps her hands around the Wedgwood cup, straining to remain composed. She has always been fiery, but playing the paramilitary First Lady has taken some of the edges off.

'Bet the boys'll be queuing up for a chance to carry her books. Now this,' he says, picking up another photo, 'must be Wendy. Sixteen?' He whistles softly as she sets the cup on the tray, placing it just so.

'They grow up fast, don't they? Jesus, a man could be arrested for what's in his mind when he sees a young girl like that. Two years and she's legal. Mind you, two years is a long time to wait.'

'Don't,' says Eileen. There is a pause and she looks wretched. He thinks she's going to leave it at that but then her face creases in a plea. 'Don't, Jackie. That's not you, that's not the talk of a man like you. Don't even pretend.'

He's pleased, despite himself. Then he fishes his wallet from his pocket and takes out a Polaroid photograph. He leans towards her and sets it image-down on the sofa next to Eileen, then stands back. Her face drains of colour and she looks from him to the photograph.

Jackie says, 'Have a look.'

She lifts it cautiously, as if it might sting, and slowly turns it over. Her blanched face tenses, then sags and something un-readable flits across her dark eyes. Now that she's confronted the image, Eileen almost looks relieved, which scares Jackie.

She says, 'Shit.' Then she glares at him and sits forward, perching on the edge of the sofa. 'You were gone – I thought dead. Billy was playing around, I knew it. I was tired, lonely. After you left I had years – *years* – of a soulless marriage with a monster. My life was hell.'

'This isn't about you,' he says. 'It's not really about me, either. But enough's enough: somebody needs to stop Billy before any more lives are ruined.'

As they face each other, she sitting and he standing, his ears pick up a low drone somewhere in the distance. As it gets closer, he realises it is a helicopter. Smaller than the Army Lynx which hung over the city in the old days, this has more of the annoying, tinny hum of a police chopper. Perhaps Rab and his friend Danny were destined for tonight's *Telegraph* evening edition. On cue, he hears the wolf whistle of police cars careening down the road.

'Hope it's no one we know,' he says.

'Did you do something, Jackie?'

'And if I did, what would that be to you?'

'Is it Rab?'

His silence, part caution, part surprise, answers the question.

'Oh, Jackie, what have you done?'

'What I had to. I'll say no more, but whatever I did, I had no choice.'

'I can believe it,' she says. 'He never forgot what you did to Tommy.'

He sags on the sofa opposite her, tilts his head back and rubs both hands over his face. Then winces as they rough up his damaged nose.

'I did not kill Tommy. Rab talked about it. Billy inferred I'd done some killing, too. But, on my mother and father's souls, I did not kill Tommy.'

'I always knew you didn't have it in you,' she says. 'I mean that in a good way. You're not a natural killer, is what I mean. Despite Rab.'

For a moment it's good to hear her say it. Then he thinks of that back room in Ardenlee Avenue and leans forward, resting elbows on knees.

'For a while everybody thought I was dead, too. Why was Rab so convinced I shot Tommy?'

Eileen leans back into the soft upholstery of her sofa, increasing the distance between them. The lines which bracket her wide, full mouth set sharply and she says, 'I don't know. You'd have to ask Billy.'

Jackie stands again with a groan. He searches in his pocket for a mobile phone and tosses Rab's on the sofa next to her. 'Aye,' he says, 'I suppose I will.'

CHAPTER 25

1993

He'd avoided the Windsor on Templemore Avenue as if his life depended on it, which it probably did. Instead, he'd checked for a tail and driven along the Down shore of the Lough, past Bangor and on to the village of Groomsport. As he had passed Bangor, Jackie had wondered if Gordon and his wife, Rebecca were at home, curled up on the sofa with the kids.

At Groomsport, he'd sat in front of Cockle Row with the old fisherman's thatched cottages at the small harbour. His head was low, shielded by the collar of his dark blue jacket from the cold night air that had swept in unexpectedly. The glow from his cigarette warmed his hands against the biting chill and he moaned to himself about the weather. Late April and he was freezing his bollocks off. Mind you, there'd been snow in mid-May one year. He'd come here in his last days of school, heartbroken by a local girl, to brood. Not much had changed, in the village or himself, other than the Walther pistol in his jacket pocket.

Jackie had always found it strange how the men and women of the force took it as read that, at any time, they could be shot in the back or blown to smithereens by PIRA or INLA. Gordon checked under his car every morning and took a different route to and from work each day. He knew a uniformed officer who refused to give his kids a lift anywhere, fearing they might be caught up in an ambush. Marty Jess had been shot in bed next to his hysterical wife. But the vast majority of officers hated keeping a personal protection weapon in the house for fear of an accident involving their children. Alcoholism and depression were common and divorce rates high, along with casualties. The uniforms took the brunt of it, one of the reasons Jackie had opted for Branch work when the opportunity arose.

Undercover with Tyrie's mob, he had never considered the possibility of becoming a republican target. Presumably the Provos didn't know he was RUC, and his position wasn't that high profile in the UDA anyway. He wasn't even recognised as a player by many of the rival UVF.

He'd informed Gordon of the IRA threat, who'd passed it on and E3A, the intelligence division dedicated to republican groups, were looking into it. In the meantime, E4A were conducting static surveillance on his father's house, but when he was out and about, he was on his own. Police manpower couldn't extend to shadowing individual officers in their daily tasks and routines. If it did, the RUC Widow's Association wouldn't have such a burgeoning membership. In any case, the rank and file thought they were surveilling a low-level loyalist in the hope of snatching a Provo hit team.

He thought back over the last weeks and months, recalling victims of the UDA's East Belfast Brigade. Everyone he could think of who'd suffered at UDA hands recently was a local and unionist, loyalist or just didn't give a shit. Shanty, Harold, James Maguire, Shanty's wee girl, Eddie McMaster.

That was it.

But the night Billy savaged Eddie's hand in the cashbox at the pub, a young Catholic fella was shot dead at the junction of Mountpottinger and Albertbridge in East Belfast. Unclaimed, but it had to have been UDA or UVF. That must be it: somehow, Cochrane and Short Strand PIRA had his name and pinned it on him. He was the tit-for-tat hit. Jackie lit a cigarette and had a quick, hungry smoke. He flicked the butt in the froth lapping onto the slipway in front of the cottages, gave the Walther a pat in his pocket, and headed for home.

#

Back in Bendigo Street an hour later, he padded up the stairs and checked in on his dozing father like a parent with a child. Sarah had popped in: there were flowers in the living room and a note on the hall table, asking him to give her a ring and telling him to buy milk. It was a little after eleven. Time to head for the arms dump at Cregagh Glen where he was scheduled to meet Sam Rainey.

They loved all of this, Rainey and the rest. All this cloak and dagger bollocks, creeping around in the middle of the night while the good people of Belfast slept. It made them feel like outlaws, living on the outside.

He pulled out of the street onto the Ravenhill Road, the heater of the car a low roar, and turned right heading out of town.

It was as the Ravenhill joined the Ormeau Road at a Y-shaped junction that he realised he was being followed. A roundabout regulated the traffic coming from the three routes and he completed two circuits, even though the road was empty. The green Sierra followed suit, then began gaining as they straightened out onto the upper Ormeau Road. He breathed out, long and slow, maintaining control. The car was probably stolen and would be found burnt out on waste ground in the morning. He prayed his body wouldn't be in it.

Dropping a gear to force acceleration, Jackie swung left into the Rosetta area, heading back into the east of the city. The Sierra followed about fifteen yards behind, the interior dark, concealing how many were inside. He killed the heater in the car: he needed to think, stay sharp. The sound of the Escort accelerating and shifting gear growled at him. The Sierra followed.

The roads were deserted. Even the customary choppers weren't up and Jackie thought madly that it might be a conspiracy. He slammed the steering wheel with the palm of his hand, spat and muttered to himself like a maniac, and fought a rising panic. His chest was tightening and he felt totally, utterly alone. Aside from the car following silently behind. He barked at himself to get a grip.

Then he grimaced and prayed for a passing police patrol as he approached a T-junction. The eastern ring road sliced through the city like a belt and cut across his current route, leaving him no choice but to turn left onto the one-way system. He came to a hard stop. A white van was approaching from his right on the ring road on the inside lane, the one closest to where Jackie would emerge. No police. The Sierra was slowing gradually behind him, now about ten yards away. The van was moving at speed on the two-lane ring road. It was approaching fast where Jackie sat stationary, waiting to turn onto the lane. The Sierra was coming on steadily, now closing on five yards. A burst of automatic fire could do some real damage at this range.

Jackie shoved the gear into first. The van was almost passing him. The Sierra was almost behind him. The interior of the car behind was still dark.

He prayed the van driver was alert as he stamped on the accelerator and shot into the inside lane. A horn blared and he glimpsed a flash of white shimmer for a moment in his line of sight. As he steadied the wheel he saw the van had swerved into the outside lane, the driver still leaning angrily on his horn. Then Jackie was increasing speed on the ring road, the van braking hard on the outside as he passed it. The Sierra was behind and gunning to stay within range.

His hands gripped the wheel and gear-stick hard. It stopped them from shaking. His heart hammering, he told himself – willed himself – to calm down. He checked the mirror and could see a little more of his pursuers on this well-lit route. There were definitely two men in the front. It was likely that there was a third in the back seat: a typical PIRA team. They were now approaching traffic lights at the junction of the ring road and Castlereagh Road.

The lights were red.

He heard the Sierra revving its engine behind.

There was a slip road on the left with no filter light and he took it faster than he should, hugging the kerb with a squeal of tyres. The Sierra, the driver surprised by the exit on the left, slowed a little to take the turn. There was an angry growl as the pursuit car dropped gear and surged to gain lost ground.

Jackie was approaching the turning onto Ladas Drive, home of Castlereagh Police Station. He could drive right up to the gates. Even ram them. But if he tried that, he could be riddled with bullets by the officers in the observation sangars armed with automatic rifles. If he drove up to the gates, the hit team behind could still strafe his car as they passed. If not, they'd be suspicious of a paramilitary, in their view a killer, seeking sanctuary in the very place where suspects were held. Word would get back to the loyalist paramilitaries, his cover would be blown. He took the turning anyway, and drove at a decent speed with the Sierra now following, again at a distance of about fifteen yards. A taxi passed them. It was the only vehicle he'd seen aside from the van since he'd spotted the tail. He thought of all the work to infiltrate the East Belfast Brigade, the hours spent with Tyrie and his hoods, running with those animals. All for nothing if he sought protection within Castlereagh station.

He passed the police station.

A large 24-hour petrol station stood a short distance ahead on the right. Jackie slowed and turned into the forecourt at the entrance, a couple of taxis and a pizza delivery car standing idle at the pumps, and stopped. He saw the clouds of breath in the chill from a couple of motorists standing at the pumps. He kept the car in gear, his foot poised on the bite of clutch and accelerator as the Sierra turned into the forecourt at the entrance. The harsh neon of the station's sign silhouetted the interior and Jackie saw he had been wrong: it was a four-man team.

He let the clutch out and turned back onto Ladas Drive at speed, continuing towards the Cregagh Road. The Sierra followed but he felt calm now, despite the odds. He knew how many he was up against and he had the edge of less weight in his car. He took the Cregagh, then cut down Ardenlee Avenue back onto the Ravenhill Road. The streets remained empty.

Turning back onto the Ravenhill, Jackie put the Escort to work. The 88 horsepower engine strained in a low gear and approached seventy miles per hour. Jackie knew the Sierra was more powerful, but gambled on its extra weight slowing it down. A distance opened between pursuers and pursued and, as he took the bend leading to the large, ornamental gates of the park, his tyres screaming in protest, the Sierra's lights were two angry insects on the road some hundred or so yards away.

Jackie grabbed a blue football scarf lying on the back seat and was relieved to feel the weight of the 32 ACP Walther PP semi-automatic in his jacket pocket. He jumped from the Escort almost before it came to a complete stop and mercifully didn't have to fiddle with his keys in locking the doors. He didn't want to return to the car and find an explosive inside. If he returned at all. Next to the high gates was a low brick wall topped by railings around head height which circled the park. He took a run at the wall and used it as leverage to get up on the railings and place a knee between the metal spikes, gouging himself, then eased over as the Sierra took the corner.

He sprinted into the park, the football scarf trailing from his right hand like a streamer. His jacket was a darker shade of blue than the scarf, but his jeans were pale; as camouflage went, it was pretty poor. A kids' playground was on the left, a large flat grassy expanse on his right, and no cover. Running on the path into the park interior, there was a distance of about three hundred yards ahead before a clump of large bushes and a cluster of trees. Jackie felt naked, his feet pounding on the concrete to match his heart as he sprinted towards the huge black forms of beech, oak and evergreens ahead. He heard, above the jagged wheeze of his breathing, the sound of a car drive off at speed. One of the team must have left rather than have the stolen vehicle sitting outside the park gates. The fourth man would probably rendezvous with the other three at another entrance on the Ormeau Road side.

Risking a look back, he clocked three figures behind, one just clearing the railings, two still clambering over. Jackie couldn't make out any rifles and assumed they had handguns. The men looked awkward and heavy as they hauled themselves over the metal spikes and he felt a flutter of hope that he might actually come through this. Then he stumbled and collapsed on the hard concrete. He landed on his knees, skinning them for sure, but recovered quickly and set off again. The Walther was mercifully still in his pocket.

The chase was almost soundless in the total still of the park. Not a rustle of wind. Jackie could hear his trainers slapping the path, the angry rasp of his breath and the indistinct hum of a city at sleep. And the grunt of men behind.

Jackie glanced back again and saw three clouds of breath gaining. Ahead was the towering black wall of heavy foliage and shrubbery. There was a tall slim silhouette resembling a gallows too: the park bell, hanging from a high pole, rung each sunset to warn the public that the gates would soon be locked. He willed his legs to move faster, work harder, and used the cold burn of the chill night air in his throat to stay sharp. The closer he got to the treeline, the harder it would be for them to see him. Moving at a crouch he went deeper into the shrubbery, then settled on his haunches and tied the football scarf tightly around his nose and mouth.

He heard the three men come to a cantering halt off to his left. They held their tongues and he knew they were padding as silently as possible on the path. Jackie quietly eased the Walther from his pocket. The triggermen were hiding their positions well and he couldn't account for two at present. But the third was a couple of feet to his left. There was the soft wheeze of a smoker regulating his breathing after a bout of running and Jackie was thankful the scarf was muffling his own breath. The scarf gave him another edge: a small fog of condensation was rising lazily into the night air, drifting up from the gunman's nose and mouth. Jackie's breath was trapped and dissipated by the football scarf.

The first man's white mist of breath was joined by a second. They were silent and likely communicating with hand signals and gestures. Now they were directly in front of him. He could have reached out and touched them at a stretch. Their clothes were just visible through the bushes. One wore blue jeans and a leather jacket and was big but with no gut. The other was in a camouflage jacket with black jeans, the cam pattern straining against a heavy-looking belly. Crouching at hip level, Jackie could open fire and probably hit both at this range, but how decisive the wounds would be was another matter. And he didn't know where the third man was.

He almost yelped when the third man appeared suddenly on his right, again almost within touching distance. This one must have circled around the trees out of sight. He was wiry and wearing a thick black sweater with black jeans. Jackie hugged the gun to his body to stop his hand from shaking.

After a short time, two of the three moved off. The remaining man paced a little and then seemed to decide there was no immediate threat and lit up a cigarette. Jackie made a mental count to two hundred before shifting his position. It seemed to take an age to settle flat on his stomach. Peering under the

225

shrubbery for a view of the surrounding area, he couldn't see the other two triggermen. Either they had pushed further into the interior of the park or were somewhere behind, in the direction from which he'd come. This one, black jeans and sweater, wasn't going anywhere soon.

Jackie had learned patience in his undercover work. Many times he had contemplated quitting, walking into Branch offices and telling them he wanted out of Tyrie's crew. But he had learned to endure. Now in the cold, maintaining a fetal position with a pistol gripped tightly to his body and shaking despite his best efforts, he could wait no longer. It was unbearable, a man standing within touching distance with the intention and means to kill him. He might lie here all night and live until morning, but it was more likely he'd give himself away soon. He had been lucky thus far that it hadn't occurred to the gunmen to search the bushes. Jackie's nerves were at breaking point and he knew that the panic bubbling inside was in danger of erupting. And with panic came loss of control. And then, he knew, he would die. Better to act and take your chances.

He unwrapped the scarf from his face, aching with the effort of controlling his movement and breathing shallowly, and moved a fraction to the left. The gunman dropped the butt of his smoke on the concrete path, so close a spark stung the back of Jackie's hand, now snaking out.

As a boot ground out the fag end, he gripped the man's left ankle with his left hand, hooked his right, still gripping the Walther, around the man's right ankle and yanked hard. The body toppled with a gasp and landed awkwardly on its shoulder. There was a clatter as the killer's pistol skittered across the concrete. Jackie grabbed his scarf and launched himself at the man, now on the ground next to him. He went for the man's face, wedging the scarf into the gunman's mouth. There was a muffled cry and Jackie prayed the others were some distance off. They wrestled, rolling on the path. The man's boots scraped concrete as he kicked and thrashed, Jackie's gun waving madly in the air as the killer gripped his right wrist and pushed the pistol away from them both. Jackie felt sure the others must hear. They were breathing hard and a cloud of breath surrounded them. The man was twisting Jackie's arm inward and he gave it a sudden jerk. Jackie pushed his midsection upwards in an inverted v-shape as a spasm jolted his hand. There was a sharp crack and the killer's left foot exploded with a wet slapping sound. The scarf was still wedged in the man's mouth as his head jolted forward from the pain of the bullet, butting Jackie in the face. The Walther went skating across the path.

There was a shout of 'Declan!' and Jackie stood in time to wipe his stinging eyes and see both of the injured man's companions running towards his position from the direction they had all come a short time before. The direction of the gate and Jackie's car.

There was a flash and another crack, louder and heavier.

There was no choice. Jackie had to run further into the park interior.

The path split in three and he took to the grass between the middle and right trails, where tree cover was heaviest. Here were great horse chestnuts weighed down with leaves and huge willow trees, their branches almost touching the ground. He heard cursing and screaming and hoped the wounded man would force one of the others to abandon pursuit. Declan wouldn't be walking out of the park without help and they would want to get away soon. It was unlikely the shot had attracted much attention as they were already a fair distance from the road, but PIRA always got in and out as quickly as possible.

He stopped to look back rather than risk stumbling on the uneven ground and saw that he was right. He had lost sight of Declan and another man in the murk of the inner park but the man in leather jacket and blue jeans was giving chase. He raised his gun at the sight of Jackie. Jackie took off again.

He'd run, walked, biked and played in this park countless times as a child. He'd fumbled with girls as a teenager in the very bushes where he'd hidden from the triggermen. It seemed surreal that he was now running for his life through the trees and shrubs where he'd played at soldier as a boy. Adrenaline coursed through his body and he felt no pain in his nose from the head-butt, but he tripped on a huge tree root erupting from the grass at the foot of a massive elm. To his own amazement he didn't go down but stumbled, pitching forward with his body parallel to the ground, before regaining control of his stride. They were approaching another large thicket of foliage partly hiding an angular black hulk rearing against the Prussian blue of the night sky: the old park-keeper's house, now derelict. As he reached the large brick house now fallen to ruin, he vaulted the waist-high, rusted garden gate.

The house was the stuff of children's nightmares. A decayed husk, all sharp pointed roof and hollow-eyed windows, inky black inside. The garden was wild and overgrown, a long-dead paddling pool discarded in a corner and a washing line still attached to one pole, the line trailing down and disappearing into the long grass. Jackie had to step over beer cans and bricks, ensuring he didn't stand awkwardly on the rubble and go over on his ankle. He could hear the gunman approaching at a cautious pace and yanked the washing line from the pole. It gave with an angry snap. It was answered by a loud, sharp crack. He ducked into the grass, easing his jacket off, leaving him in a grey T-shirt. His breathing was an exhausted rasp. He saw the large man step into the garden. The man would see him in a second. Jackie's jacket hung from his right hand. He almost laughed when he saw the killer's face shrouded in a balaclava, a walking cliché. The man caught sight of the grey T-shirt and turned, the gun coming to bear on Jackie's chest. Jackie spat an obscenity and threw his jacket at the gunman. The man fired three shots wildly, the muzzle flare tracing a short arc in the dark. Two bullets shredded the jacket. The third missed Jackie by inches; he felt the whisper of the round as it passed him. Then he ran at the man, getting in close. With the gunman momentarily confused, Jackie put everything he could into a shoulder charge. He connected, winding the man. Both of them went sprawling in the long grass. Then, gripping the rope, he encircled the gunman's neck with the washing line and moved awkwardly behind the killer. At first he thought the thin line wouldn't find purchase but, after a moment, it bit into the wool of the balaclava. There was a rasp as the gunman's windpipe felt the sudden, crushing pressure. The killer dropped his weapon and clawed at the line.

Jackie grimaced and shoved a knee into the man's back. They both sank slowly down in the grass and he kept pressure on the man's spine, using his knee for leverage as he felt the life seeping from his pursuer. His fingers felt as though they might be severed as the taut rope gouged them, but his mind was blank. Something had taken over, some animal rage, and he couldn't stop himself killing this man. Even if he wanted to.

Then two large shadows appeared and rough voices ordered him to stop. He saw more guns, one of which he dimly recognised. The new arrivals levelled their weapons at him and shouted. Their voices were a loud, brusque clamour in the stillness of the park and he snapped back to reality. A Ruger Security Six revolver. Gannex jackets. A Heckler & Koch MP5 sub-machine gun. The taller of the two policemen leaned forward and gently but firmly prised the rope from his hands.

CHAPTER 26

Saturday

'Jesus, Jackie. What have you done?'

A hand, shaking slightly, hovers over Sarah's mouth and he can see she's swallowing hard. He wonders if he shouldn't have let things be and not called. But if things go badly later, he doesn't want to never have seen his last remaining blood relative again, his big sis. He wonders at the emotion welling in him when they've hardly seen each other over the last two decades. But, blood is blood.

Even the dog walkers are sitting this one out as the weather has taken a turn for the worse. The sky is so filthy-grey it looks like the Almighty has spilt ash from His fag end all over it, and the clouds are straining hard for a heavy downpour. Jackie and Sarah sit on a bench in the grounds of Stormont Parliament Buildings in the late afternoon while the city gets its dinners ready and checks the night's TV schedule. Up on the hill to their left sits the Portland stone facade with its six classical pillars, one for each county of Northern Ireland. Formerly Parliament buildings, now home of the power-sharing executive. The statue of Carson, from this distance, looks like he's giving a two-fingered salute to the mucky weather.

Jackie gives her a lop-sided grin that spasms into a grimace as his bruised cheek rages at him. She flinches in sympathy.

'There's nothing permanent. I've had worse,' he says, pointing to his face, 'except for my nose. It hurts like hell.'

All Sarah can muster is, 'Oh, Jackie.'

He takes her hand in his, shifts to face her on the bench and says, 'I thought when I came home for Da's funeral – I hoped – the past would be left well alone. It hasn't been. It's caught up to me and matters are coming to a head. Tonight.'

'What does that mean?'

'It means I'm going to put an end to some things.'

'Some things, or someone?'

His stomach lurches: she thinks him capable of that. Then he realises that he *is* capable of that. Just ask Rab Simpson. Danny McCardle too.

At least she doesn't know. She never will, if he has anything to do with it.

'I'm just going to take care of some stuff from the past. You were never really touched by my job when I was in Bendigo Street with Da. I didn't want either of youse involved and there's no reason for that to change now.'

'But we were involved, Jackie, whether you wanted us to be or not. How could we not be, knowing what you were living with, going through? I'm your sister, for God's sake. He was your dad. We both loved you.' She says, quickly, 'Love you.'

'Sarah, I know it wasn't easy on you carrying what I did while I was undercover. And then you had to deal with the fallout when I had to disappear.'

'Da was fine when you left.' She sees his expression and adds, 'I mean he coped.'

'Coping wasn't exactly his strong point. If he had a strength it was the amount of abuse his liver could take. I thought he'd completely collapse after I had to disappear. More out of fear of Tyrie and Simpson than anything.'

'You think he was scared of that shower of cowboys?' says Sarah, laughing. It's a hard, bitter sound. 'Sure, he thought they were scared of him, the father of Jackie Shaw. You'll never know how proud Dad was of you. Me too.'

She squeezes his damaged hand.

'To live with those animals and risk what you did? There's not many could do it, Jackie. But you did. And because of who you were, because you were a policeman, Da never thought for one second that crowd would touch him if they knew the truth. For all their violence he knew them for the cowards they are.'

'It's a quaint thought,' says Jackie. He isn't sure that Rab was a coward. That flavour of psycho isn't really scared of anything. Billy, he doesn't know. But he'll find out in a couple of hours. 'But I didn't *talk* to him enough, Sarah. I didn't trust him. I never told him anything because I didn't trust him.' He looks at her with a frown. 'I thought he might speak out of turn in a bar some night and get me killed, maybe himself and you, too. I thought he was just a drunk.'

'He was a drunk,' says Sarah, 'but he was your dad and he'd have done anything for you. Anything to protect you.'

She can see that he's retreating into his head, and she knows that isn't always a healthy place for him to be. She shakes his hands to bring him out of himself.

'He told me once, you came into some pub drunk, ready for murder. He said a couple of times he was worried you were doing things that didn't sit right with you, or you were fighting with yourself over something. In his way, he tried to calm you down, or take a bit of the stress off. But he was never good at expressing himself, especially after Mum passed.' Sarah fishes in her bag for a tissue. 'He apologised to me, you know. When he knew he was dying. He said he was sorry that he couldn't leave much behind other than the house, but he was glad that Tom had done well and we were okay financially.'

She wipes her eyes, but the tissue is already damp from the drizzle enveloping them.

'He talked about you. How he had nothing to pass on to you. No heirlooms. But then he smiled and said he hoped the one thing he might have passed on to you was Belfast.' Her brow furrows. 'The Belfast he remembered. As it was and could be. I think that was it.'

Thoughts of a car ride through the city and stories of Ma Copley and 'Stormy' Weather swim through Jackie's mind. The Markets, Sandy Row, the Shankill, and his da sitting next to him, sharing his past and that of the city. And the story of a beating at the hands of the Army and a moment of kindness from a republican gunman.

Jackie is blinking hard, trying to focus on the sodden ground at his feet. There's nothing he can think to say. Sarah wraps her arms around him and hugs him tightly. They rock back and forth on the bench and he blurts out, 'I'm sorry, I'm sorry,' over and over. It almost hurts more when his sister tells him it's okay, she loves him, he'll always be her brother, no matter what.

'Why don't you just turn away from all this, Jackie? Come home with me. We'll have dinner, you, me, Thomas and the kids and you can stay in our house. We'll spend the day together tomorrow and you can fly back to England in the evening. In a wee while we'll come over and see you.'

He smiles and pulls away from her a little to look into her eyes. The fact is he can't because, if the past has been festering away for twenty years, it could fester for twenty more. And he can't leave family here without taking care of Tyrie. He has to know that chapter is closed. But he hates having to disappoint her again.

'No, Sarah. I can't. And you can't be touched by this.'

'I *am* touched by this, Jackie. I'm your sister, how can I not be? And Dad was touched by it too back then, but that was okay. That was okay for both of us, because back then it seemed the right thing to do. It seemed necessary. But now? Can't you just let it go?'

Maybe she's right. If he just disappeared again, would the machine grind on, Tyrie and Cochrane ruling their own little fiefdoms and the rest of the country left at peace? Or would Sarah and her family suffer? Billy was never interested in targeting families, and he'd done what was required: Rab Simpson is dead, by his hands.

But what about Cochrane? Jackie killed one of his too. Would he be benevolent and leave Jackie's family be? And Eileen? If Billy ever found out about Jackie's affair with her there'd be hell to pay; would Tyrie turn on Sarah and hers? Who would bring Tyrie to account for what he did? Hartley? MI5 weren't interested in prosecution, only information, 'keeping a lid on'. They wouldn't be interested in protecting Jackie's kin, either, if there wasn't an angle for them involved. No, the past has to be laid to rest. This has to be done.

'I'm sorry, Sarah.'

He expects her to rail against him. Instead, she looks sad and resigned and small.

'It was twenty years ago. You're twenty years older, you and the rest. But never the wiser. Men in this country hardly ever learn and they never grow up. And it's the women who are left with the consequences.'

She's right. The number of widows across Northern Ireland. The number of kids raised by a single mother. He thinks if his father had gone first, his mother would have coped better than Sam ever did, God love him. Billy has a wife and two kids. Cochrane is a husband.

There is nothing he can say, so he stands and manages, 'Come on. I'll see you for that Sunday dinner tomorrow,' because he doesn't want to leave with a silence between them.

The rain is gathering strength now. She stands wearily and hooks her arm through his. They walk back to the austere gates of the Stormont estate, their cars parked just beyond. Both of them are soaking. She doesn't comment on his change of car, although he knows she will have noticed. She has always been sharp in her observations, but perhaps she has reached a point where she would rather not know any more.

They embrace below the giant stone posts and black and gold wrought iron, all flames and lions. The gates to the kingdom. She's crying. It is almost camouflaged by the rain.

'Be careful Jackie.'

Then she gets into her car and pulls out into the busy current of early evening traffic.

#

The Claddagh ring comes off his finger with a sharp protest, biting the lacerated skin of his finger. He breathes in with a hiss as it comes away, and drops to his haunches next to freshly turned soil, a rich earthy musk coming from the ground. Roselawn Cemetery is empty and the light has all but faded. Jackie is self-conscious as he stares at the grave, trying to envisage the man lying six feet below. He hadn't had a chance to look at the open casket before the funeral. Hadn't really wanted to because all of the memories that had survived the bullshit filter in his head were of a much younger Sammy Shaw. Fishing off Ardglass Harbour. Kicking a football. Aborted camping trips in rain-lashed Tullymore Forest. A Northern Irish childhood in the company of a loving father.

He almost loses his balance as he grasps for a small stick to his right, really no more than a twig. Then he places the Claddagh ring heart-down on the earth and, his tongue poking out in concentration, positions the end of the stick on the flat silver.

Splinters of memory: a thin sharp object and Rab Simpson's gaping mouth. He drives them away, shaking his head and whispering curses. Then he leans down hard on the stick, pushing the ring deep into the sodden soil so that his fingers are coated in dirt when he's finished burying the silver with his father. He's glad it's still raining as he raises his face to the sky, the fresh fall of drizzle washing the tears from his cheeks. Then he rises with a groan and walks towards the car, a short clamber over the cemetery gates away.

#

Around him, the city is gearing up for a Saturday night on the town. Packs of young men and women are entering off licences, stocking up on early-evening lubrication before they hit the bars and clubs later in the night. Fathers and families are tripping out of takeaways with Chinese, Indian or deep-fried food, the Saturday-night treat while they hunker down in front of the TV. In the four quarters of Belfast local pubs are filling ready for the latest instalments of the ongoing soap operas of life in the close-knit communities of Sydenham, Falls, Shankill, Tigers Bay and New Lodge. And Ravenhill.

Jackie parks on the Ballymiscaw Road, a thread climbing to the rolling Craigantlet Hills. He sits in darkness with the city spread before him. Belfast is a huge, shimmering wishbone, clinging to the river and branching out to embrace the sprawling swell of Belfast Lough on its Antrim and Down shores. He can see the glass dome of Victoria Square, lit from within. The glass and steel tombstone of the Obel building sits across from the Odyssey Centre and new Titanic Centre. And towering over them all stand the giants: Samson and Goliath, the massive gantry cranes in the shipyard.

Jackie inserts his sim card into his mobile again and checks for texts or missed calls. Nothing. He throws Rab's mobile in the grass next to the car and puts its sim card into a plastic bag lying on the passenger seat. He performs a last-minute check that he's got everything he needs.

Then he is ready. He puts the car in first, eases onto the road and begins the steady descent into the east of the city.

CHAPTER 27

1993

Having taken the rope from his hands, the tall cop proceeded to shove Jackie to the ground, giving him a mouthful of earth. He heard a pained grunt, probably the IRA gunman getting similar treatment, then a bored, rehearsed declaration from the policeman that they were RUC, and the legal warning every peeler learns by heart.

Jackie heard the hoarse rasp of cuffs being tightened. A few moments later he got the same treatment. There was a swish of feet trampling overgrown grass and the babble of voices some way off. He heard the low squawk of police radio and then he was being lifted by several strong hands and shoved towards the gate of the abandoned garden. A couple of uniforms were milling around in the area of the park next to the deserted house. Then a man in a suit and overcoat materialised out of the dark.

Gordon Orr said, 'Are you all right?'

Jackie sighed in pure relief. He nodded as Gordon gestured for a uniform to take the handcuffs off again.

'Sorry about that,' said Gordon. 'Just a wee show for the other boys we've lifted. No reason to let them know you're a cop if they don't already.'

'No bother. Your timing couldn't have been better.'

'For you or the other fella?'

Jackie rubbed his right wrist where the cuffs had gouged into the flesh. It was a fair question, and begged another: would he have taken a life if the cavalry hadn't shown up? As far as he'd been concerned, only one of them was walking back out of that long, wild grass. He might have killed the first gunman with a second shot if the Walther hadn't gone flying. It was a question he didn't want to contemplate. He was relieved he hadn't taken a life.

'Who are the uniforms?'

'HMSU.'

Jackie was thankful there hadn't been any further violence. Headquarters Mobile Support Unit was trained by the SAS, hardly known for their restraint.

'The other three?'

'In the Land Rovers over by the Park Road entrance. We picked up the walking wounded you left back on the path with his mate. The wheelman was idling by the entrance on Park Road when we pulled up. Hard stop.'

So they'd rammed him. Jackie wondered what damage an armoured Land Rover would do to a Ford Sierra.

'Has it created a crowd? Crime scene?' He worried that word might filter back to the lower Ravenhill, where his car was still parked at the gates.

'A couple of drunk gawkers but nothing major. At this time of night,' Gordon checked his watch, 'the good people of Belfast are in their beds.'

It was a little after one a.m. Jackie felt very tired. 'And my car?'

'Unmolested, where you left it.'

Gordon took him gingerly by the arm and led him to a bench. Uniforms continued to mill around them.

'Aren't you wondering why we're here, Jackie?'

He had been so glad to see the unit and Gordon in particular that the thought hadn't crossed his mind. He said as much.

'Anonymous call, Confidential Telephone,' said Gordon. 'Referred to E Division at Castlereagh. You were named as a target for PIRA. It went through to Special Branch East in case E3A had any relevant intelligence on IRA hit lists. That's when the

Branch boys on duty heard your name and one, my superior, re-alised the target was one of our own. He called me, a Land Rover patrol was diverted to your father's house and, thank God, saw a suspect vehicle parked at the gates of the park. When they relayed the licence number your name came up on the database and we sent in the MSU boys.'

'And here we are,' said Jackie. 'Any idea who called it in?'

'None. We'll have more information soon, but the officer who took the call has been pulled for some other detail for an hour or two. Any idea why you're being targeted by the Provisionals, assuming they don't know you're a police officer?'

'This is just a theory, but a young man was shot dead a few weeks ago on the Albertbridge Road. A young Catholic. I'm thinking James Cochrane took it to be one of Tyrie's crew was the shooter. My name must have come up and maybe they thought I was a soft target in comparison to Billy or Rab.'

'It's possible. We'll get the Provos back to Castlereagh for in-terrogation and see what we can get out of them. In the meantime, I can pull you if you want. Just say the word.'

Christ, thought Jackie, just one word and this would all be over. He'd be back at the Branch, probably transferred out of Belfast for operational reasons and his own safety. He could begin learning how to be a human being again. No more living life as a shadow.

But what would happen to his father? There'd be questions, and Tyrie's mob wouldn't be gentle in the asking. The job would remain unfinished and the whole pack would be free to ruin the area and its people. There'd be more lives taken or destroyed. And he'd never see or touch Eileen again. He laughed at himself. It wasn't until he caught Gordon's concerned look that he re-alised it had been aloud.

'Sorry, Gordon, I'm just a bit shaken. Can these boys be trusted to keep their mouths shut?'

'HMSU? Oh, aye. We'll have them sign the Official Secrets Act and scare the bollocks off them. They've barely had a look at you.'

'Then I'll be all right. If anything, this might strengthen my position within Tyrie's crew, local folk hero and all.' He stood. 'I was meant to be meeting Rainey at the arms bed in Cregagh Glen. He'll hardly be there now but it might be an idea to check. Confirm he's at home if he isn't up the glen. If he wasn't named in the call, he's probably not a target, but it wouldn't hurt to make sure.'

'Will do. You sure you can maintain your cover?'

'Aye, we're lucky this was contained in the park.'

'What if your car was spotted at the gates? Local UDA won't think that's sus?'

'I'll just tell them the truth. I thought I had a tail, parked at the gates and hopped it into the park. Rainey's going to want an explanation why I didn't turn up at the bed but they know I'm on a hit list anyway.'

A uniformed officer approached them. They discussed forensics: they would be in and out of the park before it opened to the public again. There was speculation as to how contained the situation on Park Road was. A chopper was now up, hovering at a discreet height and distance, seemingly over the Stranmillis area across the river but actually monitoring the park area through the powerful military surveillance equipment on board. The players were arriving at Castlereagh and word got through that, through heat-imaging equipment on another helicopter flying over the hills, it was apparent Rainey wasn't at Cregagh Glen. A team on the ground was finishing up a sweep of the area too. A fly past would establish if he was likely at home through a count of warm bodies in the house.

'And we need to process your weapon,' said the uniform, 'as you discharged it tonight. It's been recovered with the other firearms but I can't return it to you at the minute. It's been taken to the lab at Belvoir by one of the back-up units.'

'No problem,' said Jackie. 'I suppose I'll have to go to Castlereagh now for statements if I'm to be back on the road in the morning. I'll go in through the back door incognito and I can pick it up there or draw another weapon when I'm done with the debrief.'

Gordon nodded and the uniform strolled away with the practised insouciance of law enforcement the world over.

'Do you want a lift in my car,' said Gordon, 'after you drop yours at your father's?'

Jackie lit a long-awaited cigarette and drew the smoke long and slow down into his lungs. Poison never tasted so good, he thought. 'I'm all right, Gordon. I'll drive back to my da's to look in on him, see he's okay, then drive over to Castlereagh myself. There'll be nobody about at this time of the night.'

Gordon looked uneasy but gave a curt nod and, hands on knees, rose wearily from the bench. 'Some Branch guys have arrived, men I trust. I'll tell them to shadow you from a distance.' He held up a hand in anticipation of an objection. 'Better to be safe than sorry.'

Jackie, exhausted, relented. 'Aye, all right,' he said. They strolled to the path where an ugly, clumsy struggle had been fought less than an hour ago. Jackie looked at the rough surface and thought how easily his body could be sprawled there now, nothing more than a precursor to a chalk outline. He caught Gordon's elbow and said, 'Thanks, mate.'

'Somebody was on your side tonight,' said Gordon, eyes rolling to the heavens.

'I'm just glad you were.'

They left him to walk back to the gates alone. When he looked back he could see nothing but the blur of heavy shadow, reaching into the sky, of the treeline, but he knew they were there, watching.

It was an effort to haul himself back over the gates. The car coughed to life and Jackie drove the short distance back to Bendigo Street. He parked a couple of doors down from his father's front door as the space in front was occupied by a hatchback. Sticking out like a sore thumb among the smaller cars of the neighbours, a Range Rover was near the corner of the street at the Ravenhill Road end. A flicker of annoyance: this was probably the Branch detail, most likely E4A surveillance men. They used Rovers when on jobs in the surrounding countryside. Could they be more obvious? He felt uneasy as he clambered out of his car, now without a weapon. As he approached his father's house, he caught a flutter of movement in the Range Rover. If they were his babysitters, they'd signal, maybe flash a torch or interior light.

Then the Rover rocked slightly. Someone was moving inside. The wise move was probably to continue as though unconcerned, keep the vehicle in his peripheral vision. But Jackie was tired, his nerves beyond frayed. So he stopped and squinted, staring hard at the car. The interior was too dark to discern shapes.

He knew the Provisionals rarely had a second team on hits. They lacked manpower, due to the small cell structure they employed. He began walking to the house again, fumbling for his door key. His heart was moving through the gears and he fought to calm his movements. As he reached the house he heard the hollow click of the Range Rover's door opening. Adrenaline began to kick in again and he turned. Jackie wouldn't put his father in danger. He would fight, rush whoever was slamming the driver's door shut. If it was a plain-clothes detail, they'd identify themselves. If not, it was one-on-one.

An irate voice hissed, 'Where the fuck have you been?'

The venom was a verbal slap. He peered through the dim light in the street. Tommy strode up to him with a full head of steam.

'Why weren't you at Cregagh Glen? Rainey sat up there for well over an hour waiting on you and the fat fucker started bending my ear when you didn't show.'

Jackie spat the words. 'Somebody was following me: the Provos, if Ruger's warning is true. I had to shake them off.'

He'd only spoken with Tommy a couple of times. Now the quiet man tutted, a sharp spit of annoyance. It sparked something in Jackie, the irritated sigh that followed like flint on tinder.

'Sure, I'm sorry my need for self-preservation held up my date with Ruger. What's he got for me, some out of commission piece of shit that'll misfire anyway? Too bad the Provos didn't shoot me the night and save youse all the bother of staying up past your fucking bedtime.'

He walked up to Tommy and squared up. 'And what're you doing here? Shouldn't you be back over in Mount Vernon playing soldiers with your mates in North Belfast? Why the fuck do we see you over here at all?'

Tommy, seething, hissed, 'Keep your voice down, Shaw. Don't want to wake half the street, your alco da included.' A finger drilled its way to Jackie's chest. 'And watch your mouth. I've people over here to watch my back.'

Jackie had an image of Tommy's arm around Rab's shoulders in the Tartan Star Club.

Then another, third body was there between them. It grabbed Tommy's shoulders and gave a hoarse bark at the man. There was a mumbled dialogue of a couple of seconds, a brief shuffle of bodies, and then Danny Moore turned to face Jackie with an easy grin on his open face. They hadn't met since the surveillance on James Cochrane's home and he looked leaner and more confident than when he'd been working shifts at the bus station.

'All right, Jackie, what about ye?' he said.

Jackie gaped, open-mouthed for a beat. He'd suspected Rab or Tyrie might have forced Danny's hand in helping them out when they were watching Cochrane's house. While Shanty had told him of Moore's involvement in his punishment, Jackie never dreamt the man would be along riding shotgun with Tommy.

'Danny, what are you doing?'

'Helping out again. We're fellow soldiers now.'

Jackie flashed a look at Tommy, watching for a snigger or roll of the eyes, but the man was already stalking back to the Range Rover.

'That's shocking. About the Provos,' said Danny, 'but we'll strike back for you. Tonight.'

'So you're in the organisation now? I mean a full member?'

'Aye, had my ceremony this morning, oath and all. And here's the best of it. We're going to hit Cochrane. Now.'

'Now? It's two in the morning. When was this planned? When did Billy sign off on it? And where is Billy? Where's Rab?'

'Waiting for us. Get in the car and we'll explain on the way.'

It had been a long, fraught night and Jackie prayed the Branch undercover surveillance team was monitoring them. He had shot a man and almost killed another with his bare hands, things he hadn't thought himself capable of. He knew every policeman, every soldier, questioned whether they could react if faced with a threat to life – and now he knew. He thought Danny Moore was no threat, but Tommy was another matter. Yet, if this hit was really going to happen tonight, he had to go along, because he had to prevent the murder. And that meant he had no choice but to hunch his shoulders, gesture for Moore to go first, and follow him to the car.

#

244

'The car,' said Jackie, 'whose is it?'

'Fucked if I know,' said Danny.

They were approaching the Holywood Road. The Range Rover was stolen, of course. They'd picked it up somewhere in the affluent belt of housing that formed the Balmoral area of South Belfast. Jackie was in the back, Moore driving and Tommy brooding silently in the front passenger seat. Jackie couldn't turn to see the view out the rear window and the mirror was at an awkward angle. He had no idea if his shadowers from the force had seen him climb into the Range Rover and were currently tailing them. They could be monitoring him from the air now; just because you didn't see the chopper didn't mean you weren't under surveillance. But he couldn't shake the niggle of doubt festering in his mind at the absence of the three major players: Sam Rainey, Rab Simpson and Billy Tyrie. They passed a brooding slab of concrete encircled with anti-blast bomb fencing with its huge iron gate: Strandtown police station. No sight ever looked more inviting to Jackie at that moment. He quizzed Moore on the plan of action.

Danny had overheard a couple of co-workers at the bus station, republican sympathisers, talking about an Irish dancing competition being held in the town of Portaferry tomorrow. As the men chattered, James Cochrane's name was mentioned. Cochrane had a niece who he doted on, a girl in her early teens who was a gifted dancer. She had entered the competition and Cochrane was staying in a small B&B near Portaferry tonight in order to attend the competition in the morning in support of his niece. It was the perfect opportunity to hit him. He'd have a minimal guard, and getaway would be easy as there was a scribble of country roads in the area, some not on the map, to use as escape routes. Rab, Billy and Rainey were going to meet them in Holywood at a small disused factory owned by a loyalist sympathiser on the shore of Belfast Lough. There, Rainey would arm them for the job. Danny had been promoted to the ranks of the UDA proper in recognition of his work in setting up the operation.

It was plausible and a golden opportunity to take out a high-ranking PIRA officer with a minimum of fuss. The shooting might not be discovered for days if Cochrane was the only guest in the B&B and they abducted the owners – or worse. And it was also going to be a bitch of a job to stop them carrying out the operation, if he was on his own. Even these jokers could get the job done in a lonely area of the country with an isolated target.

He cursed that he was so tired, and his judgement so blurred, by the trauma of the night and lack of sleep. A few hours ago, he was sitting by the water in a quiet fishing village, rather than calculating his chances of survival after one failed attempt on his life.

'These boys you overheard in the depot, Danny,' said Jackie. 'Do you have names for them?'

Moore flicked a glance at Tommy, who hunkered down further in the passenger seat.

'Just first names. Patrick and Hugh.'

'Local, from the Short Strand?'

'Not sure, Jackie. I only know them to see, like.'

'But you know their first names.'

'They're on their lanyards.'

'Youse all wear lanyards in the depot? Drivers usually have a name badge.'

'Aye, depot staff who don't go out on the runs wear lanyards.'

Jackie nodded. Danny's eyes sought him out occasionally in the rearview mirror as they approached the lights at the end of the Holywood Road that would lead them onto the dual carriageway heading out of the city. Danny had resolutely avoided his gaze while answering his questions. Now he kept stealing glances at him in the back seat.

'I don't remember you wearing a lanyard when I picked you up on Mountpottinger,' said Jackie.

The eyes darted ahead again.

'I take it off when I leave the gates. Can't wait to get rid of it.' A snigger, nervous.

'But you still had your uniform on. Couldn't you change that as well? Youse must have lockers in the depot.'

'Enough!' Tommy's bark was like a rifle shot. 'What are you, a fucking peeler?'

'Fuck off!' said Jackie.

'Lads,' said Danny, 'c'mon, now. There's no need.'

'There's every need,' said Tommy. 'This cunt never fit in. He's never been one of us.'

'So what am I doing here?' said Jackie.

He sounded a little desperate and was angry at himself. 'Well?' he said, more controlled.

Tommy sank down in the passenger seat again. The tall lights lining the central reservation swept over the windscreen like a visual metronome. The road was a straight shot from East Belfast to the commuter town of Holywood. After a time, an Army patrol in green Land Rovers, rather than RUC battleship grey, passed them heading into town. There was no other traffic. They drove by Palace Barracks, the largest military base in Belfast. Jackie watched as it slid past, a cross between an industrial and housing estate with observation towers and helicopter pads as added extras. Again, he hoped they were being surveilled from afar by a Lynx, although he hadn't seen or heard one.

'So, Danny,' he said, 'why have you joined up?'

'Are we getting a fucking job interview now?' muttered Tommy.

But Danny said, 'I want to do my bit, Jackie.'

'Your bit of what?'

'To defend Ulster, like.'

'From what?'

'The taigs.'

'You work with the taigs, don't you, in the depot? Do most of those boys look like we need defending from them?'

'You know what I mean, Jackie.'

'Sorry, mate, I don't.'

Tommy said, 'He's joined to keep Ulster British. And he'll do anything to make that happen.' The needle in his voice almost pricked Jackie as he sat in the back.

'Do you think you could kill someone for Ulster, Danny? Like what's going to happen tonight?'

'Here, I've just joined, you know.'

'Because you are killing Cochrane, aren't you?'

'I'm not telling you again,' said Tommy.

'I mean, you're setting him up–'

'Shut up!'

'Even if your finger's not on the trigger, Dan–'

'Shut up, Shaw!'

'You're just as responsible for his death.'

Tommy roared, 'I swear, I'll fucking shoot you now if you don't leave it!'

'As opposed to shoot me later?'

For the first time, the quiet man turned in his seat to face Jackie. The harsh lighting of the carriageway sent bright muzzle flashes across his eyeballs in the dark. Tommy probably had a gun somewhere on him. The man was calculating now, most likely weighing up the damage if he did put a bullet in Jackie's head there and then. For his part, Jackie was calculating his chances of walking away if he flung himself from the Range Rover at forty miles per hour on a tarmac surface. Danny was checking activity in the back seat in the mirror and stealing glances at Tommy next to him. They were approaching Holywood and there was a collection of rooftops and spires to the right. A set of traffic lights were looming up ahead, a stone railway bridge just beyond on the left. Tommy shifted in his seat.

Danny said, 'All right, it's a fair question. If I thought they were opposed to the organisation, and a danger to the organisation, then maybe I could do it.'

'Do what?'

'Jackie, come on.'

'*Do what*, Danny?'

'Fucking shoot him. Now turn here,' said Tommy.

They turned left, under the stone bridge and onto a narrow road, which curved to hug the shoreline of the lough. Tommy gave brief orders as they passed a bar, a post office and a couple of old terraced houses and drew up in front of a small factory. A sign above the door identified it as *Down Shire Litho Ltd*, a printing company.

They got out of the car and Tommy walked to the front door, sorting through keys on a chain. Danny brought up the rear. There was a short, narrow corridor on the other side of the door; no more than two of them could stand side-by-side. No one bothered to lock the front door as Danny closed it behind them. They walked down the corridor towards a closed door, the upper half a large pane of frosted glass with a harsh light burning through it. Jackie took in two rooms of office space on the right and two small storage rooms on the left. All were deserted, although a couple of chairs and a metal rubbish bin were left in one of the offices. The little they could see of the interiors was thanks to the lighting from the glass window of the door at the end of the corridor.

Tommy stopped and gave Danny a brief look. Jackie was sandwiched between the two men but he fancied his chances against Moore if pushed. However, if Tommy were armed he wouldn't make it to the front entrance.

Tommy opened the door to reveal the shell of what had once

been a printing works. Strip-lighting gave the room a cold appearance: more empty shelving, chipped and pitted long wooden tables, hardened ink spills on the floor. And standing next to a couple of heavy metal rollers, giving them an aimless kick while dragging on a cigarette, stood Sam 'Ruger' Rainey.

Jackie let a little of the tension seep from his body. The quartermaster was here. They were to be armed, probably with guns out back or in a van parked outside. Rab and Billy must be on their way. Now he just had to find a way to delay or abort the attempt on Cochrane.

Then Tommy drew a handgun from his waistband and shot Rainey through the shoulder.

The big man made a strange gulping sound and burning embers from his cigarette bounced off his tracksuit top as he staggered with the punch of the bullet. Jackie was shoved hard in the back and stumbled forward. Tommy cursed as Rainey refused to go down, and shot him in the stomach. Ruger grunted and collapsed in on himself, ending up in a curled heap on the floor. Jackie turned to find Danny Moore pointing a revolver at him. Rainey's cigarette lay smouldering next to a crusty tin of ink. The report of the handgun reverberated around the empty space.

'You, on your knees.'

Jackie was looking at Danny and felt a moment of confusion as the man's mouth remained still. Then he realised the order came from Tommy. He turned back to look at him.

'On your knees. Now.'

Jackie slowly lowered himself. Rainey was rocking slightly as he lay on the floor but was silent. Shock was probably setting in, fast.

'Tommy?' said Jackie.

'Grass,' said Tommy. He gestured at Rainey with the gun, then spat a gob of phlegm on the big man.

'And you, Danny?' said Jackie. 'How long have you been in on this?'

Danny remained silent.

'Since yesterday,' said Tommy.

'How do you know Ruger's a grass?' said Jackie. 'He's one of Billy's closest friends.'

Tommy said, 'Mount Vernon. This fat fucker's up there all the time, shagging that wee whore of his. Billy's thought there's a grass in Ravenhill for a while. That's why I was brought in: internal security, better if I'm not local. Gives me a clear perspective.'

He leaned against one of the pillars, folding his arms loosely with the gun dangling from his right hand.

'When the Cochrane hit was called off it confirmed the Brits or the peelers must have a source. Billy cooked up another, bogus hit and fed it to Rainey. Lo and behold, the security forces set up shop in the Fenian bastard's street. That's when we knew it was him.'

He nodded at the body on the floor. Jackie could hear a low, wheezing moan.

'So we watched his wee girl's house. Followed him from it a couple of times. He drove out to Nutt's Corner in Antrim, always late at night. Jumped in and out of different cars, met different men, always in pairs. One night, we recognised an RUC detective from CID. It just confirmed what we already knew. Two nights ago we called in on his girl, had a chat with her.' A leer sloped across Tommy's face. 'She's still alive because she didn't know what he was up to.'

'How do you know? Maybe she played youse.'

'After the treatment she got, we'd know if she was talking shite. So here we are.'

'And why am I here? Am I a grass as well?'

'I don't know,' said Tommy, 'are you?'

'Catch a fucking grip. Sure I didn't know about the second Cochrane hit until it was already aborted. Danny knew more about it than me.'

Tommy shook his head.

'No, he didn't. We never told him. Like I said, Billy just made it up to check on Rainey. But you will keep using words like "aborted". And you will keep asking questions like in the car. You sound an awful lot like a fucking peeler.'

'If I was, would I have broken Peter Rafferty's kneecaps? Would I have gone on donation runs on the Cregagh and Woodstock?'

'Well, there's the problem. You stopped Rab doing his job on that fucker owned the shop on the Cregagh. And Rab does love his job.'

Jackie knew he wasn't getting out of the room alive unless he could take control of the situation. Rainey was as good as dead; there was nothing he could do for him. Moore was a new recruit; this level of violence would be frightening to him. Danny was like most of the UDA, striving to be the big man and playing at soldiers, but essentially a coward relying on the protection of the pack. Tommy was the threat.

He tried another gambit. 'Where's Rab?'

'On the road back to Belfast by now. He brought this grass bastard out here, told him there was a meeting. When he heard me at the front door he'll have told Rainey he was popping out the back for a piss, then got in another car and driven off. Essentially, he was never here.'

'Does Billy know about this?'

'About him,' Tommy said, kicking Rainey, 'yes. About you, not yet. But Rab can spin it. You were involved with Rainey. You turned up hoping to save your mate, you had to be dealt with. Billy's known Rab a long time, he'll believe him. And Rab's a lot more valuable to us than you ever will be.'

Jackie said over his shoulder, 'And what makes you think you won't end up like me, Danny? They've nothing on me, no proof I'm a grass or a threat. But Rab doesn't like me, so I have to go. No rhyme or reason to it.'

Silence from behind. Tommy was watching Danny dispassionately.

Jackie said, 'Do the wrong thing, say the wrong thing and you'll be in my shoes with a gun pointed at your head. Am I a taig? Am I in the Provos? Or the INLA?'

Silence. Rainey rolled over on the floor.

'I know you're scared now, Danny. You're holding a gun but you've probably never been trained how to use it. You're pointing it at a man; you don't really know why. You're scared of Tommy and scared of Rab. And you should be–'

'That's enough,' said Tommy.

'–because this will be you some day–'

Tommy unfolded his arms and raised the gun, levelling it at Jackie.

'–and you'll be on your knees–'

'Just like Tommy,' croaked Rainey.

The room froze, a sealed-off capsule, the world outside non-existent for all of them. Then a scorched, gurgling laugh bubbled up from Rainey, a hideous sound.

'Tommy's on his knees,' a gasp, 'a lot of the time when Rab's about. Just in front of his crotch.'

Tommy turned to look at the dying man.

'How's the carpet burn, Tommy?' said Rainey. He was struggling to form the words.

Tommy took a position standing over Rainey, straddling him. Jackie could see Ruger's face now. It was contorted in a smile of pure agony.

Rainey said, 'You fucking homo cun–'

Tommy shot him in the face. He held the gun with both hands. His eyes were wild.

Jackie heard a whispered, 'Shit!' from behind.

Tommy squeezed the trigger again and another round took another part of Rainey's face away. The body jolted as though shocked with an electric charge. There was another bark from the handgun and this time the body hardly responded. Rainey was nothing more than meat now, the empty factory a slaughterhouse. Jackie was transfixed.

Tommy let out a yell and unloaded the magazine into Rainey's ruined face. The bullets tore through flesh, tendon and finally bone. The muzzle flared, illuminating Tommy's face distorted in a scream. The noise was deafening. Bullets were passing straight through Rainey's head and ricocheting off the stone floor beneath. There was a flash as one took out the strip-lighting above.

Then Tommy's head snapped back. His arms moved upwards, sending the last couple of shots into the wall on the left. His head lolled forward, his knees gave and he collapsed on the ground in a heap next to Rainey.

Danny Moore ran for the door. Scrambling over to the two bodies in the centre of the floor, Jackie winced and looked away from what was left of Rainey's face. A small hole was drilled in Tommy's forehead, barely graced by blood. Both men were dead.

There was a bang as Moore flung open the front door, then three sharp cracks followed by the heavy thump of dead weight hitting the floor.

Jackie walked to the corridor and saw the body of Moore lying half in, half out of the building entrance. He raised his hands and walked slowly towards the threshold, glimpsing shadows flitting in front of powerful headlights. There were other lights too, blue lamps, and he saw the snout of a Land Rover on the left of the open doorway. There were shouts coming from outside, angry commands. A hail of hoarse orders and rebukes. He edged to the doorway, standing over Moore's corpse.

'Police,' said Jackie. 'Police. I'm a policeman!'

CHAPTER 28

Saturday

He listens to the low scream and checks the magazine on the Ruger semi again. The noise from an Airbus shifts to a low roar as it skims, then touches down on the runway at Belfast City airport.

Jackie stands next to the River Conn in a steady drizzle on the southern perimeter of Victoria Park. He can see the island in the centre of the narrow stretch of water circling the park, lit by the lights of the airport on its western and northern periphery. The island is connected to land by a single footbridge. He turns to take in Samson and Goliath to his back, the giant gantry cranes towering over a swathe of powerful arc lights in the shipyard.

His target should be there any time now.

He turns to his companion. The figure stands in silence, staring at the cars flitting along the bypass, which hugs the eastern limits of the park. The Belfast to Bangor train line runs parallel to the road. Crowding beyond that are the regimented terraced streets of the loyalist stronghold of Sydenham. The four-lane road and slim rail link hold the snaking streets back like a defending wall.

Jackie had recovered the gun from his father's house, ducking into the alleyway that ran behind it and vaulting the back wall. It was a simple job to pick the lock and grab the Ruger and ammunition from its hiding place. He had exited the way he'd entered. Now Rebecca Orr's car was parked where he'd left it, at nearby Sydenham train station. It was there he'd met the silent figure standing next to him.

His companion turns at the sound of a vehicle entering the parking area at the entrance to Victoria Park through a small tunnel under the bypass. The island in the middle of the park is swept by headlights, like searchlights hunting a fugitive. There is only one car, as Jackie had stipulated on the phone. A pause is punctuated by the rising and falling clatter of a train passing on its way to Bangor. He checks his watch: 11.25 p.m.

He shoves the semi-automatic into the waist of his jeans to the right of his stomach as the headlights die and a lone figure emerges from the driver's-side door. No doubt there are more men in the car, although he'd given clear instructions that Billy Tyrie should come alone. The figure looks around. Satisfied he has arrived first, he looks back at the car, which coughs to life again and turns out of the car-park. It enters the tunnel as a large Airbus takes off, roaring overhead, undercarriage not yet withdrawn into its belly. The heavy whine of the jets swallows the sound of the car, just as the darkness of the tunnel swallows its headlights.

Jackie turns to his companion and says, 'Time to go.' The figure moves off at a crouch, mumbling into a mobile phone. The drizzle is subsiding some but the ambient noise from the airport, road and shipyard persists, the sounds of a city on the move, and will continue for a while yet before retiring for the night. Tomorrow will be quieter, the shipyard silent, Belfast nursing a Sunday-morning hangover as it traipses to the newsagent for the papers.

The figure is now standing stock still on the island looking around. His face is in shadow but his bulk and the arrogance in his stance belong to Billy Tyrie. His hands are deep in the pockets of his heavy wool coat. After a minute, he produces a packet of cigarettes from the right pocket. The flare from his lighter makes a 1930s horror film poster of his face in the dark. He succumbs to nerves and looks back at the dark mouth of the tunnel, across the footbridge, some 400 yards away.

'Hands in front of you. Turn around.'

Tyrie turns slowly, the tip of his cigarette like a warning light in the dark. Jackie can't believe it was only three days ago he strode on the beach at Cloughy, Eileen's lover neatly sliced and wrapped in bags. It seems a lifetime ago.

'Jackie, you're looking well.'

In truth, Jackie looks wretched. His jeans are soaked from wading through the moat to get to the island. His eyes are tired and raw and his face is battered and bruised from the fight at Rab's house. But he feels calm and centred and has the Ruger in his hand. For now, he's accepted that he has taken life and, while he'll have to deal with it for the rest of his days, he knows he's lucky to be breathing. At least for the moment.

'Where's your Claddagh?' says Billy.

'Turn the pockets of your jacket inside out.'

Tyrie does so. They are empty save for a packet of cigarettes and a cheap disposable lighter. Jackie waits as a large Boeing taxis somewhere behind him, its shriek passing slowly.

Then he says, 'Are you armed?'

'Should I be?'

'Hold your coat open and turn around.'

Tyrie complies, spending longer than necessary checking out the parking area and tunnel. He has a snub-nosed revolver tucked into the waistband at the back of his jeans. Jackie leans over and wrenches it out, then tosses it into the moat surrounding them.

Billy says, 'Rab Simpson's dead. The PSNI found him at his house at Ardenlee with the body of another man. There are already rumours of them killing each other in a drug deal gone wrong.'

Jackie doesn't move an inch or make a sound. He knows the lights of the airport and shipyard behind make him little more than a silhouette. Billy is growing nervous and talking to cover his discomfort.

257

'Terrible sad to see such a loyal volunteer come to such a violent end. But then, drug dealing? Rumours of collusion with republican sources in the drug business? What can you expect?'

Jackie reaches his right hand around his back, to the waistband of his jeans.

'I have to thank you, Jackie. A job well done. I warned you not to cross me and – fair play – you didn't. You're a good man.'

'There's good news and bad news.'

'What?'

'Which do you want first?'

'All right,' says Tyrie, cockiness returning, 'I've had a jar before coming here. I'm buzzing a bit. Give me the good news.'

'Your old mate, James Cochrane, is being lifted by the PSNI as we speak.'

Billy's eyebrows peak in curiosity. 'Do tell.'

'The man who was found with Rab in Ardenlee Avenue had both Rab and James Cochrane's numbers on his mobile phone. A known republican and member of RAAD, Danny McCardle.'

Jackie checks for a glint of recognition on Tyrie's face in the glow from the airport.

Nothing.

'Seems it also had the name of a young man from the Markets on it too, a Gerry Simmons. This boy Simmons was shot dead last year, a good friend of a known dealer and associate of Rab, Adrian Morgan. The cops suspected it was drug related. McCardle mustn't have bothered organising his numbers very often. Maybe he was using his own supply and got careless.'

'Is it enough to have Cochrane put away?' Tyrie can't hide the eagerness in his voice. It smacks of desperation.

'Could be. Ballynafeigh Police Station received a tip-off this evening that a house in the Holylands had evidence related to the murders at Ardenlee. The drug dealer, Adrian Morgan, was arrested at the house. He'll be more than happy to help police with their enquiries. If they don't do Cochrane for murder, they can certainly link him to Simpson. God knows what the cops have turned up already in Rab's house and they'll probably find more in Cochrane's.'

It hadn't been difficult to slip the bag containing Rab's photographs and the mobile phone sim card over the wall of the yard at the back of Adrian Morgan's terraced house in the Holylands. An alleyway ran the length of the rear of the row of houses and Jackie had moved easily in the shadows where twenty years earlier a British Army patrol might have been crouching on night manoeuvres. The thump of dance music radiated from the front of the house, along with the clatter and chatter of people in various states of inebriation. The precursor to a midnight trip to a club no doubt. Jackie had made a short telephone call, tipping off the PSNI that Morgan's house contained material related to a double murder at Ardenlee. He stressed that officers should search the yard of the house.

Now in custody, Morgan would plead he was abducted from Club Realm, perhaps set up. But he had no name to pin on Jackie, his number was on Rab's phone and it would look suspect that he hadn't reported his abduction on Friday. It was hard on Morgan but if you played with wild animals, sooner or later you'd be bitten.

'Here's the kicker,' he says. 'There was a photograph of Mrs Cochrane in a compromising position with Rab Simpson.'

Billy's face lights up in a smile that gives the oil rig at the shipyard a run for its money. Arrest and trial is one thing, but personal ruin is a whole new level of pain for a man like Cochrane. Christmas has definitely come a couple of months early for Billy Tyrie.

'Cochrane's bitch and Rab? He was shagging her, like?'

'Giving her one for Ulster.'

'You're a fucking dynamo, son.'

'I never said any of this was my doing,' said Jackie. 'You ask me, Rab and this McCardle boy shot each other. Maybe Morgan did them both. It could even have been on Cochrane's orders. Someone in Cochrane's group, probably some player in RAAD, saw a chance to make a grab for power and tipped off the peelers.'

Billy's mouth is stretched in a wide grin, but some of the light has gone out behind the eyes. He leans forward, his body language a six-foot question mark.

'Did you just say *player*?'

It's Jackie's turn to smile.

'Isn't *player* the sort of word a peeler would use?'

Jackie's hand tenses on the polymer grip of the Ruger SR9 semi-automatic. He says, 'The penny drops.'

'A fucking peeler? We thought you were a grass, but a peeler?' says Billy, his forehead a mass of ridges in the orange light of the city. 'But you killed people. You killed Tommy and Danny Moore. You killed Rab.'

Jackie levels the Ruger at Billy's face. Tyrie doesn't flinch. He has to give him credit, Billy's a gangster, but he's got some class with it.

'I'm retired,' says Jackie, 'and for the last time, I did not shoot Tommy. Or Danny.' After a second he adds, with less surety, 'Or Rab Simpson.'

'You're fucked,' says Billy. 'When you pulled that gun on me you made a huge mistake.'

Jackie nods in the direction of the dark tunnel mouth on the other side of the footbridge.

'Nobody's coming,' he says. 'The Indians have already seen to the cavalry.'

Tyrie spits a gob of phlegm at Jackie's feet.

Jackie goes on: 'See, I don't know if you knew what Rab and Tommy were up to, back then. They'd brought in Danny Moore and taken me to Holywood to kill me. But here's what I do know. Rab had a grudge. He didn't like me. It's the default position for a few people I know. Maybe he didn't like me getting in his way in the organisation. Maybe he thought I was a bit suspect, already thought I was grassing to the peelers.'

Billy's fists clench and unclench. A jet screams off from the airport headed across the water and Jackie waits until it is up and over the lough before he continues.

'I was a policeman: Special Branch. Someone called in an IRA hit on me. Branch got a tip-off, maybe from Rainey. After that night, the RUC investigated further and leaned on various sources. Turns out Rab had reached out to the Provos, and James Cochrane in particular, to have me killed. Rab used some contacts to get word to Cochrane that I was responsible for the shooting of a young Catholic lad. Rab was the real shooter. Cochrane set me up for a hit the night I disappeared. Rainey was supposed to be hit too, when I met him up in Cregagh Glen.'

No reaction from Tyrie. He could have known everything, or nothing, about that night.

'The Provos got over-zealous when they followed me, tipped me off, and Tommy rolled out Plan B: Rab gets Rainey to Holywood, Tommy and Danny take me, then we're both supposed to be shot there and then.'

'But you weren't,' says Billy.

'Maybe that was the start of Rab's relationship with Cochrane, maybe not. I think you knew and that's part of why you wanted Rab dead, alongside the drug dealing and the fact he was a homicidal maniac. He was in bed with republicans and that made him a liability.'

Tyrie's face is a granite cliff face, expressionless. His breath is seething through gritted teeth.

'But did you know,' says Jackie, 'he was up to more than the drugs? Did you know he was pimping?'

Billy fires a sharp look at Jackie, murder in his eyes. It is a more controlled ghost of the same look Simpson gave him in the house in Ardenlee Avenue this morning.

'Girls from Eastern Europe. Did you know he was running them? Using European men as muscle and the women as whores? For fuck's sake, they could have been trafficked. Did you know that, Billy? That he was running girls?'

Billy takes a step towards him and Jackie grips the Ruger more tightly. Tyrie takes another step, closing the distance between them. Jackie lowers the gun and risks a shot at Billy's feet. An ascending Boeing smothers the report. Tyrie flinches as the bullet strikes the grass – but takes another step.

'Did you know?'

Billy Tyrie stops dead at the sound of the new voice. His face crumbles, and his eyebrows knit as if in pain. Jackie's companion is stepping off the footbridge onto the island, having circled around from the far bank. Eileen Tyrie strides into the light.

'Did you, Billy? Did you know Rab Simpson was a bloody pimp?'

Tyrie looks at Jackie, momentarily broken. 'Did you bring her here?'

'You did,' says Jackie. 'She hates you. She wants you burned just as bad as I do.'

'Damn the two of you,' says Eileen. 'You'll not talk about me as if I don't have my own voice.'

She covers the ground to where they stand in long, fluid strides.

'Did you know that Rab was running girls?' she says again.

'No, I did not,' says Billy.

Jackie believes him. There was no angle for Tyrie in Rab's pimping, as far as he can see. Eileen doesn't look so convinced but keeps her counsel, drilling holes in her husband with her eyes.

'Nineteen ninety-three,' says Jackie.

Billy turns to him again. 'What about it.'

'The bomb at East End Video.'

'I remember.'

'It was intended for you.'

'Sure, we all know that,' says Billy, spreading his arms wide like a preacher delivering the good word. 'But they got the wrong address, didn't they? That cunt Cochrane wasn't as smart as he thought.'

'No,' says Jackie, 'they got the right address. They just got the wrong time.'

'What?'

'There was a flat above the rental shop,' says Jackie. 'That was your place, wasn't it, Billy? That's where you used to take the wee girl, Kim Clarke, when you wanted some private time with her.'

Eileen's mouth tightens and her eyes narrow to coal-black slits.

'Her da, Harry, hated you, especially after the bombing,' says Jackie. 'My own father never knew why. Harry never spoke of it. Maybe he was scared. Maybe he couldn't bring himself to talk about it. But I know, Billy. You were taking that wee girl up to that flat for sex. She was what, fifteen? Maybe sixteen?'

'Shut up,' says Billy, low.

'Do you remember how Rab set up surveillance gear when we were staking out Cochrane's house back then? He was good with cameras – video cameras – wasn't he?'

'You're talking shite.'

'A bit too good. He rigged your wee love nest,' says Jackie, reaching into his inside pocket. He produces a photograph and holds it up to the light. It is a couple – a coupling – on a bed, on all fours. The girl's face is mid-cry. The man behind her is grinning with a fierce intensity. He is younger and leaner but it is, unmistakably, Billy Tyrie. The girl is Kim Clarke. The photograph is dated in ballpoint pen: January 1993. An address is scribbled on the back of the photograph in Rab Simpson's hand. It is the address of East End Video.

Billy's face is a monument to rage, his lips so thin his mouth is a papercut.

Rab's photo collection was the gift that kept on giving and he'd spotted the hidden-camera-style shot of Billy and the Clarke girl among some of the oldest photographs in the set. Rab had played that one close to his chest, probably expecting McCardle to interrupt back at Ardenlee and take care of Jackie. The shot of Billy Tyrie with an underage girl was valuable leverage. It was the photograph Jackie showed Eileen that afternoon, when he convinced her to come to Victoria Park. Something changed in her then. She has been on a slow fuse since. Now she ignites.

'You bastard!'

Billy crumples under her fists. He covers his head as she pounds at him and kicks with her boots at his shins. He pleads with her, a loop of *please, Eileen, please, love*. Their hands flap at each other like children in a playground tussle. Jackie feels awkward, like a voyeur, and thinks of Rab spying on couples in other intimate moments. Billy's voice is becoming clearer, stronger. It is competing with the roar of a cargo plane landing at the airport. He finds purchase, grips Eileen's hands in his left and balls his right hand in a fist. He tenses. Jackie raises the gun again and makes to strike Billy with the butt.

'Go ahead!' screams Eileen. 'Sure, you may as well! It's about the only thing you haven't done to me!'

Her words stop her husband in his tracks. Her pure, white fury. Eileen is livid, her breathing heavy and ragged.

'Go on,' she goads, 'hit me. You've cheated on me. You've lied to me over and over. You've neglected me and left me lonely, and alone. No one will go near me for fear of you. One man who did is God knows where now, chopped up in bits.'

She drops her head.

'And you've humiliated me and your daughters.'

The part of Tyrie that took over a moment ago, the animal rage, is subsiding again and he is shrinking before her.

'Hit me. It's no worse than what you've done to me already.'

His hands fall to his sides, limp. His shoulders hunch and he sags.

'Eileen, love,' he begins.

She snatches the Ruger from Jackie and shoves the barrel into her husband's temple before either man can react. They both stare, dumbfounded, at her.

'Don't say my name. Don't say your daughters' names. You're no husband. You're a father in name only. You had sex with a bloody child. God knows who else you've been with. You're nothing to us. You have no family.'

Jackie thinks this must be over now. He waits for the sudden angry flame, the gout of blood and the ragdoll frame collapsing on the damp grass.

But Eileen belts Billy hard across the face with the pistol. Tyrie yelps in pain; Jackie flinches. Eileen looks her husband up and down with a withering glare and hands the gun back to Jackie.

'I'm done,' she says and walks off towards the footbridge. She looks beautiful, her stride confident. Jackie thinks Billy probably never wanted her as much as he does now. Or maybe that's just him.

'So, that's it,' says Billy. 'Are you going to use that gun on me now?'

'This is for personal protection only.'

'Too bad you have to hide behind it.'

Jackie keeps his gaze steady and focused on Billy's eyes as he throws the gun to his right. There is a soft splash from the moat.

'If you think you're up to it, come ahead,' he says.

Tyrie glares, fuming, desperate to rebuild some of his ruined ego. His instinct is to dominate, intimidate and destroy. To terrorise. But Jackie is not scared. He has seen, done and lived enough today to be strong in the face of Billy Tyrie. He holds the man's gaze until the blaze dies in Tyrie's eyes and the defiance in the man's stance fades. 'I didn't think so,' he says.

'So what? Do you beat me? Give me a kicking?'

'I can't be arsed. You're not worth it.'

'Take me to the police? Presumably you're going to see me punished for what I've done.'

'This isn't about punishment,' says Jackie. 'It's about accountability.'

'Where are my men? The ones in the car?'

'Alive. It depends on how cooperative they were as to how sore their heads will be.'

'Who's got them?'

'That's the least of your worries right now. There are copies of the photo of you and Kim, and a few other bits and pieces, in an envelope that's being couriered to the *Belfast Telegraph* as we speak. The rest of the boys in the East Belfast Brigade won't be too impressed.'

'They'll kill me.'

'Maybe, if they find you.'

'You're letting me go?'

'It's done. You're ruined. Eileen has called the other Belfast Brigadiers by now. You've probably got about ten, maybe fifteen minutes before they show.'

'You know, there'll just be another like me in the future.'

'Maybe, maybe not. At least these days youse aren't dignified with any title other than criminal or gangster. You, Cochrane, the whole shower of you.'

He begins walking towards the footbridge, leaving all of this, the last twenty years, behind. At the bridge he turns and looks back once. Tyrie is on his knees in the centre of the island, the grass smooth in the bald light of the industry around him, like a broken groom without a bride on a wedding cake.

Jackie breathes in the night air. His chest expands and he closes his eyes for a moment. Then he heads for the Sydenham bypass. He looks into the maw of the tunnel. The car is gone and there is no trace of life. He steps into the shadows by the side of the road and sets off, against the flow of traffic.

CHAPTER 29

1993

The room was bare concrete with a steel toilet in the corner. A holding cell. Spotless and reeking of disinfectant.

Vapid coffee and a grease-soaked bacon bap. He devoured it.

Beyond the wall he heard the muffled sounds of Castlereagh police station and detention centre as it went about its daily grind. He glanced up at the CCTV camera in the corner and thought of Rab Simpson and his electronic surveillance on Cochrane. There was every chance one of the gang would sit on this bench one day. If they lived long enough.

MSU officers had bundled Jackie into the back of a Land Rover outside the factory in Holywood and taken him straight to Castlereagh. A couple of Branch officers had driven to Palace Barracks to inform the British Army of developments and discuss a strategy for his extraction from the UDA, while some uniforms were at the Royal Victoria Morgue, finding a John Doe to match Jackie's height and build. The search would extend to other counties if a suitable body wasn't on hand. A tattoo artist in Antrim Army barracks was being driven to the city, tasked with the ghoulish job of replicating his loyalist tattoo on the John Doe's arm. A roadblock shoot-out would then be staged near Holywood and word circulated that Jackie Shaw was dead, several high-powered British Army rounds having taken his face off as he fled a UDA meet in the town.

A couple of female uniforms would now be on their way to Thomas Cowell's house where they would inform his girlfriend, Sarah Shaw, of the night's events, and tell her that her brother was being flown to a military base in Gloucestershire. Sarah would be asked to inform Samuel Shaw of the news and arrangements would then be made to fly sister and father to England at a later date to see Jackie.

The debrief had been exhausting. Gordon had been joined by a detective inspector from CID and the Deputy Head of Special Branch. Gordon's gentle encouragement had been tempered by restrained scepticism from the Deputy Head and open hostility from the DI. CID and Branch were awkward bedfellows at best and the bad blood caused by CID running Rainey without telling Branch had heightened tensions. Upon conclusion, the Deputy Head had offered a brusque handshake and strode out of the interview room. The DI had sniffed and shuffled papers before giving Jackie a stare and also exiting.

'McCandless,' Gordon had said. 'In his mind, you're a liability.'

'Bastard,' said Jackie, rubbing the tattoo on his forearm.

'One of a few I could mention. And boy, does he love his work here.' The big man gestured to the walls of the interrogation room with a dark look. 'There'll be people across the water can remove that,' Gordon had said, pointing at the red hand and *Quis Separabit* motto Jackie was still rubbing.

'I'd kill for a drink.'

Gordon had left the room, returning a minute later with a bottle of vodka. Food and coffee followed and now he waited in an empty cell for the word to leave for RAF Aldergrove.

Time passed at a crawl. It felt as though he'd been in perpetual motion over the last days and weeks and now, sitting alone in a concrete box, the minutes seemed to decompress. He fidgeted and fretted about Sarah. About his da. And he thought of Eileen.

'You're up.'

Gordon entered with a coat and black hood and muttered, 'Sorry,' before placing it over Jackie's head. The coat covered his tattoo. Anonymity was all. He stumbled into the corridor, Gordon's arm guiding him, and felt another take a grip on his shoulder. For a mad moment he thought he was going to die. Then an English voice said, 'Apologies for the inconvenience, Mr Shaw. We'll have this off you as soon as you're in the car.'

CHAPTER 30

Sunday

Morning. A hot shower after sleeping on clean sheets.

A breakfast of bacon and eggs, sausage and tomatoes, potato bread and soda bread. Eaten with gusto.

He drives into the suburbs of Belfast in under ten minutes. The city hoves into view on the Ballygowan Road like a giant patchwork of red brick and grey steel.

He parks near the rugby stadium and walks to the sturdy Victorian detached. He hasn't called ahead. He hasn't seen or spoken to her since last night, but Eileen Tyrie doesn't seem surprised to find him on her doorstep at ten o'clock on a Sunday morning. She steps aside, giving him more room than is necessary to pass her in the wide hallway, and shows him into the sitting room at the front of the house. Coffee is offered and accepted and five minutes later he's blowing on an Italian blend and fingering a biscuit. They sit at a right angle to one another on the matching sofas, Eileen facing the window. He can't believe how hungry he is.

'You okay?' he says.

She gives him a look. He takes a gulp of coffee.

'Where are the girls?'

'They stayed over at a school friend's last night. Pyjama party. They'd been looking forward to it for weeks.'

'Good timing.'

'Yeah,' she says with a sigh. 'Lucky me.'

They both have a chug of brew.

'Is he alive?' she says.

'If he isn't,' says Jackie, 'it's none of my doing. I left him at the park. What about the boys in the car?'

'They've had the fear of God put in them and they'll be none too pretty for a while, but they're still breathing.'

They'd called the Fergusons yesterday and brought them in on the proviso that no one would die. Mark, the Godfather, former lover of Mrs Tyrie and now buried at various spots around Cloughy mudflats, had originally been a culshie: a country boy, from County Antrim. The official line on Mark was that he had disappeared and was now a missing person. The Ferguson clan didn't buy that and weren't slow in taking up the offer to put the hurt on some of those involved in Mark's 'disappearance'. They'd been waiting – and when the car had entered the tunnel, Billy's boys hadn't stood a chance. Culshies were hardcore.

'Where are Billy's lads now?' says Jackie.

'Retired,' says Eileen. There is an edge to her that wasn't there yesterday.

He raises an eyebrow.

'I told you, they're alive.' Her voice is flat. Her gaze remains fixed on the hedge outside, although he doubts she is seeing it.

He takes another sip of coffee and finds himself gasping for a cigarette.

'You didn't know,' he says, 'about the room? The room above East End?'

'No,' she says with a slap of finality in her tone; he wants so badly to believe her.

'Does it surprise you that Rab did? I wouldn't have wanted Simpson to know I had an under-age lover. Too much leverage for a man like Rab to have on someone.'

'Not in those days. What's a dirty wee secret like a fuck pad in comparison to murder and torture? They were thick as thieves back then. Do you think it could have been Rab who fed the information to the IRA?'

272

'That Billy used the room? Maybe. It could have been a power play to get him out of the way; the UVF sold the Butcher Murphy out to the Provos happily enough.'

Eileen nods, chewing on a patch of her lower lip.

'Or it could have been your lot,' says Jackie.

The chewing stops and she blinks.

He says, 'MI5 are all about manipulation. They might have been looking to remove Billy.'

She begins to shake her head, still blinking. A deep frown furrows the smooth dome of her forehead.

'I'm sorry, I'm not sure what–'

'I know,' says Jackie. 'One of their men, Hartley, was at the airport when I flew in. He was giving me a warning, telling me to keep my nose clean while I was here. He talked about you having kids and said I should leave you alone. But no one ever knew about us. I never told my colleague.' He thinks of Gordon, and of Rebecca. 'You never appeared in a report. Billy and Rab didn't know about us. But that Spook knew.'

Her mouth opens a hint. He can see the glistening pink tip of her tongue on the ridge of her front teeth.

He takes a leap to see how it plays out. 'Thank you for that night.'

Several expressions appear to be battling for supremacy among her sculpted features.

Jackie continues, 'It was you who called in the attempt on my life. You knew Rab had set me up for an IRA hit. You called it in.'

The colour is draining from that beautiful olive skin again and the fine lines at the side of the wide, sensual mouth seem more deeply etched than ever, punctuating her surprise.

'I asked Billy if he knew about the set-up last night. He didn't answer but I know he did. I know because you must have found out and saved me.'

Her eyes are somewhere else again. Probably twenty years ago. 'Why?' he asks.

'Back then,' she begins, then stalls. 'At that time,' she starts, then falters again.

Finally, she says, 'What else could I do?'

Jackie understands. It was the same for him back then. But not now. They are both different people.

'Is that when Five recruited you?'

'Around that time,' Eileen says. 'I thought you were dead. I was sick of Billy and scared of Rab. I thought they'd help, take them away.'

'But they didn't.'

'They wanted to *contain* them. Keep them in place and limit the damage with my information.'

'An acceptable level of violence, right?'

She gives him a mirthless smile. 'Exactly. This was never going to end. My informing, their violence, all of this.'

She gestures to the window with both hands outstretched. She looks as though she is offering her wrists to a pair of handcuffs.

'I found out you were alive; that you didn't die that night, at least. And part of me hated you for it. You got away, clean. I lost myself then. I did some things I'm not proud of, things I'll never forgive myself for. But I couldn't give up and I couldn't disappear. I have the girls to worry about. I couldn't leave them with their father. So I'm still here.'

'And he isn't,' says Jackie. 'Billy never knew about MI5?'

'No.'

'Rab's dead. You're free now. Free of Five too, if you play them right.'

She hangs her head and looks at him out of the corners of her eyes, sideways.

He takes a breath. He puts his hand in his pocket and pulls out an envelope and hands it to her.

'That's a photograph. It's of you and Rab Simpson. One of those things you're not proud of, I'd imagine.'

She throws the small flat object on the floor as if it carries a plague strain.

'Do with that copy as you see fit.'

'Copy?' She whirls on him. 'Copy? What the fuck, Jackie, there's more of them?'

'You're part of this, Eileen. You were married to Billy, you know people. You pulled the Fergusons into last night's shenanigans. Christ, you could have a lot more clout with MI5 than I think. I have to protect myself and my family and this photograph is my insurance.'

He'd been surprised at how comfortable she was last night, her authority over the Fergusons and her callous disregard for Billy's men. Men who'd murdered her lover, but who'd probably protected her, maybe cared for her girls and played with them as children. And after the last four days, he wouldn't put anything past her, or any of them, the people who still live in that world of forty, thirty, twenty years ago.

'I would never ...' she begins, then thinks better of it. They both understand. Whatever pushed her to make that call to Branch twenty years ago has gone. They are strangers now.

Eileen says, her voice very quiet, 'I was drunk. No man would come near me and then, one night, Rab called over while Billy was away. He had to leave some package for him and he'd just bought the house at Ardenlee. It wasn't long after he'd been shot, and he was different for a while, calm. He invited me to come over and have a look at the new place and he was ... nice.' She crosses her arms and legs. 'We drank too much, he asked me upstairs and, before I knew it, he had a camera out.'

'As I said before, this isn't about you,' says Jackie. 'Anything happens to my sister or her family, this photograph goes to the local media, the PSNI and UDA East Belfast Brigade.'

Once again, she understands. He hopes she sees enough of the man she cared for back then to trust him to keep the photo under wraps. And to use it if he has to.

'Thanks for the coffee,' he says and stands to go.

She joins him, keeping her distance from the photo on the sofa.

'I have to get ready,' she says. 'I'll be taking the girls to church when they get back.'

He thinks of the small funeral church of two days ago.

'I suppose there's no point in asking you to say a prayer for me.'

'Do your own dirty work,' she says, as he steps out the door.

#

Sunday lunchtime. Beef, roast spuds, boiled spuds. Broad beans, peas, steaming carrots. Sarah glowing. Tom happy to see his wife so happy. The two kids – teenagers – wary of Jackie. Then amused by how giddy their mother is and then losing themselves in the banter. The craic is great. Uncle Jackie, he thinks.

Ice cream and jelly for dessert and now he is no longer hungry. More craic. Uncle Jackie guffaws and realises he hasn't laughed with honest-to-God joy in a donkey's age. Sarah tells a funny story from their school days and calls him 'my brother' and he feels a warmth spread through him. She and Tom talk about going back to work tomorrow and the kids ask about Jackie's job. His niece is particularly interested in the horses on the land where he lives. She wants to be a vet.

At the end of the afternoon they have coffee and a slice of cake Sarah bought yesterday and he is satisfied.

#

Evening. A coffee in the departure lounge and a hollow ache in his belly at being alone again. He'd left Sarah at her home. But he had had to drive out to Bangor to return Rebecca Orr's car and pick up the rented Toyota. He swallowed memories of the abattoir of Ardenlee as he made his way to the airport, gripping the wheel until his knuckles seemed almost translucent. The flight is one of the later departures on a Sunday night and the terminal is quiet, the shops closing. He's almost glad when his name is called over the Tannoy system: it promises something to occupy the next few minutes.

A member of the ground crew is waiting for him at the desk and accompanies him to a door along a narrow corridor. She opens it, revealing a large man in a suit who ushers him inside and steps to the left. Stuart William Hartley is sitting behind a simple, cheap-looking table. He has a blossoming purple bruise across the bridge of his busted nose and a bandage on his temple. The large man in the suit gestures towards the plastic chair opposite Hartley and Jackie sits down.

'Your nose looks almost as bad as mine,' he says, fingering the empty space where the Claddagh ring had been.

'Like mine, it seems yours has been broken,' says Hartley.

'You should see the other fella.'

'I think I have. Photographs of him anyway. Or what's left of him.'

'I'm sure I have no idea what you're talking about.'

'I'm in no doubt that you do, but it isn't an issue that concerns me.'

'If it's more information you're after, no can do. I don't move in those circles any more.'

Hartley breathes through his battered nose. The nasal burr is stronger than ever and the bruising extends out below his eyes, giving his expression a permanent, almost comical glare. He looks at the be-suited man, perhaps for reassurance, and plays with a ball-point pen.

'Billy Tyrie shot himself in the early hours of this morning.

277

Local residents heard a gunshot and called the police. They found his body draped over the railings of a memorial to the victims of a bombing atrocity committed some twenty years ago on the lower Ravenhill Road.'

Jackie looks Hartley in his dark-ringed eyes. 'Are you sure he shot himself?'

'It would appear so, according to early reports from the pathologist and crime scene boys.'

'He'll be sorely missed,' says Jackie. 'If that's all, I'll be going. I have a flight to catch.'

'By all means. I just thought you'd want to know. I suppose this means you're last man standing, quite an achievement considering your competition.'

'They were only competition if you played the same game,' says Jackie. He puts his hands on his knees, ready to get up.

'I also wanted to pass on our thanks for a job well done.'

'Bollocks.'

'I did say last *man* standing,' says Hartley. His glance flits to the suit and back to Jackie again. 'I believe you know who our asset has been in the Ravenhill UDA.'

Jackie, palms still planted on knees, looks at Hartley. The man is licking his lips. Then he waits. He knows Hartley can't help himself.

'Eileen Tyrie was our primary source of intelligence on the activities of Billy's little tribe until the end of the Troubles. As our Billy was a true believer, he cultivated some pretty nasty friends in Scotland and England in recent years. The usual right-wing headcases. Even a couple in mainland Europe.'

Jackie leans in to the table, listening hard as Hartley goes on.

'But he'd lost his way, had our Billy, and Rab Simpson was a threat to him. Simpson was a different animal altogether: unpredictable, more vicious, no beliefs or standards left but the pursuit of wealth and power. Unlucky for him he wasn't born in Surrey and working in the City.'

Hartley laughs at his own little joke.

'So when we heard you were coming back, thanks to our friends in GCHQ, we made sure Billy heard you would be in Belfast through our friend Eileen. Billy tasked you with getting rid of Simpson. We had no qualms about it.'

'And you think it was me shot him in Ardenlee.'

'Trust me, you needn't worry. We all know Rab Simpson was shot in a drug deal gone wrong.'

'And Billy?'

'Billy's a bonus. Eileen was going to try a story on you anyway, push you in the right direction. We thought you'd find it hard to resist playing the white knight. Turns out that wasn't necessary. We picked up your Estonian friends at Belvoir Forest Park, and they were only too happy to lay out Rab's proposal for you.'

And you let it play out, knowing the bastard had threatened my family, thinks Jackie. He sizes up the distance between them, gauges how much more damage he could do to Hartley before the suit pulled him off. But there is no point. It wouldn't change anything and it definitely wouldn't change a man like Hartley. Born into the right family. The right school, the right clubs. He'd always be comfortable, always have influence with the right people, always have money and a sweet retirement fund at the end of the day. Men like him had, quite literally, nothing to lose.

'And Eileen?' says Jackie. He remembers the dead, flinty chill in her voice this morning.

'With a bit of luck, she'll have a seat at the East Belfast Brigade command table. First woman in a senior role within the organisation.'

'And you won't be needing me again? I'll be back to visit family from time to time.'

'I shouldn't think so.'

Jackie rises and waves a hand behind him, a vague farewell.

Just before he reaches the door, the suit's hand on the handle, he turns.

'You realise you can't trust her. For all you know, she could have been in bed with Simpson, too.'

'Hardly,' says Hartley, superiority regained now the length of the room stands between them. 'She's quite the businesswoman. She wouldn't get into bed with someone as unstable as Simpson.'

Jackie takes his wallet out and fishes a Polaroid out of it. He looks at it and whistles, keeping the back of the photograph facing Hartley so the man can only see a scribbled date and a place name written in Rab Simpson's hand.

'Oh, I don't know, Stuart,' he says. 'You'd be surprised.'

Then he nods at the suit, who duly turns the handle and opens the door for his departure as Jackie slips the wallet and Polaroid back into his pocket.

#

The Airbus A319 roars into the sky bound for the south-west of England. As it peels away from the city below, it leaves the ship-yard, Victoria Park and the east of the city, sprawling into the Castlereagh Hills, in its wake. And as it gains height, making good speed along Belfast Lough against a lively headwind, it passes the commuter town of Holywood. The blinking lights of coastal Bangor wave a final farewell as the plane banks over the huge black chasm of the Irish Sea.

Jackie Shaw rubs his face with his hands and breathes deeply. He looks forward to collecting his car on the other side and the silent drive through the countryside to his small flat in a converted stables. He looks forward to a full night's sleep and waking in the morning without a slow twisting of his guts, and he looks forward to looking at his face in the mirror after the scars of his homecoming have healed. This trip is over, he is still in one piece and he believes his family is safe.

And he is smitten once again with the city of his birth. The hills, mountains and lough, which corral it into the Lagan Valley. So for now he makes a conscious effort not to grip the arms of his seat and wills himself to relax. He rubs a bare finger on his right hand, his Claddagh ring gone but his soul taken by the city that shaped him. Then a jolt of turbulence clouts the plane and he whispers a short prayer. An image of a gored Rab Simpson flickers in his mind's eye and, as he takes a long, deep breath, he remembers one of his mother's favourite passages from the Good Book.

Be sure your sins will find you out.

END

ACKNOWLEDGEMENTS

My thanks to: Dave Busby, for getting the ball rolling; David and Ewan Cameron for their time and honest feedback; Leslie Rich for encouragement and a great soundtrack for writing; Robert Dinsdale, my editor at Silvertail; Shona Andrew, for making the book look good; Humfrey Hunter at Silvertail, for his honesty and patience, and for taking a chance on me; Ruth Dudley Edwards; Colin Bateman; Christopher Zuk; Reza, Iman and Najiba for listening to me harp on; my mum for instilling my love of reading; and my dad for spinning so many great yarns. Now, I hope, it's my turn.

AUTHOR'S NOTE

The road to this novel began way back in the good-old-bad-old days of my youth in the Belfast of the seventies and eighties. The Ravenhill Road emerged relatively unscathed from the 'Troubles'. There was no bomb on the lower part of the road, although there was a great video rental shop, sadly long gone. The road straddles East and South Belfast and has changed a lot since then, for good and bad. Both parts of the city saw their fair share of horrors and both have worked hard to put the past behind them.

The murders which form the backdrop to Jackie's story in *Ravenhill* are fictional, but many are inspired by tragically true events. The La Mon bombing occurred as described and remains one of the most remembered atrocities in a long line of Northern Irish outrages. I have written the bombing into the novel with the utmost respect for the twelve dead and many injured. However, the hotel, like the majority of the people in our wee corner of the world, has moved on and prospers.

Half of *Ravenhill* is already an historical novel of sorts: it was a story which I wrote for very personal reasons, and to help my daughter understand the tangled, obstinate, warm, beautiful, passionate place that shaped her daddy. I hope, when she's old enough to read it, the likes of Billy Tyrie, Rab Simpson and James Cochrane are well and truly gone, and Belfast and its people are as proud, irreverent and generous as ever.

Read on for a taster of
what comes next for Jackie Shaw ...

The next Jackie Shaw thriller, ***Seven Skins***, is available now
to pre-order in paperback and ebook.

CHAPTER 1

Saturday

Somewhere beyond the reaches of the Square Mile, at eleven-fifteen on a Saturday night, London rages, but the man and woman sit in the quiet seclusion of an eight-pounds-a-glass City wine bar, twitching with anticipation. The man is in his later years, a solid but unspectacular career behind him, and the woman is at least forty years his junior. She has an eager smile that verges on greedy and the man thinks she wants to be with him in the mistaken belief that he is worth something substantial.

He has refined the anecdotes and crafted the cues. Snippets tossed into conversation: 'When I was in Zimbabwe – of course, it was Rhodesia back then ...' a rueful smile, '... or off the coast of North Korea ...' Then a few operational titbits and a shallow sigh. 'But I shouldn't go on: I signed the *Act*,' and, for those too clueless to understand, 'You know, the Official Secrets Act.'

He has the look, too: just enough calibrated dignity and the world-weary, careworn confidence of a man who has trod the darker roads of human existence and seen a world only glimpsed by others when the body of some foreign diplomat or oligarch washes up in the Thames, or lies broken in a Knightsbridge apartment. The whole package is good for a couple of free drinks from the younger City boys, and it reminds him that once he had, indeed, been a trusted operative with the British intelligence services.

The blank but polite look on the girl's face reminds Len Parkinson-Naughton that she is too young to know what or where Rhodesia was, or to have any interest in Korea. She has finished her Prosecco after taking an age to sip it – he has finished three gins in the time – and is fingering the stalk of her glass with slim, spidery fingers. Her cheekbones and slim, angular nose say Slavic, possibly Serbian, making a mockery of the name she gave him: Beatrix. He can't quite place her accent. The bar is striving for post-industrial chic and almost empty as the financial quarter slumbers between business days. The harsh fluorescent spotlighting, like the lamps in an old-school interrogation room, serve only to heighten the brilliant sheen of her coal-black hair. To all intents, despite her diminutive frame, she appears brittle and beautifully cruel, and he wants her with a restless desperation. The fact that this seems, somehow, all wrong enhances his desire all the more. After all, wrongdoing has been his forte for the last few years.

I'm a fool, he thinks. An old, proud fool who doesn't know when he's beaten. At this age, I should be gardening and building models of the North Atlantic Fleet in '43.

The Rhodesian and North Korean cues are, like many of his conversational hooks, vicarious. Derek Reid, a HUMINT man in MI6, had met Mugabe back in the seventies and related the Rhodesian story at a conference in the States. In over thirty years with MI5, Parkinson-Naughton had never learned much of the tradecraft, even during his stint in Northern Ireland. He'd attended the lectures and heard the gossip in the canteen, but senior recruitment and HR officer at Thames House hadn't been seen as a high-risk position in need of fieldcraft training. There was a brief spell of responsibility for running logistics in Ulster, but only because they were short-staffed and he was already in Lisburn doing performance evaluations. No, not much chance of being 'spotted' back in the old days, seduced by some GRU 'swallow' girl in a honey-trap, and even less now. This woman before him sees a lonely, older man in a good suit with the right accent, and smells money. And that is fine. He's been paying for it since Pat left him and he'll make sure Beatrix earns her fee.

They leave the bar and he catches her gazing at the glowing steel and glass bullet of 30 St Mary's Axe, all forty-one storeys. He lights a cigar, the tip flaring in the dim light, and glances at Mitre House directly opposite. There are no lights in the cramped offices of the consultancy where he works two days a week as a favour to an old Oxbridge friend. A former intelligence agency officer is worth the salary of a non-executive director when it comes to tenders for Home Office or military contracts. The fact that Parkinson-Naughton had been an administrative manager for most of his career is immaterial. He talks a good game. To be seen on the street with an unknown young woman in heels and short skirt, however, would never do.

Then there is the handsome civil service pension and the savings from some other, secretive dealings. For a moment his eyelids flutter at the thought of that third income, what he considers his retirement fund, and he wets his lips with a booze-coated tongue. Then his eyes widen at the thought of Pat discovering the money, how she would revel in ruining him with the undisclosed cash, and he determines to work the delicate girl beside him that little bit harder in lieu of his poisonous ex-wife.

The girl, Beatrix, takes his arm and steers him towards the larger thoroughfare of Aldgate and a taxi to his home in Twickenham. But after a couple of yards she edges him to the left past Mitre Square, where Jack the Ripper eviscerated Catherine Eddowes, and into the narrow alleyway of St James's Passage. He lets her lead him and feels a vague spark kindle in his belly. The passage is a dim trench at this time and, like much of the financial district at this hour, devoid of life. She stops him twenty yards from the far entrance of the passage, the empty avenue of Duke's Place beyond, with a gentle shove against the alleyway's wall.

She'll pay for that later, he thinks, and feels the flame below his gut burn a little brighter.

Her kiss is strong and frantic. He feels a flicker of disappointment at the clumsiness in her embrace and surprise at how angry her tongue feels in his mouth. But he draws her to him nonetheless, crushing her small body hard against his, stooping, his shoulders still broad despite his years, to lock his mouth onto hers. He feels her bony knees stab at him as he closes his eyes and her muffled, 'No. Not like this,' only serves to goad him on. He is so inflamed, so lost in the struggle for a few seconds, that it takes him a moment to register that she's been wrenched from him and that his hands are left clawing the musty air. He hears a short, stifled cry and then his world is filled by white heat and the angry bite of stinging fragments of brick. He sees a young man, pale and terrified, holding a pistol with a long, cigar-like suppressor. He smells the heavy musk of brick-dust and hears, distorted and far away, a hiss, 'Get out of the way, youngster.' Disorientated, he barely registers the harsh Irish accent.

A wiry, bearded man, perhaps in his late forties, takes the gun from the younger man and aims at the left side of Len Parkinson-Naughton's head. The ex-MI5 man feels the beginning of a dull, excruciating ache and realises that part of his ear has been shot off. Then he hears the tinny clack of the suppressor doing its job, a sound cut off as abruptly as if someone had slammed a door. It is the last conscious moment of his life.

#

The three of them had been waiting long enough for the kid, Padraig Macrossan, to get a bad case of the jitters, and for the veteran, Harris, to get bored. Alex Morgan knew what could happen when men with guns had too much time on their hands and that's why he'd insisted that only he carried; he'd give

Macrossan the pistol when the time came. Besides, he'd already decided Harris was enjoying himself a little too much to be given a gun.

The girl was taking her sweet time but they'd been assured she was the older man's type: short, scrawny and young.

Each to his own, thought Morgan. He preferred a woman with some meat on her bones but if the whore could get the old man where they wanted him, he had no complaints.

At around 11.45 they heard the couple in the passageway, her stilettos telegraphing their approach. The empty stone tunnel of the passage was an echo chamber and he worried for a moment about the noise of the shot, knowing the suppressor would mask only around 30 per cent of the report. He hoped that Macrossan would get the job done with one bullet.

They stood on Duke's Place at the entrance to St James's Passage, glancing up and down the thoroughfare for traffic or pedestrians. It was deserted. Not even a taxi. Harris smoked beside him as he took the Beretta M9 from his pocket and screwed the suppressor in place. The kid, Macrossan, stared at the weapon. The silhouettes of the couple, when they appeared, were almost comical, one tall and lanky, the other petite beside him.

The shadows merged and he heard muffled grunting as he handed the gun to Macrossan and followed him into the alleyway. Morgan grabbed the girl, slapping a hand over her mouth to smother her cry and for a moment it looked as though the kid would do as he'd been told. Stride up to the target and adopt the Weaver Stance: double-handed grip with forward pressure on the drawing hand and slight rearward pressure on the second hand to control recoil. But Macrossan stopped too close to the target and Morgan realised that the kid was holding his breath. Macrossan's hand trembled as he fired and the bullet clipped the side of the old man's head, ripping part of his ear off. The round tore into the brick behind and struck like steel on flint, sending a shower of fragments into the bloodied conch shell of the ruined ear and hurling the ricochet at a crazy angle, forcing Morgan to duck on instinct and hurl the girl behind him. The old man stood wild-eyed, his hands beginning to tremble, while Macrossan cowered against the wall. Then Harris appeared, wrenched the Beretta from the kid, clouted him behind the head as he said something in an irritated tone, and shot the target twice in the head, just below and to the right of the shredded left ear.

The old man folded in on himself. He hadn't hit the ground as they caught his body and made their way back out of St James's Passage, Harris unscrewing the suppressor from the pistol-barrel and Morgan and Macrossan dragging the corpse. The girl had already fled into the dark, vacant heart of the City.

#

It is one of a row of unremarkable, well-tended semi-detached houses on the dark street in West Belfast. Even the twenty-five-foot Peace Line wall, separating the street from its parallel neighbour, tapers off a few yards from the row of semis. Instead, the corrugated iron fence of a small industrial complex stands opposite number 85, albeit with a stencil of a gun sprayed on it with the scrawled legend, *You are here*, with an arrow pointing from the muzzle to the angry lettering.

But number 85 is distinguished from its neighbours thanks to the store of three Glock 17 handguns, an SA80 assault rifle, two Mossberg 500 shotguns, and ammunition wrapped in sacking and hidden in the loft insulation. Behind the closed curtains, the three men sitting in the small living room watching reality TV and drinking strong, bitter tea, are hard men with prison records and blood on their hands. They don't know each other. If lifted by the police, they'll have minimal information to give under questioning, should they break. All three have been diligent in maintaining a low profile in order to keep the house and its residents in good stead with the locals: the area is close knit and gossip spreads fast, particularly when strangers move in, so a minimum of attention is vital.

The street is silent and empty. It is almost midnight and most people are at home, drinking in one of the bars on the larger road nearby, in an illegal shebeen, or in one of the city centre clubs. A thick veil of cloud hangs over Belfast, as though someone has stretched a blanket from the Black Mountains in the west to the Castlereagh Hills in the east, and the sodium streetlights of the city below lend a flame-like glow to the overcast sky.

The three tea-drinkers don't hear the low grumbling as ten Police Service of Northern Ireland Land Rovers cough to life at the rear of the industrial complex opposite. The sound, and the whine of the PSNI helicopter hovering three miles away, is drowned by the wail of a mannequin-like celebrity wife in conflict with a glamour model over a pad of eyeshadow on the TV. One of the men rises to stretch and another lights up his fourth chained cigarette.

'Turn that down, Marty,' he says. 'We don't want the neighbours giving off.'

'Sure, the walls are thick.'

'Not as thick as your head. Turn it down, will you. I saw the woman next door with a wee child yesterday. You'll be waking it up.'

The tap of Marty's finger on the remote control seems to amplify as the soft clatter of men and equipment running towards the front door drifts in from the street. The third man, sitting nearest the living-room door, spills his tea at the first shout of 'Armed police! Armed police!', punctuated by the heavy thump of a battering ram on the front door. Light floods the room despite the closed curtains, infused with blue flashes, throwing bogeyman shadows of the three men on the living-room walls. The thin, insect-chatter of the helicopter above fills the air like the whine of a migraine.

Marty and his companions hear the dull explosion as the front door gives way. The men drop to their knees and place their hands behind their heads before the first officers enter the room, Heckler & Koch submachine guns at the ready. The man on Marty's right takes a look at the PSNI men in full body armour, wearing balaclavas and goggles, helmet-mounted cameras and mics, and clutching the ubiquitous H&K MP5s, and says, 'Sorry, lads, we finished playing Call of Duty a couple of hours ago.'

The boot on his neck keeps him quiet while he is cuffed along with his companions, and one of the forced entry team reads their names.

'Philip Cross. Robert "Sav" Savage. Marty Catterick.'

Twenty minutes later they are separated, Philip Cross in the back of a Land Rover on the street, Robert Savage in the forensic tent which has been set up in the front garden, and Marty Catterick in the living room, face down and kept company by two officers wearing chequered baseball caps and their enmity on their sleeves.

A tall sergeant, his face slick with sweat after finally peeling off his fire-retardant balaclava, enters the cramped space clutching a shotgun and sits on the sofa.

'Mr Martin Catterick. So, what's on the shopping list, eh?' says the sergeant. Another policeman enters the room and gives him an official-looking form then exits again. 'Three Glocks. Not any of ours, I hope.'

Marty says, 'Fuck you.'

'No thanks, I'm on duty. One SA80.' The sergeant winks at

one of the other officers as he writes something on the form and says, 'Take the paperwork up to McMahon. He's in the loft going through the ammunition now.'

The officer leaves with the document. His companion shifts position slightly, getting a better grip on his submachine gun.

The sergeant says, 'And, finally, two Mossbergs: check.' He pats the shotgun. 'I believe the Yanks were fond of using these, although that's changing now. We prefer the Remington 870 ourselves. Still, I suppose a shotgun's a shotgun, at the end of the day.'

He smiles at Marty and stands, lifting the black, murderous Mossberg. Behind his back, Marty Catterick's hands fidget. He needs to piss.

The sergeant says, 'Unless they have one of these in the barrel.' The tall policeman tips the shotgun muzzle-down and a small, plastic, rectangular object falls out, landing on the beer and fag ash-stained carpet. The cop drops to his haunches in front of Marty and picks up the black and green memory stick. As Marty stares at the device, held between the tall sergeant's thumb and index finger, the policeman leans closer to him, his Kevlar flak jacket straining against his chest.

'Let's you and me go up to Serious Crime in Antrim, Marty, and have a wee chat about this.' The sergeant sniffs, like a bloodhound, his nose in the air. 'And we'll give you a change of clothes to wear, seeing as your jeans are covered in piss.'

CHAPTER 2

Monday

Jackie Shaw scratches his arse, places the shotgun in the back of the Range Rover and straps in for a bumpy ride. He starts the vehicle and begins the drive down the stubbled lane leading to an eight-furlong grass gallop that will be pummelled by several thoroughbreds later in the morning.

Neither the gun, nor the car, is his. Nor is the land he now crosses or the bed he woke up in twenty minutes ago. Jackie doesn't own much at all, but the bad dreams are his and his alone. Sometimes he wakes moaning to the dim, sparse contours of the stone-walled room and functional wooden furnishings in his small flat, the loft of a converted barn on the farm. At others, the upper half of his body springs forward, like the blade of a flick-knife. The flat is his cocoon, his solace. It contains a large wooden wardrobe with a mirror on the door, kitchenette, shower cubicle, sofa and wooden coffee table. There are two photographs propped on top of the chest of drawers: his mother and father, both buried back home in Northern Ireland, and his sister with her husband and kids. The quiet purity and solitude of the bare, whitewashed walls calms him and there are no curtains on the windows. He doesn't want to feel entrapped: there should be no veil over the world outside.

At the end of the lane, the car's headlights pick out a sign, wreathed in a gossamer mist: *Garbella Hill Farm*. He's been working as a nominal security guard on the farm, with its racehorse stables, yard and training facilities, for a couple of years now and enjoys the seclusion which the location in the

Cotswolds hills affords. He remembers years ago, staring out across the Irish Sea, a beautiful woman sitting next to him. He'd told her he could never live in England, it could never be home. But that was a long time ago. He's always liked hill country and he feels as at ease here as anywhere he's been in the last twenty years. And he's been around.

In the open-featured countryman's face he sees each morning in the mirror, his brow is knit like the knotted skin of the large scar on his right forearm. Since last year, there is a little more salt in the dusting on his dark crew-cut.

The Range Rover begins to lurch on the lane, the ground puckered by man, machine and beast. In the glow of the head-lights, the lane is a shattered spinal column of loose stone and muck. After sixty yards it splits and Jackie takes the left branch, heading for the gallops rather than the main road. He wills the sun to rise, to bleach the night shadows.

As he approaches the gallops, Jackie can discern the small stone rectangles, sprouting at crazy angles from the ground on the left of the lane. All thoroughbred winners laid to rest on this spot on the 1,000 acres of Mack Stevenson, racehorse trainer extraordinaire. The millions of pounds now stirring in the stables is a fraction of the fortune buried in this patch of long, grasping grass. It's still too dark to read the names, the cobalt sky still some time from dawn, but he knows many of them from memory. Flashing Blade. Call for Empties. Duke of Windsor. Ernie's Cat.

'Sickbag' Simpson. Another name; a very different animal.

'Ruger' Rainey; 'Big Dog'; Billy Tyrie. Killers, abusers, pushers, terrorists. The victims, too, and friends shot down or blown to bits: a lifetime of memories from a couple of years in the RUC.

He pulls over onto the grass verge and lifts a shotgun, wrapped in a leather cover, from the back of the Range Rover.

Locking the vehicle, he sets off on the mile-long course used to give the thoroughbreds a workout. The Beretta semi-automatic is mostly used for pest control, and is light for a shotgun. Jackie holds it crooked in his arms, patrol-style.

As Jackie strides across the dark plain of Hogg's Hill, the world around nothing more than a shadow, he takes comfort from the gun in his arms, its weight and finality. He hates firearms, and yet he can face down the dark with his finger on the trigger, an ounce of pressure and the terrible bark of the weapon; its savage discharge.

The open space, ringed with the black husks of the Gloucestershire hills, is a world away from the terraced streets and fierce, tribal murals of his youth. Then the ground becomes clogged with thick, unruly grass and clumps of bracken, and he's forced to concentrate on threading his way through the thicket. He can see the dark mass of the copse beyond, the trees like storm clouds anchored to the earth. The sky is a lighter hue and sunrise will be upon him in another twenty minutes or so. He unwraps the Beretta.

Jackie doesn't like guns, but he respects what they can do. He knew men in the Army who obsessed over them, studying makes and models, comparing calibre, magazines, sight radius, muzzle energy and trigger pull. Many of those in paramilitary groups had a terrible fascination with weaponry and the damage it could inflict. Jackie is repulsed by it. But, on days like this, when he awakes with the shadow of his past looming over his bed, he comes out here to shoot.

He's already loaded the shotgun and creeps into the copse, sighting on some targets he fashioned out of rusted iron left lying around the yard. Mack gives him free rein on the land and has insured him for all the vehicles. Ian Sparrow, the gamekeeper who owns the gun, is fine with him using it, so long as it is back in the cabinet, cleaned and oiled, by mid-morning and

Jackie pays for the ammunition. Tight oul' bastard, he thinks with an affectionate grunt.

Sparrow, a Londoner by birth and twenty years Jackie's senior, served in the Gloucestershire Regiment back in the eighties and feels a profound, if sentimental, kinship with Jackie thanks to his service in the Royal Irish Rangers. Both men know their regimental history: the ferocious fighting of the Royal Ulster Rifles, while the Glosters clung to Hill 235, at Imjin, Korea. A battle long past in a war not yet over, fought a world away.

There is no cloud and the day is going to be a beauty. The ear protectors block some of the morning chill and Jackie finds his grip on the moulded chequering of the stock and fore-end of the shotgun, breathing evenly as he does so. This is why he comes out here to fire off a few shells: the concentration drives all other thoughts, whether good or bad, away. The repetition, too: sight, breathe, squeeze; absorb the buck of the weapon, and start the sequence over again. For a while, at least, he can stop living in his head.

The first shot sends a murder of crows soaring. It also tears the iron trowel target out of the soil thirty yards away. Jackie works steadily with the gun, alternating a sequence of slugs at distance with double-ought buckshot at larger, closer targets. Each heavy blast, still deafening despite the ear protection, takes a little edge off his morning. Each punch of recoil on his shoulder works some more tension out. The mechanical cycle of fire and reload drags him from the violence of his past into the cold, crisp light of the present just as the daylight chases the dark from the Cotswolds hills. As the weapon spits each spent cartridge out the side of its ejection port, another flashback of his brutal past spins away.

After thirty minutes he has almost finished the ammo and, for today at least, has settled his soul some. The early-morning target shooting is a workout and a purge. He wraps the Beretta in leather and searches the ground for the spent cartridges, feeling a chill graze his back. He has worked up a sweat and his T-shirt and sweater are not enough protection against the fresh bite of early morning country air. Working quickly, he takes a plastic bag from his pocket and fills it with the empty cartridges, then walks back to the Range Rover. Once at the vehicle, he places the bag of spent cartridges and the semi-automatic on the back seat. Fishing in his pockets for the keys, he realises that he has forgotten his mobile, left back in his flat at the farm. Then he smiles. He has no one to call. His sister, Sarah, is in Australia with her family, a long-cherished trip. A year ago he wouldn't have known she was out of the country, they communicated so little. Now they speak regularly. It's one of the better outcomes of the trip home for his father's funeral last year and he is glad that some good came of Samuel Shaw's passing.

The colours hang limp on the tall spike of aluminium rising from the champions' graveyard. Rifle-green and scarlet. Mack Stevenson's racing colours, the silks worn by the jockeys when his horses run at Aintree, Newbury and Cheltenham. As the vehicle sways along the worst of the lane, a young woman on a chestnut mare canters towards him in the field beside the track. He recognises the wiry brush of blonde hair erupting from under her riding helmet: Kelly, one of the stable staff. She is fit, her thighs strong and lean in her jodhpurs, and he can see her working to boss and steer the horse. She wears a tight-fitting cream sweater which accentuates the pale pink of her face, now flushed with the sting of morning air. An open and simple face. An English face, with a strong, angular nose and thin, well-set lips. She is also, in Jackie's eyes, obscenely young at twenty-five and he has kept his distance, despite her attempts at flirtation. She is like this countryside: gentle, uncomplicated, perhaps a little raw and privileged. He is tainted.

As Jackie pulls up next to her, Kelly leans over in the saddle and says, 'Mack is looking for you. He's been calling your mobile for the last half hour.'

'Is there a problem?'

'Only some dark, handsome Irish guy brooding around the yard. What are we going to do about him?'

'If I see him, I'll let him know you were asking for him.'

'You do that. You let him know *the craic*,' she says, her voice deep with an exaggerated rise in tone at the end of the sentence.

It's an abysmal attempt at a Belfast accent but he grins as she canters away and he puts the Range Rover in first. The grin stays with him until the farm buildings and stables appear around the bend in the lane. Mack is waiting in the yard, hands on hips, in a checked shirt, mud-spattered quilted vest, corduroys and Wellingtons, flat cap on head. Ian Sparrow is there beside him, a warning in his eyes. Behind them are parked two BMWs and, standing in front of them, four men in jeans and spotless suede boots wearing new-looking Barbour jackets. They all sport short, ordered haircuts and are clean-shaven – a uniform of sorts. And, as he pulls up a couple of yards away, Jackie can clearly see the bulge of a shoulder rig and handgun under one of the shiny, green waxed jackets.

SEVEN SKINS is available for pre-order NOW

Lightning Source UK Ltd.
Milton Keynes UK
UKOW04f0727031117
312088UK00001B/159/P